"Do you want

That was a loaded question. [obscured] said instead of answering. "[obscured] of your day. I'd understand i[obscured] want to go home."

Jake looked between her and the food. "*Home* is a tricky word. It's not in the DC area anymore. It's not in Peony Cottage, which I've stayed in for less than forty-eight hours. Home is more about a feeling, in my opinion. For me, it's all about feeling loved. And safe," he added.

Trisha tilted her head. "Safe?"

Jake leaned against her kitchen counter. "Feeling safe is also about being free to just be you, no veils or pretenses. And knowing that the people around you won't judge you or make you feel crazy. That's what home feels like." His gaze was still locked on hers, holding her hostage in this moment. "At least to me."

Trisha swallowed. If that was what home felt like, she hadn't been there in a very long time.

"If you're looking for a sweet romance set at Christmas about finding love after loss, look no further. Annie Rains brings us a book that captures the Christmas spirit perfectly."

—ThatHappyReader.ca

Sunshine on Silver Lake

"Readers will have no trouble falling in love with Rains's realistically flawed hero and heroine as they do their best to overcome their pasts and embrace their futures. A strong cast of supporting characters—especially Emma's stepmother, Angel, and the many returning faces from earlier books—underpin Rains's engaging prose and perfectly paced plot. Lovers of small-town tales won't be able to resist."

—*Publishers Weekly*

"*Sunshine on Silver Lake* was an endearing second chance romance that pulled at the heartstrings as often as it tickled my funny bone!"

—TheGenreMinx.com

"Annie Rains delivers hope."

—ReallyIntoThis.com

Starting Over at Blueberry Creek

"This gentle love story, complete with cameos from fan-favorite characters, will enchant readers."

—*Publishers Weekly*

"A sweet, fun, and swoony romantic read that was both entertaining and heartfelt."

—TheGenreMinx.com

Christmas on Mistletoe Lane

"Top Pick! Five stars! Romance author Annie Rains was blessed with an empathetic voice that shines through each character she writes. *Christmas on Mistletoe Lane* is the latest example of that gift."

—NightOwlReviews.com

"The premise is entertaining, engaging and endearing; the characters are dynamic and lively...the romance is tender and dramatic... A wonderful holiday read, *Christmas on Mistletoe Lane* is a great start to the holiday season."

—TheReadingCafe.com

"Settle in with a mug of hot chocolate and prepare to find holiday joy in a story you won't forget."

—RaeAnne Thayne, *New York Times* bestselling author

"Don't miss this sparkling debut full of heart and emotion!"

—Lori Wilde, *New York Times* bestselling author

"How does Annie Rains do it? This is a lovely book, perfect for warming your heart on a long winter night."

—Grace Burrowes, *New York Times* bestselling author

THE
SUMMER
COTTAGE

Also by Annie Rains

Sweetwater Springs

Christmas on Mistletoe Lane

A Wedding on Lavender Hill (novella)

Springtime at Hope Cottage

Kiss Me in Sweetwater Springs (novella)

Snowfall on Cedar Trail

Starting Over at Blueberry Creek

Sunshine on Silver Lake

Season of Joy

Reunited on Dragonfly Lane

THE SUMMER COTTAGE

ANNIE RAINS

FOREVER

NEW YORK BOSTON

Copyright © 2021 by Annie Rains
Preview of *The Christmas Village* © 2021 by Annie Rains

Cover design by Daniela Medina
Cover images © Trevillion; Shutterstock
Cover copyright © 2021 by Hachette Book Group, Inc.

Bonus novella *Kiss Me in Sweetwater Springs* copyright © 2019 by Annie Rains

Grand Central Publishing
Hachette Book Group
1290 Avenue of the Americas, New York, NY 10104
grandcentralpublishing.com
twitter.com/grandcentralpub

First Edition: May 2021

Grand Central Publishing is a division of Hachette Book Group, Inc. The Grand Central Publishing name and logo is a trademark of Hachette Book Group, Inc.

The publisher is not responsible for websites (or their content) that are not owned by the publisher.

The Hachette Speakers Bureau provides a wide range of authors for speaking events. To find out more, go to www.hachettespeakersbureau.com or call (866) 376-6591.

ISBN: 978-1-5387-0342-7 (mass market), 978-1-5387-0343-4 (ebook)

Printed in the United States of America

CW

10 9 8 7 6 5 4 3 2 1

For my grandmother Nannie—
the first book lover in my life

Acknowledgments

I wish I could say that writing a book gets easier each time, but each new story comes with its own set of challenges. That's why I'm so grateful to have the people in my life who help me climb these proverbial mountains (because that's how they feel in the beginning. And the middle. And the end).

Thank you to my family for a million and one reasons. These books would never get written without your steadfast support and encouragement.

Thank you to my editor at Forever, Alex Logan, for making my heroines tougher, my heroes sexier, and my books the very best they can be. I am so thankful for the entire team at Grand Central Publishing / Forever, including Estelle Hallick, Jodi Rosoff, Mari Okuda, Carrie Andrews, and Daniela Medina.

Thank you to my amazing agent, Sarah Younger, for all that you do to ensure that I can continue doing what I love. I'm so fortunate to be on #TeamSarah.

Thank you to my critique partner and friend, Rachel Lacey. You're my first reader and your input is so valuable to me. I so appreciate you reading this one in three days and giving me feedback. Wow! You're AMAZING!

Lastly, I want to express my gratitude and love to all my readers. I can't tell you what it means to me that you take the time to read my work, review it, and spread the word. Thank you from the bottom of my overflowing heart.

THE
SUMMER
COTTAGE

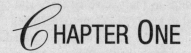CHAPTER ONE

This wasn't a good way to start off the day.

Trisha Langly grabbed a towel and hurried out the door and down the steps just as the sun rose over the Blue Ridge Mountains. She'd accidentally overslept this morning and needed to get to the west side of Somerset Lake quickly—before some poor, unsuspecting person happened upon a sight that couldn't be unseen.

As property manager of the Somerset Rental Cottages, Trisha had the unique job of heading out every morning to make sure Mr. S wasn't lying on the shore in his full glory.

This wasn't a nudist colony by any means, and Mr. S was in his eighties. In his thirties and forties, however, he'd lived on a nude beach. And apparently old habits die hard.

Trisha quickened her step. She'd left her son Petey in bed as usual. She'd only be gone long enough to toss the towel over Mr. S, nudge him awake, and convince him to go home. Then she'd hurry back to have coffee and make breakfast for her son.

Trisha had done a lot of things to make ends meet in her adult life, including housekeeping and running a women's shelter in her hometown of Sweetwater Springs. She was technically the property manager here, but the job description included a lot more than tending to the twelve cottages and sparse tenants. She also tended to her boss, Vi, an older woman in the house next door. Trisha kept Vi's garden and purchased her groceries, as well as those of two other homebound tenants. She retrieved the mail every day from the boxes at the end of Lakeshore Drive and delivered it to the addressees' doorsteps.

And every morning at dawn, Trisha woke a naked elderly man from his slumber.

The blurry image of Mr. S came into view.

Trisha picked up speed. The sun was rising and so would the folks who lived on Somerset Lake. Her gaze caught on movement in the distance. *Oh no.* Someone was approaching from the opposite direction. Making sure no one happened upon Mr. S was one of Vi's most important requests from Trisha. Apparently, the last time someone had seen him, it'd caused quite a stir. So much so that an ambulance had to be called.

Trisha started running now. "Mr. S!" she whisper-shouted. "Mr. S, wake up!"

He didn't move. Over the month that Trisha had been working here, she'd discovered that he was a sound sleeper. It usually took several long minutes to wake him up. That was time she couldn't afford this morning.

She reached him now, tossed a towel over his midsection, and tapped his shoulder. "Mr. S!" She glanced up and saw the approaching man getting closer, walking a dark-colored dog off leash. Trisha tapped Mr. S a little harder. "Wake up!"

Mr. S cracked an eye. "There you are, T. My beautiful alarm clock." Mr. S had a thing for calling people by their first initial. It was another oddity in the growing list of the older man's quirks.

Trisha shook her head. "I'm not the only one here this morning, Mr. S. Please return to your cottage or I'll have to talk to Vi."

Vi was tough, although physically she was tiny and medically frail. Mr. S sat up. "Please don't tell Vi. I'm going. I'm going."

He turned to look in the direction of the man walking his dog. "Oh, it's just you, J," he called down the shore. "You don't mind me being naked, do you?"

The other man stepped toward them with his dog at his side. Trisha had never seen him at Somerset Lake before, but that didn't mean anything. Vi and the Fletcher family owned her house and the twelve cottages on the west side, but there were other, larger lakeside houses that rounded the lake. "I don't mind, but I think the lady's probably right. You should go home before the folks here wake up."

Mr. S huffed loudly. "All right, all right." He stood and secured the towel around his waist before making his way to a nearby cottage that was bordered by a thick wooded area.

Trisha faced the man that Mr. S had called J. "Sorry about that." She folded her arms across her chest, feeling the need to distance herself from the man in front of her.

"Not your fault. You can't control Mr. S any more than his wife can. Or Vi." The man chuckled, his hand absently petting the head of his medium-sized dog, who tipped its head back and let its tongue hang out, seeming to love every second of the attention.

Trisha inspected the man more closely. He was tall with golden brown hair that was slightly overgrown and curling at the tips. His T-shirt hugged his broad chest and not because it was too small for him. He didn't have bulky muscles, but they were there, begging for her attention just like that dog, whose eyes were now rolled back in its head.

Trisha blinked and willed herself to stop checking out the handsome stranger. She swallowed and glanced down at her bare feet. She hadn't taken the time to put on shoes or even brush her hair. Mortification quickly flared up through her chest and neck.

Here she was checking out the hottest guy she'd seen on the lakeshore so far, and her just-rolled-out-of-bed look must be making his eyes sore. She was pretty sure she'd coated an oncoming zit with white benzoyl peroxide cream last night too. She suddenly felt as naked as Mr. S.

Trisha glanced over to make sure Mr. S had gone back inside his cottage and was relieved to see that he had. Then her thoughts jumped to her son, who was alone in bed. Or awake and wondering where she was. Somerset Lake was safe, of course. There was no reason to be concerned. Just the constant mom-worry that no one ever told you came along with being a parent. "I have to go," Trisha told the man she only knew as J. "Enjoy your day."

Trisha took a step backward, ready to run for more than one reason. A handsome man with no ring on his finger—she'd gotten that far before she'd yanked her gaze—couldn't lead to anything good for her right now. She'd only been in Somerset Lake for one month. She and Petey were finally starting to settle in, and staying here depended on keeping their distance, and their pasts, locked away. Any kind of romantic interest was definitely off the table.

* * *

"Where were you?" Petey looked up a few minutes later as Trisha stepped into their little two-bedroom cottage. The place was quaint, although it needed a few repairs and renovations just like the rest of the cottages on the lake. A hurricane had swept through the central and western part of North Carolina last year, causing flooding and damage in its path.

To this point, Vi, the trustee of her family's rental cottages, had struggled to complete the repairs. That was the reason Trisha was hired—to pick up the slack. In return, Trisha received a modest salary and a home here at Juniper Cottage.

Trisha ruffled Petey's hair as she walked past where he sat on a barstool. "Just helping Mr. S find his way home," she said, not mentioning why that task was so important.

"Why does he sleep outside when he has a bed inside his cottage?" Petey looked up from the sandwich he'd made himself.

"Good question, but I don't have an answer. I was going to make you pancakes," Trisha said, eying the mess he'd made.

"But isn't it against the law to sleep outside without your clothes on?" Petey asked.

Trisha's mouth dropped open as she spun to fully face her son. "How did you know about that?"

Petey took another bite of his sandwich. "Vi told me," he said.

"*Mrs.* Vi," Trisha corrected. This was the South, and in the South, it may as well have been against the law for a youth to address their elder without a proper *Mr.* or *Mrs.* salutation.

"She told me to just call her Vi," Petey said as he chewed. "She said it makes her feel old when I call her *Mrs.*"

Well, Vi wasn't exactly young. She was in her late seventies.

Trisha headed to the back counter and started preparing her coffee. She needed it extra strong this morning. She'd slept restlessly last night, thinking about all the things on her to-do list for this week. It was a hefty job for one person, and she was surprised that she was the first property manager ever at the Somerset Rental Cottages. "It's respectful to use *Mrs.*," Trisha told Petey.

"Not if using *Mrs.* makes her feel old, Mom. I don't want to hurt Vi's feelings."

Trisha flipped the coffeemaker on and turned, leaning against the counter and looking at her son. Maybe she was a bit biased, but he was the sweetest boy in the whole wide world. There was no risk of him coming off as disrespectful. "Okay, but she's the only adult you can call by just their first name."

"Okay." Petey bit into his sandwich again. He chewed and swallowed before talking again. "But it's illegal, right? To sleep outside naked? He could go to jail like Dad?"

Trisha hesitated a moment before answering. "Remember, we don't talk about your dad being in prison around other people here. That's very important."

Petey looked down at the counter of the kitchen island for a long moment. "I know. But no one else is here right now. You're the only one who can hear me."

"I'm just reminding you. We don't want other kids picking on you the way they did at your last school."

Petey's shoulders slumped forward as his chin tipped toward his chest. "What other kids, Mom? I haven't seen any kids my age here."

Trisha sighed softly. "It's summer. Other kids live in Somerset Lake, I promise. And when you start school in the fall, you'll meet them and make new friends. And to answer your question about Mr. S..."

Petey looked up at her.

"I guess it is a crime," Trisha said, "but it's not like Daddy's."

"Daddy's is worse?" Petey asked. "Because he stole money from people?"

Trisha turned back to the coffee maker, which wasn't brewing fast enough. "That's right. He hurt people with his actions. But he's still your dad," she said, like she always did when the subject came up. Her ex-husband, Peter, was far from perfect.

But Petey deserved a father, even if his father had embezzled, lied, and robbed people of their life savings. Petey also deserved to be able to go to school without other kids reminding him of that fact every day.

"Mom?" Petey asked.

Trisha braced herself for another hard question as her coffee-pot grumbled to a stop, signaling that her French roast brew was finally done. She reached for a mug from her cabinet. "Yes?" she called behind her.

"There's a man with a big dog standing at the door."

* * *

Jake Fletcher waved from where he stood on the porch of Juni-per Cottage. The Somerset Rentals were owned by the Fletcher family, but as the last of her generation, his grandmother Vi was the trustee. She handled all aspects of business, including management of the property and the money it brought in, which in recent years wasn't much.

Jake didn't think anyone who wasn't of retirement age stayed in these old cottages, but he supposed he was wrong. Where had the beautiful brunette come from? He held up the bracelet that she'd dropped along the lakeshore when she'd poked at Mr. Santorini. Jake's dog, Bailey, had sniffed the item out and alerted Jake to it once the woman had left. And Jake had to admit that some part of him was relieved because he'd hoped to run into her again. She'd hurried off so fast. He hadn't even gotten to ask her name.

The woman squinted at him through the glass door, but she didn't come to answer it. Instead a little boy with a mop head of black hair came running toward him, plastering purplish fingerprints to the glass that Jake guessed was from jelly residue.

The woman finally walked over to peel her son away. Then she opened the door and looked up at him. "Hello."

Jake was taken aback for just a second, like a teenaged boy being awestruck by a pretty girl. He hadn't gotten a good look at the color of her eyes on the beach earlier because he'd been wearing sunglasses. Now he saw that the woman's eyes were a bright brown that matched a small splattering of freckles along the bridge of her nose and cheeks.

Jake cleared his throat and offered the bracelet. It had a silver turtle dangling from one of its links. "Hi again. You dropped this on the shore. Just returning it to you."

She lowered her gaze to his palm. While she did, he took a second to look at her more closely. She'd obviously just woken up when he'd run into her earlier. Why she'd left her home so quickly, he wasn't sure. But even with her unbrushed dark hair and pillow creases running diagonal to her high cheekbones, it was plain to see that she was beautiful.

She took the bracelet, her fingers briefly brushing against his skin. Then she looked up at him. "Thank you. I would have missed this bracelet. I never take it off."

"You're welcome. Mrs. Jenkins down the way likes to take her metal detector out every now and then. If she would have found that, she'd have added it to her treasure chest."

The boy's eyes lit up comically. "She has a treasure chest?"

Jake chuckled as he looked down at him. There was the same purplish jelly at the corner of his mouth. "That's right. One man's junk is another man's treasure."

"Isn't that wrong though? Finders keepers isn't a real thing. It's stealing," the boy said, frowning deeply. "And we don't steal in this family."

Jake rubbed the side of his cheek where a new growth of hair was filling in. He'd just rolled out of bed before heading down the beach this morning as well. "That's a good family policy to have," he told the boy, who couldn't have been older than seven or eight. He looked back up at the woman. "I should've introduced myself to you earlier, but there wasn't really a chance. I'm Jake. Otherwise known as J." He gestured at his Labrador retriever mix at his side. "And this is Bailey."

Her gaze flicked to his dog and back to him. "Well, thank you again for returning my bracelet, Jake," she said with a too-quick smile. She took a tiny step backward. "Now, if you'll excuse me, I have to make breakfast for my son."

Jake's gaze dropped to the purple jelly evidence on the boy's mouth again. As a lawyer, Jake wasn't one to miss details. It was his job to notice.

"I've already eaten," the boy said.

"Well, I also need to, um…" The woman trailed off, not meeting Jake's gaze again.

"Brush your hair and get dressed for the day?" Jake supplied. He was usually a lot more charming than this with a beautiful woman. The brunette standing in front of him looked anything but charmed.

"Yes." She smoothed her hand over her mussed hair. "That too." A shy smile curled at the corners of her mouth. Before he could appreciate it too much, it disappeared. "It was nice to meet you," she said, looking at him now.

"We didn't meet, actually. I introduced myself, but you never told me your name."

The woman hesitated. Maybe she was just shy, but the impression he got from her was one of guardedness. "I'm Trisha."

Jake offered his hand for her to shake. She looked at it for a moment and then seemed to take a breath as she slid her palm against his. "I've never met a Trisha before," he said. "You'll be hard to forget." He released her hand and took a step backward. He would've asked the boy's name, too, but something told him he'd be pushing his luck with the inquiry. Instead he waved at the two of them. "See you around the lake."

Jake walked Bailey for another good twenty minutes. Bailey needed the exercise as much as he did. Plus, Jake was stalling. Grandma Vi didn't know he was back yet, and she certainly didn't know the reason he was here.

But he couldn't delay going to see her forever. He turned and headed toward his grandmother's house beyond the twelve cottages. He didn't suspect she would love the idea of selling the Somerset Rental Cottages. But Jake agreed with his parents, aunt, and uncles. Considering Vi's recent health issues and the fact that the property was edging closer toward foreclosure with each passing month, there was no choice.

And since his family had nominated him to come here and convince Vi, he didn't really have much choice either.

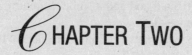

CHAPTER TWO

ᴊake!" Grandma Vi moved a lot slower than she had at Christmastime when Jake last saw her. She still moved faster than most people he knew in her age group though. "I didn't know you were coming to town," she said as she opened the door for him.

Jake stepped inside. "Sorry I didn't call," he said, noticing that Vi wasn't alone.

"We're family. You don't have to apologize for visiting." Vi turned toward Trisha, who was standing in the living room, adding to the growing mystery of who she was and why she was here. "Trisha, this is my favorite grandson, Jake."

Jake chuckled and narrowed his eyes at his grandmother. "I bet you say that to your other eight grandchildren too."

"You are the only boy, so that makes you the favorite grandson."

This was true. Jake was the only male grandchild, but there were seven other grandchildren. Half of them were defense lawyers at what used to be Fletcher and Sons. Now it was called Fletcher Law Practice. Jake was the only one in his family who'd become a prosecutor. He guessed that made him the black sheep of the family.

Jake gave Trisha a nod and a smile. In return, she lifted her hand and offered a slight wave.

Vi's gaze bounced between him and Trisha. "It appears that you two have already met."

Jake slipped his fingers into the pockets of his jeans, rolling his shoulders out until they felt more relaxed. "Trisha and I ran into each other on the lake this morning. She was waking Mr. Santorini."

Vi frowned. "You know he prefers to be called Mr. S. Was he"—she lowered her voice—"clothed?"

Jake grinned. "Is he ever dressed before dawn?"

Vi shared a glance with Trisha. "You've only been here a month, and you already deserve a raise."

Jake felt his smile drop as he looked between them for answers. "What does that mean?" His grandmother was a one-woman show when it came to running the Somerset Rental Cottages. She'd always refused to hire anyone for anything. There were some things she couldn't do herself, of course, but those were times she got friends and family to pitch in.

Vi gestured at Trisha, who had taken the half hour since they'd met to change clothes and brush her chestnut-colored hair back into a ponytail. "Trisha is my new property manager. After my little...medical issue, I decided it was time for some assistance. She has been so much help to me already."

Jake was speechless for a moment. "That little medical issue, Grandma, was a stroke that could have killed you."

"Could have, but didn't. A colonoscopy can kill you, too, by the way. It's been documented," Vi said.

Jake's mouth dropped. The lawyer in him took over. "No, that

THE SUMMER COTTAGE

would be medical negligence that killed whoever you're talking about. Not the procedure, which saves many lives each year."

Vi laughed quietly. "Oh, it's so good to have you home, Jake. We have the best debates, don't we? Always have."

Jake wanted to argue more. He wasn't home. Somerset Lake hadn't been home to him in a long time. Neither was the DC area, where he was coming from. He'd wanted to make his own way in life so he'd stubbornly gone north when the rest of his relatives had gone south. But there was nothing up there for him anymore, and after years of his family tugging on him to join them, he'd finally agreed. He was headed in that direction and aiming to take Vi with him.

He looked at Trisha again. This woman was going to complicate things. It would be a lot easier to convince Vi she wasn't up to handling the family's rental properties if she was still handling it on her own. "You hired someone to help? That's a surprise."

"Well, it was time. And it's been amazing to have someone here to relieve me of some of the daily chores involved in running these properties." Vi clapped her hands together at her chest. "Why don't we catch up over breakfast?" She turned to Trisha. "You and Petey can join us, too, of course."

Jake noticed that the boy, Petey, was sitting on Vi's couch with a book in his lap. A boy after Jake's own heart.

Trisha shook her head, a beautiful smile blooming on her lips. "No, thank you, Vi. Petey ate earlier, and I need to take this list of yours to Hannigan's Market."

"You'll check to see if Tammy needs anything?" Vi asked.

Tammy lived in Ivy Cottage right next to Mr. S.

"Of course." Trisha was still smiling.

For a moment, Jake couldn't take his eyes off her. She possessed an unassuming beauty that seemed to grow the more you looked at her.

"So breakfast?" Vi turned back to him.

"I would never turn down a home-cooked meal from you," Jake said, partly relieved that Trisha had declined to stay. The other part of him was disappointed though. Sharing breakfast with a beautiful woman wouldn't be a bad start to his day.

* * *

"What are you doing, Mom?" Petey stepped over to where Trisha was sitting. They'd already been to the market, picked up groceries for Vi and Tammy, another cottage resident, and delivered them. Now Trisha was holding an old camera that she'd found while packing up her home in Sweetwater Springs last month. It was a nice camera. Expensive. And she felt a little guilty owning it because maybe her ex had purchased it with money from cheating his clients.

"Just looking at this old camera." It wasn't old though. It'd never even been used.

"Dad gave it to you, right?" Petey leaned in to get a better look at it.

"Yep." After Peter's arrest, the feds took most of the things of value that Trisha owned. "I don't even know how to use it. I can't find the manual that came with it." Trisha laid the camera on a small outdoor table in front of her.

The table was part of the porch furniture. It had taken Trisha a good hour when she'd moved in just to clean this one table from the grime that had set in from being outside. Then she'd done the chairs, working her way through all the porch furniture. She'd also cleaned Vi's, and now she was going to Mrs. Beaver's house once a week and slowly reviving hers as well. The job description as property manager here wasn't set in stone, but Trisha didn't want for anything to do either.

"Hi there!" A voice floated on the air toward Trisha, coming from the south side of the lake. A woman with long, auburn hair in a ponytail was headed toward her. She looked to be in her thirties or maybe her late twenties.

Trisha didn't invite her up her steps, but the woman climbed up anyway, stopping at the top stair and resting against the banister. She was holding a plate of something that looked and smelled delicious.

"Hello, neighbor. I'm Lucy Hannigan," she said. "I live down the lake. I heard there was a newcomer in Somerset so I came to see for myself. I'm ashamed that it took me this long to get here." She lifted the plate. "But I come bearing cinnamon buns hot from my oven. Hopefully that makes up for my rudeness."

Trisha stood and stepped closer, leaning in to get a better look at the tray of treats. "Wow, that's very kind of you."

"Full disclosure, because there's no such thing as secrets in this Hallmark town, I bought these sticky buns at the market and warmed them in the oven before heading over."

Trisha tried to ignore the whole no-secrets-in-a-small-town line. Maybe she should've moved to the city, but she'd never been a city girl at heart. She liked the slow pace of a town that only held a thousand people or less. Somerset Lake's population was a little over five hundred. Trisha also liked knowing everyone's name and their story; she just didn't want people to know *her* story.

Lucy offered her the plate of cinnamon buns. "Careful. They're hot," she warned.

"I'm Petey," Trisha's son said first, making Trisha realize that for the second time today, she hadn't introduced herself to someone she was in a conversation with. "I'm seven years old, and I want to be an engineer when I grow up. Or an architect. I like to build."

"Wow. That's ambitious." Lucy looked down at him with a warm smile.

"Or I want to be a veterinarian like my uncle Chase because I like animals. But my mom won't let me have a pet."

Lucy shared a look with Trisha. "Well, pets are a lot of work," she offered, helping Trisha's case. "You have to feed them, walk them, bathe them." She tapped the list out on her well-manicured fingers. "I have a little dog at home, and she's very demanding."

"Why didn't you walk her down here?" Petey asked, ever ready with a question. For that reason, Trisha thought he'd make a better lawyer or reporter.

"Well," Lucy said, "because she would've tried to eat your cinnamon buns. And they're for you and your mom." Lucy looked back up at Trisha.

Time to introduce myself. "Thank you for these." Trisha offered her hand to shake. "I'm Trisha. It's nice to meet another neighbor."

Lucy shook her hand and seemed to look around the deck, which had very little on it. Just a couple chairs and one drooping plant that needed watering. "You'll meet us all eventually. The crowd on my stretch is younger than the folks over here. This stretch of property used to be more of a place for retirees on vacation. You know, the whole live in the south in the summer and fly farther south for the winter."

Trisha surprised herself by laughing. "Yeah, I've heard that about the Somerset Rental Cottages. I'm the property manager here."

"Oh?" Lucy apparently hadn't heard that bit of information. "Interesting. So what are Vi's plans for these old cottages?"

Trisha set the plate of cinnamon buns down on the outdoor table. "Renovate them and rent them out. To anyone. Vi would actually like to attract a younger crowd, just to change the perception of this place."

Lucy's gaze roamed over Juniper Cottage, no doubt taking in the wear. There was a lot of work to be done before people would flock to live here. Trisha wasn't in charge of doing all that work herself. Vi wanted her ideas though. She wanted Trisha to do the legwork and find the necessary and cheapest contractors. Vi didn't have a lot of money to invest so frugality was important.

Trisha's first priority in her job title was caring for those who already lived on the lake though. And those residents were needier than Trisha would've expected.

"So anyway"—Lucy pointed down the shore—"if you ever need anything, I'm in a neighborhood called The Village. Turn in there and head straight down Christmas Lane. I'm in the pink house at the end. You can't miss it."

"Christmas Lane?"

Lucy grinned. "We love the holidays around here. Just wait." Lucy looked between Trisha and Petey for a moment. "So just the two of you, huh?"

Tension rolled back between Trisha's shoulder blades. "Yes, it's just us." And she hoped Lucy didn't ask the next obvious question: Where was Petey's father?

Lucy apparently had more class than that. "Well, maybe you'll come downtown with me one Friday night. There's live music and dancing in the summers. It's a good time. We call it Sunset Over Somerset. You'll meet a lot of people, and I'd be popular if I was the one to lure the town newbie down there."

Trisha smiled because it seemed like the polite thing to do. But she had no intention of going downtown with Lucy, even if she seemed nice. And even if Trisha missed having a close friend nearby. Her best friend Sophie in Sweetwater Springs was only a phone call away, but it wasn't the same.

"What an amazing view this stretch of lake has," Lucy said with a long sigh as her gaze roamed over the lake and then snagged on Jake, who was sitting on the neighboring deck. She looked at Trisha with wide eyes and an open mouth. "Jake is back?"

Trisha couldn't figure out if Lucy looked shocked or excited. "Just for a couple weeks or so. You know him?"

Lucy's expression was unreadable. "Of course I do. He was one of those guys that all the girls had an eye for growing up. He only ever had eyes for my friend Rachel though." Lucy's gaze lowered for a moment. Then she looked back up at Trisha with bright eyes and a brighter smile. "Well it's official, my new friend. You definitely have the best view on this lake."

*　*　*

Later that morning, Jake headed down Vi's pier, where his amphibious seaplane was tied to the end post. It'd been kept in a large garage, getting tended to whenever Jake came to visit. Now he'd have access to it for a decent stretch of time. In his experience, there was no better way to relax than to immerse yourself in the clouds.

He walked toward the plane with Bailey matching his pace. When he reached the end of the pier, he opened the door to his plane. He'd started flying these birds when he was fifteen. His grandfather had owned one, and he'd taught Jake everything he knew.

Bailey jumped up onto the seat of the seaplane, knowing the routine. Jake unwound the rope securing the plane to its post and prepared to cast off. Then he walked around to the pilot's side, hopped in, and took a seat, his hand moving to pet Bailey's head before turning the key.

The plane purred to life. It was a smooth sound, clearing all of Jake's troubles immediately. *Ah, yes.* This was one of the things Jake still loved about being here at Somerset Lake.

He taxied the plane slowly, keeping his speed below seven knots and making sure the area was clear of other seacraft or swimmers before gaining momentum. Then he operated the gears on autopilot, bringing the plane in a nose-up position. The rudders dipped below the lake's surface, and then... *Liftoff!* They were airborne. The buzz, like music, filled Jake's ears.

Once they were leveled out, Bailey started shifting around restlessly, which wasn't like her at all. Usually she kept her tongue out and her gaze pinned forward, enthralled by the experience. This time, she twisted to look in the small back area of the plane, panting more loudly than normal. An emergency kit and some life preservers were the only items back there.

"Whatcha doin', girl?" Jake petted her back. "It's okay."

Maybe some kind of animal had stowed away with them. A rabbit or a cat.

Ah, geez. If that was the case, Bailey would go nuts, and this plane would take a dive in no time.

Bailey's panting increased. She seemed excited about something. Jake kept his gaze forward, steadying the plane until they reached twelve hundred feet. Then he turned to see what was going on.

Two dark eyes peeked out from behind a seat.

Jake's heart took its own sort of dive straight to the bottom of his stomach. "What are you doing in here?" he snapped. He didn't mean to, but this was not good.

What was the kid's name again? Jake tried to remember.

The boy didn't respond. His eyes were wide, and his complexion was paler than Jake remembered.

"Kid? Are you okay?" Jake moved his gaze from the cabin to the front windshield and back. "Kid? What are you doing here?"

The boy opened his mouth. "I…I was just…I was…I was just playing," he finally stammered. And if Jake wasn't mistaken, he was on the verge of tears. "I didn't know…"

Jake looked forward again. The last thing he wanted was to lose control of his plane. "I'm guessing you didn't know we were going to have liftoff, huh?" He patted the passenger seat where Bailey was. "Want to come up here so I don't have to keep looking back? It's safer if I look forward when operating this thing."

Jake heard the little boy shift around as he moved to the front of the plane. "That's better, huh?" He glanced over at the boy's wide-eyed expression. Jake didn't think it was terror so much as excitement.

"What's your name?" Jake asked.

"Petey. I don't think my mom is going to like this," the boy said shakily.

Jake suspected that was true. That's why he was circling around and heading straight back to the dock. He couldn't get around telling Trisha that this had happened, but it wasn't his fault. He never would have willingly given a ride to a minor without parental permission. Or without the parent coming along.

"Don't worry. We're going back," he told Petey. "You'll be on land before she even knows you're missing. But we still need to tell her. You can't go hiding in strange places. That can get you into all kinds of trouble."

Petey leaned forward, watching the land below them. His breathing seemed to even out, and a small smile curled at the corners of his mouth. "This is so cool!" He petted Bailey's head as they shared the passenger seat. "I've never been up in a plane before."

"Never? Well, this is a different kind of plane than you're probably used to seeing. This is what's called an amphibious seaplane. It can land on water or on the ground."

"Amphib-ous like a frog?"

Jake glanced over and chuckled. "That's right. Smart boy."

"You should just call this a frog plane," Petey suggested. "That would be easier to say."

"That's not a bad suggestion. I'll think about it." Jake glanced over at the awestruck expression on Petey's face. The boy was loving this. It would only take a few minutes more to fly once around the lake. "Want a tour of Somerset Lake?"

Petey's mouth dropped open. "I thought you said we had to go straight back."

"And we are. We're just taking the long way," Jake told him. *Wrong, wrong, definitely wrong.*

But the grin on the kid's face was 100 percent right. Jake remembered being a kid flying with Gramps. It was the stuff that good memories were made of.

"Awesome!" Petey exclaimed, placing a hand on the passenger window.

Jake searched for something interesting below to show the boy. "Let's see." He pointed out the front window. "Those are the Somerset Cottages. Have you counted them yet?"

"Twelve," Petey supplied. "We live in the first one because Mom says that Vi's house doesn't count. Vi lives in a mansion."

"It is pretty big, especially next to the cottages." From this distance, the cottages didn't look old and run-down. They looked scenic against the ever-blue water, each one a different color. Jake was reminded of looking down at the cottages when his grandfather used to take him up in his plane. There'd always been pride evident in Gramps's voice as he pointed and named each of them.

Juniper Cottage. Peony. Laurel. Tea Rose. Ivy. Orange Blossom. They were all named after some sort of flower or plant, except for the last one. "That's Bear Cottage, where Mr. Santorini lives."

"Mr. S," Petey said.

"That's right. When I was around your age, there was a story of a black bear from the woods getting inside the cottage and making himself at home. It was kind of like 'Goldilocks and the Three Bears.'"

"That's why it's called Bear Cottage instead of some sort of flower?" Petey asked.

"Yep." Jake wasn't sure what the cottage was named before, but after that day, it became known as Bear Cottage.

A wave of sentimentality crashed over him as they passed his family's rental properties and skimmed over the small copse of hickory and sassafras trees beyond. He kept his altitude somewhere between twelve and fifteen thousand feet as they flew over other lakeside houses, acres of lake water, rivers, and small canals.

Jake didn't venture past the actual lake. The town of Somerset Lake was a sight to behold, but he didn't want to upset Petey's mom by keeping the boy MIA for too long.

"There's a pink house!" Petey pointed as they flew over the other side of the lake. The Village was a prestigious neighborhood in Somerset. "That's Lucy's house!"

Jake glanced over. "You know Lucy?"

"She came over to introduce herself this morning. She said my mom had the best view on the lake, but she was looking at you when she said it."

Jake glanced over. "Did she now?" He chuckled as he slowly started descending and prepared to land back on the lake. "Where did you live before Somerset Lake?" he asked, hoping to find out more about Petey and his mother.

Petey hesitated for a moment. "In Sweetwater Springs. But you probably shouldn't ask me any more questions."

"Why not?"

"Because you're a stranger. Mom says I really shouldn't talk with strangers."

"How else are we supposed to become friends if I can't ask you questions?" Jake asked.

Petey draped an arm around Bailey, giving her a gentle hug. "I don't know, but my mom won't like it if I air our dirty laundry."

Jake laughed unexpectedly. "Her exact words?"

"Yep." Petey continued to pet Bailey.

"Well then, we'll just talk about other things. Like fishing. Do you know how to fish?"

"Not really."

Jake wondered where the boy's father was. The fact that Petey didn't know how to cast a line was evidence, in and of itself, that he didn't have a father in his life. Jake's father and grandfather had taken him fishing from the time he could walk.

"Well, maybe I'll teach you while I'm here." Assuming Petey's mom ever let Jake near the boy again once they landed.

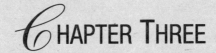HAPTER THREE

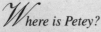*here is Petey?*

Trisha had looked everywhere. She'd told him not to run off, and he was usually pretty good about listening. For the most part, Petey was an obedient child. He rarely misbehaved on purpose.

The thing that usually got him in the most trouble was his inquisitive nature. Petey asked a lot of questions, and there were a dozen unasked questions in his little mind for every one he did ask.

"He's around here somewhere," Vi said from where she was standing in front of the stove, stirring something. The aroma wafted in the air, but Trisha couldn't begin to appreciate it because she was so worried. "Did you check with the neighbors?" Vi asked.

"I did." Only four of the Somerset Cottages were rented, and she'd checked with all the residents. "Petey wouldn't have ventured beyond the Somerset Rentals. He knows that's against the rules."

"You said he met Lucy from The Village this morning. It's quite a ways down the lake, but possible. You're sure he wouldn't have gone to see her?"

"I'm sure." Trisha nervously fidgeted with the silver bracelet on her wrist. Her best friend had given it to her before Trisha had moved. The turtle charm signified home.

"*Turtles never leave home because they carry their homes with them wherever they go,*" she'd told Trisha. "*As long as you have Petey, and he has you, you'll always be home.*"

Trisha didn't have Petey right now though, and that was the problem. "What about beyond Bear Cottage? In the woods. Is there anything back there?"

Vi glanced at her. "Well, there's a path back there, but I don't think Petey would have gone that way. The woods are a scary place when you're alone."

Trisha suspected Vi was right. Petey never would have stepped into the woods without an adult. "What if he fell into the water?"

"You said he was a good swimmer." Vi stopped stirring and turned to face Trisha. Why was she so calm right now? Petey was missing. He could be hurt. Someone could have kidnapped him.

"He is a good swimmer. But he could've hit his head and fallen in."

Vi stepped away from the stove, moving slowly. Unevenly. When she reached Trisha, she put a hand on her shoulder. She had to lift her arm because Vi was a good five inches shorter. "You're on lake time now, which means things move at a slower pace around here. The worst-case scenario is rarely the truth." She lowered her hand and headed to the lakeside window. "Did you check with Jake?"

Trisha shook her head as Vi turned to look at her. "He wasn't at Peony Cottage when I knocked. But I can't imagine Petey would be with him. He barely knows Jake, and he knows not to talk to strangers."

"Jake isn't a stranger; he's my grandson," Vi said. "And he's a lawyer. As such, he is one for details and facts. He makes it his business to know everyone and everything that goes on around him. Your son reminds me of him a lot in that regard."

Trisha folded her arms over her chest. "What responsible adult would take a kid from his home without asking a parent?"

Vi frowned as she looked at her.

Trisha shook her head. "I'm sorry. I'm just worried about Petey."

Vi looked out the window again. "Hmm. Jake's seaplane is missing from the dock."

"Seaplane?" Trisha followed her gaze. "I haven't seen a seaplane."

"He brought it over early this morning. When he's here, he usually brings the plane with him. I always said his head was in the clouds, and his heart was there too. He must be flying."

"Well then, Petey definitely isn't with him," Trisha said. "He's never flown, and he would check with me before doing anything like that."

Vi glanced over her shoulder. "You're probably right."

"Should I call the sheriff?" Trisha really didn't want to get on any law enforcement's radar in Somerset Lake. She wasn't a criminal, but her ex-husband was probably known by most officials in North Carolina. If they ran any kind of check on Trisha, they'd see that she was formerly Trisha Lewis. And then they'd see Peter's crimes. And if word got out to the locals here, Trisha might find herself defending her innocence again. And Petey would have to do the same.

A loud buzzing sound grew louder outside. Trisha turned to watch a seaplane descending and preparing to land on the water. The plane was white with a thick purple stripe along the side. There was cursive writing on the door that Trisha couldn't quite read.

"Let's go out there and check with Jake anyway." Vi didn't wait for Trisha to respond. The older woman headed to the door and stepped onto her porch, waving at the plane as it skimmed the water.

Trisha stepped onto the porch beside Vi, her gaze roaming the beach for any sign of Petey. She returned her gaze to the seaplane. It took several minutes for the plane to dock. Then Jake stepped out with his long legs and lean body.

An unwanted attraction whirred inside Trisha. This was not the time for that, but her body and her mind never seemed to be on the same page anymore. Her breath caught as a smaller figure stepped out behind Jake along with a dog. "Petey!" Trisha hurried down Vi's porch steps and sprinted toward the dock. "Petey!"

When her son looked up and saw her, he started running in her direction, plowing into her stomach and wrapping his little arms around her waist, his hands fisting in the fabric of her long T-shirt. He hadn't fallen and hit his head. He hadn't gotten lost in the woods or been attacked by a wild animal beyond Bear Cottage. No, Petey was in the very last place that Trisha ever would have looked—the sky.

Trisha snapped her gaze up to meet Jake's, fury funneling inside her chest. "Who do you think you are taking my son up in a plane without asking me first? My answer would have been *no* by the way." Heat flared red-hot in her body. She could feel it climbing through her chest, neck, and face as she continued to hold tightly to Petey.

Jake held up a hand. "Now, hold on just a minute. I didn't 'take' your son anywhere. Not on purpose at least."

Trisha furrowed her brow. "What's that supposed to mean?"

"He stowed away with me. I had no idea he was in my plane

when I took off half an hour ago. He was there without my permission." Jake gestured at Petey. "I didn't see him until I was twelve thousand feet in the air."

Trisha suddenly felt nauseous. Her son was twelve thousand feet in the air?

Petey peeled away from Trisha's body, and she saw now that he was crying. "I'm sorry, Mom. I didn't mean to go on a plane. I was just playing. Vi said I could go anywhere in her yard, and the dock is part of her yard." He sucked in a shallow breath as he cried harder. "Please don't be mad at Jake. It's not his fault."

Trisha lifted her gaze to the man in front of her. He was wearing dark sunglasses. She wished she had something covering her eyes right now too. Some say the eyes are the window to the soul, and right now she guessed there was a television screen of emotions visible for him to watch.

She lowered her gaze back down to Petey. "You were in his plane without his permission?"

"I didn't know he was going to take off. Then he got in, and I was worried I would get in trouble so I hid. Then the plane started moving. I didn't know what to do."

"As soon as I realized your boy was on board, I redirected my path back home." Jake grimaced slightly. "In full disclosure, I did take the long way back so he could see the lake. He's new to town, and I thought he'd enjoy it. Sorry 'bout that."

Trisha felt frazzled and frayed. She wasn't sure if she was supposed to be upset with Petey or Jake, or just be happy that he was safe.

Vi reached them now. "Petey was on your plane?"

Jake gave a brief nod. "A stowaway."

Vi put her hands on her hips as she looked at Petey. "Well, did you see anything interesting up there in the clouds?"

Petey blinked up at her, the tears on his cheeks drying quickly in the sun. "Yes," he said almost shyly.

Vi chuckled softly. "Wonderful. You can tell me all about it over lunch. I made farmer's stew from my garden."

Trisha opened her mouth to protest. But Vi was her boss, and technically Petey was the one who'd done wrong. Trisha was wrong too. She looked at Jake, discomfort tightening her chest. "I'm sorry for yelling at you."

He lifted his sunglasses onto the crown of his head, revealing blue eyes the color of the lake behind him. There was no mistaking that he was a handsome man—and her mind and body agreed. "You can make it up to me by saying yes to my grandmother's lunch. Farmer's stew is my favorite, especially when she includes a side of cheese drop biscuits."

"They're in the oven." Vi turned back to the house as if the answer was already yes.

Trisha guessed it was. She didn't really see how she could possibly say no.

* * *

Grandma Vi's farmer's stew tasted like home.

Jake's spoon paused before reaching his mouth. He was surprised that he still thought of Somerset Lake as home. This was where he'd grown up, though, and these rental cottages along the lakeshore brought back memories—mostly good, but there were one or two weeds in the lot.

Jake refocused on the bowl of colorful vegetables in front of him. He lifted his spoon to his lips and let the tangy taste of tomato, corn, beans, and spices hit his tongue. "So you moved here for the job?" he asked Trisha.

Vi was the one who answered. "I placed an online ad, and Trisha interviewed for the position here. As soon as I met her, I just knew she was meant to work at the Somerset Cottages with me."

"I didn't know you even knew how to turn on a computer, much less place an ad, Grandma."

Vi lifted her chin high, looking down her nose at him. "I should take offense to that. I'm old, but not too old to learn new tricks. Since your grandfather has been gone, I've taken up lots of new hobbies, including computers. It keeps my mind young." She reached for a cheese drop biscuit with her right arm. Her left side was still weak from last year's stroke.

"You didn't want to hire someone locally?" Jake dipped his spoon into his stew. "No offense to you." He looked at Trisha.

The newcomer stiffened. "None taken," she said, but he could tell by her posture that her defenses were up.

Vi bit into her biscuit while catching the crumbs with a shaky hand. "Well, I interviewed Cristina Meadows," she said after chewing and swallowing. "You remember her, right?"

Jake nodded. He'd dated Cristina for about a month in high school when he'd been on a small break from his longtime girl-friend, Rachel. And Rachel had dated a guy named Miles Bruno during that brief time; Jake had never liked Miles again.

"But when she toured the cottages, Cristina decided she wasn't interested in the job after all," Vi said. "I guess there's a lot more work to be done than she'd expected." Vi reached for her glass of sweet tea. Even though it was with her strong arm, her hand shook. Maybe it was just age.

"So Trisha came to interview, and I couldn't be happier that she did." Vi beamed at her new employee.

Jake tried to stay casual as he turned to Trisha. "So you just up and moved your entire life for this job?"

Trisha shifted. If he wasn't mistaken, her hands shook as well. "Um, well…We were looking for a change of scenery, and the town of Somerset Lake seemed like a wonderful place for a fresh start."

"Why would you need a fresh start?" Jake asked.

"Jake," Vi said sternly, "what are you doing?" She looked at Trisha. "I'm so sorry. As a lawyer, Jake thinks it's his job to cross-examine everyone."

"I'm just asking a friendly question, Grandma. I'm trying to get to know my new neighbor."

Trisha looked at Petey for a moment. "Sweetwater Springs is our hometown," she said. "I'm sure you understand the need to get away and experience a new place."

Jake grabbed the biscuit on his plate. "Perfectly. I left Somerset Lake when I was eighteen years old. I haven't spent a summer here in over a decade."

"It's overdue. There is no life like lake life." Vi smiled crookedly, the left corner of her mouth not quite reaching as high as the right. "I'm glad I have you both here together. I need to ask for your help."

Jake straightened. "What's wrong?"

She waved a hand. "Nothing is wrong necessarily." Vi slid her bowl of soup away and folded her hands on the table in front of her, looking between him and Trisha. "It's just, the cottages are dying."

Jake was glad to hear she agreed. Maybe talking her into selling would be easier than his family suspected. It was better to sell than lose them to the bank.

"Only four are rented out, and two are occupied by the two of you." Worry creased the area between her blue eyes. "So I've decided it's time for a change."

"I couldn't agree more." Jake reached for his glass of tea. "And I'll help you in any way I can."

Vi looked pleased. "There are six that are open right now. I've already told Trisha this, but I want to reinvigorate them. A few still have damage from last summer's hurricane. They need minor repairs, painting, and landscaping. They need a good cleaning too."

"That would definitely increase their market value when we sell." Jake bit into his biscuit.

Vi frowned at him. "Sell?" she repeated in disbelief. "These cottages are part of our family. Our legacy."

Jake chewed and swallowed. "I thought that's why you wanted to fix them up."

"No. I want to rent them out. It's much too big a job for one person though. I can't expect Trisha to take care of everything on her own. I want you both to work together to spit shine them and get new blood living under their roofs."

Jake looked at Trisha, who seemed as taken aback by the idea as him, although he was sure her reasons for being shocked were probably different. "Grandma, the cottages haven't been updated since before I was born. It won't happen overnight."

She pulled her bowl of soup back toward her and picked up her spoon again. "Well, you said you'd be here for a good month. A lot can happen in that amount of time," she said, eyes twinkling.

* * *

Even though it was evening now, Trisha was still trying to relax after the long lunch at Vi's house. She walked out on her front porch overlooking the lake and sat in one of the red Adirondack chairs. Then, without thinking, she glanced over at Jake's house.

He wasn't sitting outside. *Thank goodness.* Then she would've been forced to wave at him politely, and all her efforts to calm down since their last encounter would've been for nothing.

He'd interrogated her. She was a good person. She'd never even gotten a speeding ticket. She'd worked at the women's shelter in Sweetwater Springs for the last several years helping women who were trying hard to rebuild their lives. She didn't need an award, but she also didn't deserve to be treated like she belonged in a prison cell. Like her ex.

"Mama?" Petey pushed through the screen door and stepped onto the porch. "What are you doing?"

Trisha glanced over. "Enjoying the view."

Petey looked out on the lake as well. "It's pretty here. You should see what it looks like from the sky." As soon as the words left his mouth, he looked regretful, lowering his chin to his chest.

Trisha reached out and tugged him toward her. "I bet it was a lot of fun up there, huh?"

He wasn't too big to crawl into her lap just yet. She wrapped her arms around him, and they both looked out into the night.

"So fun. Scary, too, but more fun than scary."

Trisha laughed quietly. "I'm just glad you're okay."

"Jake took good care of me. He's really nice."

"Mm-hmm," Trisha said, not exactly agreeing.

Petey grew quiet for a moment. In that moment, the night seemed to thicken as the sun continued its descent behind the mountain ridgeline. "Mom?"

"Yes?"

"When are we going to visit Dad again?"

Trisha had been traveling up to the prison, two hours away, once or twice a month, but they'd missed last month's visit due to the move. "Soon. I'm sure he misses you."

She'd filed for divorce pretty quickly once she'd realized the charges against Peter weren't a big misunderstanding like she'd been telling everyone who would listen. She'd never yelled. She'd never cried—not in front of anyone at least. Despite his failings, Peter was still Petey's father, his namesake even, so she'd done what she thought was the right thing and she'd driven Petey up to the prison for monthly visits.

Family and friends told Trisha how impressed they were with

her strength. Trisha wasn't sure if it was a strength or if she was just really good at pushing her feelings down. She was a mother after all. She didn't have time for breakdowns. Petey was her first priority. He needed the basic necessities, which were all her responsibility now. And he needed as much love as she could give him because he only had one parent most days.

"I miss Dad," Petey said, resting his head against her chest. "When will he get out?"

Trisha had been asked this question before. Petey knew the answer, but maybe he thought the answer might change if he asked enough times. "Five years."

"I'll be twelve years old," Petey said.

"Mm-hmm."

They grew quiet again, looking out on the lake. It was peaceful here.

"Will you ever get married again?" Petey asked after several minutes.

That was something Petey hadn't asked before. "Where did that question come from?"

He shrugged against her. "I had friends at my old school whose moms married guys who weren't their dads. Will that happen to me too?"

"I don't know. Not anytime soon," Trisha said. "Would you be sad if I did remarry?"

"I guess not. As long as he's cool. Jake is pretty cool. I've never met a pilot before. He's really good at it too. He said he's only ever crashed once."

Trisha stopped breathing for a moment. "He's crashed before?"

"Yep. Neat, huh?"

This made Trisha laugh. "No, not neat."

"Well, I was wondering. Since I've already been up once, shouldn't I be able to do it again?"

Trisha squeezed him in a hug. "No, you shouldn't. And if you do, you'll be grounded until you're one hundred years old. Maybe longer. Now go inside and get ready for bed."

"Already?"

"Yep. It's a big day tomorrow."

Petey stood and faced her. "Why?"

"Because we have a long to-do list for the empty rental cottages. You're my helper."

"Jake too," Petey noted. "Vi told him so."

Yeah, Trisha was trying not to dwell too much on that fact right now. She didn't mind giving Jake a list of things to handle for the cottages, but she didn't intend to do any of it together.

"Go brush your teeth and change into your pajamas," she told Petey. He disappeared back inside the cottage. Then Trisha turned toward a noise coming from the cottage to her left and sucked in a sharp breath. Jake was standing there on his porch. Bare-chested with a pair of low-slung jeans.

Trisha gulped. How was she going to focus on the cottages if he was around? Next question: How was she going to get rid of him?

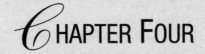CHAPTER FOUR

$\mathscr{T}$risha rolled out of bed with her alarm clock the next morning. She tiptoed half asleep down the hall and grabbed her cardigan off the back of a stool at her kitchen island. Then she walked to the lakeside door and slid her feet into a pair of flip-flops.

As usual at this hour, Petey was still sleeping. Trisha would venture to guess that so was Mr. S somewhere down the lakeshore.

The sun wasn't quite up so the air held a slight chill to it as Trisha hurried down the steps with a towel draped over one arm. Her gaze stayed on the water for the first leg of the walk. There was something magical about Somerset Lake. It eased some space inside her that had felt restless and achy since the whole thing with Peter. Watching the water gave her serenity for the moment she focused on it.

Trisha looked forward just in time to keep from tripping over a sleeping, naked man. *Poof!* There went the fleeting serenity. She tossed the towel over his midsection and dipped down to tap Mr. S's shoulder. "Wake up. Time to go home, Mr. S."

He groaned as he cracked open one cataract-glazed eye. "T, my beautiful alarm clock."

"Yep. Afraid so. Vi doesn't like you sleeping out here, and it's my job to—"

"Yeah, yeah. I know." He sat up, and Trisha looked away, trying not to get more of a look-see than she wanted as the towel slid off the mound of his belly. The memory of her eyeful of Jake last night came to mind.

She'd gotten a good look at Jake's chiseled abs. He'd had a little patch of golden chest hair too. Not too much, but he wasn't the kind of guy who waxed, which she liked. Lucy from The Village was right. Jake was quite the view when he wasn't giving Trisha the third degree.

Mr. S stood and secured the towel around his waist as if he'd just stepped out of the shower. "See you tomorrow, T."

"Or you could just stay in your bed tomorrow," Trisha suggested. "That would make Vi happy." And her.

Mr. S grunted, which Trisha took as a no. She felt a frown tug at the corners of her mouth. Every job had its downsides. This was one of being the property manager here.

She hurried back up the shore toward Juniper Cottage and took the steps two at a time.

"How's Mr. S doing this morning?" a voice asked as she reached the deck.

Trisha turned to face Jake, who still wasn't wearing a shirt. He was holding a steaming mug in his hand. Trisha had succeeded in quickly looking away from Mr. S, but she couldn't pull her gaze from Jake. "He's, um, well, he's back inside Bear Cottage now and hopefully putting on pants." She swallowed as her eyes traveled down Jake's bare chest. "And a shirt."

Jake looked at her. "In this town, the signs don't read *No Shirt, No Shoes, No Service*."

Trisha folded her arms over her chest, squeezing herself in a barely perceptible hug. "No?"

Jake sipped his beverage, taking his time in answering. "It's *No Shirt, No Shoes, No Problem*." A slow smile crawled onto his cheeks, creating dimples. "I guess Mr. S took that literally."

"Apparently so. Well, have a good morning." Trisha offered a smile that felt forced because she was still a little peeved about the way Jake questioned her over lunch yesterday. She gave a quick wave and headed inside to check on Petey, who was still sleeping. Good. She could get started on making breakfast and have her first cup of coffee, too, if she was lucky.

Predictably, Petey shuffled down the hall within five minutes of hearing the rattle of pots and pans. His hair was a sight to behold, poking into the air in various directions.

"Coffee?" Trisha asked, laughing when Petey's pillow-creased face twisted adorably.

"Yuck, Mom. I drink orange juice."

"Oh, that's right." She grabbed a glass and poured him a healthy serving, setting it on the counter. Then she prepared him a bowl of cereal. "I'm getting dressed. Once you're done eating, I want you to get dressed too. We have a busy morning, remember?"

Petey gave an enthusiastic nod. "We need new blood in the cottages for Vi."

Trisha laughed and then turned toward a knock on her door. Jake was standing on the other side, wearing a T-shirt now. Even with *shirt and shoes*, he was a big problem.

* * *

Jake knew an irritated woman when he saw one. He'd thought they'd cleared up the misunderstanding about Petey's plane ride with him, but maybe Trisha was holding a grudge. Or maybe he'd asked too many questions at lunch yesterday. Yeah, that was probably true.

Trisha walked toward the screen door but didn't open it. "Hello again." She appeared to be waiting for him to explain why he was standing on her porch.

"I'm here to work," Jake told her. "Vi said she wanted us to get started on the rental cottages today. I figure that means we need to go through each of the vacant ones and make a list of what needs fixing." And he fully intended for that list to be so long that Vi realized she was in over her head with renovations. It would only help to prove that selling was for the best. He also intended to find out more about the Somerset Cottages' beautiful new property manager.

Trisha folded her arms over her chest like she'd done earlier as they'd stood on their respective porches talking to each other. "I don't think we need to assess them together."

"We should be on the same page when we make our recommendations to Vi."

Trisha seemed to think on her answer. "I've been working here for over a month. I've already determined what needs to be done."

"Then you can show me." He gave her a polite smile.

"Well, I'm afraid we're not ready yet. I need to get dressed and so does my son," she said.

Jake glanced past her to Petey, who was watching their conversation from the kitchen island. "Hey, Copilot."

"Hey, Jake. Are you flying today?" Petey got up and ran toward the door.

"Maybe. Not this morning though. We have work to do, you included."

Petey grinned. "My mom says I can't fly with you again until I'm one hundred years old."

Jake lifted his gaze to meet Trisha's. "That's a long time."

She played with the bracelet on her wrist. He'd seen her do this a couple times now and wondered if it was a nervous habit. "By then you'll be back home, wherever that is," she said.

"That's right." Once upon a time, he would've said Somerset Lake was home. But not these days. Neither was the DC area or Florida. He was currently without a place to call home.

"Where's Bailey?" Petey asked.

"She likes to sleep in," Jake said. "I'll grab her while you and your mom get ready for today. Maybe you can be in charge of Bailey while we're at the cottages. What do you think, Copilot?"

Petey bounced slightly on his heels. "Yes! I'll go get dressed right now."

Jake watched the boy race down the hall that had once been his own stomping ground. Then he looked at Trisha again. Her features were soft, but her expression was hard. She didn't like him all that much. That was easy to see. He wanted to not like her, too, because that would make his role here easier.

He did like her though. She had grit, and from what he'd seen, she seemed to be a hard worker. "Why don't you just stop by my place and get me when you're ready?"

Trisha hesitated. "I'll have my son with me, and he's a lot to deal with. He asks lots of questions and gets into trouble sometimes."

Jake chuckled as he turned to head down her steps. If he let her, he supposed she'd continue to make excuses until she found a viable one. "I don't mind. I like kids," he called over his shoulder. Then he paused, looked back, and met Trisha's gaze. "Meet me at my place then?"

Trisha hesitated. "Give us fifteen minutes."

"You got it." Jake headed over to Peony Cottage and climbed the steep set of steps. Bailey was waiting by the screen door.

If a dog could pout, she was. Her expectation was that anytime Jake left home, he was to take her with him.

He opened the sliding glass door and patted her head. "Jealous?" he asked, running his hand down her coat of dark brown and black. "Don't be. I was setting up plans for our morning that include you getting to play with our copilot next door."

Bailey didn't understand him, of course, but she looked excited anyway. And despite the friction between him and Trisha, he was excited too. Trisha felt like a challenge somehow. If she smiled and gave him the time of day, he would win.

It was silly. And dangerous. He didn't need to get involved with someone who was on the opposing side of his mission at Somerset Lake.

His phone dinged with an incoming text.

I've changed my schedule. I'm coming to town sometime in the next two weeks, depending on how this case I'm working plays out. It was from his uncle Tim. If you can't convince Vi to sell, I will.

Jake muttered a choice word under his breath. Then he whirled to the sound of a soft gasp on the other side of his screen door, where Petey was standing, mouth gaping.

"You said a bad word." Petey pointed and grinned mischievously. "Don't worry. I won't tell my mom."

Jake liked this kid a lot. "Where is your mom, Copilot?"

"She's coming up the steps. She said a bad word, too, right after you left."

A laugh kicked its way out of Jake's belly, unexpected and unannounced. Then he laid eyes on Trisha as she cleared his porch and another feeling kicked its way through his chest, unexpected, unannounced, and unwanted.

A camera hung from around her neck.

"Are you a photographer?" he asked.

She shook her head. "Aspiring, I guess. I've owned this camera for a while and haven't learned the basics yet."

Jake dropped his gaze to the nice Canon. It was a pricey piece of equipment, which struck him oddly because nothing else about Trisha screamed money. "Maybe you'll be an expert by the end of the summer."

She looked down at her camera and back at him. "That's the goal. Not an expert, but maybe just competent enough to snap the *after* pictures of the cottages once they're renovated."

Jake stepped onto the porch with Trisha, Bailey following at his heels. "I think that's a great goal."

Trisha smiled. A real, genuine smile. As quickly as the smile bloomed, however, it dropped into a straight line across her lips. "I think we got off to a bad start yesterday. I'd like to try again. If we're going to be temporary neighbors and working together for Vi, we should get along." She offered him her hand.

They might be working for Vi, but they had two very different goals. "Well, from my viewpoint, we're already getting along just fine." Jake slid his palm against Trisha's, finding her skin smooth and soft. "But you're right, our first impression of each other was a little shaky. I don't mind starting over. My name is Jake Fletcher."

The corner of her mouth curled slightly upward—another win for him. "I'm Trisha Langly."

Her last name was a new bit of information. Maybe he'd run an internet search on her later this evening. No harm in knowing who your neighbors were, especially ones working for his grandmother. Vi had a reputation for being open and trusting. Jake just needed to make sure Trisha Langly didn't take advantage.

* * *

Trisha didn't trust Jake. Of course, it was quite likely he was a very nice man, and the only factor in her not trusting him was that he was good-looking and charming. Those qualities set off little alarm bells inside her. Her ex was good-looking and charming too. Those two qualities were an easy mask to hide huge character flaws.

As they'd walked over to Jake's place, Trisha had reminded Petey of their rules.

"Remember what I told you," she'd said, looking down at him. "We don't talk about Daddy. Or why we left Sweetwater Springs. We don't talk about the past at all, okay?"

Petey's boyish grin had slipped away. "I know, Mom." Then he'd run off ahead of her to Jake's place.

Trisha felt horrible for asking her son to keep secrets. But it was for the best. They'd had a taste of living their truth in their last home.

Petey wasn't the only one who'd been bullied. Trisha had kept two jobs. One at the women's shelter and one cleaning houses on the weekend. One of her housekeeping clients used to follow her around as she'd cleaned once she'd found out about Peter's crimes. Then she'd let Trisha go, based on nothing but the supposition that she might be guilty too.

Jake closed his cottage door and stepped onto the deck. Bailey jogged over and sniffed Trisha's thighs and then returned to sniffing Petey's chest and neck where there were likely a few crumbs from the breakfast he'd gobbled down. "Sorry, she has no manners at all," Jake said of his dog.

Trisha shook her head. "She's fine."

Jake handed the leash to Petey. "Here you are, Copilot. We probably won't use this. Bailey is really good about not running off."

Petey took it and nodded, taking his job very seriously.

They headed down the steps and along the shore in front of the cottages.

"Which place do you want to start with?" Trisha asked.

Jake gestured toward the end of the shore where the woods popped up beyond Bear Cottage. "I figured we'd go all the way to the end and work our way back. Sound good?" He glanced over.

When he did, Trisha didn't look away fast enough. She found herself staring into those blue eyes of his. This was a working relationship, she reminded herself. That was all.

She pulled her gaze away. "Yes, that sounds like a plan." They walked for a few moments in silence. Then she asked, "What brings you here? I mean, not many people can afford to take off an entire month for a lake vacation."

Jake shoved his fingers into the pockets of his jeans. "I recently got out of a romantic relationship. It seemed like a good time to make a few life changes. I'm heading to Florida to work with my family."

"So you decided to break up with everything in your life?" she asked.

"Actually, my ex is the one who broke up with me."

"Really?"

Jake looked over and grinned. "You sound surprised. You don't think I'm capable of running a woman off?"

Trisha shook her head and answered a little too quickly, "Oh, I'm sure you are. What did you do to make your ex dump you?" Not that it was any of her business. She didn't want to talk about her past so she really shouldn't be prying into his. But since he was being so open, she had to admit that she was curious.

"Nothing really. We just grew apart. Parting ways felt like the next right step in our relationship."

Trisha found herself suddenly sympathizing with Jake. "I'm sorry."

Jake looked over. "It's okay. At least I got to keep the dog."

They were now standing in front of Bear Cottage, the last of the family's property. Trisha gestured. "Mr. S lives here, of course. So we'll go to this one." She pointed at Magnolia Cottage. "Ready?"

"Lead the way," he said.

They walked inside Magnolia Cottage, and Trisha stood back while Jake walked around and Petey played with Bailey.

Jake's gaze roamed the open floor plan, no doubt taking in what a fixer-upper the place was. She'd already seen what needed to be done, and it was extensive—more than she could do on her own.

Jake craned his neck back and stared at the ceiling, where there was a hole in the roof. A bright blue tarp could be seen covering it from the other side.

"A guy that Vi knew helped me get the tarps up there a couple weeks ago," Trisha explained. "Before that, I placed buckets around the room whenever it stormed."

Jake chuckled as he looked at her. "That's an unusual job requirement."

"It was kind of fun," she said with a shrug. "Wasn't it, Petey?"

Petey looked up from playing with Bailey and grinned. "I miss using the buckets to catch the rain."

Jake laughed and returned to scrutinizing the roof. "I can get up on the roof and patch that hole this week."

Trisha felt her lips part. "What? You're going to fix it?"

Jake looked at her. "You seem surprised."

"Well, I mean, you're a lawyer. Fixing a roof isn't exactly something they teach you in law school."

"No, but it's something I learned growing up around here," Jake explained. "Gramps was always working on repairs of some sort for these cottages. It just requires a trip to the hardware store and a day's work." He acted like that was no big deal.

But it felt like a big deal. Trisha had been trying to figure out how she was going to work with the leaks with the small budget that Vi had given her for repairs. It was basically only enough to cover supplies. "That would be wonderful," Trisha said. "Thank you."

Jake gestured at the hole again. "Is this the only roof that leaks?"

"No, Jasmine Cottage also has a spot. There isn't a visible hole, but when it rains, the floor has a puddle."

"I'll do that one too." Jake continued to look around the cottage. "The walls need painting," he said.

"Definitely. I already have that on my list. I think these walls used to be white at some point." This made Jake laugh, which did something funny to her chest.

"What else is on your list?" he asked.

"Well, um, the appliances are old."

"You mean ancient?" he asked with a wide grin.

"Yes, exactly. I was thinking I'd check out the Habitat for Humanity ReStore that Vi told me about. They might have some used appliances that can be switched out with these."

"Good idea," Jake said. "Maybe I should go with you when you check that place out."

Trisha shook her head. "That's not necessary. You're already fixing the roofs, which I really appreciate."

"I have the truck," he said matter-of-factly. "If you find an appliance, how will you get it back here?"

Trisha grimaced. She was hoping the thrift store delivered, but judging by Jake's question, they most likely didn't. "That's a good point."

"Besides, this is my family's property, and Vi is my grandmother. I should be helping as much as I can. I'm here, so use me," he said.

Something else loosened in Trisha's chest. He was being overly nice, but he seemed sincere. "Thank you again."

"You're welcome. We'll handle the insides of these places and leave the exterior for last. Except for the roofs, of course. Those need to be done as soon as possible."

She nodded. "That was my plan too."

"Great. Sounds like we're on the same page." They headed out of the cottage and down the deck's steps. Then Trisha and Petey started to head in the direction of the next empty place.

Jake called out to them. "Since we're all the way out on this stretch of the lake, I want to show you something," he said, standing rooted in front of Magnolia Cottage.

Maybe she'd found Jake to be nicer today, but she still felt guarded where he was concerned. "What is it?"

He tugged the ball cap on his head a little lower to shield his face from the sun, which was now out in full force. "I'd rather show you." He pointed toward the woods beyond Bear Cottage. "It's down that trail."

Trisha's mouth dropped open. "You want us to go into the woods with you?"

"If you're going to be part of the town of Somerset Lake, you should know the ins and outs. Things that only locals can show you."

Trisha looked at the trail again. "Aren't there bears in there?"

"They're very unlikely to be on the trail. And we can be noisy to alert them we're coming." Jake gestured at the camera around her neck. "Might be good photo ops for that camera of yours. Trust me."

Trisha swallowed. She didn't trust Jake. And she didn't trust herself where he was concerned either.

"Come on, Mom," Petey said, already leading the way with Bailey at his heels.

Jake chuckled. "I didn't nickname him Copilot for nothing." He turned and began to follow her son.

Trisha stood just a second longer. Then she started walking, too, picking up speed to catch up. Just in case there was a bear nearby. The sun seemed to disappear behind the canopy. The air became cooler too.

"Are you a romantic?" Jake asked a couple minutes later.

Trisha's steps slowed on the path. "Excuse me?"

He pointed at a wooden sign on a tree as they approached. ROMANTICS ONLY. CYNICS TURN BACK.

Trisha furrowed her brow as Jake looked at her.

"Well? Are you?" he asked.

Trisha looked at him. "I used to be. Not anymore."

CHAPTER FIVE

It's been forever since I've been back here." Jake kept his gaze forward, waiting for the first glimpse of the old gated area he and his friends used to visit.

"Is this part of your family's property?" Trisha asked.

"Yep. Gramps made this trail, but he didn't make what we're coming to see. It's a mystery who did." Jake chuckled. "My grandfather was so angry when he discovered it back here. He was going to tear it down, but the place became kind of a landmark around Somerset Lake."

The gate came into view now. The sign was crooked like it always had been.

"*Lost Love Cemetery*," Trisha read. She stopped walking. "You're taking me to a cemetery?"

Jake grinned at the shock and mild horror in Trisha's expression. "Don't worry. There aren't people buried in there. Just the memories of those that someone used to love. Which I think is pretty romantic."

"How do you bury memories?" Petey asked. The kid was always listening and asking questions.

"Well, you take something that belonged to them. You get a box or a bottle, and you bury that item in it. It's kind of symbolic of letting go of that person's hold on your heart."

"Have you buried a memory in there?" Petey asked next.

Jake looked up to span the cemetery, his gaze holding on a spot in the back where a metal spoon poked up out of the ground. "Yep, I have."

But he didn't want to talk about that relationship. He'd tried to bury it, but his first love's ghost still haunted him from time to time, especially when he was in town visiting.

Jake opened the gate to the cemetery and gestured at Trisha. "Come on. It'll be fun. This is the kind of thing that small towns are known for. Their hidden oddities that make city folks scratch their heads."

Trisha laughed, and it felt like he'd hit the lottery. "You're not telling me anything I don't already know. I grew up in a small town, remember?"

"Right." Jake put his fingers in his pocket. "Sweetwater Springs. That name is familiar to me, but I can't pinpoint why."

Trisha slid a lock of hair behind her ears. "Well, four or five years ago, it was named the most romantic town in America. Just in a magazine's list, but it got a lot of national attention."

Jake shook his head as they stepped down little rows of mementos sticking up out of the ground, marking individual plots. Some people made homemade signs. Other spots had plastic flowers marking where something was buried. "No, that's not ringing a bell. But I don't read magazines or watch much TV." Jake glanced over at Petey, who was exploring the opposite side of the little patch of land. "Hey, Copilot, just don't let Bailey dig up anything. Stay in the aisles." He lowered his voice and looked at Trisha. "This is sacred ground in Somerset Lake."

"I'm not sure I've ever seen a place like this."

For a reason he couldn't explain, he began to lead Trisha to the back corner where the metal spoon poked up out of the ground. He stood in front of it for a solid minute. This was always where he felt Rachel's memory the strongest—not at her real grave.

"I buried the memory of my lost love here when I was eighteen," he said, squatting down in front of the spoon. He looked up at Trisha. "Rachel and I were together from our freshman year of high school until almost graduation. We had a few breakups in there, of course, where she saw another guy or I flirted with another girl. She was always it for me though. She was *the one*." It hurt to breathe suddenly. Jake cleared his throat, hoping that would clear his emotions too. "Rachel died a month before she could get her high school diploma."

Trisha's hands flew to her mouth. "I'm so sorry."

Jake looked at the tarnished spoon, almost black after all this time. "Me too. She was amazing. I'm sure I romanticize her in my head, but she was smart, nice, beautiful. Everything I ever wanted in a relationship. We used to joke that we were going to be that couple who got married the day after graduation and never left their hometown."

A pang of regret hit Jake in the chest harder than he'd expected.

Trisha's hand touched his shoulder, surprising him. "I'm so sorry," she repeated.

"Thanks." Jake reached out and touched the spoon. "This spoon fell out of her lunchbox before we were dating. I picked it up and used it as an excuse to drop by her house and give it back. The next day, she dropped it again." Jake stood because his legs were tired from squatting. "So I picked it up and brought it back to her. It became a sort of game until I got up the nerve to ask her out."

He looked at Trisha, who was quietly smiling. Jake shook his head. "Rachel said no."

Trisha's smile slid away as her eyes widened a touch. "Oh."

"Rachel wasn't old enough to date yet," Jake explained. "So she kept dropping the spoon, and I kept bringing it to her house after school to return it."

"That's a sweet story," Trisha said.

"She was a sweet girl. Anyway, that's why there's a spoon there. And buried under that is a bottle with a few trinkets and notes we'd exchanged when we were together."

"You're not afraid someone will take it?" Trisha asked.

"Nah." Jake shook his head. "I wasn't kidding when I said this was sacred ground. People love this place."

Trisha lifted her camera off her chest. "Do you mind if I take a few pictures? Just for practice. I'm not that good."

"Go ahead. Just keep inside the aisles." He winked, which made Trisha visibly stiffen. Winking was something he'd always done. It wasn't flirty. Not usually, at least. But *yeah*, with Trisha, without meaning for it to be, it was.

* * *

Trisha realized too late that she was putting herself in an awkward position, trying to take pictures with this fancy camera when she didn't know the first thing about photography. She'd always loved pictures. They represented home to her, which was something that always felt elusive. Until Peter came along and showered her with his love and attention. For the first time in her life, fleeting as it was, she'd felt like she belonged.

She wanted to learn photography. But she didn't want to do

so in front of a man she barely knew. She preferred to look like an idiot when she was alone.

Trisha lifted the camera off her chest and looked around the Lost Love Cemetery for an object to focus her attention on, hoping Jake wouldn't notice that she was even less than an amateur.

She wanted to snap a picture of the spoon because it represented so much emotion. A simple spoon carried so much weight once she knew the story behind it. But it felt wrong to aim her camera there with Jake watching, so she looked for something else. There was a little spot with an orange flag blowing in the breeze. She stepped over and looked at it. There was a message attached to it, weatherproofed by clear masking tape.

Trisha squatted and pinched the tiny flag to read. "'Here lies the memory of the guy who cheated on me with my sister.'" Trisha grimaced as she looked up at Jake. "Now that's a story."

He chuckled. "I can probably guess who put that one there."

Trisha moved on to another marker since that one wasn't really the most romantic. She found a glass jar with two marbles inside. She read the label on the jar. "'I lost my heart and my marbles.'" This one made Trisha laugh.

"I bet I can guess who put that there too."

Trisha looked at him again. "I thought you've been gone for a while."

"Doesn't mean I'm not on Facebook like everyone else. And Reva Dawson has her own blog devoted to Somerset Lake, filling everyone in on all the small-town gossip. Have you met Reva yet?"

"No." Thankfully. Trisha wasn't a fan of gossip. She continued looking at the "grave" markers. "Okay, I can take a picture of that one." She pointed at a large river stone with a couple's initials written in black Sharpie. Pulling her camera up in front of her face, she prepared to take a picture. But everything was black.

"Might want to, uh, remove the lens cap," Jake suggested.

Heat flooded Trisha's cheeks. Such an amateur. "Right." She took the lens cap off and glanced over to look at Petey, who was sitting on the ground outside the gate with Bailey. He appeared to be talking to the dog, which was sweet, and also sad. Petey needed a real friend. Real friends were hard to have when you held secrets though. Secrets kept a superficial shell around you, making it hard to get too close.

"A Canon SLR, huh?" Jake asked, bringing Trisha's focus back to him.

She slid her gaze sideways. "You know your cameras."

Jake had his fingers in his pockets, which seemed to be his normal stance. "I study things," he said. "It's been kind of a hobby since I was a kid."

Trisha straightened and let her camera rest on her chest. "What do you study?"

"Any subject I'm interested in. I read manuals and how-to books. That's my thing."

"Photography?" Trisha asked.

"And gardening, mechanics, carpentry, welding, anything and everything. I've never planted a seed in my life, but I know how to." He gestured to Trisha's camera. "I've never held a fancy camera like yours, but I know exactly how it works."

Trisha's mouth fell open. "That's a strange hobby."

He chuckled. "Yeah, well, I also fly planes."

"That one's a bit cooler," she said, a teasing tone in her voice.

"You didn't think so yesterday."

"Yeah, well, I was worried my son was drowning or being eaten by a bear at the time."

"Do you always assume the worst?" Jake asked.

Trisha's lips parted. "I'm a mom," she said, as if that

explained it. "It's kind of my job to make sure he's safe. But I will admit that flying planes is cool."

"Your hobby is photography?" Jake asked.

She glanced at her camera. "I wouldn't say that. I barely know how to turn this thing on. And I can't find the manual it came with. It was a gift."

"Someone must think an awful lot of you to give you something so expensive."

Trisha looked down at her feet. She took a breath and pulled her gaze back up to meet his. "I guess so."

He seemed to wait for her to say more. She didn't. She'd already said too much.

"Do you mind?" He gestured to the camera.

"No." She took the strap from around her neck and handed it to him, listening as he rattled off jargon about the camera's features. Then he held it up to his eyes. He turned the dials around the lens, back and forth, back and forth, until he finally seemed satisfied. "There." He handed the camera back.

Trisha hesitated before grabbing it and holding the viewfinder up to her eyes. She aimed the camera at the jar of marbles. The image was clear and focused.

"You, uh, need to put your finger on the shutter release," Jake said.

Trisha stiffened as his hand took hers, guiding her index finger to rest over the button. She pressed it, maybe a little too quickly, to get him to remove his hand. But as soon as his hand left hers, she wanted it to return. The feel of his skin on hers was intoxicating. It left her mouth dry, her body warm, and little sparkles resonating throughout her chest.

This wasn't good at all. Once upon a time, she would've thought that was the best feeling imaginable. An insta-crush complete with the kind of warm tingles that left her wide awake in bed, dreaming of the next look, next touch, next everything.

She was older now though. Wiser. And yeah, a little bitter from her heart's battering and wear. These fluttering-heart feelings weren't welcome.

She focused her camera again, aiming it at the jar of marbles. It would be a quirky image with a story all its own. Someone lost their marbles in a relationship. She could relate. Only, she'd lost a lot more than marbles. That's why keeping Jake at a safe distance was necessary.

His hand slipped over hers again, the feel of his skin brushing over hers.

"What are you doing?" she asked, breathless.

"Showing you the dials. You have to turn them to focus the lens."

"Yeah, I know that," she said. But he was right. The camera wasn't even focused on the jar. The image was blurry. She took a breath. Then she turned the dial, her fingers under his. She looked in the viewfinder and waited for the perfect picture to emerge. When it did, she pushed the button again.

"There." Jake winked at her. "That's going to be a keeper."

She ignored that little jump in her pulse. Then she felt a sense of dread wash over her for seemingly no reason. She turned frantically to look outside the gate. "Petey!" She started running, not bothering to stay in the aisles like Jake had said repeatedly. "Petey!" she called again, flying out the gate and around the corner where he was sitting. His hands were clutching his throat.

Trisha scanned him, trying to figure out the reason for his distress. All she saw were tiny ants.

Jake caught up to her. "What's wrong?"

Trisha squatted next to Petey. "Can you breathe? Talk to me!"

Petey's eyes were large and frightened. "It's hard...to breathe."

But he was talking. Which meant there wasn't any object obstructing his airway. Her gaze went back to the ants. Then she noticed a couple on Petey's leg. She swatted them away.

"Is he allergic?" Jake asked.

Trisha shook her head quickly. "I don't think so."

Petey was still gasping for air, his throat making a scraping sound with each quick, sharp intake of breath.

"We need to get him to a hospital," Jake said.

Trisha was about to pick Petey up to carry him, but Jake beat her to it.

"It'll be faster if I do it." He picked Petey up like it was nothing and started racing back toward their cottages, leaving Trisha working hard to keep up. Her heart was beating so hard that she thought it might explode inside her chest.

"Do you have an EpiPen?" Jake called behind him.

"No." Why would she? Petey wasn't allergic to anything. Or he hadn't been.

"I have one in my truck," Jake said. "Almost there, buddy," he told Petey.

"Why do we need an EpiPen?" Trisha asked frantically, feeling like it was hard to breathe herself.

"Because he's in anaphylactic shock."

Trisha was pretty sure the meaning of the word was every bit as scary as it sounded.

"I'll give him the shot and drive you both to the hospital. It's faster than nine-one-one out here. Trust me," Jake said for the second time today.

She didn't argue. She was just glad he had a plan because she felt helpless right now, and she needed someone to take charge of the situation. In this moment, she had no choice but to trust Jake Fletcher.

* * *

The last hour had been a whirlwind of what seemed like life and death, and now Jake sat in one of the chairs situated along the wall of Petey's hospital room. Trisha sat in another that was scooted up to the bed. Petey was seemingly oblivious to the commotion he'd caused and was sleeping soundly.

Jake could only see the back of Trisha, but he thought maybe he heard a few sniffles coming from her direction. "You okay?" he asked for the tenth time.

"I'm fine. You don't have to stay," she said, also for the tenth time.

He shifted in the hard chair. Why hospitals couldn't afford comfortable chairs, he'd never understand. "I'm not leaving you alone here. I'll go sit in the waiting room if you'd prefer."

She turned to look at him now. When she did, he saw that his suspicions were right. The whites of her eyes were bloodshot. He reached for a box of tissues and passed it to her.

"You don't have anyone else here in Somerset Lake. You shouldn't be alone. Just in case you need water or a snack. Or if you need to go to the restroom and don't want to leave Petey alone. Or if you need a Kleenex."

She took the box and pulled out a tissue. "Thank you."

He watched as she dabbed under her eyes.

"I don't know what I would have done if you hadn't been there today."

"Well, you wouldn't have been in the Lost Love Cemetery if it weren't for me so this is kind of my fault."

Trisha clutched the wadded tissue in her hand. "Petey is alive because of you. If you hadn't had that EpiPen…" She trailed off. "Petey has never had an allergic reaction before. To anything. Why did you have an EpiPen in your truck anyway?"

Jake kicked his legs out in front of him, crossing one shoe

over the other. "Because I'm allergic to peanuts." He always felt a little weak when he told people. "The kids used to have a field day with that fact when I was younger. I sat at a separate lunch table because of all the peanut butter and jelly sandwiches. It was—*it is*—my kryptonite."

Trisha looked at him with interest. "You've had an attack like Petey did?"

Jake glanced at Petey, his heart squeezing at the sight of the energetic boy lying there so helplessly. Then he looked at Trisha again, his heart squeezing for a different reason. She looked so devastated. His first instinct was to lean in and give her a hug, but he didn't think she'd allow him to. "Yeah. A couple of times. It's pretty scary."

Trisha's eyes teared up. She reached for another tissue as her expression crumpled. "I'm sorry. That was just"—she shook her head—"terrifying. He couldn't breathe." The tears started streaming down her cheeks. She used the tissue to wipe them away with a shaky hand. "And there was nothing I could do to help him."

Jake scooted up closer. "Hey, it's okay. It's going to be okay. These things happen all the time. The doctor will prescribe you an EpiPen to have handy if it happens again."

A startled noise came out of Trisha's throat. "Again?"

Jake reached for her hand and squeezed it, his gaze narrowing on hers. "Petey is okay. My copilot over there is going to be just fine."

"Thank you." She met his gaze. She looked so vulnerable right now. Far from the closed-off woman he'd met yesterday on the beach. She'd started warming up to him before Petey's attack, but now her guard was gone, shredded away by the stress of the day.

"Want me to call someone for you?" he asked.

She shook her head. "My closest friends and family are two hours away."

Was that where Petey's dad was? Wouldn't she at least call his dad to let him know what had happened?

Instinctively, Jake knew the answer was no. For whatever reason, the dad didn't appear to be in the picture. For another unknown reason, Trisha was all alone in a new town, where it seemed she hadn't made any friends aside from his grandmother. That raised all kinds of questions in Jake's mind. He didn't want to interrogate her right now though. All he wanted to do was be a much-needed friend.

CHAPTER SIX

An hour later, the physician walked in to check on Petey. Dr. Paschall was middle-aged and wore a long white lab coat with pens and lollipops poking out of the front pockets.

"You're awake," Dr. Paschall said. "That's a good sign."

Petey's eyes were open, but the usual spark of endless excitement was gone. He looked completely drained. Poor kid. Jake knew the feeling. The last time he'd gone into shock was when he was dating his ex in DC. He hadn't yet told her about his peanut allergy. It wasn't something that usually came up on a first date, or even the second.

She'd made him dinner at her place. When he'd asked what the menu was, it'd sounded safe enough. Steak, potatoes, and salad. A hearty meal with no indication that peanuts were involved. She'd made this vegetable dish to go with the meal, though, and Jake hadn't seen the peanuts until his throat started to close.

He'd wondered if he was being paranoid at first. He'd cleared his throat for what felt like a million times. Then his tongue began to feel like it was thickening. When he'd asked his date to call an ambulance, she'd looked horrified.

Jake leaned forward now and watched as the doctor checked Petey's neck and throat, listening to his heart and scribbling things down on his clipboard. Finally, Dr. Paschall looked at Trisha and Jake.

"Your son looks good," he said as his gaze floated between them.

Dr. Paschall thought Jake was Petey's dad. Trisha didn't correct him. Jake presumed it was because she thought it would've only made things awkward. The most important thing was to hear what the doctor was saying.

"I'm prescribing an EpiPen for Petey. He's allergic to ants so please keep this boy of yours far away from the insects."

Trisha leaned forward in her chair to get the doctor's attention. "But he's never been allergic to ants before. I'm sure he's been bitten in the past."

"He likely has. His response has just escalated with each bite. Today was the tipping point for him." The doctor looked back at Petey. "Little bites, big response. Steer clear, okay, buddy?"

"Yes, sir," Petey said.

Dr. Paschall reached into his pocket, grabbed a lollipop, and handed it to Petey. Then he grabbed a pen and scribbled more on the chart he was holding. When he was done, he looked at Trisha and Jake once more. "You can take him home. Might want to rest for the remainder of the day. A reaction like Petey's takes a toll on the body. Keep him indoors this evening."

Trisha nodded quickly. "We will . . . *I* will. Thank you, Doctor."

"You're welcome." The doctor offered Petey a high five and left the room.

"All right, sweetie," Trisha said to her son. "You heard the doc. Indoors and in bed for the rest of the day."

"He didn't say in bed," Petey corrected, looking at Jake for confirmation.

Jake held up his hands. "I'm staying out of this." He was only here for moral support. "But I think you should be sitting or lying down today. Speaking from experience."

Petey looked at Trisha. "Can we tell Dad what happened? He'd probably want to know that I was in the hospital and almost died."

Jake slid his gaze to Trisha. He could practically feel the tension rolling off her. She didn't look at him.

"We'll tell your father the next time we see him," she said. "Now get dressed, sweetheart. It's time to go home."

* * *

On the drive to the hospital, Trisha had been too worried about Petey to notice the scent of the interior of Jake's truck. Now, as he drove Petey and her home, she noticed the smell of his leather seats. It was a newer vehicle. That or kept nice, which Trisha guessed was much easier to do when you didn't have kids.

Jake didn't scream money when she looked at him, but he owned nice things. A nice vehicle. A plane. Nice clothes and a leather watchband on his wrist. She'd never been one to care about that sort of stuff, but after what her ex-husband had done, she purposely didn't keep expensive things. Except for her camera, which she'd left in Jake's truck as they'd raced into the emergency room hours earlier.

Trisha glanced over at Jake as he drove. "What did you do with Bailey?" She hadn't noticed or wondered about that on the way to the hospital. Honestly, the whole day was one big blur.

"I left her on the lake."

"By herself?" she asked.

Jake glanced over. "I texted Vi to bring her in. She's got her."

"Oh." Trisha met his gaze. "So Vi knows about Petey?"

Jake gave a subtle nod. "She does. If she still drove, I'm sure my grandmother would have rushed up to the hospital to sit with you."

"Vi is so thoughtful. She's a wonderful boss and friend." Trisha glanced over her shoulder to check on Petey, who seemed to have melted into the cab's back seat. The poor guy was exhausted. Trisha was tired too. All she wanted to do was go inside her home, make a warm bath, and cry in the tub.

The bathtub was her crying place. It was the only quiet space she got where Petey didn't interrupt her with a need or one of his questions. A single mother did what she had to.

Jake pulled in behind Juniper Cottage. "Home sweet home." He pulled the key from the ignition and looked over. "Let me help you get Petey inside?"

It was a question. Trisha could say no, but help sounded good. She had a bag of medication and papers, and she wasn't sure if Petey was woozy. Plus her son was a growing seven-year-old boy. Her days of picking him up were over.

"Thank you," she said in answer. "For everything."

"It's good to have people in your corner," Jake said, his gaze serious. Had he already figured out that she was deficient in that area? She'd been here for a month, and she'd stayed closed off. That seemed like the right thing to do to keep people from asking too many questions. If they wanted to make this their home, they couldn't risk getting too close to anyone. That had been her thought process at least.

But that mentality could've led to a disastrous situation with Petey today. If Jake hadn't been around, Trisha would have called 911, not knowing that it would take longer for them to reach the area. Not knowing that she needed an EpiPen and not having one. She wouldn't have been able to carry Petey up the shore on her own. She would have only had Vi's number programmed into her phone.

Vi wouldn't have been able to walk to where Trisha was. She probably could've called people in her contacts list to help, but Trisha wouldn't have known those people. They'd have been strangers, which didn't seem right anymore.

Jake pushed open his door and stepped out. Then he opened the cab door and helped Petey out while Trisha walked around to where they were. She led the way up the steps to her cottage and fumbled with her keys to let them inside.

"Where do you want him?" Jake wasn't carrying Petey. Instead, he had wrapped an arm around Petey's shoulders in case he lost his balance.

"My bedroom," Petey said. "Can I watch your iPad in there?"

"I'll set you up." The iPad was another thing Trisha had gotten to keep after Peter's imprisonment. The FBI took it and looked at every bit of information on it. It was mostly used for Petey so they'd given it back.

Jake walked Petey into the cottage, down the hall, and to his room. Trisha stepped ahead of them and fluffed a pillow before Petey lay down. Then she pulled a thin sheet over him, grabbed the iPad, and set it up on his nightstand.

"What do you watch on that thing?" Jake asked Petey.

Petey was so worn out that he could barely muster a smile. "Videos about how to do stuff."

"There's a parental control on it," Trisha offered in case Jake judged her. Single men weren't typically the mom-shamers though. It was women of a similar age with kids and a husband to help out. Women who seemingly had everything, including time to spend shopping for hours, multiple times per week.

Had she been one of those women? Once upon a time, she'd left Petey with her mother-in-law and went to get her nails painted on a weekly basis. There was nothing wrong with that, but she'd also often spent a mortgage payment at her best friend's boutique in Sweetwater Springs, buying clothes she might or might not even wear. She'd worked at the women's shelter, not out of necessity for a paycheck but because she had so many resources, including time, that she felt like it was the right thing to do to give back.

Trisha's mind-set and lifestyle were so different two years ago. Then suddenly she was a single mom with very little income and time, and with all eyes cast on her with pity, judgment, or both.

"What kind of how-to videos?" Jake asked. He slipped his fingers into his jean pockets.

"Everything," Petey said. "Since you took me in the sky yesterday, I've watched a couple videos on flying planes."

Jake looked pleased. "Cool. Maybe you can teach me what you know."

"You already know that stuff." Petey rolled onto his side under the thin sheet.

"At least I hope you do," Trisha added. "Seeing that you took my son flying yesterday."

Jake looked at her and winked. "There's always more to know." His phone dinged in his back pocket. He pulled it out and glanced at the screen. "It's Vi," he told Trisha before placing it to his ear. "Hello?"

Trisha watched him walk out of Petey's bedroom. She turned back to Petey. "Let me know if you need anything, sweetie. I'll be in the living room or the kitchen."

Petey pressed his lips together the way he did when a question was bubbling up.

Trisha waited for it.

"Why can't you call Dad and let him know what happened?"

Trisha glanced back at Petey's bedroom door, making sure that Jake wasn't standing there. She looked at Petey again. "I guess I could. But there's no need to worry your dad since you're okay. Tomorrow morning, you'll be as good as new."

Petey looked disappointed.

Trisha knew he was missing his father. She'd have to plan a trip down to the prison sometime soon. "Right now, you need to rest, okay? We can talk more about your dad later." When Jake wasn't in the next room.

Petey sighed quietly and tapped the iPad's screen.

"Just call out if you need me." Trisha walked out of his room and headed down the hall. Jake was nowhere to be found as she stepped into the living room. He wasn't in the kitchen or the bathroom. Trisha stepped out onto the porch for a moment. She didn't want to go too far in case Petey called out so she headed back inside.

It appeared that Jake had left. That was just as well. Trisha had inconvenienced him enough today. She walked into the kitchen to figure out what to cook. They'd missed lunch, and now it was past dinnertime. Petey would likely be hungry. Or maybe not. Maybe he'd just fall asleep until tomorrow morning.

Trisha's stomach clenched at the thought of food. She pulled open the fridge and dipped inside, peering at condiments and containers of leftovers. Nothing looked appetizing. Then she straightened and turned at the sound of a knock behind her. Jake was standing at the door. Her heart unwittingly lifted.

He held up two bags as he opened the door and stepped inside. "Dinner is served!"

"What's that?" she asked.

"This is how my grandmother cares for people. It's enough food for a small party instead of just you and Petey." Jake carried the bags toward the kitchen island and laid them down. "It's barbeque chicken, string beans, mashed potatoes, and biscuits."

Trisha's mouth watered. "Wow."

"I know." Jake chuckled. "Enjoy."

Trisha looked up at him. "You're not staying?"

He narrowed his blue eyes. The color of them seemed to change depending on the lighting. Right now, they were more of a blue-gray shade. She liked the little squint he had with one eye when he smiled. She also liked the subtle wave his hair made right at his left temple. "It's not for me," he said. "She made it for you."

"But your day was just as long and hard as mine. And like you said, there's more than enough." Plus, she couldn't send Jake away hungry after all he'd done for her today. Even if that's exactly what she needed to do.

"Do you want me to stay?" Jake asked.

That was a loaded question. "I mean, you don't have to," she said instead of answering. "We have certainly taken up enough of your day. I'd understand if you just want to go home."

Jake looked between her and the food. "*Home* is a tricky word. It's not in the DC area anymore. It's not in Peony Cottage, which I've stayed in for less than forty-eight hours. Home is more about a feeling, in my opinion. For me, it's all about feeling loved. And safe," he added.

Trisha tilted her head. "Safe?"

Jake leaned against her counter. "Not just keeping the bogey-men out. Feeling safe is also about being free to just be you, no veils or pretenses. And knowing that the people around you won't judge you or make you feel crazy. That's what home feels like." His gaze was still locked on hers, holding her hostage in this moment. "At least to me."

Trisha swallowed. If that was what home felt like, she hadn't been there in a very long time.

* * *

Petey wasn't interested in eating, so Trisha and Jake sat at the kitchen island, side by side. The only word Jake could use to describe their meal was awkward. But it was a good kind of discomfort. The kind that crackled with sexual tension between two attracted single people.

"So, uh"—Jake reached for his glass of water—"tell me more about yourself."

Trisha stopped eating and gave him an odd expression. "Like what?"

"I don't know. I know you came from Sweetwater Springs. What kind of work did you do there?"

She reached for a napkin and wiped at the corner of her mouth. "I worked at the women's shelter."

Jake found this interesting. "That sounds like a rewarding job, helping women get back on their feet."

Trisha returned her attention to her food. "It was. I really enjoyed it."

"I bet you saw a lot of tough situations in that line of work."

"Maybe too much. I burned out on it. It was time to let someone else take on that job."

"I understand." Jake lifted his fork and stabbed at a few string beans. "What kinds of things did you do for fun in your last town?"

Trisha gave him another odd look. "Why are you asking me so many questions about myself?"

Jake's hand and fork froze midway to his mouth. "Because that's how people get to know each other."

"Why do you want to know me?" He could see her defenses rising as he asked questions. It wasn't like the first day he'd met her though, when he'd been asking because he was suspicious of her intentions toward Vi. These questions stemmed from a sincere desire to know her.

"You're going to be my neighbor for the next few weeks."

She narrowed her eyes. "I really appreciate your help today. I appreciate your grandmother giving me a job working on your family's property. But you should know that I'm not up for more than being friendly neighbors."

Jake set his fork down. He was pretty sure she was talking about romance, which surprised him. He hadn't so much as flirted with her. At least not much. "I'm always up for making new friends, but nothing more than that right now. I think I told you, I'm just getting out of a relationship."

Her eyes were wide as she looked at him.

"I don't know your story," he continued, "but I'm guessing you've been in a bad relationship too." He took her lack of response as a yes. "So I'm just asking you questions to be friendly. To be friends. Nothing wrong with that, is there?"

She hesitated. "No, I guess not."

He picked his fork back up. "I just want to be your friendly neighbor. Like Mr. Rogers."

Trisha laughed quietly. "Well, to answer your question, I didn't really do anything specific for fun in my last town." She returned to eating her food. "My best friend came over a lot. I went to her place too. I worked two jobs in Sweetwater Springs so there wasn't a lot of time for hobbies or going out."

"Two jobs?"

"Being a single mom has its difficulties. I cleaned houses on the weekend."

"I see. You don't have to do that here?" he asked.

Trisha's shoulders were slowly coming down. "Vi has been so generous. I get paid on top of having a free place to live. That's one of the reasons I took this job. It's better for me and Petey."

Jake nodded as he listened. That was just like Vi to give more than she needed to. But in this case, he understood why, and he couldn't seem to find the flaw in helping a single mom spend more time with her child. "Sounds like you have time to have a little fun here in Somerset Lake. And after today, I'd say it's deserved. How about you let me help you with that?"

Trisha's forehead wrinkled as her brows lifted in question. "What are you talking about?"

"Sunset Over Somerset. It happens during the summers on Friday nights. Petey will love it."

"Lucy told me about that. She invited me earlier this week, but I didn't say yes."

"You turned her down?" Jake asked.

Trisha nibbled on her lower lip as her fingers reached absently for the bracelet that always dangled at her wrist. She located the silver turtle charm and ran her fingertips over the smooth metal. "I guess it's taken me a while to warm up to the social life here."

Jake hoped she wouldn't turn him down. "Let me take you and Petey there tomorrow. There are children there. Petey seems interested in meeting other kids his age."

"Yes!"

Both Jake and Trisha lifted their heads to see Petey standing in front of them. Jake hadn't even heard Petey walk up. Bailey hadn't either because she stood on all fours now and jogged over to the boy.

"I want to meet other kids, Mom. Please!" he said, showing more energy than he'd had earlier. "I really think that would make me feel a lot better."

Using the whole sick card was a smart move. Jake glanced at Trisha, who still seemed to be looking for a way to remain in this reclusive world that she'd created in Somerset Lake so far. But why? What was she so afraid of? It wasn't good for her or her son if she planned to make this town their home.

And the bigger question for Jake to answer for himself was why did he care?

* * *

A half hour later, Jake left Juniper Cottage with plans to pick Trisha and Petey up tomorrow afternoon for Sunset Over Somerset. First thing in the morning, however, he was planning on going to the hardware store for supplies and getting started on repairing the roofs of Magnolia and Jasmine Cottages.

Jake headed up his steps now and stood for a solid second, trying to figure out what to do with himself this evening. He wasn't ready for bed just yet so he grabbed the latest book he'd purchased from Lakeside Books and walked back out onto the deck to read. It was another how-to book. He didn't really want to know how to start up and run his own fish farm. He just liked the technical language of a nonfiction, instructional book. It was somehow soothing. His form of a lullaby.

He flipped the book open to the beginning of chapter one and tried to read, but the words blurred together as his frayed focus wandered to Juniper Cottage next door and the woman inside.

Trisha was beautiful. And mysterious. Something about that element of mystery drew him in like the title of a how-to manual. There were facts and information that he didn't know, which made him yearn to open the book and read.

His phone rang, pulling him out of his relaxed state. He held his breath, checked the caller ID, and sighed. It'd been a long day, and he really didn't want to argue right now. He tapped the screen anyway and connected the call. "Hey, Uncle Tim."

"Hey, Jake," his uncle drawled in an exaggerated Southern accent. "How's it going in Somerset Lake?"

Jake leaned back in his Adirondack chair and gazed out on the water. The lake water captured the moonlight, making it look like there were tiny diamonds scattered across its surface. Once, when he was about little Petey's age, Jake dove into that water after sunset to see if there were, in fact, diamonds out there.

"Vi isn't even thinking about selling the property," Jake informed his uncle. "She wants me to help renovate the vacant cottages and bring in new blood to rent them out."

"New blood?" Tim asked.

Jake draped his hand over the chair's armrest and petted Bailey's head. "She wants me to help her new property manager revive the place."

"She's hired a property manager?" Tim asked, his voice rising. "I just spoke to her a few days ago. She didn't tell me about any property manager. What is my mother thinking?"

Jake glanced over at the porch of Juniper Cottage to make sure Trisha couldn't overhear. He was just starting to gain her trust, and he didn't want to lose it. "The woman's name is Trisha Langly."

"I don't know any Langlys in Somerset Lake," Tim said.

"She's not from around here," Jake told him.

"Well then, she needs to go back to wherever she came from. And Vi needs to sell the family's rental cottages. It's the only thing holding her to that sleepy nowhere town. My mother would be so much happier here with the rest of the family. You will be too."

That was Jake's plan. "I have to admit, Grandma Vi seems pretty content."

Tim grunted. "You didn't see her right after her stroke. She was scared and alone. She had too much on her plate and no one to help her long-term." Right after Vi's stroke, the family took turns checking up on Vi. "We have the law practice to maintain," Tim said.

"I guess that's why Grandma hired a property manager," Jake said. "If she's not going to sell, I think hiring Mrs. Langly was a good move."

"You're missing my point, Jake. Vi *is* selling the Somerset

Rental Cottages. And you're there to convince her. Then she can move down here where she belongs."

Jake already heard this spiel from both his uncle and his parents before, of course. He just needed the reminder because, so far, Vi didn't seem ready to give up the family's property. On the contrary, she seemed determined to save it.

Jake talked with his uncle for a few more minutes and then they disconnected their call. Instead of returning to his book, Jake pulled up a browser on his phone and tapped in SWEETWATER SPRINGS, NORTH CAROLINA.

That was the town where Trisha said she was from. He didn't know much about it, and he wasn't sure if his motivation was because he wanted to know Trisha, the beautiful woman, better. Or because he was still collecting information on Trisha, the inconvenient property manager.

CHAPTER SEVEN

The next morning, after waking Mr. S and sending him home, Trisha sipped her first cup of morning coffee as she looked out the window at the lake, her mind lingering on thoughts of Jake. He was a handsome man, and despite her first impression of him, he was a nice guy. That didn't mean she needed to give in to any romantic notions, of course. That period of her life was over. She'd done the whole happily-ever-after thing, and it wasn't what everyone made it out to be.

So why did she agree to go downtown with him? She knew the reasons. There were more than one, but the main one was that Jake was right. If she and Petey were going to call this place home, they needed to know people. Petey needed friends. He was homesick, and that wasn't going to change if they kept to themselves on the little strip of shore along Somerset Lake.

Petey set his spoon down as he finished his breakfast and wiped his mouth with the sleeve of his shirt. "Are we going to see Dad at the prison today?"

Trisha sucked in a sharp breath. There was no one else

listening right now, but next time there might be. "Let's get the word *prison* out of our vocabulary, okay? Let's just say 'visit Dad.'"

Petey visibly deflated, making Trisha feel like an awful parent. Maybe she was a little homesick too. Maybe she'd made a mistake by moving to Somerset Lake. Yeah, there were people in Sweetwater Springs who'd judged her and Petey based on Peter's actions, but there were also people who didn't.

"Are we going to visit Dad?" Petey asked again.

"Not today. I'm sorry, sweetheart. But we'll go soon, I promise."

His body folded even more. "Are we going to see Jake this morning?"

Trisha shook her head. "No, but we will this afternoon," she added, hoping this would cheer her son up. "We're going downtown with him, remember?"

"Yes!" Petey practically squealed.

Trisha looked at him long and hard. He missed his father. She was sure he missed his uncle Chase in Sweetwater Springs too. A little boy needed a male figure to look up to. Petey hadn't had much of that since they'd moved here. Jake was the first man in Somerset Lake that Petey met and spent any amount of time with. "You like Jake, huh?"

"He flies planes and has a really nice dog. Can we get a dog too, Mom?"

If Trisha thought adopting a pet would fix everything that was missing in her son's life, she'd take him to the local animal shelter right now and let him pick out ten dogs. Okay, maybe not ten, but definitely one. Doing so would only be a Band-Aid though. Time and love were the only true salves for his kind of heartache. Hers too, she guessed.

"Jake also saved my life yesterday," Petey said. "I heard you tell him so."

Trisha felt her heart drop at just the thought that Petey's life had been in danger. One small ant bite had held huge repercussions. "Yes, Jake did save your life."

"So he's my superhero, right?"

Trisha nodded. "That's right." And that made Jake her hero because she wasn't sure what she would have done if something more serious happened to Petey. Her son was her whole world. Everything she did centered around him. His needs. His wants. His hopes. His fears.

She swallowed and pushed away the thought of anything bad happening to Petey. He was fine. He was sitting on his stool and making a huge mess of breakfast, and she wouldn't have it any other way. "Go on and get dressed. We have a lot to do today."

Petey took one more spoonful of cereal, hopped off the stool, and hurried down the hall toward his bedroom. Trisha was already dressed. She took a moment to walk to the window and look at the lake view. When she'd interviewed for this job, it seemed like getting hired would be equivalent to winning the lottery. It came with a fresh start and a free place to live. On the water.

She'd read everything she could on Somerset Lake before taking the job. Somerset Lake had a population of little more than five hundred. A majority of the town was age sixty-five and over. According to the town's website, younger generations were slowly moving in, thanks to the booming neighboring town of Magnolia Falls. Businesses in Somerset Lake consisted more of mom-and-pop kind of shops, which suited her just fine.

Trisha had researched all the recent crime stories from Somerset Lake that she could find as well. There was hardly anything to uncover. The town was wholesome, idyllic, and the perfect place for Petey to grow up. The lake stretched acres and offered all kinds of activity, including swimming, wake boarding, fishing, kayaking—anything a boy could want, minus the dad to do them with.

"Ready, Mom!" Petey dropped to the floor beside Trisha and tugged his shoes onto his feet. Then he stood and opened the door. The lake air seemed to rush over Trisha as she followed him out onto the deck. Petey hurried down the steps, healthy and energetic as usual. No one would have known he'd spent a portion of yesterday in the emergency room.

Bailey ran up to greet him as soon as his feet hit the ground. Trisha's heart stopped. She looked around for Jake. Instead, she saw Vi walking toward them, her gait uneven and slow.

"Good morning," Vi said warmly. "As you can see, I'm baby-sitting my grandson's dog this morning while he's repairing a couple roofs on the cottages."

Trisha released the breath that had gotten lodged in her lungs at the prospect of seeing Jake unexpectedly. "Morning, Vi. Yes, I'm so grateful that Jake offered to help with the renovations. I've been looking for a reasonably priced contractor to do the roofing, but now I don't have to."

"Oh, Jake is better than any contractor you could have found anyway," Vi said, her voice full of pride. "The man seems to know how to do just about everything, just like his late grandfather." This made Vi chuckle.

"It's all those how-to manuals he likes to read," Trisha joked.

This seemed to grab Vi's interest. Her blue eyes lit up. "Sounds like you two have been getting to know each other pretty well, hmm?"

Trisha's cheeks burned a little and not from the full sunshine overhead. "Well, we've spent some time together going over what needs to be done for the cottages. Like you asked us to. Then Jake helped out yesterday with the whole Petey emergency."

Vi's expression pulled into one of concern. "I was so worried about him. He's doing better this morning?" she asked.

"Much better," Trisha agreed. "Jake was so helpful. I'm really grateful that he was there and knew exactly what to do. He had an EpiPen and everything."

"Oh yes. Jake gave us quite a scare a time or two when he was Petey's age. I'm glad he was there for you both as well. And that you're getting along so well," Vi said, her eyes a little more twinkly than usual.

Trisha hoped Vi wasn't getting the wrong idea about her and Jake. She was debating clearing up any misunderstanding when Petey ran over and cut into the conversation.

"If you don't want to babysit Bailey, I can watch her for you," Petey offered, his arms fully wrapped around the Lab mix's head. Bailey didn't seem to mind. Instead, her tongue lopped out with a long string of drool pooling onto the ground below.

"You two like each other, huh?" Vi asked. "A boy and his dog. I remember Jake was always like that at your age. There's something about a dog that heals the soul of a little boy."

Trisha felt a pain deep in her chest. She didn't want her little boy to need soul-healing. And what did it mean that Vi seemed to understand that's what they needed? Trisha hadn't told Vi anything of her past. She hadn't told anyone here.

"I would love for you to care for Bailey today," Vi said. "Jake would appreciate that as well, I'm sure."

"Jake is my superhero. He saved my life," Petey told her.

Vi smiled. "So I've heard. Maybe you want to do something else for him this morning."

"Like what?" Petey asked.

"Well, I was planning on bringing Jake this snack and drink while he's working on the roofs. I don't want him to get dehydrated up there in the hot sun." Vi held up a small brown paper bag. "Maybe you can bring it to him for me."

"Sure!" Petey said. "We're going down the lake anyway. Right, Mom?"

Trisha hadn't planned on stopping in and seeing Jake—she needed a little distance from him before they got together tonight—but she didn't want Vi to have to walk all the way down the shore in the heat. "We'd be happy to take it to him."

"Oh, thank you. It would be a lot of help." Vi gestured at Petey, who was back to playing with Bailey. "Bailey wanders a bit. But don't worry if she does. She takes care of herself."

"And she comes back?" Trisha asked.

"Oh yes," Vi said. "Always. She knows where home is."

Something ached deep in Trisha's chest again. The dog in front of her knew that better than her.

* * *

Jake didn't mind hard labor. He actually enjoyed it. It didn't require too much thought. Planning, yes, but when he was in the moment, his mind was free to roam just like it did when he was flying.

Today his mind was roaming to Trisha. He adjusted his position on the roof and nailed another shingle into place. He'd already replaced some of the wood framing, which had deteriorated from weather exposure. He should've gotten down here sooner. He'd been busy in DC though. His client load had grown exponentially over the last year, which was good, he guessed. But it didn't feel good. It left very little time for actual living. Hopefully in Florida, things would be different.

"Jake! Jake!" a small voice called down below.

Jake peered over the roof's edge to see Petey and Bailey running toward Magnolia Cottage. He pulled his ball cap over his head to shade his face and looked a little farther down the shore where Trisha was following behind. Since it looked like they were coming to talk to him, he put his hammer down, crawled across the roof, and climbed down the ladder on the side of the cottage. He met Trisha as she was approaching.

Naturally, Bailey stormed the space between them first. He gave her a gentle pat and continued walking toward Trisha.

"Hey, neighbor," he said. "Couldn't wait until tonight to see me?" he teased, loving the way her cheeks grew a dark shade of pink.

She held out a brown paper bag. "We have a delivery for you."

"Wow." He took the bag and shook his head. "You didn't have to do that."

"I didn't. Vi did." Trisha grinned. "But I'll take the credit of walking it down the beach to hand it to you. Can't have you getting too hot or hungry. You might not come back to help me with the second roof or the other stuff that needs repairing."

Jake pulled the water bottle out of the bag and twisted off the cap. "You don't have to worry about that. I'm a man of my word. And I want to help." He tipped the bottle back and took a long drink of water. When he lowered the bottle, his gaze went to Trisha just in time to catch her staring at his bare chest. He'd stripped his sweat-drenched shirt off over an hour ago.

Trisha snapped her gaze away when she realized he'd seen her. And if he wasn't mistaken, her cheeks grew an even darker shade of pink. "So how's the roof coming along?" she asked.

"Good. It's an easy patch. I replaced some of the beams up there, added new insulation, and now I'm just nailing down the shingles. No more blue tarp."

Trisha laughed. "Vi will be very happy about that."

"I might not get to the second roof today. If not, I'll do it early next week. I checked the weather forecast over the next seven days. No rain so we should be all right. Though an unexpected shower in the summer is pretty normal."

"As long as the tarp is there, it'll be okay," Trisha said.

Jake set his water bottle down and peeked inside the brown bag. "Let's see what else Vi packed me. A sandwich. Perfect!"

"You like sandwiches?" Trisha asked a bit awkwardly. There was a nervous edge to her voice.

"Doesn't everyone? Bologna and cheese is my favorite."

She made a face, which he found slightly adorable. "Peanut butter and jelly for me."

"And me!" Petey called, reminding Jake that he was ever watching and listening.

"Well, thank you for saving my grandmother a trip down the shore. It would be a long walk for her. Although I suspect she saw you coming and planned it this way. She's sneaky like that."

Trisha looked surprised. "You think she was waiting for Petey and me to leave the cottage so she could happen to run into us?"

"There's a good chance." Jake pulled the sandwich from the bag and opened the Ziploc. "We still on for tonight?" he asked before biting into his bologna and cheese.

"Unless you want to cancel," Trisha said.

Jake took another bite, chewed, and swallowed before answering. "I don't. I'm looking forward to it. Do you want to cancel?"

She hesitated, her eyes strictly above his shoulders now. "No. It'll be fun. We'll have fun. Petey will have fun." She was talking quickly, which made him further suspect that she was nervous.

He was used to seeing her irritated or standoffish. But nervous was new. He wondered if it had anything to do with his lack of shirt and maybe a little bit of attraction she might be feeling. Or maybe that was just on his end.

He took another bite of his sandwich.

Trisha cleared her throat. "Well, we'll let you get back to work on the roof. Petey and I are going to do a bit of deep cleaning in Jasmine Cottage this morning."

"And Bailey is coming with us," Petey offered up. "Vi said that I could take care of your dog for you today," he told Jake.

"Thanks, Copilot. She'll enjoy your company a lot more than mine, seeing as I'll be on the roof trying not to fall."

Trisha sucked in a sharp breath, and her eyes rounded a touch.

Jake winked. "Just joking. I don't plan on falling today." At least not off the roof.

* * *

Time had ticked by too fast today. Trisha and Petey had cleaned Jasmine Cottage until it was spotless, and Trisha made a list of next steps to get the rest in prime renting condition. She'd wanted the day to stretch out longer because of her plans with Jake looming ahead.

She'd considered canceling at least once every hour. Seeing Jake without a shirt on, up close and personal, was her undoing. The attraction she felt for him was off the charts, and if she wanted to keep things platonic, then maybe she needed to limit social outings.

She hadn't canceled though. This wasn't a date. It was just Jake being nice and showing her and Petey more of the town, which was something she needed. And she could ignore her attraction to Jake. As long as he kept his shirt on.

"Why are you walking so slow?" Petey asked, looking up at her as they made their way back to Juniper Cottage.

Trisha glanced over. "I'm just tired, I guess." Which was true. They'd swept and mopped. Windexed windows. Scrubbed and polished until her nails were chipped.

Trisha nibbled her lower lip. Was she going to have time to file and paint those nails before Jake picked her and Petey up?

"We're still going out tonight, right?" Petey asked.

"We are," Trisha confirmed. Because she was not canceling their plans.

"I can't wait. Maybe Jake will take us there in his plane."

"Nooo," Trisha said.

Petey's excitement didn't falter. "Maybe Bailey can come with us," he said, patting Bailey's head.

"Probably not." Trisha picked up her pace. No more dragging her feet. Tonight was happening, and she needed to get ready.

How did one dress for a nondate to downtown? She was just as nervous about being out with Jake as she was coming in contact with new people. In her old job, she dealt with people all day. Women who needed help were her specialty. Somehow along the way, however, she'd become one of those women. No, Peter never physically hurt her, but the emotional harm was done.

She climbed the steps to her cottage with Petey close behind. Once they were inside, she turned to him. "Go put on clean clothes."

"These are clean. I just put them on this morning."

Trisha made a shooing motion. "That was before rolling around on dusty floors with Bailey. Go." She watched as Petey dutifully headed to his bedroom. Then she retreated to hers and stood in front of her closet. Her best friend Sophie in Sweetwater Springs would know exactly what to wear tonight.

Trisha plopped down on her bed and pulled out her cell phone. It'd been a few days since she'd spoken to Sophie. Not a day went by without at least a few random texts. Trisha pulled up her contact list and tapped Sophie's name.

"I was just thinking about you," Sophie said in answer a moment later.

"Oh yeah? Why is that?" Trisha asked.

"Chase and I were just thinking that we need to get over to Somerset Lake to visit you sometime soon." Chase was Peter's brother. Now he was married to Sophie. Trisha was happy for them. They'd earned their happily ever after.

"I'd love to see you." Even if Trisha didn't want her past

mingling with her present. Sophie and Chase knew how Trisha felt about people in Somerset Lake knowing her whole back-story. They wouldn't tell anyone. Chase had a hard time dealing with the repercussions of his brother's crimes as well.

"I'm calling because I need your assistance." Trisha continued to stare inside her closet.

"Oh. On what?" Sophie asked.

"I'm going out tonight."

"What?" Sophie squealed into the receiver. "You have a date?"

Heat flooded Trisha's system. "I didn't say anything about a date."

She could hear Chase in the background though. He'd overheard Sophie's exclamation, and he wanted details.

"Tell him it's not a date. I'm just going downtown tonight. Petey is coming," she added to prove it wasn't romantic in nature.

"You and Petey are going downtown alone?" The disappointment in Sophie's voice was evident in her tone. The high-pitched squeal was gone.

"No. We're going with a, um, friend."

"Male or female friend?" Sophie asked.

Trisha sighed. Her friend was the best, but Sophie was also the worst person when it came to keeping secrets. Trisha never kept anything from her best friend though. They told each other everything. "It's a guy, okay? But it's not a date."

"A guy, huh?" Sophie sounded giddy again with the news.

Trisha could still hear Chase asking more questions in the background. "I was just calling to ask you what I should wear to a nondate downtown."

Sophie hummed softly into the receiver. "Let me think on what you have."

Most of Trisha's nice stuff was from Sophie's Boutique, so Sophie would know exactly what Trisha had to choose from.

"What exactly goes on downtown?"

Trisha shook her head. "All I know is there's music, dancing, and lots of people."

"Dancing, huh? That sounds romantic to me."

Trisha rolled her eyes. "I shouldn't have called you."

"Yes, you should have," Sophie said. "Let's see. You should wear your tangerine-colored skirt with your white cotton top. It's fun, casual, and very summery. You could wear that ensemble to volunteer at a nursing home, to go on a lunch outing with friends, or"—she trailed off and Trisha knew exactly what was coming next—"to go on a first date with a handsome guy."

"You don't even know who he is. I didn't call him handsome, and he could be forty years my senior."

"As long as he treats you nice, I don't care," Sophie said.

Trisha swallowed past the sudden lump in her throat. Her ex had treated her nice. As their marriage matured, he'd spent way more hours at work than with her though. The last year they were married, before he'd been arrested, Trisha only saw him at dinnertime. He was usually late, and he almost always retreated to his home office afterward to do more work.

She'd thought he was working hard to provide for his family. Instead, he was working hard to steal from other families.

"It's not a date," Trisha reiterated, standing up and walking to her closet. "But the tangerine skirt and white top is perfect. What shoes?"

"Do you still have the silver strappy sandals?" Sophie asked.

Trisha looked at her closet's floor where one strappy sandal poked out from a pile. "Yes, I do."

"Those will be perfect for tonight. Have fun and call me tomorrow. I want all the details."

"All the boring, nonevent, *nondate* details?" Trisha asked, pulling the items from her closet. "You got it."

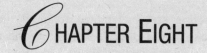CHAPTER EIGHT

Trisha inspected her reflection in the mirror. Soft white top. Tangerine skirt. Strappy sandals. Her hair was down and flowing past her shoulders. She felt feminine for the first time in a while.

"Mom, you look beautiful." Petey stepped into the doorway.

The compliment had the opposite effect of what it should. It made Trisha want to trade out the skirt for a pair of long shorts and the sandals for her favorite Converse sneakers. Beautiful was for dates. Which tonight was not.

Trisha looked at Petey and then her gaze jumped to her closet, trying to think quickly of what she could change into. Sophie's advice was all wrong, and that was because Sophie was assuming, despite Trisha's objections, that this downtown outing was romantic.

The doorbell rang, and both Trisha and Petey turned in that direction.

"He's here! He's here!" Petey took off running down the hall that led to the lakeside door.

Trisha didn't budge. She could delay things by changing, but she'd have to walk out there and explain first. And how could she explain needing to change out of her current attire for something...less.

She released a soft breath and followed the sound of Petey and Jake talking. Jake looked up as she approached, and something shifted in his laid-back demeanor. His gaze seemed to narrow in a way that made her want to run and hide.

"Wow. You look really nice," he said.

Trisha swallowed and looked down for a moment.

"I told her she looked beautiful," Petey said, bouncing on his heels.

Jake slid his gaze over to meet Trisha's, the corners of his lips curling up just enough. "You were right, Copilot. Your description is more accurate than mine."

Petey seemed proud that Jake would approve. Her son was hanging on every word Jake said. It was sweet. But also concerning. He missed his father.

"I don't want to be overdressed for downtown. Maybe I should change." Trisha gestured back down the hall. "I wasn't really sure what to wear. Maybe shorts or capris would have been better." She felt like she was babbling.

"No, that's great as long as the shoes are comfortable. There's no driving on the main downtown stretch. We'll have to park and walk. There'll be dancing too."

"I'll probably just watch," Trisha said, burning from the inside out. Because who would she dance with? Jake? "I have Petey to look after," she explained.

"Mom, you and I can dance together," Petey said.

Even better. Trisha looked at her son. "Okay then. I guess we're ready to see what all the fuss is about."

Jake reached to open the door for them. "Now, don't expect

anything fancy. We're a small town. We make our own music, our own food, and our own fun."

"You keep forgetting I come from a small town too."

"That's right." Jake held the door as she and Petey walked through. "I looked up Sweetwater Springs online. Somerset Lake is smaller."

Trisha froze on the middle step. "You searched for Sweetwater Springs? Why?"

Jake's eyes narrowed again. "Because I'd heard of Sweetwater Springs but couldn't remember where or why. I was curious why anyone would choose to move to Somerset Lake."

Trisha forced her shoulders to relax. And the defensiveness out of her voice. Searching Sweetwater Springs wouldn't automatically bring up Peter's story. Would it?

"It sounds like an amazing town," Jake said.

Trisha turned and continued walking down the steps and then followed him to his truck. "Sweetwater Springs is a wonderful town," she agreed as Jake held the rear passenger door open for Petey and then opened the front one for her. "Thank you." She waited nervously as Jake shut her door and headed around the truck to get in on the driver's side.

He cranked the motor and put the truck in motion. "Sweetwater Springs seems like a quaint little place," he continued. "Lots of shops along Main Street," he said as he pulled out of the driveway.

"My best friend, Sophie, owns a boutique," Trisha said.

Jake's gaze dropped before returning to the road. "Is that where you got that nice"—he glanced in the rearview at Petey—"correction—beautiful—outfit?"

Trisha turned to watch outside the passenger window. She'd gotten this skirt before Peter went to prison. When she'd felt free to purchase nice things without people wondering if they'd been purchased with stolen money. "I did. My best friend gives me discounts."

"Ah. The BFF perk." Jake glanced over. "Sweetwater Springs has some nice parks advertised on the town's home page too."

"The dog park is my favorite," Petey said from the back seat. He was definitely paying attention to every word they were saying. "Bailey would love to go there. My aunt Sophie used to take me there with her dog, Comet."

Jake glanced over at Trisha. "Your best friend is Petey's aunt? That makes her your sister-in-law, doesn't it?"

"It's complicated," Trisha said, wishing Jake would slow down with his questions. "If you wanted to know more about my hometown, you could've just asked. You didn't need to do extensive web research."

The corners of Jake's mouth turned down. "It wasn't extensive. I couldn't sleep, and I typed your town's name into my phone. I guess you intrigue me, which means everything about you, including your hometown, intrigues me. I'm sorry if I upset you."

Trisha swallowed. "No, you didn't. And to answer your question, yes, Sophie is my best friend, and she's also family now. She married my, uh..."

"She married my uncle Chase," Petey supplied from the back seat.

Jake glanced at Trisha. "Your brother?"

This was getting too personal for Trisha's comfort. She resisted squirming where she sat with every fiber of her being.

"No." She turned to look out the passenger window again just in case her face gave away how uncomfortable she really was. "Chase is my former brother-in-law," she answered. But that was as close to talking about her ex-husband as she was getting tonight.

* * *

Former brother-in-law told Jake a lot. He thought that was more than Trisha wanted him to know.

She was divorced. Her best friend was married to her ex's brother. Was her ex still living in Sweetwater Springs? Is that why she'd moved away?

Jake didn't ask all the questions circulating in his brain right now because the tension rolling off Trisha was as thick as the walls she'd built up around her. Instead, he slowed at a common parking area. It was already half full with vehicles. "We leave the truck here. The village green is about a half mile down. See why I told you to wear comfortable shoes?" He winked at Trisha without thinking, and the air seemed to buzz to life. His goal tonight was conflicted. He wanted to help her get to know the people of Somerset Lake because she seemed all alone here. But he also wanted to push her out of town. For Vi's sake. At least if he listened to the rest of his family.

Jake opened his truck door and stepped out. He was a gentleman, but Trisha didn't give him time to walk around and open her door. She was already on the ground and helping Petey climb out. Instead, Jake headed to the tailgate to grab the supplies he'd brought with him. He pulled out the large basket that Vi had insisted he bring tonight.

"What's that?" Trisha asked.

"A picnic basket."

She folded her arms over her chest. "Well, I can see that. What is it for?"

Jake laughed softly. "To have a picnic."

Trisha didn't seem to find his answer funny. "Petey and I already ate."

"Just a sandwich," Petey said. "I'm still hungry."

"Knowing my grandmother, there's something really good

in this basket for you, Copilot. And she always includes some-thing sweet."

"Yes! This is going to be the best night ever!" Petey said. "At least since we moved here."

The boy's excitement was contagious because Trisha was smiling again. "That was nice of Vi."

"She's the most thoughtful woman I know. I'd guess there's enough food for a week in here, judging by the weight of this thing." He laughed nervously, some part of him want-ing Trisha to be happy and also happy that she was here with him.

They walked while Petey dominated the conversation. Jake found that if he listened well, Petey gave him a few clues into who the Langly family was.

"My uncle Chase is a veterinarian. He came to my class last year and talked about animals. But he had a black eye so my friends were kind of more interested in that."

"A black eye?" Jake repeated.

"Yeah. Uncle Chase punched a guy, and the guy swung back," Petey said. "Then they went to jail."

Trisha's hand moved to Petey's shoulder, an obvious message that Petey received loud and clear.

"But it wasn't Uncle Chase's fault," Petey said quickly.

"It was a misunderstanding," Trisha agreed.

"My uncle Chase is going to come visit us soon. He and Aunt Sophie will bring Comet, and Comet and Bailey can play together."

"That would be fun," Jake said. "What kind of dog is Comet?"

Petey looked up at Trisha, who was mostly quiet. "A border collie, right, Mom?"

"Mm-hmm. A mix," she added.

"I think your boy here loves dogs. He might need one of his own," Jake told her.

She shook her head. "Not right now. We're still getting settled."

But she'd been here for a month. In Jake's mind, she should already be settled. She should've seen the downtown area and experienced the goings-on here.

The music grew louder as they approached the end of the street, which veered off into another large, open, grassy field enclosed by towering loblolly pines. There was a stage about a football field's length away. The current music was a local blue-grass band complete with banjos and harmonicas. The field was speckled with picnic blankets and lawn chairs, lots of people and laughter.

"Looks like a good spot there." Jake pointed and led the way, weaving through blankets with people sprawled out and enjoying themselves. He was thankful for the breeze tonight. Sometimes in the summer, the heat was sweltering out here. That didn't prevent people from gathering though. The only thing that turned people away on a Friday night was one of the summer storms.

Jake had been caught many a time out here during a sudden downpour, and he'd walked the half mile back getting drenched while the lucky few with golf carts zipped by.

Jake stopped walking and gestured at an open spot he'd led them to. "Good?"

Trisha looked at the spot and nodded. "Yeah." Then she looked out at the crowd of people scattered across the field on blankets and in lawn chairs. She watched the music for a moment before Petey tugged on her hand.

"Mom, this is so cool! We should have been coming here every week."

Jake set the basket down and pulled out the picnic blanket that was folded inside. "I guess your mom didn't know about this scene. That's why I'm taking you two tonight. Next time you won't need me to give you the tour."

"You won't come out with us anymore?" Petey asked, his tone making it clear that he wasn't happy.

"I didn't say that. I said you wouldn't need me to." Jake lifted his gaze to meet Trisha's, and something sparked inside his chest.

Careful there. Sparks in the summer can lead to a wildfire.

Jake pointed at Trisha as his brain suddenly made the connection it'd been searching for. "That's it. That's how I recognize your hometown's name!"

* * *

Trisha's heart stopped beating. It was hard to breathe, and the noisy surroundings grew quieter. It felt as if she were floating away on the night air. "Excuse me?"

"The town of Sweetwater Springs sounded so familiar to me, and I just realized why," Jake said.

Peter's crimes had made national news more than once. And that always cast a spotlight right on the town of Sweetwater Springs. What if Jake had heard about the financial planner who'd skimmed money from his clients' accounts, stealing hundreds of thousands over the years? What if Jake followed that trail and it led back to Trisha?

"How?" she asked, bracing herself.

"I saw the news story about Sweetwater Springs on TV last year."

Oh no. This was her worst fear. She wanted a home for her and Petey without her ex's shadow. She knew better than anyone that, once one person knew the truth, it was only a matter of time before others started talking. "What news story?"

"The wildfire," Jake said.

Trisha blinked. "What wildfire?"

Jake gave her a strange look. "A spark caught, and the whole

Christmas tree farm in your town went up in a blaze last year. You were there, right?"

"Oh. Right." She exhaled softly. "Yeah, it was only half the tree farm, but it was a big deal. Granger, the owner, is one of my friends. His daughter accidentally caused the fire."

Jake shook his head and spread out the picnic blanket. "It was quite the story. I think our local tree farmer sold that farm some evergreens last holiday."

Adrenaline was still shooting through her veins. She'd felt that fight-or-flight feeling so strongly that—even though the threat was gone, had never been there at all—she wanted to get up, pull Petey to her, and start running.

She could relate to all the women she'd helped at the women's shelter over the years. Even after you were out of a bad situation, your body still responded. Everything still sent your guard flying back up.

"You okay?" Jake asked once they were seated. Petey seemed distracted by the surroundings, which was good.

Trisha looked at him. "Yeah. I'm fine."

"You looked a little upset at the mention of that tree farm in Sweetwater Springs. I'm sorry if I brought up a difficult topic."

If only that was the reason her mood had taken a downward dive. "No. I guess a little homesickness crept up on me."

"I know the feeling," Jake said. "I've been away from Somerset Lake a long time. My family moved south to Florida, and I went up north because I've never been one to follow the herd, I guess. I only come back to the lake a few times a year to see Vi." He directed his attention to the music, sweeping his gaze to her every few words. "There's something about being home that heals you. There's also something about it that opens the wound and pours in salt."

Trisha swallowed. "You feel that way because of your high

school sweetheart? The one you made a spot for in the Lost Love Cemetery?"

Jake picked single blades of grass that poked up beyond the edge of the blanket. "For the most part, yeah. She was killed by a drunk driver. I guess that's why I became a prosecutor instead of a defense lawyer like the rest of my family. I can't defend a criminal. I want to be on the side of the victim. The ones who are hurt by someone else's crimes." He met Trisha's gaze and held it.

She hoped he couldn't see the emotion surging just below the surface. If Jake knew her story and what her ex-husband had done, would Jake defend her? Or would he find her guilty by association?

CHAPTER NINE

Trisha tried to focus on the music to calm her nerves. She wasn't ready for any of this. Being out in town, getting submersed in the nightlife, and staring into the soulful eyes of a man who made her feel things she also wasn't ready for.

"This isn't going to solve your problem," Jake finally said.

She looked at him. "What problem?"

One corner of his mouth kicked up. "The reason I invited you and Petey out tonight. You need to experience Somerset Lake. You need to meet people and have fun. Right, Petey?"

Petey turned at the sound of his name. "Can we dance?"

"Vi packed us a basketful of food. Shouldn't we eat that first?" Trisha asked.

Petey's demeanor slumped. "I'm not hungry, Mom."

"That's not what you said back at Jake's truck," she reminded him.

"I'm actually not that hungry either," Jake said. "The food can wait. Let's rip off the Band-Aid."

Trisha gave him a questioning look. "What Band-Aid?"

"Somehow I think you'd be content to sit on this blanket all night and just watch. That's not the point of being here though." Jake stood and looked around. He seemed to find what he was looking for. Or rather who. He waved, and the person came walking toward them.

Trisha recognized the woman.

"Hey, Lucy," Jake said.

Lucy smiled widely at him. Trisha remembered Lucy's comment about Jake's good looks when they'd met. "Hey, Jake. I heard you were back. Actually, I saw it with my own two eyes from Trisha's deck."

"Not back," Jake corrected. "Just here for maybe a month."

"That's too bad," Lucy said. "The town isn't the same without you in it." She looked at Trisha. "Hey, Trisha. Looks like you came out after all. I tried to invite her to come with me," Lucy told Jake. "I'm not sure how you got her to say yes." She folded her arms over her chest. "Actually, I can guess how. Women have always had a hard time saying no to you."

Trisha shook her head. "Oh, we're just, um, neighbors." She couldn't even say that they were friends. They hadn't crossed into that territory yet, but she thought they were going in that direction. The vibe between them had changed yesterday when he'd been so great during Petey's emergency. And with her.

Jake had also opened up to her. He'd told her about his first love. But Trisha hadn't shared anything, and that's why they weren't exactly friends. Their relationship was one-sided.

"I took Trisha and Petey here tonight because they haven't experienced Somerset Lake until they've experienced a summery Friday night downtown," Jake said, his voice a little more Southern when blended with the nightlife and old friends.

Lucy laughed. "That's true. I never plan on coming out here, but the thought of not being here on a Friday evening just doesn't feel right. I drag my feet, and once I reach the village green, I'm having the time of my life." She pointed at a blanket a few yards away. "I came with Moira and Tess, of course."

Jake looked over at the other blanket and waved at the two women who were watching them. Then he looked at Trisha. "Have you met Moira and Tess yet?"

Trisha shook her head. "No, I don't think so. The one with dark hair looks kind of familiar."

"That's Tess," Lucy said. "She owns Lakeside Books on Hannigan Street."

Trisha didn't think that's where she'd seen Tess. Maybe it was at the market because that's really the only place that Trisha had ventured since moving to town. "I haven't been to the bookstore yet."

Lucy put her hands on her hips. "How long have you been here?"

"A little over a month."

Lucy shook her head and reached down her hand, wriggling her fingers in a come-on gesture when Trisha didn't immediately take it. "Up you go. I'll introduce you to my two best friends. Moira is an emergency helpline operator. You'll love both of these ladies, I promise."

Trisha reluctantly let Lucy pull her to stand. Then she looked at Petey. "I can't leave my son though."

"Of course not. Come on, Petey," Lucy said.

They followed Lucy to the blanket with the other two women, and Lucy introduced Trisha.

"Trisha has been hiding out at one of the Somerset Rental Cottages," Lucy told the two. "She's the one I told you about. Vi's new property manager."

"Oh, you'll have to talk to Della Rose," the brown-skinned woman with dark hair and eyes said. "Della is a real estate agent. Maybe she can help you get those places rented once you've fixed them up. I'm Tess, by the way."

She bumped her arm against the woman beside her. "This is Moira."

"Nice to meet you both. And that's good to know about the real estate agent. Maybe she can give me some pointers on renting the places out." Trisha grimaced. "*If* we ever get them fixed up. I'm so glad that Jake is here to help me. I was beginning to wonder if the job wasn't bigger than I'd bargained for."

The ladies looked at Jake and back at Trisha, their eyes not so subtly widening just like their grins.

"Jake is helping you, huh?" Something playful twinkled in Tess's eyes.

"I'm helping *Vi*, okay? Trisha and I are both helping *Vi*." Jake emphasized his grandmother's name and put his hands on his hips, shaking his head with playful exasperation.

"Speaking of the cottages, when do you think they'll be ready?" Lucy asked. "I have a friend who's considering moving to Somerset Lake. Maybe I'll tell her to contact you."

"That would be great." Trisha glanced over at Jake. "Now that I have help, I'm hoping they'll be ready next month." She nibbled her lower lip and turned to Jake. "Or is that too ambitious? You seem to have experience with the kind of work that needs to be done."

He shrugged a shoulder. "We're a two-person team and there are six empty cottages. It's ambitious, but not impossible."

"Great," Lucy said. "Then I'll give my friend your contact information." She sat back down on her blanket beside the other two women, who were looking up at Trisha.

"Do you like to read?" Tess asked.

Trisha's mouth fell open. "Yes, when I have free time."

"Which probably isn't often as a working single mother," Moira offered. "I'm just guessing. I don't have kids of my own. None of us do," she said, gesturing at the other two. "But Della Rose does. The real estate agent we told you about. And her boys are about your son's age. You two will make fast friends."

Trisha nodded. "I can't wait to meet her."

"Well, I have a book club going on at my store every Thursday evening," Tess said. "Six p.m. We'll all be there. You're welcome to join us this coming week."

"I don't have the book selection. And Petey..." Trisha trailed off with her excuses.

"Della Rose brings her boys too. There's a kids' section with LEGOs and games. They'll have a blast. Us too." Tess reached into the bag at her side. "And I just happen to have a copy of our current selection on hand. We only read romance and only three chapters a week. If you don't get to those pages, you can still come." Tess nudged the book into Trisha's hands.

"Um, thank you. I'll try to make it," Trisha said, knowing she probably wouldn't, but she was fresh out of excuses right now.

Jake bumped against her shoulder. "And I'll remind her." He winked as Trisha looked over at him.

"Mom, people are dancing. Can we dance too?" Petey asked.

Trisha was about to jump at the opportunity to dance with him herself. Then Tess stood up and reached for his hand.

"I thought you'd never ask," she told Petey. "Will you be my dance partner?"

Petey looked at Trisha for permission.

Lucy swatted Trisha's shoulder. "Stop worrying. Tess will take good care of him."

Trisha didn't feel like she could say no. "Don't step on her feet, okay?"

"I won't!" Petey tugged Tess's hand as he led her away. He'd never met a stranger in his life. He was still a happy-go-lucky boy despite everything that had happened in his short life.

Trisha turned back to Lucy, Moira, and Jake, her nerves buzzing louder than the music.

Lucy reached for Jake's hand. "Okay, if Trisha here isn't going to snatch you up for a dance, I will."

Trisha thought she'd feel relieved with two of the three heading off to dance. Instead, something different buzzed in her awareness. Something irritating. Jealousy?

"Don't worry about those two," Moira said. "Lucy isn't interested in Jake."

Trisha didn't know where to start with her response. Did she argue that she wasn't interested either? Or did she ask the other obvious question. "Why isn't Lucy interested?"

Moira seemed entertained by this question. She patted the blanket beside her. "Sit. Let's talk."

Trisha took a seat and faced the crowd, moving her attention from Petey and Tess to Jake and Lucy.

"Lucy and Jake go way back," Moira explained over the music. "They're just friends. He dated her best friend in high school."

"Rachel?"

Moira looked at her with interest. "Jake told you about Rachel?"

Trisha noted the surprise in her new friend's voice. "Just a little bit."

"Wow. I didn't think he ever talked about that part of his life anymore. How'd you get him to tell you about her?"

"He took me to the Lost Love Cemetery."

Moira gave her a knowing look. "Ah, yes. I've buried a few exes in there."

A laugh tumbled off Trisha's lips. "That sounds like a crime."

"The crime was dating those guys." Moira cast her a mischievous grin. "Rachel and Jake were the perfect couple. They never fought. They were always holding hands and making goo-goo eyes at each other. They were never apart. It was kind of disgusting actually." Moira shook her head. "At least until she died. Then Jake was always alone." Moira grew silent for a long moment, focusing her attention back on the music. Then she looked over at Trisha. "Are you and Jake really just here as friends?"

"I...well, we..." she stammered. "Jake is staying in the cottage next to mine," she finally explained.

"And you're staying there as the property manager?"

"That's right. It's part of the deal."

Moira leaned back on her hands, looking relaxed and happy. Trisha envied her a little bit in that respect. "Tending to a few cottages on the lake sounds like fun. Especially if Jake is helping." Moira cackled softly.

The conversation continued to ebb and flow until Trisha found herself leaning back on her hands, too, almost as relaxed and happy as Moira seemed to be.

Then a man came to stand in front of their blanket and reached a hand out to Trisha.

Trisha didn't take it immediately. She'd never met the man before.

"Trisha, this is Miles Bruno," Moira said.

"Nice to meet you," Miles said, still offering his hand. "You're new in town so I thought we'd share a dance and become fast friends."

Moira gave Trisha's shoulder a playful shove. "I'll vouch for this guy. Plus, he's a deputy sheriff. A good person to know in case you're ever in trouble."

All the relaxation that Trisha had worked hard to conjure within her body drained in a mere second. She didn't want to get up. Didn't want to dance. And she especially didn't want to put herself on law enforcement's radar around here.

Moira gave her a gentle shove though and Trisha found herself reaching for Miles's hand. "Okay. One dance."

* * *

"Feels like we're teenagers again." Lucy looked up at Jake with a wide grin.

Jake chuckled. "That was a long time ago, huh?"

"Seems like forever ago," she agreed.

"How've you been doing, Luce?"

She looked away, which told him everything he needed to know. She was still struggling after losing her mom last year. Lucy had come home when her mom got sick. Now she lived alone in her childhood house in The Village.

"You decided to stay?" he asked.

"I haven't decided anything. I'm just taking one day at a time." She looked up at him again. "You?"

"Oh no. I'm definitely not here to stay."

"That's what they all say," she said in a singsong voice. "So if you're not staying, why are you here? What are you up to?" She narrowed her eyes as one corner of her mouth curled.

"What makes you think I'm up to something?"

She swatted him playfully as they swayed back and forth, two old friends who'd been through a lot together. "Our teenage years were maybe forever ago, but you haven't changed that much, Jake Fletcher. You were always up to something. I'm guessing that's still true."

"I'm here for Vi." Which was true. It just wasn't the whole truth.

"Fine. Don't tell me then." Lucy glanced out into the crowd. "Looks like Trisha has been swept off her feet while you weren't paying attention."

Jake followed her gaze to where Trisha was dancing with Miles Bruno. His body tensed uncomfortably. He and Miles weren't exactly friends. Miles was a former Boy Scout, a sheriff's deputy, and a volunteer at the youth center. Somerset's Most Eligible Bachelor according to the little blog that Reva Dawson ran now in her retirement. Jake subscribed to it online because it was like a little extension of the small-town grapevine that he'd managed to escape but couldn't let go of completely.

There was no good reason to dislike Miles Bruno. Except for the fact that his hands were on Trisha right now—and Jake didn't like that one bit.

"Go on." Lucy pulled her arms away from him. "She came with you. She should be dancing with you."

Jake looked at Lucy. "You don't mind?"

"Of course not. In fact, let's both break that dance up. I wouldn't mind a dance with Miles. I've got a beef to pick with him."

"Of course you do." Jake chuckled and started walking, picking up speed as he drew closer to Trisha and Miles. They both noticed him and Lucy at the same time.

"We're cutting in," Lucy said, taking the lead. Jake was grateful. There was nothing wrong with Miles. He'd just gone on a couple dates with Rachel back in school, which had rubbed Jake all wrong.

Trisha and Miles dropped their arms. Lucy didn't waste a second stepping in front of Miles. She tossed a you-owe-me look over her shoulder at Jake. He'd make it up to her before he left town.

Jake met Trisha's uncertain gaze. "Sorry to intrude."

"It was just a friendly dance." She gestured at Miles. "And Miles has offered to get the youth center to help clean the rest of the cottages as part of their community service."

"It's a good opportunity for the kids to help others," Miles agreed, overhearing.

"That's a great idea." Jake held out his hand. "So, care for another friendly dance with your friendly neighbor?"

Trisha looked at his outstretched palm for a long moment and then back up into his eyes. Jake noticed the golden flecks in the brown color of her irises. Fool's gold, but tempting all the same.

"One dance," he said. "Everyone's doing it."

Trisha smiled. Then she finally took his hand, and their arms fell into place around each other. "If your buddy jumped off a cliff, would you do that too?" she asked. It sounded like something his mom would've asked him once upon a time.

Jake thought for a moment. "It depends. How high is the cliff?"

Her smile stretched wider. "Really high."

"Is there water below?" he asked, loving the easy banter that he and Trisha hadn't had until now.

"Shallow," she said.

Jake grimaced. "Then it's a hard no. I would not jump off that cliff."

Trisha felt light in his arms as they moved to the beat of the music. "Smart man," she said in a playful tone.

"Good-looking too," he joked. "From what I hear, at least."

Trisha laughed easily. He was glad to see that she was enjoying herself tonight. He'd hoped that would be the case. She looked over at Tess and Petey, who were still dancing and also seeming to enjoy themselves.

"I have a feeling that boy of yours could dance all night," Jake said.

"And you'd be right." Trisha met his gaze again. They were close. At this distance, he could smell the soft flowery scent of her hair. Her body seemed to buzz beneath his hands. There was an electricity running between them like a live wire.

"So you've met Lucy, Moira, Tess, and now Miles."

Trisha lifted an eye. "And you don't like Miles," she said. It wasn't a question.

His gaze narrowed. "That's not exactly true. He's a nice enough guy."

"I saw the look you gave him a few minutes ago. It was much worse than the one you gave me across Vi's dinner table the first day we met."

Jake grinned. "I guess I'm a bit wary of strangers."

"That explains why you were suspicious of me. But Miles isn't a stranger."

Jake looked over at Miles, who was now twirling Lucy. As far as he knew, there was no romantic potential there. They were both from the same small town. They'd dated and fizzled more than once. They were just two friends having fun. "He was kind of like the teacher's pet in every class growing up. He was the star athlete for every sport. He didn't have a lot of money, but he had all the girls' attention. He was such a charmer."

Trisha blew out a breath. "I know the type."

Jake heard a hint of something in her voice that made him wonder if she'd dated the type before. Or maybe married the type. Jake glanced at his archenemy again. "My main beef with him though is that he took Rachel on a date once when we were broken up. And he kissed her. I guess I'm still holding a grudge about that."

"I see. I guess that's fair."

"Not really. We were all just kids. It's in the past." Jake looked around the crowd, needing to find a less painful subject. "What do you think about Sunset Over Somerset so far?"

Trisha looked around. "It's fun. This happens every Friday night?"

"During the summers, yeah. During the year, a lot of folks are at the local high school games and events too. And it gets too cold for this kind of thing in the winter." Jake tipped his head at the stage. "I used to play up there sometimes."

"Really?" Trisha met his gaze again. He felt a little shock to his chest every time she did.

"Yep. Harmonica. Self-taught."

"A how-to manual?" she asked on a small laugh.

He loved watching her laugh. The way her head fell back and her hair caught in the wind. "That's how I learn everything for the most part."

"You're an interesting man, Jake Fletcher," she said as her laughter died down.

"And you are an interesting woman."

Her eyes grew serious. "You don't know anything about me."

"I guess that's part of what makes you interesting. I want to know more about you. I don't guess there's a how-to manual on Trisha Langly, is there?"

She shook her head. "I hope not. It would be awfully boring."

"Something tells me that's not true."

The song ended, but another one started up. Their dance was slow. The space between them tense.

"You want to learn about me so that you can decide if I can be trusted to work for your grandmother?" she asked.

"I do trust you." Maybe he hadn't when he'd first met her, but that had changed. He had a good feel for people and whether they were trustworthy. As much as he'd wanted to find something not to trust about Trisha, because that would make it easier to get rid of her, he'd failed. "I was a lot like your son growing up. I had questions that needed answers. That's the appeal of those manuals I read." He swallowed, hoping this didn't come out wrong. "That's part of the appeal of you."

* * *

Trisha reminded herself to breathe. Was Jake hitting on her? She didn't think so because he was likening her to a how-to book. "Okay." She glanced over to check on Petey. He was dancing with Moira now. Tess was dancing with Miles. Lucy was swaying with an older gentleman. *Mr. S?*

"Since there's no book at Tess's bookstore about you, you stand a mystery to me." He looked around the crowd before returning his gaze to her. "This is a small town. I already know everyone else's stories."

Trisha swallowed, her mouth suddenly dry. "Okay," she said against her better judgment. Maybe it was the music and commotion surrounding them, clouding her thoughts. "Ask me anything."

Jake's eyes subtly narrowed.

She braced herself for something invasive.

"Favorite band?" he finally asked.

She blinked up at him for a moment, unable to think. That wasn't the question she was expecting. "Bluebirds. It's a local band in Sweetwater Springs."

He nodded approvingly. "I like local best too. Favorite food?"

Trisha laughed nervously. She was all too aware of his hands on her waist, encircling that place where butterflies were fluttering around. "I guess I'd have to say nachos."

"Interesting choice. Creamy and crunchy at the same time. No peanuts involved so I approve." He grinned. "Favorite movie?"

Trisha tilted her head. "Are we playing twenty questions?"

"Something like that. You said ask you anything."

She held her breath for a moment. "Let's just skip to the last question. You want to know why I left my idyllic hometown for a place that I knew nothing about."

Jake's expression grew serious. "You don't have to tell me that. If you don't want to talk about the past, I'm fine to just get to know you in the present."

Trisha swallowed. She was so tired of hiding everything about herself from everyone in this new life of hers. "I left Sweetwater Springs because Petey's father hurt some people. Even though we divorced, some folks still connected me to him. Petey was getting picked on at school. We needed to start over, where no one connected us to my ex-husband."

Jake's gaze was steady on her.

She expected another question. She expected him to ask what her ex-husband had done that was so wrong.

Instead he reached for her hand and squeezed it. "I'm sorry you had to deal with that."

Trisha felt tears prick behind her eyes. "Thank you."

"Are you okay?" he asked.

She shook her head. She felt like she was going to explode suddenly if she didn't tell someone the heavy secret she was carrying. She needed to tell him all of it. "Petey's father is in prison."

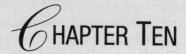

CHAPTER TEN

The music stopped. Everything stopped. Or maybe it was just Trisha's world that seemed to freeze.

Jake's expression revealed nothing. His hands were still on her waist. Her arms were still on his shoulders. She wanted to step back, run away, hide.

"Wow. I didn't realize. I'm sorry."

That was the second time he'd apologized to her in the last five minutes.

She shook her head and looked down at their feet, toe to toe as they swayed to the music. "How would you?"

"I just assumed he was deceased or MIA for some other reason, like being a lowlife dad."

Trisha laughed. "Prison doesn't automatically put you in that last category?"

"It depends on what he did to get himself there," Jake said.

She looked up at him. She'd already said too much. She didn't want to get into the details of Peter's crimes. "Enough to put him behind bars for five years if that tells you anything."

Jake's eyes widened. "That's a long time."

"Petey will be twelve when his father gets released. Petey is already going to miss out on having a dad in his life. I didn't want him to grow up with constant reminders of the reason why. So I decided to give us both a fresh start. I answered Vi's ad, she interviewed me, and we seemed to click. When she offered me the job, I didn't give myself time to second-guess. Not until recently, at least."

"You're second-guessing being here?" Jake's brow dipped.

"Petey's homesick," Trisha said. "I'm a little homesick. I know it's my fault. We've mostly stayed at the cottages. We haven't ventured out that much until tonight." She looked over at Petey, who seemed to be enjoying himself. "Tonight is good for him. We need people in our daily lives. And he also needs friends his own age."

Jake followed her gaze. "There are kids here. We'll search them out and introduce him to them all."

Trisha looked at him. "Thank you. You didn't have to take us here tonight. You're being so nice to us."

His gaze connected with hers, and she felt something deep inside her chest. She didn't want to acknowledge it, but at the same time, it felt good.

Moira and Petey stepped up to where they were. "My dance partner wanted to come check on you," Moira said.

Trisha was grateful for the interruption. She couldn't process what was stirring between her and Jake, and she didn't want to. Now was not the time for romance.

Jake touched her arm as he talked to Moira. "I told Trisha I would introduce Petey here to some of the kids in Somerset Lake."

Moira pointed. "Della Rose and her boys arrived a few minutes ago. They're sitting over there. They have twin boys your age," she told Petey.

Trisha turned to Jake to confirm that was a good choice for Petey. "I was told that I needed to meet Della Rose anyway."

Jake set his gaze on the woman and two boys that Moira had pointed out. "Great. Let's head over and say hello."

An hour later, Petey had two new best friends, and Trisha was sitting on the blanket with Jake, keeping a close eye on her son.

Jake pulled over the basket that Vi had packed for them and opened it. "Let's see. Your choices are fruit or a sandwich."

"What kind of fruit?" Trisha asked.

"Strawberries. She packed some whipped cream to dip them in." He grinned wide, almost like an excited child. "I'm sold." He pulled the container of whipped cream out of the basket along with a container full of huge strawberries.

Trisha reached for one. So did Jake. They both reached to dip their berry in the whipped cream at the same time, their hands accidentally touching. The contact zipped straight through Trisha as she pulled her hand away and took a breath.

Jake was watching her.

"I need to say something," she said.

"Okay." He bit into his strawberry.

Trisha slid her hair behind her ear. She felt shaky and nervous. "I need you to know that I'm not looking for romance right now."

Jake's eyes darkened. "I feel like you've already informed me of this. Maybe more than once."

Trisha nibbled at her lower lip. "I know, but that was before I really knew you. Now we're here having a picnic and sharing a dance. And people are mistaking us for a couple, possibly."

Jake grinned.

"I just wanted to make it clear that all I need is a friend, Jake. I'm divorced, and I've got Petey to think about."

"We're on the same page." Jake took another bite of his strawberry.

She hadn't taken her first bite yet.

Jake chewed for a moment, and then he narrowed his gaze. "We'll just have to ignore what people are saying about us."

"Right."

"And also ignore the undeniable attraction between us," he added. "It won't be easy, but I can if you can."

* * *

The stars were out by the time Jake led Trisha and Petey back to his truck. There was a tension pulling in his chest, like a rope wrapping tightly in a crank. What he felt for Trisha was just attraction. Although it was strong, he planned to do just like he said and ignore it. It was already getting in the way as it was.

Trisha had told him she was homesick earlier. He could have used that to his advantage to get her to move on so that Vi would be receptive to selling the cottages. Instead, he'd encouraged Trisha. He'd helped Petey find two same-aged friends who the boy was currently rattling on about.

"Can they come over, Mom?" Petey looked up at Trisha as they walked. "Or can I go to their house?"

Trisha seemed to be happy as she walked, holding her son's hand. "I got their mom's number. We can plan something next week."

"Yes!" Petey lifted a triumphant fist. "I can't wait."

Trisha caught Jake's eye as he watched her.

The proverbial rope on the crank stretched tighter. It was more than attraction. There was something deeper there. He'd recognized the pain in her eyes, and now he knew why. She'd been hurt by her ex. Something about Trisha's story made him want to shield her from further pain.

They reached his truck, and he opened the door for Petey first. Trisha helped her son get in while Jake walked around to the passenger side to wait for her. As she approached, he opened her door too.

She gave him a hesitant look.

Jake lowered his voice. "Can't a friend show good manners?"

This made her smile. They were still on the same page. They were just friends. Even if he felt more than friendly toward her.

He drove back to the Somerset Cottages and parked in front of his place.

Trisha glanced in the back seat. "Petey's asleep."

"I'll help get him inside. I did it last night. I don't mind doing it again." Jake stepped out of the truck.

She didn't argue.

Jake opened the cab door and dipped inside to unbuckle Petey. The boy's eyes cracked open sleepily. He got out and walked alongside Jake sleepily. Jake wrapped his arm around the child, making sure he got up the steps safely. Then Trisha opened the back door, and Jake led Petey down the hall to his bedroom. Trisha pulled the blankets down for Petey and tucked him in with a kiss.

Jake stepped back to watch. There was that rope on its crank, tightening, tightening his chest. He ran a hand through his hair and turned away, stepping back into the kitchen area.

Who am I kidding? Ignoring his attraction for Trisha was impossible. The goal was instead to resist it.

"Hey." Trisha stepped up behind him.

He turned to look at her, finding her standing closer than expected. "Is he asleep?" Jake asked.

"His eyes were shut as soon as I pulled the covers over him," she confirmed.

"That's good. It was a busy night." Jake wasn't sure what to do. Stay and make polite conversation or say good night and go back to his cottage.

"Well, thank you for giving us the full downtown experience. You were right. It was fun."

"I'm glad you thought so."

They stared at each other for a long moment. Then Trisha broke into a yawn. That was his cue to leave. He turned and headed toward the lakeside door.

"I guess we should meet soon to discuss what's next for the cottages," Trisha said at his back.

Jake's steps slowed. He turned to look at her. "I thought I'd run some errands tomorrow. But we can meet in the evening if you want."

Trisha looked unsure. The evening was maybe more romantic than she would like. With the stars shining overhead the way they were now and the cicadas singing softly in the background. Yeah, he could see why she was hesitating.

"It can wait until early next week," she finally said. "Enjoy your weekend."

Why did the thought of not seeing her again all weekend disappoint him? "You too." He opened the door to leave. He didn't want to. He wanted to stay a little longer, which was exactly why he needed to go to his own place across the way.

"Um, Jake?"

He turned back to face her.

"Please don't tell anyone what I told you. About my ex and Petey's dad. We're here to get away from all that." She shook her head. "I'm not even sure why I told you."

"Maybe you just needed to tell someone here. I'm glad you trusted me."

Trisha met his gaze. "I do. Thank you."

Jake felt the pull, tugging on his heart and making him want to step toward her and put his arms around her. The night beyond the open door was dark, the sounds of wildlife and water thick in the air. This was his idea of romance.

Time to go.

"Good night." He stepped onto the deck, increasing the space between them.

"Good night, Jake." He heard her door close behind him as he descended the steps. Bailey was resting at the landing. She lifted her head and stood, walking alongside him as he made his way to Peony Cottage. "Did you miss me, girl?" he asked his dog.

She gave him an adoring look.

Jake laughed. Then he looked back at Juniper Cottage for a reason he couldn't explain. And found another female looking back at him from the window.

* * *

Saturdays always felt light and carefree to Trisha, no matter what tasks lay ahead. Even if she still worked early and still had responsibilities, there was something about the start of a weekend that felt hopeful.

After waking Mr. S earlier, Trisha stepped outside on her deck with her cup of coffee for a quiet moment before Petey started vying for her time. Last night was a turning point. Petey gained two new friends, and Trisha had made acquaintances with other women in town as well. She'd even been invited to a book club.

Trisha sighed happily at the thought. Lucy, Tess, and Moira seemed like nice women. They reminded her of her friends in Sweetwater Springs. Miles Bruno was a good person to know, too, even if she felt skittish around law enforcement these days. He'd offered to have the kids at the youth center help with cleaning the cottages, and she fully intended to contact him next week and take him up on that offer.

A noise grew louder above the typical morning sounds. Trisha lifted her gaze and noticed a plane in the sky. She glanced to the lake where Jake's plane normally bobbed on the water beyond the pier. It was gone. He'd already gone up to the clouds and appeared to be preparing to land again.

Her heart skipped a moment as she watched, part of her wishing that she was up there with him. She'd only ever been on a plane once, and it was a long time ago. She wasn't scared of flying, but she wasn't one to take unnecessary risks either.

Being friends with Jake felt like an unnecessary risk. She was attracted to him. On a scale of zero to ten, she was feeling a full eleven on the attraction meter. Dancing with him last night might have kicked it to a twelve.

She sipped her coffee, the smooth bitterness satisfying her early morning taste buds. She finished off her first cup and then went inside to check on Petey, who was still sleeping. Trisha prepared a second cup and sat at the kitchen counter with her notebook and the list of things that the vacant Somerset Cottages still needed.

One of the things she'd been looking forward to in moving to Somerset Lake was that she wouldn't be working weekends anymore, and she'd have more time for Petey. Today was the exception. Vi held a vision for her family's cottages, and Trisha wanted to make it a reality. It was the least Trisha could do for all that Vi had done for her.

"Mom?"

"Hey, sleepyhead." Trisha turned to Petey as he shuffled down the hall. "We are going to have a great day."

His sleepy eyes widened just a touch. "What are we doing?"

"Cleaning."

He blinked, and his head lowered a notch. "Oh."

Trisha hadn't expected him to jump up and down about the news—she was just teasing—but she didn't think it would make him look so forlorn.

"I was kind of hoping we were going to see Dad."

Trisha's heart sank. Petey was right to be disappointed. It'd been over a month since he'd last seen his father, and that was too long. Resolution sucker-punched her. "Eat and get dressed. We're going on a trip today."

Petey gave her an excited look. "In Jake's plane?"

"No. Not in Jake's plane," she said for what felt like the hundredth time. "We're going to see your dad. In our car."

Petey's little eyes rounded like he was running into Christmas morning. "Yes!" he called as he raced down the hall.

He'd always been Daddy's boy.

Trisha rubbed the sore place in her chest where her heart ached beneath the surface. A boy needed his father, and after all this happened, she'd promised herself that she'd make sure Petey got what he needed. As much as she could give him, at least.

He needed to play ball in the backyard with his dad. He needed to go fishing, hiking, camping—all of it. She couldn't offer those things, but she could allow Petey to sit in a prison community room and see his father across a small table.

"I'm ready!" Petey raced back into the living room a few minutes later.

"Okay, let me get ready too. It'll just take a minute." Trisha went to her bedroom and looked in her closet. She didn't waffle on what to wear like she'd done before last night's outing with Jake. Instead, she pulled on a pair of jeans and a striped T-shirt and slid her feet into a pair of Converse sneakers.

Vi told Trisha that the weekends were hers as long as she handled Mr. S on the shore each morning, which she had.

Taking one day off wouldn't be a setback, especially now that Trisha had so many people offering to help her with the renovations.

"Let's go," Trisha told Petey, walking back down the hall into the living area. She grabbed her keys and purse as they headed out the door. Petey raced down the steps. She didn't even have time to yell "be careful" before he was on the ground. Bailey jogged up to meet him.

Trisha sucked in a sharp breath. If Bailey was out, so was Jake. She glanced around and met his gaze. Her heart skipped before her brain reminded her that they were just friends. "Hey."

"Heading out early, huh?" Jake asked, walking over.

"Not as early as you," she said. "I saw your plane in the sky earlier."

"Early morning flying is the best. Where are you two off to?" Jake asked casually.

"We're going to see..." Petey trailed off, no doubt remembering that he wasn't supposed to tell anyone where his dad was.

"We're going to see Petey's dad," Trisha said.

Petey's mouth fell open as he looked up at her as if she'd forgotten her own rule.

"I told Mr. Jake about your dad last night," she told Petey.

Petey beamed at Jake. "I'm so excited. I can't wait to tell Dad about the plane ride you took me on. And all the dancing I did last night. I can't wait to tell him about my two new best friends either," Petey rattled on.

"Well, we'll see you later," she told Jake.

Jake shoved his fingers in the pockets of his jeans. "Have a safe trip," he told her. "Have fun, Copilot," he told Petey.

Trisha continued walking Petey to her car behind the cottage. She opened the car door for him to get inside, and then she started to climb into the driver's seat but her gaze caught on the front tire. It took a moment to process that it was flat. Not just low on air, but the rim was digging into the ground. "Oh no."

It would take half the day to have a new tire put on. She'd have to get her car towed or call AAA to come help. Vi had warned her that everything took longer on this stretch of the lake.

Trisha looked back at Petey in the back seat, ready and eager to go see his dad. She was going to have to disappoint him because there was no way that was happening today.

Jake stepped up beside her. "What's wrong?"

She turned, surprised to find him standing there. "I didn't know you were still hanging around."

"I was waiting on Bailey to do her business. I saw your expression and headed over to see if I could help."

She pointed at the front tire. "Our trip is canceled. I'm just trying to figure out how I'm going to break the news to Petey."

Jake looked between the tire and her. "You don't have to. I'll take you."

Trisha shook her head. "It's over two hours of driving each way, depending on traffic. It'll take all day. I couldn't ask you to do that."

Jake gestured to the pier. "So let me fly you."

"What?"

"My plane is amphibious. It lands on land and water. There's a little runway near the prison that a friend of my grandfather owns. I've been there many times before. We can fly and be at the prison in an hour."

Trisha was still shaking her head, but her mind was considering the only option that meant Petey wasn't stepping out of her car with a broken heart.

"My grandfather's buddy will let us use one of his spare vehicles. That's what they're for. I'll drive you to the prison and wait in the parking lot. Then I'll fly you both home. All in half a day's time."

"I…" She looked at Petey who was still buckled in the car, ready to go. "I…" She really wanted to say no, and she had a million reasons why no was the right thing to say. But looking at Petey, she understood that she needed to do whatever she could to make sure he got to see his dad today.

Trisha looked at Jake. "Okay. Thank you."

"You're welcome." Jake tipped his head toward his plane in the water off Vi's dock. "Let's go. It's a beautiful day to fly."

CHAPTER ELEVEN

Jake glanced over at Trisha in his copilot seat. He hadn't even started the motor yet, and she was already gripping the sidewall. The whites of her knuckles pressed against her skin.

"You know, I could just drive you there. It would take longer, but I don't mind," he said.

Trisha looked over at him. As if realizing her nervous posture, she relaxed her hand and pulled it into her lap. "No, I'll be fine."

"Have you ever flown before?" he asked. The last thing he wanted was for her to pass out fifteen thousand feet above land.

"Yes. I have once. Just never in a little plane like this one."

Jake continued to visually assess her. "Maybe it'll help if you go sit in the cabin with Petey. I don't mind."

She seemed to consider this. "Yeah, that might help," she finally said. "You're not going to crash, right?"

He felt the corners of his lips curl. "I've only ever crashed once."

"Not helping." She laughed. "And Petey already told me about that."

"It was just a tiny crash. Didn't even total my plane." Jake reached for her hand, the sensation of her skin against his igniting those flames he was steadily putting out. "I'm not going to crash. I've been flying since I was fifteen with my grandfather. It's in my blood."

She exhaled softly. "I'm going to sit back there and pretend like Petey and I are just passengers in your truck."

"Great idea. I'll be up here, not crashing."

Now she smiled. He felt her smile inside his chest, like it had jumped from her lips to his heart. Once she was settled in the back, he cranked the engine of his plane and cleared his thoughts of everything except the mission at hand. Blue sky and a family friend's landing strip. Then a trip to the state prison.

What had Trisha Langly's husband done to get himself locked away? Jake didn't recall any Langlys in the news, but he'd been out of state and only kept up with the news that Reva Dawson put up on her blog pertaining to Somerset Lake. The most recent crime she'd spoken of was the financial planner who'd robbed Vi of a huge chunk of her personal savings and the money that the rental properties brought in.

Jake would love to find himself face-to-face with that guy. In fact, Jake was pretty sure Peter Lewis was in the same prison that he was flying to today.

Jake put his little plane in motion and took off, skimming across the lake while his thoughts buzzed around in his mind.

Jake's gaze flitted to Trisha, who still looked tense. She would most likely relax once they reached altitude. He was supposed to be spending his day doing other things, like talking to Vi about the future of Somerset Cottages, and not in the way that Vi envisioned the family's property. But in a split second of Trisha needing help, Jake dropped all his plans.

The nose of the plane tipped up, the rudders dipped down. Then they took off. A few minutes later, they reached optimal altitude, and Jake leveled out the plane. He glanced at Trisha again. What was it about her? Attraction obviously, but there was also something more stirring inside him every time he looked at her.

He moved his gaze forward and kept it there, along with his thoughts, until he was near their destination forty-five minutes later.

"Five minutes to land," he called back to Trisha and Petey. Surprising him, Trisha came to sit in the copilot's seat. He glanced over. "You okay?"

He heard her suck in a deep breath. "Yeah. You're a good pilot."

"I told you I'd get us there in one piece."

"You did." She laughed beside him. Then she took a moment to look around. "Wow. It's beautiful up here, isn't it?"

"Yep. There's just something about being up here in the clouds that sets my soul at ease." Maybe that's what it was about her too. She didn't exactly set his soul at ease, but whatever it was about her spoke to him in the same way.

"This was your grandfather's plane?" she asked.

"It was. Not the one he taught me in. That one is in storage. This is a newer one he got right before he died. I'm the only grandkid who learned to fly, so his planes went to me."

"I bet you get a lot of female attention flying this thing," Trisha teased.

He glanced over. "If I remember correctly, you wanted nothing to do with me and this plane when I first offered you a ride."

"That's different. I'm not one of the women I was talking about."

Maybe that's what it was about her. He'd always loved a

good challenge. Trisha made it clear she wasn't interested in him so maybe some part of him wanted to see if he could change her mind.

Without thinking, he reached over and touched her hand. The touch echoed through him. "Time to land. Do you want to go sit back there with Petey?"

She looked down at his hand on hers for a moment. Then he heard her suck in another breath. "Yeah. For Petey's sake. I want to make sure he's secure as we go down."

Jake resisted telling her that was a good idea because if, *big if*, they were to crash, it would most likely happen during takeoff or landing.

Jake called over his radio to his grandfather's friend. "You ready for me, Harold?"

"All clear. Come on in, Jake."

Jake started to descend. The open field was in sight. There was no need to worry Trisha about crashing because he had perfected smooth landings. It was his pilot's specialty.

He continued to lower until the wheels hit the ground, propelling them all forward at a high speed. He slowed the plane gradually and brought it to a stop. "We're here," Jake finally called back.

Petey cheered. "That was amazing! This is going to be the best day ever. Flying and seeing my dad."

Jake was glad he could make the boy's day. Looking at the other passenger in his plane, however, something told him that those two things didn't combine to make Trisha's perfect day.

* * *

Trisha was glad to have her feet back on the ground. She exhaled and tipped her face back to feel the sunshine on her face.

"You can kiss the ground if you want. You wouldn't be my first passenger to do that," Jake said.

Trisha turned to him and laughed. "You've had a passenger get out and kiss the ground?"

"It was turbulent weather." He folded his arms over his chest. His big, muscled chest that she did not want to step into. Nope. Not one bit.

Liar.

She noticed a man walking in their direction now. He was older with white puffs of hair that caught the breeze. He wore rimless glasses, his bushy black eyebrows curving over the lenses.

"Harold!" Jake met him halfway and shook his hand. Then they walked toward Trisha and Petey. "Trisha, this is Harold. He was a friend of my grandfather's. He owns this place."

Trisha shook the older man's hand. "Nice to meet you. Thank you so much for letting us land here. It definitely made our trip shorter."

Harold put his hands on his hips. "No problem at all. Anything to help out Jerry's grandson and his friends." Harold looked at Petey. "Hey there, buddy."

Petey shook Harold's hand too. "Are you a pilot like Jake?"

Jake laughed. "Actually, Petey, I'm a pilot like Harold. Harold has been flying planes since before I was born."

Petey looked impressed.

"But Jake has a nicer plane than mine. I've been eying that beauty since the day Jerry bought it," Harold said. "It's one of a kind."

"She flies smoothly too. I didn't even make my passengers sick," Jake teased.

Harold chuckled. Then he gestured toward the end of the property where there was a house in the distance. "Take your pick of my vehicles. They're all gassed up and ready to drive."

"Thank you," Jake said.

They followed the older man to the garage, and he handed Jake the keys to an old midsize SUV. "It's good to see you, Jake. You should fly out to see Doreen and me more often."

Jake took the keys. "I will. I'm in Somerset Lake for a little bit so I'll be closer."

"Somerset, huh? What brings you there?"

Trisha saw Jake's hesitation in answering that question, which she found interesting.

"Vi had a stroke last year," Jake said in answer.

Harold nodded. "Yeah, I know. She's doing better now though, right?"

"She is," Jake assured him. "It was a small stroke. I guess I just wanted to make sure she was okay, living alone and managing the cottages all by herself."

Trisha cleared her throat. "Not all by herself." She looked at Harold. "I'm Vi's property manager."

"Oh." Harold gestured between Jake and Trisha. "I just assumed you two were an item." He chuckled dryly, breaking into a cough. "I've gotta quit the cigars," he finally said. "Doreen has been telling me they'll be the death of me for decades now. I hate to prove her right."

"According to my late grandfather, a woman is usually right," Jake said. He looked at Trisha. "You ready?"

"Yes!" Petey answered instead. "I can't wait! I'm going to see my dad."

Harold's bushy black brows lowered. "At the prison?"

Jake patted Harold's shoulder. "We'll be back in a few hours," he said, steering the conversation in a more pleasant direction.

Trisha was thankful. Harold wasn't part of her new community, but she still didn't want to get into her messy past. That might raise questions that she hadn't even answered for Jake yet. "Ready," she said.

Twenty-five minutes and a dozen questions from Petey later, Jake pulled the old SUV they'd borrowed from Harold into the prison's parking lot.

Trisha looked across the seat. "I hate to leave you out here waiting for us."

Jake held up a book. "I won't be bored."

She read the title: *How to Start Up a Fish Farm*. The manuals he read were kind of endearing. "You're a lawyer, not a farmer. What do you do with all that knowledge?"

"Mostly use it to impress women," he said.

"Well, I'm impressed so far." She turned back to Petey. "Okay, you know the drill. Empty your pockets."

Petey's expression turned crestfallen for a moment. He removed a few coins and some LEGO figurines. Then he pushed open the door of the SUV and stepped out.

"Thank you," Trisha told Jake before getting out as well.

"You're welcome." He leaned back in the driver's seat as if to make a point and opened his book. "Take your time. I'm not going anywhere."

Trisha tried to rationalize the feelings running rampant through her body as she and Petey walked toward the prison to see one selfish man who'd broken her heart, while another sat in the car waiting for them, selflessly giving up his day for their needs.

Don't fall for him, Trisha.

She patted her chest softly, right above her heart.

"Are you okay, Mom?" Petey looked up at her, his eyes squinting with concern.

"Yeah. Just, um, heartburn. From flying." He seemed to accept her answer as they walked inside and went through the motions, passing through metal detectors and the guards'

watchful eyes. Finally, they ended up in a large room where
families came to see their loved ones in blue jumpsuits. They
sat at a small table and waited.

"Where is he?" Petey asked after ten long minutes. "Why
isn't Dad here?"

Trisha shook her head. "I don't know. I'm sure he's coming.
It's just taking a little while." She saw Petey's mouth purse
to ask another question but she held up a hand. "Just wait
patiently, okay? You're going to see your father today."

Petey closed his mouth, and then he folded his hands in his
lap and looked around. He looked nervous, which tugged on
Trisha's emotions. Everything about having to be here broke
her heart on his behalf.

Finally, Peter walked into the room, tall and lean just like
he'd always been. He looked tired even as his wan cheeks
stretched into a weak smile. Trisha watched the interactions
between him and Petey. It was good for Petey to see his dad, no
matter where that was.

"How are you?" Peter finally asked her.

She folded her hands on the table in front of her. "Good."

"How's the new home?"

She'd told Peter that they'd moved to Somerset Lake last
time they'd come. She hadn't gotten into a lot of details, just
that she had a new job and a fresh start. He had their address so
that he could write Petey, and that was all he needed. "Great,"
she said.

"One-word answers, huh? That always meant you were
upset."

She was over being mad at Peter. She'd forgiven him, or at
least she'd done her best to do so. There was really just nothing
left to say between them anymore. She let Petey take up the
conversation. He rattled on about the two boys he'd befriended
on Friday night downtown. "Jake took us," Petey added.

"Who's Jake?" Peter looked from Petey to Trisha and back.

"He's our neighbor. He's a pilot. I'm his copilot. He flew us down here today to see you."

Peter's brow hung heavily. Was he jealous? Because he had no right to be. "Are you dating this guy?" he asked Trisha.

"No. And that's not your business." Trisha felt her spine straighten. She folded her arms over her chest.

Peter looked away for a moment. "No, it's not any of my business." He looked back at her. "I just don't want to see you get hurt."

"Again, you mean?" Trisha narrowed her eyes for a moment and then expelled a breath. "Jake is just a friend, okay? He's a nice guy."

"I know how important this change of scenery is for you. Are you sure you can trust this guy?" Peter asked.

Trisha narrowed her eyes. "What's that supposed to mean?"

Peter rolled his lanky shoulders and lifted his hands to rest them on the table in front of him. "I'm just looking out for you. And for Petey. I want to make sure that there are good people in his life who have his best interests in mind. He's been hurt enough." Peter pressed a hand to his chest. "My doing, and I'm sorry about that."

Trisha wasn't sure if she should be mad, offended, or grateful for the advice. What Peter was saying wasn't exactly out of line. She *should* be careful who she trusts, and yet she'd already told Jake more about her past than she'd ever planned to. Jake was getting too close, and that could have grave repercussions.

"You're a good woman, Trisha," Peter went on. "You have a good heart, and you want to see the best in people. I know I took advantage of those qualities."

She didn't argue because it was true.

"I'm just making sure your eyes are open to the negative

qualities of the people you let into your life now," Peter said. "Not just for your sake, but for Petey's too."

* * *

Jake had barely gotten a word out of Trisha as he drove back to Harold's home. She was upset, and he was pretty sure it was due to her ex-husband.

Petey, on the other hand, was talking a mile a minute.

Jake glanced at him in the rearview mirror. "Hungry, buddy?"

"Yeah!"

"What about you?" Jake reached over and tapped Trisha's leg.

"I guess it is past lunchtime."

Jake veered toward a business strip in town where he knew there were some restaurants. Good food wouldn't fix Trisha's sullen mood, but maybe he could get her to talk. He pulled into the parking lot for a diner and cut the engine. "Burgers and shakes are good flying food."

She fidgeted with the bracelet on her wrist as she looked at him with a hint of skepticism. "Really?"

He chuckled softly. "That's my excuse to find a diner that serves those two things in every town I fly to."

They stepped out of Harold's SUV and walked inside. Then they ordered and ate. Trisha still didn't say very much. He wanted to ask her directly what was wrong, but Petey seemed oblivious and Jake doubted she'd want to talk about anything in front of her son.

Jake's cell phone buzzed on the table as he dipped a fry in ketchup.

Trisha looked at him. "What's wrong?"

He'd never had a good game face. "My uncle is calling. No doubt to check on my grandmother."

"And that upsets you," Trisha said, the skin between her eyes pinching softly. "Why is that?"

He drew in a breath and released it before speaking. "We have different ideas about what's in Vi's best interest," he said. "It usually leads to a little friction in our conversations."

"But you have Vi's best interests at heart?" she asked.

It felt like a strange question, and Jake locked eyes with her. "Always."

Trisha seemed to swallow. "That's good. Me too."

"I believe you."

Trisha diverted her attention to Petey beside her. Whatever had happened in that prison visit made Jake want to go in there and have a chat with Trisha's ex. That wouldn't fix anything for her though. The guy was out of her life, and even though Jake didn't know who her ex was or what his crimes were, Jake was fairly certain the guy's absence in Trisha's life was for the best.

The waitress came and laid down the bill. Before she could leave, Jake handed back the bill with his debit card.

"Oh no. I can't let you pay for us," Trisha argued.

Jake looked at her. "Yes, you can. And I want to."

The waitress looked between them and then walked away with his card.

"You've done too much for us already." Trisha looked worried. Or maybe it wasn't exactly worry. She held that look of a broken heart. Was she still in love with her ex? Was that what was bothering her since they'd left the prison?

"I was going to go for a flight today anyway. You just gave me a purpose. So I should thank you," Jake said.

She tilted her head and looked at him skeptically. "So you're just a genuinely nice guy? There's no catch or hidden agenda?"

A slither of guilt slid through him. He didn't answer because she wasn't asking him the questions. She was more talking to herself, the questions being their own answers.

He liked to think he was a nice guy, but would a nice guy keep his real agenda hidden? He was only looking out for his grandmother, but the last thing he wanted to do was cause Trisha more pain. He could tell she'd already been through a lot.

"I'm sorry that I was suspicious of your intentions." She shook her head. "It's hard to trust my instincts about people anymore." She glanced over at Petey, who didn't seem to be listening. He was the kid with a million questions, but he was also a kid, and sometimes adult conversation was boring. "Thank you for flying us. And for lunch." A smile curled at the corners of her mouth.

"It was my pleasure," Jake said.

* * *

The plane landed on Somerset Lake an hour later, and Trisha stepped off with Petey. She'd been too tired and exhausted on the return flight to even be nervous.

She turned back to Jake, who was closing up his plane. "Thank you again for today. Petey really needed that visit."

Jake looked toward Petey, who was running down the dock toward Bailey. He returned his gaze to her, and she saw his expression shift to something more serious. "And what about you? You've been quiet since you left the prison. Are you okay?"

Trisha resisted rubbing her chest. She was as okay as one could be taking her son to visit his father in prison. But Peter had made her second-guess everything, and everyone, new in her life for a moment. "I think I'm just tired. It's been a long day."

"Well, I'm going to church in the morning. How would you

two like to come with me?" Jake asked. "It's an outdoor service. I think you'd enjoy it."

Trisha hedged. "My in-laws are picking up Petey first thing for a family reunion on his father's side. And honestly, I'm not sure I'll be up for it."

Jake's gaze was steady on her. "Sometimes doing those things you're not up for anyway helps."

Trisha seriously doubted that. If she argued or made any more excuses, she might start crying though—her emotions were that raw. And Jake had sacrificed a huge portion of his day for her and Petey. Peter had made her doubt Jake a little bit, but that was wrong. Jake was completely trustworthy, and she didn't want to disappoint him. So instead of looking for another excuse, she said, "Okay. Yes, I'll go with you."

"Great. It's a date." Jake winked at her. "Just kidding. If I took you out for a real first date, it'd be somewhere a little more romantic than a golf cart ride to an outdoor church."

Trisha wanted to ask where he would take her. But that question was irrelevant. Because they were never going on a first date.

CHAPTER TWELVE

$\mathcal{J}$ake thought that old expression "you can't go home again" was right in a way. The memories of Rachel and his grandfather were like ghosts here, haunting him at every turn. Staying for any length of time would be difficult. That's why Jake's main goal today was to talk to Vi about the cottages.

He'd gotten derailed by giving Trisha and Petey a flight that had eaten up most of his daylight hours. But there was still time to set out and do what he'd intended before hitting the sack tonight.

Vi was a rational woman. Maybe she'd hear him out and agree that it was time to leave Somerset Lake behind once and for all. For all Jake knew, Vi was tired of entertaining ghosts here on the lake as well.

Jake walked past Juniper Cottage until he was standing in front of Vi's place. Then he climbed the steps to the back deck. He took a deep breath before stepping up to her door and knocking. "Vi? It's me, Jake."

Bailey barked and ran toward the sliding glass door from

inside. Vi had kept his dog for him today while he was gone. He appreciated the help. Bailey was self-sufficient for the most part, but she was also a social dog who needed human interaction.

Jake waited for Vi to follow Bailey to the door. When she didn't, Jake knocked again. After a several moments, he pushed the door open, knowing that Vi didn't lock her doors during the day.

"Vi?" Jake called again, patting Bailey's head as he entered the house. Bailey ran ahead of him as if showing Jake where Vi was.

Concern knotted in the pit of Jake's stomach. His steps were heavy, shaking the old house as he walked. It needed a few renovations, too, if Vi was going to continue living here.

Bailey stopped in front of Vi, who was sleeping on the couch. She hadn't heard Jake come in, which was concerning if she was going to keep her door unlocked. Jake noticed her hearing aids on the table beside her. A lot of good they did there. These were the exact reasons his family wanted Vi in Florida with them. To ensure her well-being and safety.

Jake sat down on the couch beside Vi, noting the open album on her lap. He leaned in closer to see what she'd been looking at.

Vi's eyes cracked open. She blinked at him sleepily. "I didn't hear you come in."

"You were asleep," Jake said.

She chuckled softly. "I suppose I was. Are you hungry?"

"No." He shook his head even though, yeah, he was starving. The late lunch he'd eaten with Trisha and Petey at the diner was already gone. "Just came to check on you and get Bailey."

Vi shifted and sat up. "You don't need to check on me. I'm fine, you know."

Jake wasn't so sure. How fine could she be living alone with no family nearby? Leaving her doors unlocked, her hearing aids out, and falling asleep on the couch before sunset? "Looking at pictures?" he asked.

"Oh yes. I look at these old albums all the time." She chuckled again. "It's good to see your grandfather's smiling face. Yours too." She looked over at him.

"Grandma, you don't have anyone here in Somerset Lake anymore. Maybe it's time to think about moving to Florida where my parents are. Uncle Tim and Aunt Dawn would be around too. You have at least a half-dozen grandchildren down there now. I'll be there soon enough too."

Vi's smile wasn't quite as big anymore. "Move? Don't tell me you're going to try to feed me that garbage about being too old to run the Somerset Cottages too. Tim and the others have already offended me enough."

Jake folded his hands in his lap, his gaze falling on the album. "Aren't you tired of being reminded of him everywhere you turn?" His eyes suddenly burned. He blinked the sting away.

Vi reached over and placed a hand on his knee. "When you reach my age, memories are the most valuable thing you have. Some might hurt, yes, but if I avoided remembering altogether, then I'd miss out on the good memories too. I could run away to Florida...or DC"—she narrowed her eyes at him—"but I'd miss being here and remembering all the little things, good and bad, at every turn. I'd probably begin to forget how the air smelled and how it felt on my bare arms. The same air that your grandpa once breathed in every morning before looking at me and saying, 'It's a great day to be alive...because I get to spend it with you.'"

Vi looked down at the photo album, trailing the pad of her index finger over Gramps's picture. She took a shuddery breath and then looked up at Jake. "Now, every morning when I wake up and walk out onto my deck, I breathe in all the fresh air and feel the coolness of it on my skin. And I whisper, 'It's a great day to be alive because I get to spend it with you.' He's still with me, every place I look. Why would I ever leave?" she asked.

"Gramps will be with you anywhere you go," Jake said gently.

"You're missing the point, Jake. I'm *not* going anywhere." She patted his thigh again. "I'm getting older, yes, but don't think for a moment that I don't know the real reason you're down here visiting me for an entire month. You could've gone ahead to Florida to start your new life and job."

"That's true," Jake said.

"But you didn't because the family is worried about me." Vi gave him a knowing look as he met her gaze.

Jake didn't argue. He couldn't.

"I know that you're here to convince me to sell the Somerset Cottages."

Jake didn't blink, didn't breathe. He'd been looking for an opening to this conversation, and here it was.

"But I also know that you're here because some part of you wants to convince yourself to stay," Vi said.

Jake shook his head. She was right about some things, but not that. "No, Grandma. I'm not staying. This isn't my home anymore."

"So says your head." Vi lowered her gaze to his chest. "But your heart never got a chance to heal. And nothing heals a broken heart like being home." She met his gaze and held up a finger. "And before you start arguing with your head, listen to your heart for just a moment. Somerset Lake is still your home, whether you think so or not."

* * *

Petey's eyelids were drooping as he seemed to actively resist letting them shut for the night. "Can I read until bed?" he asked. "Jake let me borrow his book about fish farming."

Trisha laughed. "Just brush your teeth first, okay? I don't want you to fall asleep without doing that."

"'Kay!" He disappeared down the hall.

Trisha walked out onto the deck to look at the lake. Despite knowing she was failing Petey in some areas, she was succeeding in other areas. He was smart and enthusiastic about life. He was respectful, dutiful, and the sweetest boy she could want.

Trisha breathed in the cool night air. There was a bubbly lightness in her chest. She and Petey were finally getting settled here in Somerset Lake. She was finally beginning to feel like she belonged. She was so happy she could cry right now.

The last six months in Sweetwater Springs hadn't felt like home anymore, even though that's where she'd grown up. The only family she had there was her ex-husband's family. She had friends, of course, but she also had a few of her ex's enemies.

Everyone here in Somerset Lake treated Trisha and Petey like instant friends, even when Trisha hadn't initially extended the same courtesy to them.

Her phone pinged with an incoming text. Trisha pulled it from her pocket and read the message from Sophie.

How are you?

Trisha tapped her index finger along the screen. I'm good. Really good.

The message dots started bouncing as Sophie formed her reply. How was your date last night?

Trisha rolled her eyes and laughed. Then she tapped Sophie's number and called her instead of texting back. "It wasn't a date," she said as soon as Sophie answered.

"A single guy that you needed to call your best friend for clothing advice for? Okay," she said in a tone that suggested she wasn't buying it. "But I'm glad to hear things are good down there."

"They are. Both Petey and I are making friends." Trisha looked out on the water, her gaze moving to a dark shadow on the dock. She blinked and realized it was Jake sitting on the end with his arm draped around Bailey at his side.

"So this guy that took you out. The nondate. When are you seeing him again?" Sophie asked.

Trisha didn't even want to answer that question because it would only confirm what Sophie was already assuming. "Tomorrow morning," she finally said. "He's taking me to church."

"Church? That sounds serious."

Trisha laughed, the sound traveling out into the night. "Stop it. We're friends. Nothing more. He's not even staying in town for long."

"Maybe you could convince him to stay," Sophie suggested, her tone climbing an octave.

Trisha saved her argument. It wasn't going to work, and, well, it wasn't as if that thought hadn't skipped across Trisha's brain. Which was silly. Trisha barely knew Jake. She was attracted to him, of course, but according to Lucy, so were half the women in town. The last thing Trisha needed was the drama of a new romance when she was just getting settled.

"Anyway," Sophie said, "is it still okay for Chase and me to pick up Petey tomorrow morning?"

The Lewis family reunion had always been a fun time for Trisha. She loved the Lewis family, but it didn't seem right for her to attend this year. Petey still needed to know his relatives though. "Yes, of course. Thank you for offering to take him with you. I know it's a little out of your way to come get him."

"Nonsense. We're just thrilled to get a whole day with our nephew. We're leaving pretty early in the morning," Sophie said. "We'll grab Petey before you go to church, if that's okay. I can't imagine church starts before eight."

"I think Jake said it starts at nine."

"Ooh, another detail about this guy that you're totally not dating. Jake is his name, huh? Sounds rugged and handsome."

"You got all that from a name?" Trisha laughed. "Anyway, thank you, Sophie. And thank Chase for me too."

"I will. Can't wait to see you tomorrow," Sophie said. "Maybe we can have dinner tomorrow night when we drop Petey back off? What do you think?"

"I think that sounds wonderful. I'll cook," Trisha said.

"Great. And maybe if I'm lucky, you'll introduce me to this guy *friend* of yours."

Trisha's gaze moved back to Jake's shadow at the end of the pier. Then, as she disconnected the call with her best friend, she headed inside to check on Petey. After that she returned outside and started walking in Jake's direction, needing to see him— unable to resist.

* * *

One thing about life that never seemed to change was the starry sky over Somerset Lake.

Jake stared out at the water. He'd walked out here after visiting Vi, hoping to clear his head. Their talk was making him second-guess his reasons for being here. His parents and Uncle Tim and Aunt Dawn were so sure that moving to Florida was what was best for Vi. But maybe they were wrong. Maybe Jake was fighting for the wrong side.

He sighed, the sound drifting off into the night along with a mix of others.

"Lost in thought?"

Jake turned toward Trisha, surprised that she was able to sneak up on him. He must have really been spaced out. "I guess so."

"You want to talk or are you hoping to be alone?" she asked.

That surprised him too. It was usually him encroaching on her territory, not the other way around. "I won't turn down good company."

She looked unsure.

"I consider you to be good company." He tipped his head to the spot beside him. Bailey was on his other side.

She lowered herself to sit on the dock and swung her legs over the edge. "Petey fell asleep reading your fish farming book. It was an eventful day for him. Last night was pretty eventful too. I'm glad we went. Thank you for everything."

Jake glanced over at her. "You're welcome. Will you go to another Sunset Over Somerset?"

Trisha nodded. "I think Petey would have a fit if I didn't. It was good for me too."

Jake grinned. "Uh-oh. I dragged you out kicking and screaming last night, and now you can't get enough of us Somerseters, huh?"

She grinned right back at him. "You say that as if you're one of those Somerseters. I thought you weren't staying."

He looked back out on the water. "Vi reminded me tonight that wherever I go, I'll always belong here."

He heard Trisha release a breath beside him. "I guess that's true for everyone and the place they grew up. There's some things that are just ingrained in us. You can't escape them, no matter how hard you try."

Jake had an urge to reach out and touch her. A comforting touch, yeah, but there was more to it than that. "I don't want to overstep. Shove me off this dock if I do."

Trisha gave him a questioning look. "Okay?"

"Can I ask why your ex is in prison?"

There was something sad in her eyes that immediately made him regret his question. His curiosity had finally gotten the best of him though.

Trisha inhaled and exhaled before answering. "Because he stole money from people. His clients." Her eyes grew shiny. "He was a prominent financial planner in the area. I guess he was skimming money off clients' accounts for years. They had no idea."

Jake felt his body stiffen. That was exactly what had happened to Vi. There was no way Trisha's ex was Vi's financial planner though. That would be too much of a coincidence. "He just had clients in Sweetwater Springs?" he asked anyway, just to relieve his mind.

She shook her head. "No. All over the western part of the state. Most of his business interactions were handled over the phone so distance wasn't really an issue. The list of people he hurt is long, with Petey at the top of that list," she said quietly.

Jake noticed how her hands shook as she held them in her lap. "You too," he said.

She looked down for a moment. "The thing is, I was proud of my husband. I bragged about him to my friends. He worked so hard. He was so dedicated. He was so good at what he did." Trisha laughed humorlessly. "And I was such a fool."

Jake couldn't resist anymore. He reached over and laid his hand over hers. "You trusted your husband. That's not a crime."

Tears brimmed in Trisha's eyes. She exhaled. "Well, according to some, it was. That's the main reason I left my hometown. I was guilty by association, just because I married someone who wasn't who I thought he was."

Jake didn't want to ask. He'd already asked too many questions tonight. But he needed to know. "What is your ex's name?"

Trisha gave him a questioning look. "Why does that matter?"

"I'm a lawyer," Jake explained. He didn't want to deceive her, but he also didn't want to push her away when she was just letting him in. "I read a lot of legal cases. I'm just wondering if I've heard of him."

Trisha seemed to accept this explanation. Her shoulders lowered as she looked out onto the lake. "Peter Lewis."

Jake grew very still. He was glad Trisha wasn't looking at him at the moment because his game face was likely shattered. "But your last name is Langly."

"Langly is my maiden name." She tipped her face up to the starry sky and sliver of moon. "Both Petey and I changed our names just to help with the fresh start. I mean, Lewis is a pretty common surname, but I didn't want us to have any tie to my ex's crimes."

Jake wasn't sure he could take any more revelations tonight. "Peter Lewis," he repeated.

Trisha looked at him. "You've heard of him?" she asked.

Jake offered a slow nod. Trisha was just as much a victim as Vi. He could tell by how guarded she was. She'd already been through a huge ordeal. Jake didn't want to add to her burden by telling her that her ex-husband was responsible for Vi's financial struggles. Peter Lewis was the reason the cottages weren't repaired after the hurricane. The stress he'd caused Vi had likely contributed to her stroke.

Jake looked down at his lap, taking a moment to reset his game face. "The name sounds familiar," he finally said.

"Well, it was all over the news. That's why I don't want to be tied to it here." Trisha wrung her hands in her lap. "I hope you understand."

"I do. What I don't get is how anyone could blame you for what he did. You weren't the one who stole from people."

"No, but some wondered if I knew about it."

"Did you?" Jake asked. He didn't mean any harm. He wasn't thinking. It was just the next obvious question.

Trisha whipped her gaze to meet his, her eyes narrowed and full of pain. "No."

"I'm sorry." He held up his hands. "I didn't even need to ask that question. I already know you would never do anything like that."

"How do you know? You only just met me."

"Maybe, but I'm a good judge of character. You have to be in order to be a lawyer, which is in my blood." He winked. "You've been amazing to my grandmother. You're a great mom. Lawyer or not, anyone with two eyes and a heart can tell that you're a good person. If anyone ever doubted you or made you feel otherwise, they were wrong."

More tears glimmered in her eyes, but he didn't think it was a bad thing. "Thank you."

"You're welcome."

They held each other's gaze for a moment that stretched as long as the lake before them and seemed to plunge just as deep. He could feel that rope on its crank tightening in his chest again, pulling him toward this woman even though he knew all the reasons why allowing anything romantic between them was a bad idea.

"I'm sorry he hurt you," Jake said quietly.

She visibly swallowed. "You've experienced your share of pain too. I guess it comes with the territory of opening yourself up to another person."

"Yeah." Jake couldn't take his eyes off her suddenly. He just wanted to kiss her right now. "You didn't have to tell me about your ex-husband. You could've told me it was none of my business. You could have pushed me into this lake."

"I could have," she agreed.

"So why didn't you? Why did you open up to me?"

She lifted a hand to swipe a strand of hair from her face, securing it behind her ear. "Maybe you've convinced me that keeping to myself isn't good for me or Petey. Even if I was completely wrong about my ex, I'm hoping that I'm not wrong about you."

Jake's heart ached in a feel-good way. "What are you thinking about me?"

"That you're a good person too," she said.

"I'm not perfect."

"Neither am I," she whispered. And unless he was totally misreading the situation, she wanted to kiss him as much as he wanted to kiss her.

He looked down at her lips. So close. When he looked up, he caught her looking at his lips too. They were thinking the same thing.

"It's probably a bad idea," he said.

Her dark eyes held his. "I know."

"I'm not staying." He couldn't. When he'd left this town, he'd never planned to make it his home again. He had his family and a job waiting in Florida.

"I know that too," Trisha said.

Jake swallowed. He was laying out the facts like a good lawyer. But he wanted this kiss more than he wanted anything, maybe ever. "I don't want to be just another guy who hurt you, Trisha."

She leaned in, a breath away from his mouth. "Then don't hurt me."

* * *

It felt good not to think for just a moment. Jake's lips on Trisha's felt good too. She leaned into him, surrendering herself to the kiss.

When they pulled away, Jake's gaze was heavy on her. The man could be as intense as he was laid-back. "You okay?"

"Better than."

The corners of his lips curled up. "It's been a long time since I've kissed a girl down on Vi's dock."

Trisha laughed. She wasn't a girl. She was a woman. A single mother who had no business being out here kissing on her boss's dock. Or kissing her boss's grandson.

Trisha stiffened. Maybe she wasn't okay. "I better get back inside to check on Petey," she said, standing quickly. Her legs were shaky. Her whole body trembled like a leaf in the lakeside wind. What had she just done? She wasn't sure. All she knew was that it felt amazing in the moment. But now she felt confused and frazzled.

Jake was still sitting on the dock, watching her. Bailey too.

"Good night, Trisha," he said easily, as if she hadn't just pulled away from the kiss and started rattling off nervous excuses to get away.

"Good night, Jake." She turned and walked away, doing her best not to run. She took deep breaths, in and out. It was just a kiss. It didn't have to mean anything, except somehow she wasn't convinced of that. She was already attracted to Jake. She already liked him. And she'd already told him her secret.

Wow, she'd really thrown caution to that wind blowing around on the lake, which wasn't like her at all.

She climbed the steps to Juniper Cottage and hurried inside, closing the door behind her. Then she crossed the living room to check on Petey in his bedroom. He was sleeping peacefully. She was a little jealous. After that kiss with Jake, she doubted she'd get much rest tonight.

Trisha sat on the edge of her bed and stared at her open closet, which reminded her of her best friend. She lifted her cell phone and tapped out a text.

I accidentally kissed Jake!

Trisha's heart was still racing.

How do you kiss by accident? Sophie texted back a minute later.

Trisha nibbled at her lower lip. That was a good question, and she wasn't sure of the answer. Maybe the kiss wasn't an accident at all. But it was most definitely a mistake.

CHAPTER THIRTEEN

On Sunday morning, Trisha woke, pulled on her cardigan, and slipped her feet into her flip-flops. Then she headed down the lakeshore to nudge Mr. S back inside as usual.

Her steps slowed as she approached the usual spot. He wasn't there, which she found odd. He was always there, from the first day she'd started this job. She guessed for once he'd woken himself and had gone inside on his own.

Good. Maybe he'll make a habit of that.

Trisha turned back toward her cottage. Sophie and Chase would be coming early to get Petey. Trisha was glad, but some selfish part of her regretted that she'd be left all alone to deal with the after-kiss. Maybe she should cancel going to church. Skipping church just felt like another wrong that wouldn't fix the first one though.

She climbed the steps of Juniper Cottage and went inside. Petey was up, eating a banana and reading his book.

"Better hurry up and get dressed," Trisha said. "You have a big day ahead."

Petey seemed to think on what was happening today. To a kid, all days ran together, especially during the summertime.

Trisha laughed as she flipped her coffee maker on. "Aunt Sophie and Uncle Chase will be here in about thirty minutes to take you to the Lewis family reunion. Remember?"

Petey jumped off the stool. "Yes! I can't wait to spend the day with them!" He rushed down the hall toward his bedroom to get ready, his feet landing heavily on the floor.

Trisha turned back to the coffee maker and watched the dark brew as it poured into the pot. After last night's restless sleep, she was so ready for a mug of caffeine. She could practically taste it on her lips.

Lips.

Jake.

That kiss.

Trisha lifted her fingertips to her mouth at the memory.

"Mom?"

She turned toward Petey's voice.

"How do I look?" Petey was dressed in dark navy shorts and a striped T-shirt. He wore white socks and his sneakers, which were already tied loosely.

"Look at you. You already brushed your hair too. You got ready in record time," she noted, hearing the coffee maker grind to a stop. "I don't even think that took five minutes."

"I already brushed my teeth too," he said proudly. She'd have to get him to brush them again because she seriously doubted he'd taken the full two minutes to clean all of his teeth.

"Great job, bud." Trisha grabbed a mug from the cabinet and poured herself some coffee. "I think you look great. I know your relatives will be amazed at how much you've matured since the last time they saw you." Which was months ago. Too long. She'd try to do better for Petey's sake.

"I can't wait to tell them all about Somerset Lake and the boys I met downtown. My new best friends."

Trisha turned back to him as she sipped her coffee and listened to his excited chatter.

"And I can't wait to tell them all about Jake and the plane ride he gave us. They're going to think that is so cool."

Trisha held her tongue. She wanted to ask Petey to leave Jake out of the conversation with her former in-laws. The last thing she wanted the Lewis family to think was that she was already moving on romantically. Before she could say anything to her son though, there was a knock on the door.

Trisha turned to see her best friend standing there. She practically spilled her coffee as she quickly set it down and hurried in that direction. She released the metal latch and opened the screen door. "Sophie!"

"Hey, stranger!" Sophie gave her a big hug, and they didn't let go until Chase stepped up behind her. Trisha released Sophie and hugged him next. Once her brother-in-law, always her brother in heart.

"What a view you have here," Sophie said, turning to the window. "It's even prettier with the sunrise."

"You should see the sunset," Trisha told her, once again thinking about being with Jake last night on the dock.

"Well, you promised us dinner tonight so we probably will." Sophie opened her arms for Petey to barrel into. "Hey, you. You're getting so big!" She squeezed him tightly, the way Trisha knew Petey loved, and then she released him.

"Mom says I'm going through a growth spurt," he told his aunt. Then he made a show of looking around. "You didn't bring Comet?"

"Sorry, buddy. Comet doesn't like long car rides," Chase told Petey. "He's home guarding the house."

"I don't mind long rides," Petey said. "Especially when I'm with you. Let's go." He stepped out onto the deck.

They'd arrived earlier than Trisha had expected. So much for another round of tooth brushing or coaching Petey on what to say—and *not* to say—to his relatives today.

"Do you want a thermos of coffee to go?" Trisha asked Sophie and Chase.

"We brought some." Sophie looked regretful. "This is a quick hello and goodbye, but tonight we'll sit and chat." She gave Trisha a meaningful look. No doubt she wanted more scoop on the kiss that Trisha had told her about last night.

"I look forward to it," Trisha said.

"Me too."

Trisha watched them go down the steps and disappear, leaving her alone. She returned to her barstool and her mug of coffee. She didn't have a good excuse to cancel church with Jake, so she'd go. But as soon as they had a chance to talk, she'd explain how that kiss shouldn't, *couldn't*, happen again.

* * *

Jake saw the SUV pull away with a couple and Petey inside. Trisha was alone next door, which rarely seemed to happen. He'd gotten her alone last night, and they'd ending up kissing.

Jake didn't regret a single second. Yeah, he probably should for a lot of reasons, but it felt good to hold Trisha in his arms. Kissing her felt like that moment in a plane when you were climbing, climbing into the sky. Then in a single heartbeat, you broke through the clouds and reached altitude. Trisha's kiss was as close to that feeling as he could get with his feet still on the ground.

And he wanted to kiss her again.

He leaned against the deck railing and sipped on his first cup of coffee. When he was finished, he went inside to get dressed for church, which was more casual than the big brick-and-mortar one on Hannigan Street. The church at the Point was set on the water and took place under a canopy of huge oak trees. There were no instruments. No pews. Most folks sat on lawn chairs or stayed in their golf carts, which they drove right up to the small makeshift altar.

When Jake was cleaned up and dressed, he walked next door, hoping that Trisha wasn't going to make an excuse to send him away. The need to see her was intense. Being close to her felt invigorating. And sometimes life came down to just doing what felt good.

He climbed the steps of Juniper Cottage and knocked on Trisha's lakeside door. A moment later, she answered, wearing a sundress and sandals.

Jake swallowed as he tried not to let his gaze linger too long below her face. "You look ready for church," he said, hoping that meant she wasn't going to back out of their plans.

"I am. And I'm excited. I haven't been to a service since I left Sweetwater Springs."

Jake exhaled softly. "I saw Petey head out with a nice-looking couple earlier."

Trisha shifted as she stood in the doorway, the sway of her dress making Jake glance down. Attraction buzzed through his veins. "Petey left with his aunt and uncle," she said. "They're driving him up to the family reunion I told you about." She nibbled on her lower lip. "Before we go, I think we should talk. About last night."

Jake felt his stomach drop. "Okay. Which part?"

"All of it." She fidgeted with the bracelet on her wrist. He had to resist reaching for her hand because he understood that she was anxious, and there was no need to be around him. "I told you things that no one else knows," she said.

"I already promised you that I won't tell anyone."

"Thank you. And we, um, we..." She trailed off as she broke eye contact.

"Kissed?" he asked.

"Yeah. We did that." Trisha smoothed a strand of dark hair out of her face, her eyes lifting to meet his. "And while it was..."

"Amazing?" he supplied, suppressing a grin.

She smiled shyly, a soft pink darkening her cheeks. "Amazing," she agreed. "While it was that, we probably shouldn't kiss again."

He wasn't surprised, but he was still disappointed. "All right. If that's what you want."

Her gaze stuck to his. "Isn't it what you want?"

He chuckled quietly. "One amazing kiss leads to another in my book," he said. "But I get where you're coming from, and you're probably the voice of reason here."

"Right." If he wasn't mistaken, she looked a little disappointed too. "So I just wanted to clear that up so there's no weirdness between us."

He held out his open palms. "No weirdness. We're just two friends going to church and having brunch at my grandmother's afterward."

Trisha tilted her head. "I never agreed to brunch."

"No, but we did say we'd review more to-dos for the cottages. Plus, I need backup when it comes to Vi. Unless you have something else to do today."

She gave him a skeptical look. It was totally fair because whatever she was thinking was most likely right. He was just angling to spend more time with her.

"Nope. My schedule is open." She reached for her bag on the counter. "Let's go."

Jake led her onto the deck, where Bailey was waiting. Then

they went down the steps and headed over to one of two golf carts parked under Vi's carport.

"Why does Vi have two golf carts anyway?" Trisha asked.

Jake patted the seat beside him. He meant it for Trisha, but Bailey hopped up to his side.

Trisha laughed as she shifted out of Bailey's way. Then she stepped closer to the cart and sat down.

"One of the golf carts is for Vi, and the other was my grandfather's. Vi was always running late for church, and he was always the first one there. So they rode separately."

Trisha scooted in closer to Bailey. "So they have these golf carts just for church?"

"No, they used to ride them along the shoreline too. As far as I know, Vi hasn't really done that much since her stroke." Jake swallowed past the bitterness he felt every time the stroke came up. The stress that Peter Lewis had caused was a contributing factor. And now he knew that Peter Lewis was Trisha's ex-husband.

Jake reversed the golf cart out of the covered area behind Vi's home, and then he put it into forward motion. Once they were on the path and headed to church, he glanced over to catch Trisha smiling. "It's fun, isn't it? The wind in your hair and on your face?"

She glanced over. "It is."

"A bike is a perfectly acceptable form of transportation to church at the Point too. Unless you're wearing a dress, which I usually don't," he teased.

"Good to know," she said on a laugh.

His heart skipped around at the sound.

"I'm curious about this church we're heading to," Trisha said. "The church I attended growing up had four walls and a roof with a steeple at its center."

"This one is nothing fancy."

"I don't need fancy." Trisha swept hair out of her face. "After my marriage ordeal, I don't even want fancy."

Jake drove the cart beyond Lakeshore Drive. "You lived a rich life, huh? When you were married?"

"Well, it wasn't a millionaire's lifestyle by any means, but it was much more than what I grew up with. It seems bizarre to think of how I lived just a couple years ago. I was never the person who wanted material things. I was a tomboy growing up. I didn't need expensive things or clothes. All I wanted for my life was the normal stuff. A family and someone to grow old with."

She fell silent as he turned the golf cart down a dirt path that cut through the woods and led to an opening along the lake where church services were held every Sunday morning. He pulled to a stop behind an old Southern oak with large, flat rocks encircling it. Those were used for seats. He looked over at Trisha.

"This is church?" she asked. She gave him an uncertain grin.

"Yep." Jake pointed across the way at a man with a long, dark scraggly beard wearing jeans and a T-shirt. "That's Pastor Lance."

"That's the pastor?" Her tone was thick with disbelief.

Jake chuckled. "I told you things were dressed down. At least on the outside. Don't be fooled though. You'll leave here feeling like you've gotten a sermon. The kind that makes you feel like you need to do better. Be better." Jake glanced around at the other golf carts and folks in lawn chairs. They wore sunglasses and ball caps like they were here to watch a ball game, and with the same kind of excitement and hunger.

"From where I'm sitting, you're already pretty great."

Jake leaned behind Bailey to whisper, "That's just the after-kiss talking," he said, knowing he shouldn't. They'd agreed this morning to leave the kiss behind them.

Her laugh sounded nervous. Her cheeks blushed faintly as she looked at him, lips slightly parted. "Are you telling me there was some type of spell attached to last night's kiss?"

Jake straightened back into an upright position. "That's right. It'll wear off eventually." He kept his tone casual even though his heart rate was picking up. "Unless, of course, we kiss again."

* * *

At the end of the church service, Trisha was sold on outdoor sermons. It was similar to the sunrise services that were traditional on Easter Sundays when she was growing up, except this apparently happened every week, rain or shine.

Trisha released a sigh after the dismissal prayer and then turned to look at Jake.

"I told you," he said. "You'll never want it any other way."

Her mind went to that kiss of theirs as she looked at him at this close proximity. Then another golf cart pulled up beside them, interrupting the moment. It was Mr. and Mrs. S.

"Mr. S," Trisha said. "I missed you this morning." She'd almost forgotten that he'd been missing on the shore when she'd hurried down that way at the crack of dawn.

Mr. S gestured at Jake. "He got to me before you could."

Trisha turned to Jake. "You woke Mr. S?"

"I did," he said. "I was trying to help you out. I guess I could've texted you to stay in bed, huh?"

Trisha felt a warmth radiating from inside her chest, imagining Jake rolling out of bed earlier than he'd like on her behalf. "I see. Thank you for helping."

"So you two are a thing now?" Mr. S asked, bouncing a finger between them.

Trisha looked at Mr. S and shook her head. "No, Jake was just showing me the best-kept secret on Sunday mornings."

Mr. S chuckled. "Sharing secrets sounds like a thing to me."

Mrs. Santorini elbowed him and made him howl in mock pain. Then she looked at Jake and asked, "Where's Vi?"

"She can't always get out of bed this early anymore," Jake explained. "We're going to check on her once we leave here."

"Well, do me a favor and don't tell her that I was lying on the beach this morning," Mr. S said. He'd said that to Trisha a few dozen times since she'd started the job, obviously thinking that Vi didn't know what went on along her stretch of the lake.

Instead of elbowing him again, Mrs. Santorini jabbed a finger into his shoulder. "Maybe you should just stop lying out there in the buff."

"You can't change a man's habits after so many years. Living at the nudist colony was the best thing I ever did besides marrying you," he told his wife. Then he looked at Jake. "I was about your age when I started. I'd recommend a colony life to anyone."

Jake held up his hands. "I'll pass, Mr. S."

The old man chuckled. "The only reason I ever left was because I couldn't get my lovely bride to join me out there."

It was kind of a sweet story. Kind of.

"You can take the man out of the colony, but you can't take the colony out of the man. We men don't change. Right, Jake?"

Jake raised his palms outward. "I'm staying out of this argument. But I won't tell Vi a word about your early morning habits."

"Good boy." Mr. S nodded approvingly. "Well, we'll leave you two lovebirds alone," he added before zipping away on his golf cart.

Trisha felt embarrassed. She looked around and noticed that others were also watching them. "Just because we came to church together, people think we're lovebirds?" she asked Jake quietly.

He laughed. "Oh, come on. You grew up in a small town. You know the drill."

She dodged Bailey's wet nose to her cheek as she narrowed her gaze. "I was hoping it was just a Sweetwater Springs thing that people started planning your marriage as soon as they saw two singles sharing a conversation."

"Afraid not." Jake looked around at the dispersing crowd. "At least some of them are watching us and just talking about the fact that I'm home. They're probably wondering if I'll stick around. Or if I'm taking over for Vi. And maybe they're wondering where Vi is, like Mrs. S was." He lifted his brows at her. "And half are talking about you. Who are you? Where did you come from? Why are you here?"

Trisha felt a familiar uneasiness settle over her. "Oh."

"Small-town talk." Jake put the golf cart back into gear. "The talk doesn't bother me. Does it bother you?" he asked after a moment as the golf cart bumped along the uneven ground.

Trisha thought about it. "I guess I'm used to it. Or I should be by now." They grew quiet again. Then after several minutes, Trisha asked, "Are you worried about Vi?"

"A little." He rested one hand on the steering wheel and one on Bailey's back. "She's not one to miss church."

"I've been here over a month now. I've never seen her take the golf cart out on a Sunday morning," Trisha said. "I would've driven her myself had I known."

Jake's lips pulled into a slight frown. "My whole family is worried about her being here all alone."

"One of your aunts came to visit last month. I think her name was Dawn?" Trisha asked with uncertainty.

"That's right," Jake said.

"She seemed like a nice woman with good intentions," Trisha

said, "but Vi seemed a little bothered by all her hovering. I really think she's glad that you're here though."

"I'm glad I'm here too." Jake glanced over. "So Mr. S is really lying on the shore naked every morning?"

Trisha laughed at the unexpected change of subject. "Yes, he is. Vi asked me to make sure he's gone before anyone else happens upon him. It's part of my job, and I take it very seriously," she said as she laughed harder, resting her hand on her chest to catch her breath.

"That's the craziest job description I've ever heard." Jake grinned over at her. "And I've heard a lot of crazy things as a lawyer."

"Well, I love being the property manager for the rental cottages, so I don't mind. Much."

Jake pulled the golf cart under Vi's carport behind her house. They both stepped off and walked around to the back of the house. Jake led the way up Vi's steps and onto her deck. He knocked before entering the unlocked door.

"Good morning. How was church?" Vi looked up from the dining room table, where she was having coffee and a plate of eggs. And she wasn't alone.

Trisha didn't recognize the man, but Jake visibly stiffened beside her.

"Uncle Tim. I didn't realize you were coming today," Jake said.

Tim gave him a wide smile that struck Trisha as insincere. "Well, I tried to call you yesterday, but you didn't answer," the man drawled in a thick Southern accent that also felt a touch insincere. He glanced at Trisha and back to Jake. "I'm guessing you were pretty busy."

Jake didn't respond to that last comment. Instead, he said, "It's good to see you, Uncle Tim. How long will you be staying?"

"A week. Maybe two." Tim looked at Trisha again, his gaze sticking this time. "You must be the new property manager I've been hearing about."

"Trisha Langly," she confirmed.

"Vi told me I could stay in one of the vacant cottages. Do you have one that isn't going to crumble around me while I sleep?" Tim asked on a quiet laugh. Trisha didn't think the question was funny though. "Because these cottages look like bulldozer fodder to me."

"Well, Jake and I have been working on them. Jake just fixed the roof of Magnolia Cottage so that one's in good shape right now. It needs new paint on the inside and updated appliances would be nice, but I think you'll find it in livable condition."

"Jake fixed the roof?" Tim's brows rose high on his forehead. "A man of many talents, huh?"

"He's proving to be," Trisha said, feeling a bit defensive on Jake's behalf, but she wasn't sure why. "And I'm very grateful for his help."

"I bet you are. Makes your job a lot easier, huh?" Tim asked.

Trisha took offense at whatever he was suggesting.

Vi tapped the table in front of her to gain Trisha's attention. "What did you think of the church at the Point?"

"I thought it was amazing." Trisha wondered if Vi was having similar thoughts to Mr. and Mrs. S's. Was she also wondering if Trisha and Jake were getting romantically involved? Was Tim wondering the same? Trisha didn't want to do anything to compromise her job.

"Good." Vi picked up her fork and stabbed at a mound of eggs on her plate.

"Well, we won't interrupt you two any longer," Jake told Vi. "Do you need help with anything? I've got the whole day. Give me a list, and I'll take care of it for you."

"Such a sweet grandson. No, I'm fine. Why don't you and

Trisha do something together? I saw young Petey go off this morning." She gave Trisha a questioning raise of the brow.

"Yes, his aunt and uncle took him for an outing. They'll drop him off later tonight." She hoped Vi wouldn't ask questions, especially with Tim watching and listening. Trisha instinctively didn't trust Jake's uncle.

"Well then, you both have the whole day to do as you please. I imagine you want to take that plane of yours up in the sky," Vi suggested. "Why don't you give Trisha a ride?"

"I actually took her up yesterday. Her and Petey," Jake said.

"Oh?" Vi looked between them, her eyebrows lifting shakily on her forehead.

Panic swept over Trisha. Was Jake going to tell Vi about her ex being in prison? In front of Tim too. She'd trusted him with her secrets, but maybe Peter's warning had been right yesterday. Was Jake now going to use her past against her?

"That's right," Jake said. "But I didn't give Trisha a decent tour of the town. I think everyone who lives here should get to see Somerset Lake from the clouds. What do you say, Trisha?" He looked at her, lowering his voice just a notch. "Fly with me? Again."

Trisha exhaled softly. No, her ex-husband was wrong when he'd made her question the new people she was surrounding herself with. She could trust Jake with her secrets. And her life.

CHAPTER FOURTEEN

Jake glanced over at Trisha beside him in the plane. "Why do you look more nervous today than you were yesterday?"

Trisha nibbled her lower lip, seemingly searching her brain for some faraway answer. "Maybe because I was mostly in the back of the plane yesterday. And Petey was distracting me."

"It's just like driving a car," he teased, hoping to lighten the mood. "Except we're several thousand feet above the ground."

"And you're the one steering," she pointed out.

The plane was bumping along the water's natural current. He hadn't even started the engine yet. He wanted to gauge if Trisha was truly up for this. Her son was fearless when it came to flying, but Trisha didn't seem as comfortable. She'd gone up with him out of necessity yesterday, but today was different.

"Would you rather steer?" he asked.

Her eyes widened. "No, you're the pilot. I'm just going along for the ride."

"I want you to enjoy yourself though. That's the whole point. Here, maybe it'll help if I give you a little lesson on flying."

"A flying lesson?" she asked.

"Why not?" He pointed at the control panel, which was admittedly intimidating to someone who knew nothing about planes. "This is the ignition."

She was looking at him as if he were crazy right now.

He continued anyway, pointing out the various buttons and levers and telling her what their function was. He tried to keep the technical names and language to a minimum, opting for layman's terms. Levers, buttons, and liftoff. Altitude, visibility, and landing.

"I don't want to pilot this plane," she finally said. "We'd crash for sure."

Jake gave her a steady look. Her eyes were a brighter shade of brown in this light. They were almost copper. "What if I promise to catch you if you go down?"

Trisha's lips parted. Had he said too much? He started backtracking. "Sometimes there's comfort in knowing how things work and what will happen." He pulled his gaze from hers. "The first time Gramps took me flying, he sat me in the copilot seat and told me everything there was to know. After his instruction, I could have flown that plane if I'd wanted to."

"How old were you?" Trisha asked.

"Eleven. Hungry for knowledge. Eager for adventure. He didn't let me actually operate the plane until I was fifteen, and even that was legally too young."

"I won't tell Deputy Bruno."

Jake chuckled under his breath as he looked out on the lake through the front windshield. He didn't dare look at Trisha again right now. He couldn't seem to control his mouth when he did. "Any kid growing up in Somerset Lake is eager for something exciting."

Trisha sighed beside him. "I guess the same is true for Petey."

"It's a sleepy little town, but a boy with a big imagination can find things to do." Jake sucked in a breath and looked at her. "Are you ready now? I know you only went with me yesterday because you kind of didn't have a choice."

"Not unless I wanted to break Petey's heart," she agreed.

"You have a choice this time," he said. "You can still change your mind about this trip."

Trisha hesitated and then shook her head. "No. It's not just little boys who are eager for something exciting." One corner of her mouth kicked up, and a fire seemed to ignite behind the golden brown of her irises.

Jake felt breathless for a moment. Trisha was beautiful in every way. If Jake wasn't already worried that he could fall for her, he was now. Which spelled trouble—but it also felt like that same adventure and excitement he'd been looking for as a boy on this very lake. Some part of him was still looking, but finding it in different ways.

"Okay. Buckle up. I'm about to take us into the clouds." He waited for Trisha to click her belt into place. Then he turned the ignition with a key and a press of a button. The propeller began to spin.

Jake put his headphones on and pointed at a pair for Trisha to wear as well. Slowly, Jake transitioned the plane into motion. It skimmed the water for several hundred feet before its nose tipped up, its rudders dipped low, and they moved forward, brushing over the lake's surface until they had takeoff.

Jake's heart lifted right along with the plane. *Best feeling in the world!* Except for maybe last night's kiss. "You doing okay?" he asked into his headphones after a long moment. "Are your eyes open?"

He heard her breathe a laugh that sounded equal parts nervous and giddy excitement. "I'm doing fine, I think. Eyes wide open, but my heart might explode."

"Just breathe," he said.

"That wasn't part of your initial instructions."

"That initial part was the manual version of how to fly a plane. Some things you can't learn in a manual. You have to experience them."

"Good to know." He heard her sharp intake of air and then her exhalation a moment later. It repeated, finding a steady rhythm.

They grew quiet as the plane ascended, and then he leveled it off a few minutes later. "Okay, we're flying. I can put this thing on cruise control and nap in the back." He slid his gaze over just in time to catch Trisha's eyes go wide.

"Don't you dare." She shook her head as she glanced out the window. "Wow," she said, voice thick with awe. "This is really amazing."

"Yep. It never gets old. You can see the cottages." He gestured out his window. "I'll circle back in a bit, and they'll be on your side."

Trisha leaned toward him to look out the pilot-side window. "They're so pretty." She reached for the camera looped around her neck. "I'm not sure if the pictures will do the actual view justice, but this will be good practice for me. Do you mind?"

"Not at all. Go for it," Jake said. "I'd love to have an aerial view of the Somerset Cottages and the lake." Maybe it wasn't his home anymore, but this trip had changed his perception of this place, bringing back all the sentimentality he'd once held for it. Being here didn't make him ache this time. He guessed it was because he was too distracted by helping the woman beside him.

Trisha lifted her camera, aimed it out the window, and started snapping pictures. Jake watched her from the corner of his eye. She seemed happy and relaxed, which gave him a sense of satisfaction because he was responsible in some small way. From what he'd seen, she rarely took a day off. She deserved a day to enjoy herself while Petey was with family.

"I can't wait to develop these pictures and see what they look like," Trisha said excitedly. "Wouldn't it be nice if I framed them to decorate a few of the cottages?"

Jake slid his gaze over. "That's a good idea. The living rooms could all have the same aerial shots. Maybe three or four each in frames."

"Yes! I'm going to develop these pictures and buy frames this week," she said. Then she lifted her camera and aimed it again.

"Whoa. What are you doing?" Jake asked when he realized the camera lens was directed at him.

"Eyes on the sky, Mr. Fletcher. I'm just taking a photo of you in your natural habitat."

Jake found himself grinning as he returned his gaze forward. "That's a true statement. Being up here is addictive. If I'm not careful, you'll snatch my keys and take it up when I'm not looking. I just explained how this thing works, after all."

"You don't need to worry about me stealing your plane. Or anything for that matter."

He glanced over just in time to see her look down for a moment. No, the only thing she might steal of his was his heart. Maybe she already had.

Another beat of silence passed between them. "So the guy I saw this morning was your former brother-in-law?"

"Mm-hmm. Chase Lewis. He's a veterinarian in Sweetwater Springs. My best friend, Sophie, married him last year."

"So I guess you'll be connected to your in-laws indefinitely then."

"Just them and my mother-in-law. Chase and Peter's dad passed away when they were young. And staying connected to the Lewis family isn't a bad thing. Chase and Sophie are amazing. And my former mother-in-law has been good to me. She's just like a real mother."

Jake realized he didn't know about Trisha's parents yet, and he wanted to. He wanted to know everything and not because he was trying to undermine what she was doing here anymore. He just wanted to know more about her because he couldn't seem to get enough of Trisha Langly.

"What about your parents? You said you didn't have any family of your own in the town you grew up in. Where are they?"

"Well, I was raised by my grandparents. They had kids very late in life. I think my grandmother was forty-two when she got pregnant with my mom. So by the time I came around, they were older. I think my grandmother was seventy-eight when I graduated high school. She only lived a couple months after that."

"I'm sorry." Jake felt a deep sense of regret for Trisha. "That must have been tough."

"It was. People told me that my grandparents hung on long enough to make sure I was okay. I think that's probably true."

Through his headphones, he heard Trisha take another breath. "My grandparents were wonderful. They did everything they could for me. I can't really complain about my upbringing."

"What about your parents?" Jake asked.

From his peripheral vision, he saw Trisha shake her head. "I don't know. My mom got pregnant, had me, came home to live with my grandparents. That was the plan. Then, the story is, my grandmother woke up to me crying in my crib early one morning. My mom was gone. They never heard from her again."

Trisha laughed beside him but Jake didn't think it was because she thought the story was funny. Sometimes the only thing to do was laugh if you didn't want to cry. He knew that from experience.

"My mom never told my grandparents who my father is, so I never knew him. When I met Peter in high school, I was just so needy for someone other than my grandparents to want me. The entire Lewis family accepted me as one of their own. It was like I finally had somewhere to belong, and I guess I just held on to it blindly."

Jake reached over and squeezed her hand. "You belong here," he said, unable to control his mouth again. He believed what he was saying though. Trisha belonged in Somerset Lake. It was a town of good people who would make sure she was taken care of. If he wasn't second-guessing his mission here already, he was now. In fact, he was abandoning his family-directed mission altogether. Vi deserved to stay in her home. And so did Trisha.

* * *

Trisha kept looking at Jake instead of what he was trying to show her. She couldn't help herself. He seemed to be getting more handsome by the second, at least in her mind. It was like she was twisting the dials of her camera, finding an even more perfect viewpoint with each turn.

"There's The Village," he said, pointing.

"That's where Lucy lives, right?" Trisha asked.

"Yep. That's where Rachel's mom lives too. I plan to visit her before I leave town."

There was yet another subtle reminder that he wasn't here for the long-term. "I'm sure she'll appreciate that," Trisha said.

"Oh yeah. Going over there is always bittersweet." He glanced over. "As much as I'd love to, we can't stay up here forever. What should we do at the cottages today?"

"Well, I need more paint for the cottages' interiors. And since you have the truck and offered, maybe we can go check out the Habitat for Humanity ReStore and see if they have any used appliances in good condition."

Jake nodded. "That actually sounds like fun."

"I think so too." He heard Trisha's camera click beside him again. "I love thrift-store shopping. And it'll save us money on renovations."

Jake glanced over. "Us? Sounds like you're invested in the property."

Trisha's gaze darted from Jake to the view outside the plane's windshield. "Well, I am the property manager. I'm so thankful to your grandmother for giving me the job and the cottage to live in. It's the perfect situation for a single mother. I want to do a good job for Vi. I don't want to let her down."

Jake was quiet for a moment. "Maybe we can find some flooring material too. I want to fix the floor in Pansy Cottage. I noticed that it was peeling when I did a walk-through the other day."

"You can work on floors too?" Trisha sounded impressed. "Are you sure you're really a lawyer? Because no one can be skilled in that many areas."

Jake chuckled. "I didn't say I was skilled. It might not look pretty, but it'll be functional."

"That's okay. The lake view is the main attraction," Trisha said.

"And by view, you mean Mr. S at sunrise?"

Trisha felt her jaw drop. "No, not that view." She swatted Jake's shoulder playfully. Just that simple touch lit a blaze within her. She may have told him with her words this morning that they couldn't kiss again, but her body wasn't listening. "And while Mr. S's behavior is weird, I think he's harmless."

"I agree."

"And you're a good judge of character," Trisha said, reminding him of what he'd told her last night. Right before that kiss that she couldn't seem to get out of her mind.

"I like to think I am. So," Jake said, "I guess when we land this thing, we can hop in my truck and go to the hardware store for paint and then to the thrift store. Maybe we can grab a late lunch too."

"Sounds good. I'm starving." Trisha felt a happy buzz in her chest. And all of it was because her entire day would be spent with Jake.

She mentally reviewed the reasons she shouldn't, couldn't, develop feelings for the man beside her. Jake was temporary. He was Vi's grandson. He was another potential heartbreak that she wasn't sure she could survive.

"Then let's get the food first." Jake circled the plane back and started its descent toward the water.

Once the plane landed safely, he cut the engine, got out, and stepped around to her side to open her door. He offered his hand to help her step out. That required that she slip her hand into his. Another touch that only made the attraction she felt grow more intense. The fluttering of her heart was a dozen hummingbird wings combined.

She found her footing and sighed as she pulled her hand away from his. Then Bailey jumped out of the plane behind her. "Are you sure you want to give up your entire Sunday for me?" Trisha asked. "I mean, I took up all of your day yesterday too."

"One hundred percent positive. I'm all yours." Jake led her to his truck and opened the passenger door for her. While she waited for him to move around to the other side, she checked her phone. No missed calls or texts from Sophie or Chase. They would just be arriving at the Lewis family reunion now. Unless they stopped off for some reason.

"Everything okay?" Jake slid into the truck behind the steering wheel.

"Just checking my phone to see if I've missed any messages from Sophie or Chase about Petey. No word."

"I'm sure he's fine then. He seemed pretty excited when I saw him running for his aunt and uncle's car this morning."

"Oh, he was. He adores them."

Jake directed the truck down the gravel path behind the cottages. "So he's fine, and it's my job to take your mind off of any worries."

She dropped her cell phone into her purse. "What will people in town think if they keep seeing us together?"

"I know the answer, but I don't think you'll like it."

Trisha lifted a questioning brow as he glanced over at her. "Tell me anyway."

"They'll think we're falling in love," Jake said.

She swallowed. "That's crazy. We barely even know each other."

"I don't know," he said. "Two single, attractive people living next door to each other. That sounds more inevitable than crazy to me."

"Good thing you're not staying in Somerset Lake then because I'm not ready to fall in love again just yet. Are you?"

Jake took his time in answering, which was just like him. He never seemed to be in a hurry about anything. "I haven't been in love since I was eighteen," he finally said. "I'm past ready. It's the heartbreak I'm not ready for. The next time I fall in love, I want it to be forever."

* * *

Trisha finished the last bite of her shrimp scampi and set her fork down. "That was delicious."

"I told you." Jake chuckled as he picked up his napkin and wiped his mouth. "I love this place. It ties with Choco-Lovers."

"Oh, I've heard about that place. I've been wanting to take Petey there," Trisha said.

"You should. Jana is always adding to the menu. It's crazy what she can find to dip in chocolate."

"Jana's the owner?" Trisha asked.

"Yep. She was a couple years behind me in school. Even back then, I remember she always had something chocolate with her. The guys tried to flirt with her by giving her chocolate, but that was never the way to her heart."

"How do you know that?" A thread of jealousy ran through Trisha as she wondered if Jake had tried that tactic too. Where had the jealousy come from? Jake was all hers for the day, but not for much longer than that.

Jake took a bite of his meal, chewing and swallowing before answering. "I know because my best friend was really into her."

Trisha reached for her glass of lemon water. "Did she ever give him a chance?"

"Not really. They went out a few times, and he was stupid. As his best friend, I can say so."

"What did he do that was so wrong?" she asked.

"It's a long story." Jake folded his arms over his chest.

Trisha recognized the look. He was keeping his friend's secret. Would he guard her secrets just the same? He hadn't told Vi earlier, when Trisha had worried that he was about to. From what Trisha could tell, Jake was a trustworthy guy. Then again, unlike Jake, Trisha wasn't a great judge of character. Especially considering the man she had married.

The waitress came up to the table and looked between them. "So I have a dollar on this being just a casual meal you're sitting down to. But Gene is betting that you two are on a date."

Trisha looked at Jake.

Told you, he mouthed. Then he raised his voice normally,

talking to Trisha. "Gene is the cook." He looked at the waitress. "Des, tell Gene that Trisha is my neighbor for the next few weeks."

She put a hand on her waist. "That doesn't explain one way or the other."

Jake reached into his pocket and pulled out two crisp one-dollar bills. "I'm not a gambler, but I'll cover both your bets."

Des looked disappointed. "You know it's not about the money, Jake. It's about the knowledge."

"Aka the gossip," he said, lifting his brows.

Des looked at Trisha again and offered a sugary smile. "It was nice to meet you, sweetie. I hope you'll come back here real soon."

"I likely will. The food is delicious."

"Neighbors, huh?" Des asked again, still prying. "That means you're staying at the Somerset Cottages."

"I'm the new property manager there," Trisha said.

Des lifted her razor-thin eyebrows. "Until the family sells. Tim was in here earlier this morning talking about that prospect. He said it's just Vi who's being stubborn."

Trisha hesitated before looking at Jake. She hated gossip as much as the next person, but sometimes it had its advantages.

Des continued talking. "Your uncle Tim said he wants Vi to move down to Florida with the rest of the family. Is that true, Jake? Is your family going to put the cottages up for sale after all these years?"

Trisha turned to Jake and studied his stiff posture. He was working his jaw, but not because there was food in his mouth.

"Vi is stubborn, you know that," Jake finally said. "She won't go along with that plan anytime soon. Trisha and I are actually heading to Hannigan's Hardware next to get some supplies for renovating the cottages. Then we'll work on getting them rented out. Since you're so good at passing on information," Jake said pointedly, "please let anyone that's looking for a place to stay know there will be six rental cottages available soon."

Des didn't appear to take offense. "I'll do that."

Trisha noted that Jake only mentioned six cottages. His was the seventh, and it would be open once he was gone.

Unless he's considering staying longer.

CHAPTER FIFTEEN

Later that evening, Jake leaned against the deck's railing and looked out onto the water. Today had been a Top Ten kind of day. It had almost been magical because everything Trisha had wanted for the cottages they'd found at two different thrift stores. She'd filled the bed of his truck, chattering excitedly. She'd found so many things that he'd actually made two trips to get it all back to Lakeshore Drive, where he'd stored the finds under Vi's shelter.

Jake replayed those earlier hours in his mind. Trisha was so invested in the Somerset Cottages, and her enthusiasm was contagious. He couldn't wait to install the new-to-them dishwashers, washers and dryers, and even granite countertops this week.

Trisha stepped up beside him and leaned against the railing as well. "I just spoke to Sophie," she said, her voice floating on the evening air. "They'll be here in about thirty minutes or so. Petey had an amazing time with the family, and he's doing well."

"That's good news." Jake looked over. He'd seen a million

sunsets over this lake, but none compared to the beauty in Trisha's face.

How long had it been since he'd first laid eyes on her? A week? Two? And already he was having crazy thoughts that both scared and excited him. He wasn't the guy who fell in love at first sight, and he hadn't with Trisha. The more he got to know her though, the more he was intrigued. The more he wanted to know. "Well, you've been stuck with me all day. I'll leave you to prepare for your family's visit. I have a lot to do this week," he said on a grin. "I might need to rest up anyway."

"Jake?" Trisha looked at him nervously, which in turn made Jake nervous. "Is there something you're not telling me?"

"Like what?" he asked.

"Like why you're really here this summer?"

Jake had been expecting this conversation. He'd actually been shocked and relieved that Trisha hadn't brought it up after what Des had said at the diner. Jake didn't want to tell her the truth. But he wanted to lie even less. He exhaled slowly. "I came to Somerset Lake because my whole family is concerned about my grandmother, which I already told you. Vi is getting older. She's a widow. And these cottages are a lot of responsibility."

Trisha's brow line dipped. "You told me all of that, yes, but Des said that your family wanted to convince Vi to sell. Is that what you're doing here? Are you and your uncle Tim here to convince her to move to Florida to be with the rest of your family?"

Jake hesitated, but if anyone deserved the full truth, it was Trisha. She'd been lied to enough. He wasn't going to deceive her in any way if he could help it. "Yes. That's why I came back to Somerset Lake."

Trisha's lips parted as she pulled away from him just slightly. "I see. So all the work you're doing on the cottages with me is just so you can get a better deal when you sell them?"

Reflexively, Jake reached for her hand. "No. Trisha, maybe that was my motivation on that first day, but I've changed my mind since then. This is Vi's home. She doesn't want to move to Florida. She doesn't want to leave the place where she feels my grandfather's presence the most. And who am I to ask her to? All I want now is to help her get what she wants, which is to stay and rent out all the cottages."

Trisha narrowed her eyes. "Really?"

"Yeah."

"When you arrived, were you trying to find out more about me so that you could figure out a way to get me out of the picture?" she asked.

Jake was still holding her hand. He hadn't let go, and he didn't want to. "I wasn't trying to hurt you. I didn't even know you at the time. But now that I·do..." He swallowed as he trailed off.

"Now that you do?" she repeated in a quiet voice, prompting him to continue.

"This isn't just Vi's home. It's yours too. And Petey's. Now that I know, I want you to have what you've been missing since you lost your grandparents."

Trisha's eyes were shining now. She looked like she was fighting back tears. "What's that?" she asked.

"A place to belong. Trisha, you deserve that, and you have that here in Somerset Lake. I'm not going to try to take that away. All I want to do while I'm here is help you find it."

She stared at him for a long moment, her face expressionless. "Why?"

Jake wasn't even sure of the answer to that question himself. "Sometimes you can know someone for years and not really know who they are. Then you can meet someone for the first time"—*What am I doing?*—"and feel like you've known them for a lifetime."

He wanted to kiss her again, but he wasn't going to. He'd agreed this morning that he wouldn't cross that line. They both had good reasons not to want to be romantically involved.

She stepped closer. His gaze unwittingly fell to her lips. Good thing he had steel willpower.

"Mom!" The sound of heavy feet stomped up the steps. "Mom!"

Trisha stepped back, but Jake stayed rooted, wondering if she'd been considering kissing him.

Petey arrived on the deck and ran to throw his arms around Trisha's waist. "Today was the best day ever!"

Trisha lit up from the inside out at the sight of her son. Prettier than a sunset in Jake's mind. He was in so much trouble this summer. He wasn't on his way to falling for her. *Nope.* This proverbial plane of his was on its way down, and he didn't have a parachute handy to break his fall.

"I'm so glad," she told Petey.

A man and a woman also reached the landing. Jake recognized them from this morning.

The man stuck out his hand to Jake. "Hi, I'm Chase Lewis, Trisha's brother-in-law."

Former brother-in-law, Jake knew, but he appreciated that the man didn't see it that way. "I'm Jake Fletcher." Jake shook his hand. "Trisha's neighbor for the time being." He pointed at Peony Cottage.

The woman outstretched her hand as well. "Sophie Lewis. I'm Trisha's oldest friend. I'm also Petey's new aunt." She grinned at the boy before looking at Jake again. Suddenly, he felt like she was scrutinizing him. She gave Trisha a look that seemed to convey approval. Then she returned her gaze to Jake. "We're having dinner with Trisha. I guess she told you."

Jake nodded. "I was just on my way back to my cottage."

Sophie shook her head. "Nonsense. Knowing my best friend,

I'm sure she made more than enough food. Please stay. I need to know the man who is making sure my best friend is okay here in a new town."

Jake turned to Trisha, looking for her to give him an excuse.

"Yes, please stay, Jake," Trisha said instead. "There's more than enough for all of us. And after your help today, a meal is the least I can do."

"Help, huh?" Sophie grinned. "You two will have to give us more details over dinner. I'm starving."

"Me too." Petey ran to the door and opened it. He turned back before hurrying inside. "And I want to tell you all about the family reunion," he called behind him.

Jake wasn't sure he wanted to hear all about the family of the guy who'd broken Trisha's heart. But he did want to spend more time with her. He wasn't ready to say goodbye just yet. He wasn't looking forward to saying those two words at all.

* * *

What was I thinking?

Trisha slunk lower in her chair as dinner progressed and Sophie and Chase took turns telling embarrassing stories about her growing up in Sweetwater Springs.

"What about that one time"—Sophie looked at Chase, barely containing her laughter—"when Trisha was the school's news-caster for our homeroom period?"

Chase covered his mouth as he started chuckling too. "You're going to love this story," he told Jake, who seemed to be having a great time at Trisha's expense. It was all in fun, but Trisha was growing tired of the endless dredging up of her less-than-finer moments.

"No, he won't," Trisha protested, but also laughing at the memory. "Why are you guys boring Jake with all of these stories?"

"Mom, I've never heard these stories about you either. You were pretty funny when you were young," he said, as if she were old now. "I had no idea."

Trisha shook her head. "Last story, okay? But I'll be the one to tell it." She inhaled and looked at Jake. "I was the homeroom newscaster. The camera was on, and I wasn't aware. So I complained about how mean my homeroom teacher was before giving my report on the lunch menu and the weather for that day." She covered her eyes momentarily, remembering how horrified she'd been when she'd realized what she'd done. "Mrs. Tawny didn't like me for the rest of the school year. I got a low B in that class when I deserved an A. End of story."

Sophie pointed at her across the table, another comment on the tip of her tongue. They'd all finished eating ten minutes ago, but no one was moving to get up. "This was funnier, Jake, because Trisha never spoke bad about anyone. She rarely ever has. Trisha is so forgiving and protective of everyone's feelings. But that day…" Sophie held a hand to her chest as she giggled to herself. "I don't know what Mrs. Tawny did to make you so mad, but you were going on and on in front of the entire school." Sophie looked at Jake. "And by on and on, I mean a full monologue worthy of a Shakespearian play. She was waving her arms in the air and ranting about how unjust Mrs. Tawny had been to her."

Trisha couldn't help but laugh too. "Not my finest moment. None of those are. I'm never inviting you two to dinner again," she told Sophie and Chase.

"Well, they were the guests," Jake said. "I'm not even supposed to be here."

Trisha looked at him. In her mind, this was exactly where he belonged. It'd felt good having him balance things out. Trisha was usually with Petey, but she still usually felt like the third wheel with Sophie and Chase.

Not tonight. It seemed Jake was good at making her feel like she belonged.

"Well, we better get back on the road." Chase pushed back from the table. "It's another two-hour drive, and I need to be at the clinic early in the morning."

"You're right." Sophie pushed back and stood as well. "Plus Comet is probably wondering where we are."

"I miss Comet," Petey half whined. "Mom, can we go home soon so I can see him?"

Trisha swallowed at the mention of the h-word. She looked down at her hands for just a moment and hoped no one else noticed. She was working so hard to make Somerset Lake their home. It was starting to feel that way to her, but maybe Petey wasn't quite as settled yet.

After collecting herself, Trisha looked up. "We can go visit your aunt Sophie and uncle Chase very soon. And Comet too."

"Yes!" Petey got up from the table and followed his aunt and uncle to the door. "Thank you for taking me to the reunion today. I wish we didn't have to wait a whole 'nother year to see everyone again."

"You're welcome, sweetie." Sophie bent to hug him. She moved stiffly. No doubt she'd physically outdone herself today. In high school, she'd gotten in a bad climbing accident and had injured her leg. Sometimes when she did too much or sat too long, such as for a long car ride, she limped.

Trisha hugged her next. "You're the best friend ever."

Sophie pulled back from the embrace and pointed at her. "And don't you forget that. You're not allowed to replace me here in your new home." She gave Trisha a serious look.

"I could never replace you," Trisha said.

"But"—Sophie cocked her head—"you are allowed to have friends. Just not another best friend."

Trisha laughed for the hundredth time tonight. Her ribs were already aching from too much fun. This whole weekend had been amazing from start to finish. "The same applies to you," she told Sophie.

They hugged again, and Trisha did her best not to cry as she watched Sophie step onto the deck to leave. She hugged Chase next.

"Hey," he said, "you'll see us again soon."

She punched his shoulder softly. "Thanks for the warning."

Chase turned to Jake. "Trisha is a lot like Sophie. Neither of them asks for help easily. Will you make sure to let me know if there's something Trisha needs?"

Trisha felt her mouth fall open. "That's not necessary."

Chase gave her a meaningful look. "I just want to know you're not alone here."

"Of course I'm not. I have Petey, and I have Vi next door."

"Petey is seven, and Vi is eighty," Chase said, as if age made any difference in their ability to help her.

Trisha scoffed. "Vi isn't eighty. She's in her late seventies."

Jake stepped up beside Trisha. "She's not alone here," he told Chase. "I'm right next door, and she knows I can be here in a flat second."

Trisha felt her body warm.

"That's a relief." Chase reached into his pocket and pulled out a business card. He handed it to Jake. "That number is for the vet clinic. It has my cell on there too."

Trisha tried to snatch it away, but Jake pulled it to his chest. She gave Chase a frustrated growl. "I miss you two, but the overprotective brother-in-law routine is getting old."

Chase chuckled. Then he joined Sophie on the deck. "We'll be going now."

"Bye, Uncle Chase. Bye, Aunt Sophie!" Petey followed them to the steps for one more long goodbye. Trisha stayed inside though. She turned to Jake and held out her open palm. "You don't need that card."

Jake shook his head. "It's mine. Chase gave it to me."

"Because he wanted to make sure I'm okay. And I am." She wriggled her fingers in a gimme gesture.

Jake tucked the card into the pocket of his jeans. "There's a man code I have to adhere to."

She lifted a brow. "What does that mean?"

"If a man asks another man to look after a woman in his life and he agrees, he has to do it. It's part of having integrity, and I happen to take it seriously."

Trisha lowered her hand. "A woman can look after herself, you know."

Jake grinned. "And you've been doing that for a while. It's not a bad thing to have others look after you too. It just means you have people in your life who care." He gave her a look that made her want to step away or step closer. There was a little war going on inside her chest, with different emotions tugging at her heart.

"Fine," she finally said. Their gazes locked for an intense moment. Then Petey walked inside the room, his mood appearing suddenly deflated.

"What's wrong?" Trisha asked.

"Now I won't see Aunt Sophie or Uncle Chase for weeks. Maybe months." Tears shimmered in his eyes. "Or Comet. I'm going to bed."

"I'll come tuck you in." Trisha started to follow him.

Petey turned and shook his head. "No thanks, Mom."

Jake cleared his throat. "How about Bailey and I get you settled, bud? You're too old for bedtime stories, and I don't do those anyway. But pick your topic. I'm pretty sure I can get you halfway to dreamland by talking about it."

Petey's mouth curled just enough to make Trisha exhale. "I want to know about camping," he said.

"You're in luck." Jake started walking toward Petey's bedroom, glancing back at Trisha over his shoulder. "I happen to be an expert on camping."

* * *

Trisha waited a solid five minutes before creeping up to Petey's bedroom door to eavesdrop. She slid down the wall to sit on the floor and turned her ear in the direction of Jake's voice. It was low and soothing as he discussed Camping 101 skills.

Trisha instinctively knew that Petey wanted to know about camping because it was something that a kid did with their dad.

Jake rattled on about selecting the perfect camping spot first and knowing your surroundings. A camper needed to research which wildlife to look out for. "*In Somerset Lake, for example…*"

Trisha closed her eyes for a moment, listening to the sound of Jake's voice. It was low and deep—calming. Petey was no doubt eating this information up. Tomorrow, she suspected, Petey would ask her when they could pitch a tent of their own in the woods. Being a single mother was hard. She always felt like she was letting Petey down in some way. She'd never been camping a day in her life. She wouldn't know where to even begin, and she certainly didn't have the necessary equipment.

Petey's tiny voice interrupted Jake. "Will you take me camping sometime?"

Trisha's eyes opened.

"Well, you'll have to talk to your mom about that, Copilot. But if she says yes, I'd be happy to take you."

"Where will we go?" Petey asked next.

Trisha closed her eyes again.

"What kind of animals do we need to look out for?" her son's little voice asked. More questions and answers followed until

Trisha barely heard them because she was falling asleep. The next thing she knew, a hand touched her shoulder. She startled awake and met Jake's gaze as he squatted in front of her in the dimly lit hallway.

"Looks like I put you to sleep too."

"Petey's asleep?" she asked.

"Yeah." Jake watched Bailey stroll past them, heading toward the living room. Then he returned his attention to Trisha.

"Thank you for that," she whispered.

"Sometimes it helps to give someone something to look forward to instead of something to miss."

"Have you read a manual on child-rearing too?"

Jake shook his head and grinned. "No. But it's not just kids who need that. Everyone does."

She swallowed as she peered at him in the dark. "If we kiss again, it's going to change things between us," she finally said.

His gaze was steady. "I think things are changing between us regardless of whether we kiss again, Trisha."

Her heart kicked. "What if I'm not ready for that? I mean, this can get messy, and I'm tired of messy things."

"I don't have all the answers. I just know how I feel when I'm with you."

"How is that?" she asked, a little breathless. "Because I'm not really sure what I'm feeling right now."

Jake reached for her hand. "Every time I look at you, my heart skips a beat. You make me feel a little nervous, but in a good way. I feel at ease and energized at the same time."

Trisha swallowed. "I can relate to all of that."

"Every time I learn something new about you, it only makes me want to know something more," Jake continued. "I feel insatiable."

"That's a good word for it," she agreed. She also felt

breathless. "What else do you want to know about me?" she asked. "Since you're insatiable."

Jake's gaze finally broke from her eyes, glancing down at her lips. "Well, if you want the truth…"

"Preferably."

"Right now I want to know what a second kiss with you would be like."

Trisha looked at his lips too. "I want to know the same thing."

"There's only one way to find out." He didn't lean in though. She understood that this was her decision. Crossing the space, and the invisible line, was completely her choice, and he wasn't going to make it for her. She was in control.

Only, it didn't feel like she had a choice at the moment. It felt like this attraction between them had gained so much momentum that she couldn't stop what was about to happen even if she wanted to. Which she didn't. No, she'd been halfway asleep when he'd stepped out, and it felt like she was still in some sort of dream. The good kind that you wanted to keep going.

She leaned in toward him. He leaned in as well, meeting her halfway.

"You sure?" he whispered just before their lips touched.

"I'm not sure of anything anymore." She swallowed. "Just promise that whatever happens between us, we won't let it affect Petey. He's been through too much instability."

"The last thing I want to do is hurt either of you. We don't have to kiss, Trisha. We can just keep fighting this attraction between us."

She shook her head. "I'm tired of fighting. I'm tired of resisting. I just want to surrender," she whispered. "Is that so wrong?"

"Not in my opinion. But I may be biased." He winked at her. Then his gaze fell to her mouth.

Before she could second-guess herself any more, she crossed the rest of the distance and pressed her lips to his.

The kiss was soft and gentle, growing more intense with each passing second. He'd taken her flying earlier today, to the sky and the clouds. Now she felt like she was flying again, and she wasn't in a hurry to return to earth.

Jake's hand touched the side of her face, trailing down the curve of her neck and stopping at her shoulder. He finally broke away from the kiss and looked her in the eye. "I think it's best if I go now. Kissing can lead to a lot of things if we're not careful."

And maybe she was ready for a second kiss, but she wasn't ready for anything more. "I'll walk you to the door."

He let go of her hand. "I'll see myself out and lock it behind me. If you follow me to the door, we'll end up kissing again. And again. Like I said, I'm a little insatiable when it comes to you."

Trisha's heart skipped in that way he'd described. "Okay, I'll see you in the morning."

"I'll wake Mr. S and join you for coffee before we get started on painting the cottages."

"You don't have to wake Mr. S. That's my job."

Jake brushed another quick kiss on her lips. "While I'm here in Somerset Lake, it's now my job."

Her skipping heart dropped a notch. *While he was here.* She'd be smart to remember that. She was making this town her home, but Jake was not.

"Good night," he said.

"Night." She watched him walk away. Then she entertained something even riskier than sharing a few kisses with Jake. She entertained a small spark of hope that maybe Sophie had been right. Perhaps Jake could be convinced to stay.

CHAPTER SIXTEEN

Jake returned to Peony Cottage but didn't go inside. Instead, he and Bailey sat on the deck, looking out on the view. Jake wasn't sure what Bailey was watching or thinking about. Knowing Bailey, probably the next trek down the shore.

Bailey loved chasing the birds—even if she'd never catch any of them—and splashing through the small wake caused by a rough wind or a boat going by.

Jake, however, was thinking about that last kiss with Trisha. Their second, third, and tenth kiss.

He was also thinking about Vi and his grandfather. And Petey. And even though Rachel had been gone for a long time, he was thinking about her too.

He tried for a moment to remember her face. Over the years, the mental image he held of her had gotten blurry. In his rare dreams about her though, her features were sharp and detailed.

He released a breath he didn't realize he was holding.

"You okay?"

Jake blinked Rachel's image into view. It was just a figment of his imagination, of course. He was halfway to sleep and exhausted from the day. Right after Rachel's accident, he'd pretended to have conversations with her at night. And the conversations he'd had felt so real that sometimes he woke forgetting for just a moment that she was gone. Sometimes he thought her death was just a nightmare.

"Yeah, I'm okay," he whispered. "Just thinking about life." He blew out another breath. "And death."

He imagined Rachel smiling at him the way she used to. Her ghost was still eighteen years old, but he was much older now. Wiser. "I left because I couldn't deal with you not being here."

Rachel held her arms out to her side. "I'm always here."

Jake didn't want to blink because it might break his dream-like state. "Yeah, I left for that reason too. And because I missed my grandfather." He exhaled and finally blinked. "Sometimes home is just one big haunting ground," he whispered.

Rachel's apparition began to fade. She didn't speak. Just smiled at him. A young eighteen-year-old girl who'd made him laugh as much as she'd made him cry. Time and distance had been his salve, and he was surprised being here didn't hurt as much as it used to. On the contrary, being home felt like the finishing balm to that last little bit of pain that had stuck around, lingering like a phantom limb.

Jake closed his eyes, his hand dropping to his side to pet Bailey. The next thing he knew, his phone's alarm was going off. He'd set it to wake himself up so that he could head down the shore and get Mr. S on his way before anyone else saw him.

Jake stirred and stretched, remembering his waking dream of Rachel, brief as it was. Then he remembered his kiss with Trisha. It had been long but not nearly long enough.

He stood, feeling energized and eager about the day ahead.

"Come on, Bailey. You can do the honors of waking Mr. S for me."

They climbed down the steps, and Bailey ran ahead of him along the beach. As they approached Mr. S, she nudged her nose to the old man's cheek.

The old man stirred and swatted the dog away. Bailey continued until Mr. S sat up and saw Jake approaching.

"I'm going, I'm going," he called. Then he stood. Jake directed his gaze to the water, using his peripheral vision to ensure Mr. S walked inside his cottage. Then he called Bailey back. Jake needed to return home, shower and change, and head to Trisha's for that first cup of coffee they'd discussed. And if Petey was still sleeping in his bedroom, maybe Jake could sneak another kiss with Trisha.

After returning home and freshening up, Jake walked next door and knocked on Trisha's door.

She answered with a bright smile. No regrets of last night in sight. "Coffee?"

"That would be great." He and Bailey followed Trisha inside. He sat at the counter and watched her prepare them both a mug. "Where's Petey?"

"He's getting dressed. He won't be joining us today though."

"Oh?" Jake waited for Trisha to explain. "Where will he be?"

Trisha slid a mug in front of him. The aroma of fresh brew wafted under his nose. "Della Rose called me last night after you left and asked if Petey could go with the twins to the skating rink. We exchanged numbers at Sunset Over Somerset. I barely know her, but Petey is so in awe of her boys. And I want him to have friends here." Trisha cupped her hands around her own mug of coffee. "So I agreed. Della is picking him up this morning. She also said she'd look at the cottages once she brings Petey back. I could use her real estate expertise. She might be able to give me some advice that'll give us an edge over the rental competition."

"That's great," Jake said. "Della Rose is very respected around here. If she recommends a property, people listen."

"So I hear. Miles Bruno also called. He's bringing the kids from the youth center over to clean the cottages that I haven't gotten to yet while we paint."

Jake brought his mug to his lips and sipped. "Maybe I didn't like the guy in school, but this completely changes my viewpoint. As long as he doesn't flirt too much with you." Jake winked.

Trisha looked away shyly for a moment. "We probably won't even see him today. We'll be working in different cottages."

"Forgive me if I'm not sorry that I'll be spending the day with you alone again."

Trisha's eyes met his over his cup of coffee. And if he wasn't mistaken, she looked as happy about that prospect as he did. "We'll get a lot more done alone," she agreed.

Jake chuckled.

She tilted her head. "Why are you laughing?"

"Because I'm not sure if that's true."

* * *

Trisha had never minded painting. It was actually pretty relaxing. Or it would be if her heart wasn't jumping every time she looked at Jake, who was painting the other side of the wall.

He put his brush down in the pan and headed toward her.

"What are you doing?"

He stopped just a couple feet away. "I thought we'd get a lot more work done if we just go ahead and get the next kiss out of our system."

Trisha laughed. "We have been making googly eyes at each other, haven't we?"

"That's one word for it."

Trisha placed her paintbrush in the pan as well. She wiped her hands on the smock she was wearing and faced him. Then they stared at each other awkwardly.

"Spontaneous is better, huh?" Jake asked.

She stepped closer. "I think it's supposed to be awkward when you're first getting to know each other. Here, let me help." She reached for his hand and brought it to her waist. The air between them seemed to electrify. "We've only kissed in the dark. That might be part of the newness here."

"Good point." Jake stepped closer and lowered his head, bringing his mouth to hers.

The awkwardness melted away as their lips touched and their hands wandered.

"Maybe getting it over with wasn't the best idea. We might not get the rest of our work done today because all I'll want to do is kiss you."

Trisha gave his chest a little shove. "Back to work, Fletcher." She bent and grabbed her brush again. Her heart was skipping around in her chest. She was completely falling for this guy, and she couldn't bring herself to be sorry about it.

When they were finished with the first cottage, they moved on to the second one, working until Trisha's arms didn't want to move anymore.

"That's it for me," she told Jake. "I can't lift that paintbrush one more time."

"What time is Petey returning home?" Jake asked.

"He's having pizza with them. Della Rose is dropping him off afterward. We're going to check out the cottages tomorrow instead. By then the paint from our work today should be dry."

"I need to check on Vi and make a couple calls. But after

that..." Jake trailed off as his gaze locked on hers. "Since Petey is having dinner with friends, how about letting me cook you a meal tonight?"

She had been hoping he'd suggest more time together. She wasn't ready to return to reality again just yet. "I'd like that."

"Me too." He bent and kissed her lips. The kiss was slow and easy, like a gentle dance.

She looked up at him as she pulled away. Things were already feeling complicated. He was her boss's grandson. He was only temporary. "What happens tomorrow when Petey is with us?"

Jake ran a hand down the side of her arm. "Well, the rest of the work on my list are solo jobs. I'll be installing those appliances we picked up from the thrift store yesterday. I'll also work on installing some flooring and the countertops we got. I might call a buddy of mine to see if he can help out."

"That's not what I'm asking and you know it," she said.

He gave her a steady look. "When we're together, we'll just keep our hands to ourselves when Petey is looking. You're pretty irresistible, Trisha Langly, but I do have willpower when I need it."

She gave his chest a little shove, but he came back quickly with another brief kiss.

"My place in an hour?" he asked. "We can eat on the porch. We'll be able to see if Petey gets home early."

Trisha nodded. "Your place in an hour sounds good."

They left the freshly painted cottage with the windows open to air it out. Then they broke off in different directions as they reached their own cottages. Trisha took the time to shower and change. Then she grabbed the romance novel that Tess had loaned her for the book club on Thursday night. She guessed she should get reading so she had some idea of what the story was about. Because she was going.

She was making more friends. She was digging her roots deeper here.

Trisha glanced over at Peony Cottage where Jake had disappeared to shower and make his phone calls. She loved her new home, but he was quickly becoming her favorite thing about Somerset Lake. And he was as fleeting as her footprints along the lakeshore.

She'd already made the mistake of hoping he might stay, but she needed to brace herself for the reality that he wouldn't. She'd be wise to just end things now, but it had been so long since she'd felt this feeling buzzing through her body, energizing her and making her feel more alive than she had in such a long time. She didn't want to lose this feeling just yet. Who knew when or if she'd ever experience it again? Before Jake, she was pretty certain she never would.

Trisha's phone buzzed with an incoming call. She checked it quickly because what if it was Della Rose calling about Petey? Instead, it was Sophie.

Trisha answered. "Hey."

Sophie didn't bother with reciprocating a hello. "He was so cute!" she practically squealed on the other line.

"My son? Yes, I think so."

"Not Petey," Sophie said. "I mean, yes, my nephew is adorable, but I'm talking about Jake. He was so cute and nice and funny. He's perfect for you, Trisha!"

Trisha patted her chest right above her heart. As if she wasn't already having a hard time not completely falling for Jake. "We're not dating," she reminded Sophie.

"What do you call it then? Because I saw sparks. The tension between you two was so thick and yummy." She sighed on the other line. "I remember that newness in my relationship with Chase."

"I'm sure you do. It was just last year." Trisha laughed.

She didn't continue denying what was going on with her and Jake though. "Petey went to play with friends today. Two friends actually. And Jake and I spent the day together. Again."

"I want all the details," Sophie begged.

"There aren't many. We kissed last night after you left. A lot. And...I don't know. I have to be careful. Another broken heart is the last thing I need. Petey too."

"What makes you think he'll break your heart? I mean, yes, I know he's supposedly leaving soon, but plans change, Trisha. You and I both know that probably better than anyone. He could stay. You could go."

"No, I'm not leaving. We just got here. And Petey needs stability."

"Okay. If you two fall for each other, then you'll find a way to make it work. That's Jake's hometown, right?"

Trisha looked out the window on Somerset Lake. "Right. But he left for a reason." Probably more than one.

"Is that reason still a factor?" Sophie asked.

Trisha knew that Jake had left after losing his first love. That was a long time ago though. She didn't know if it still kept him from wanting to be here. "I'm not sure. But anyway," she said, "it's not like we're falling in love. We're just kissing." That felt like a lie though.

"I know you," Sophie said. "Just kissing is not a thing you do. You have always been one to feel first, kiss later. It's why you only had one boyfriend all through high school."

Trisha scoffed. "And that worked out so well for me. Maybe I need to kiss more, feel less."

"Good luck with that," Sophie said. "When are you seeing Jake again?"

Trisha glanced at the time on her phone. "In ten minutes. He's cooking dinner."

Another squeal from Sophie pierced Trisha's ears. "Okay, keep kissing and stop worrying. Things will work out the way they're supposed to. They always do."

Trisha held her tongue. If that were really true, then her marriage was doomed from the get-go. And maybe this thing between her and Jake was also doomed. These wonderful feelings didn't promise a happily ever after. So as good as they felt, she was treading lightly and enjoying them for what they were—fleeting.

* * *

Jake dialed his father's number and waited as he sat on his back porch, watching the lake. When his dad didn't answer, he called his mom's cell phone. He wanted to talk to them sooner rather than later about his change of plans. He needed to explain his rationale and make them understand his point of view.

No answer.

He dropped his phone back to his lap and blew out a breath. Then he noticed his uncle walking toward his cottage.

"Hey, Jake. How's it going?" Tim climbed the steps to Jake's deck. "Whatcha up to?" he drawled once he was standing in front of Jake.

"Just trying to get in touch with my parents. Have you spoken to them by chance?" Jake asked.

"I have, in fact. Just last night," Tim confirmed. "I wanted to let them know how things were going down here." Tim sat in the chair beside Jake's.

Jake glanced over. "So you told them that Vi is doing really well and that she's hired someone to help her manage the properties?"

Tim chuckled and patted Bailey's head. "I told your mom and dad that Vi hired some out-of-towner. A single mom with a kid," Tim said, as if that was a bad thing. "And that the woman is a freeloader who's getting free room and board up here."

Jake felt his defenses rise. "I wouldn't call it free. It's part of the arrangement. It's part of her pay."

Uncle Tim chuckled. "Well, your grandmother doesn't have a good track record with financials these days. That woman seemed nice enough, but I'm sure she talked Vi into paying her more money than she's worth."

Jake took a breath. Arguing wasn't going to convince his uncle that selling the Somerset Cottages was the wrong course of action. "I've been helping Trisha with renovations. There's already interest from two new potential tenants, and Trisha is meeting with a real estate agent about stirring up more interest."

"We don't need more interest," Tim said sharply. "We're not renting—we're selling. Whoever is interested in these properties can either buy the place or rent it from whoever does."

Jake stood and walked over to the railing, needing to distance himself from his uncle. "This is Vi's home. This is where she feels Gramps's presence the most. How can we even consider taking that away from her?"

"Your grandfather isn't here anymore. No one is," his uncle said from behind him. "After you're gone, Vi will be all alone up here again. She may have a property manager to help, but that woman is a stranger. She's certainly not family, and that's what Vi needs more than anything. She needs to have her family close by. No one should grow old alone."

His uncle raised valid points. "She's a nice woman."

"Uh-huh. I think I see what's going on. The property manager is a beautiful woman, but please don't tell me you're sleeping with her."

"What? No." Just kissing her. But Jake wasn't going to allude to that. He was a little peeved that his uncle would even suggest it. "Trisha would never hurt Vi, Uncle Tim. I came down here to make sure my grandmother was okay, and she is."

"Wrong. You came down here to convince her that it's time to sell and move. She's in her late seventies, and she's had a stroke. If and when she has another, she needs to be with family. You're young, Jake. Maybe you don't understand how prudent this is. She's your grandmother, yes, but she's my mother. I want what's best for her even more so than you."

Jake stared out on the water. Then he saw Trisha descending her steps to head over and meet him for dinner. "We can talk about this later, Uncle Tim. I have plans tonight."

Tim stood and noticed Trisha approaching as well. "Just be sure that you keep your eye on the bigger plan. 'Night, Jake." He turned and headed down the steps, passing Trisha on the way up. He paused and had a polite exchange with her that Jake knew was insincere.

"Everything okay?" Trisha asked when she reached the deck.

Jake rubbed a hand across the back of his neck and released a heavy sigh. "Tim still thinks Vi should sell. And apparently he's already spoken to my parents to make sure they think the same."

Trisha's forehead wrinkled with worry. "Well, you're family too."

"Not that generation," Jake said. "Vi's generation has always run the family's rental properties. She's the last of her generation. After that, my parents, aunts, and uncles will take over. My generation won't have anything to do with these cottages if they sell."

He reached for her. "You're safe here, okay? I'm going to show my family what I see."

"And what is that?" she asked.

"Promise." He wasn't talking about the cottages as much as he was referring to her right now. "We'll convince them."

"We?"

Jake narrowed his eyes. "I thought we were in this together. We're painting the cottages and nailing boards. Kissing in between."

She lowered her gaze shyly for a moment. "I'm not part of your family. It's not my fight."

"We're both fighting for Vi's best interest. And for what's ours. This is yours and Petey's home now, and I'm not going to let anything change that."

* * *

After dinner, Jake and Trisha went for a walk along the beach. The moon was out and shining brightly on their path.

"I've forgotten how beautiful this place is."

Trisha glanced over. She was barefoot, and there was something strangely attractive about the nakedness of her feet. Her toenails were painted a light pink that shimmered against her skin. "People always appreciate things more after they've been away awhile. It's human nature."

Jake chuckled. "I guess that's true."

Trisha stopped walking and stared down at her feet. Then she dipped to pick up a penny on tails.

"That's bad luck, you know," he said.

She shook her head. "How can finding money ever be unlucky?" She handed it to him. "Here. A penny for your thoughts."

Jake held out an open palm, and she placed it at the center. "You sure you want to know what I'm thinking right now?"

She tilted her head. "Pretty sure."

Jake's heart swelled as he continued to look at her. "Okay.

I think you're beautiful. Maybe the most beautiful woman I've ever seen." Or ever known.

Something shifted in her gaze. "Wow...That's the best money I've ever spent."

"Just telling you the truth as I see it." And Jake planned on always telling Trisha the truth, no matter what. He stepped closer, wrapping his arms around her and dipping toward her lips for a kiss that seemed to circumvent time. Then they continued walking until they reached their cottages. They enjoyed another long, lingering kiss and said good night.

When Jake got inside, he retreated to his bed and stared at the ceiling, waiting for sleep to come.

There were too many thoughts circulating in his brain. What was he still doing here if he wasn't convincing Vi to sell? Maybe he could appease both sides of his family by staying and helping Vi. At least for a little while. Jake never had a reason to stay for any length of time after he'd left town.

But maybe he had two good reasons now. Vi and Trisha.

CHAPTER SEVENTEEN

On Thursday evening, Jake arrived home after hanging out with a couple of lawyer friends he knew in Magnolia Falls. It'd been good to see them and toss around legal talk.

The cases around here weren't as high profile as the ones he'd taken in DC. His buddies talked about disputes over wills and estates, marital and family disputes, and even a case about a neighbor feeding the foxes in the woods, which resulted in another neighbor's pet going to the vet for a rabies check.

It was a different world here. Slower. Easier somehow. Harder in other ways.

By the time he'd left, they'd offered Jake a position. He wasn't looking for a job, but he also hadn't said no. Some part of him had actually wanted to say yes because that would give him a reason to stay.

Was he looking for a reason?

Before going back to Peony Cottage, he drove over to The Village and turned onto Christmas Lane. The Village was a quaint neighborhood in Somerset Lake. The houses varied in size but not in charm.

Jake drove slowly down the all-too-familiar road that once led him to his high school sweetheart's home.

He realized he was holding his breath as he approached the old green house where Rachel used to wait for him on the porch. She wasn't there anymore. Only the ghost of her memory lingered against the porch railings in Jake's imagination.

He rubbed his chest for a moment and then pulled into the driveway of the home where Rachel's mom still lived. Jake stepped out of the truck and headed up the drive to the porch. Rachel had been gone for twelve years. If she had lived, would they still be together? Would she have become a teacher like she'd wanted to?

He rang the doorbell and waited. After a moment, the front door opened, and Mrs. Carroway stepped out. "Jake!" She opened her arms to greet him as if he were her family.

Jake gave her a tight hug, feeling his heart squeeze just as tight.

"Come in, come in," she said as she pulled away from the embrace and turned back inside the house. "How are you? Would you like some coffee? Tea?"

"I'd love a tea," he told her, passing framed pictures of Rachel at various ages in her life. They all stopped the spring of her eighteenth year.

"Good. I'll have a tea as well." Rose led him into the kitchen, and he sat down at one of the barstools at the counter. There was a certain kind of pain that came with being here. It made him want to walk right back out of the house and avoid it. There were too many memories, some bitter, some sweet.

He felt the same way about Vi's house. About the whole town really. Or he had felt that way until recently.

"Here you go." Rose pushed a mug across the counter toward

him. "These kettles heat water in one minute. Can you believe that? They think of everything to save time, but what for?"

Jake wrapped his fingers around the mug. "It's a fast world beyond Somerset Lake."

Rose sat on a stool on the other side of the counter. "So I hear. Are you still in DC?"

Jake drank his tea. "I'm in the process of moving."

"Here?" Rose's eyes widened as something hopeful crossed her expression.

"I'm just in town to visit Vi," Jake said, feeling a bit guilty. "My family is worried about her."

"Well, I imagine so. A stroke would put a lot of people down, but your grandmother is one tough cookie." Rose laughed. "I've gone to visit her several times. She ended up helping me more than I helped her though. She told me you were dating someone. A lawyer, right?"

"Yes, but we broke up," he said.

"Oh." Rose's expression fell. "That's too bad. I was hoping you'd find someone nice to heal that heart of yours."

She was talking about the heartbreak of losing her daughter, of course. Jake hadn't thought his heart would ever heal, but his feelings for Trisha were making him second-guess that opinion.

The steam fogged Rose's glasses as she lifted her mug to her lips and paused. "Maybe you'll find a nice woman here in Somerset Lake," she said hopefully. "Someone who'll make you consider moving home."

If Rose had said that last month, he'd have argued with her. Today, he just smiled because that wasn't such an inconceivable notion. "So what can I help you with while I'm here?" he asked.

Rose gave him a sheepish look. "Well, I was hoping you would ask. I'm thinking about getting a home security system,

but I don't even know where to start. And I know you are
the jack-of-all-trades. Or the Jake-of-all-trades." She grinned.
It wasn't the first time she'd made that joke, but she couldn't
seem to help herself. "Do you have any ideas?"

"Why are you looking for a security system? Have you had
problems?"

Rose sipped her tea and sighed softly. "Not exactly. But
I watch a lot of shows about unsolved crimes, and I get so
paranoid staying here all alone."

"Why don't you just stop watching the shows?" Jake
suggested.

Rose laughed quietly. "That would probably help, hmm?
I love the little jolt of adrenaline I get from watching them
though. It's hard to think about anything else when you're
looking at something so intense." Something sad crossed
her eyes.

Jake understood exactly what she was trying not to think of.
"For home security, you probably want something basic, just to
calm your fears at night."

Rose cupped her hands around her mug as if it were winter
and she was soaking in the heat. "That sounds good."

Jake outlined a security system that he'd installed in his last
home. When he'd done so, he'd read a how-to guide on home
security, of course. "It's fairly simple. You set the alarm when
you're in the house, probably just at nighttime. If someone
breaks in, the cops are immediately alerted and they'll show up
at your door."

Rose was nodding a lot but saying little.

"What do you think?" Jake finally asked, taking another
sip of tea.

"I think that's exactly what I need. Then I can continue
watching my shows at night and sleep safely. Should I get a
guard dog too? It does get a little lonely around here."

Jake chewed on his thoughts for a moment. "A dog's bark will definitely make a burglar think twice."

Rose sipped her tea. "Maybe I'll look into that too. I've always liked poodles. They make Labs mixed with poodles now. Did you know that? Designer dogs, they call them."

Jake nodded as he listened. He loved visiting with Mrs. Carroway. She would've made a great mother-in-law. They finished their drinks and talked a little more. Then an hour after walking inside the house, Jake headed toward the front door. "I'll get the supplies, and I'll be back before I leave town to install the system for you. It'll just take a couple hours to set up, and you'll be good to go."

Rose gave him another hug. "You know I don't expect you to do that for me, but I'll never turn down a visit from you. It's always so good to catch up, Jake. It's good to have you home."

"It's good to be home," Jake said without thinking. He stepped out onto the porch, and his heart squeezed as he passed by the porch railing where Rachel's memory lingered, her soft brown hair blowing in the ever-present breeze in Somerset Lake.

Rachel's ghost was part of what had kept him away all these years, never visiting for more than a week at a time. Maybe time did heal a broken heart after all. Maybe he was finally ready to let go and move on. Maybe, just maybe, he was finally ready to come home for good.

* * *

Trisha had been at Tess's bookstore for half an hour already, and no one had even mentioned the selection for tonight's book club yet.

Trisha had stayed up late last night reading so she'd be prepared. Instead, the ladies, five in total, were having lemonade and chocolate fudge that reminded Trisha of Dawanda's Fudge

Shop back home in Sweetwater Springs. They were laughing and telling stories about their week and their lives.

Trisha was enjoying herself for the most part, except for the fact that she hadn't shared anything about herself just yet. She was just listening like a fly on the wall. Listening and learning about her new friends.

Tess, the bookstore owner. A widow by age twenty-two.

Lucy, a midwife who lived in The Village. She seemed to long for a family of her own but was, in her words, so single that she only shaved her legs once a month.

Moira, a tough 911 operator. The kind of tough that happened when life had been less than kind. She seemed to have thick skin, but Trisha suspected there was a huge heart below the surface.

Then there was larger-than-life Della Rose, with twin boys who were keeping Petey happy in the kids' corner tonight.

"The boys don't know it yet, but"—Della Rose lowered her voice, which cracked a little bit—"I've filed for divorce."

The women's chatter and laughter ceased.

"What? Why?" Tess set her glass of lemonade down beside her. "I thought you and Jerome were solid."

Della Rose's eyes grew shiny. "I did too. But he's been"—she turned to make sure her boys weren't listening—"he's been seeing someone else."

The women gasped. Trisha didn't. A traitorous husband living a lie was no surprise to her. What was more surprising was how intimate this group of women were, sharing their secrets so openly. No one else knew about Della Rose's divorce or husband's affair yet. But Della trusted these ladies. She trusted Trisha without even knowing her yet.

How had Trisha been invited into this small group tonight? She hadn't grown up with these women. She hadn't shared life experiences with them.

"Do you know who the other woman is?" Lucy asked.

Della Rose looked at her. There was a definite exchange of silent information in the look.

Lucy's mouth rounded. "Oh. I know who she is?"

"I do believe she's one of your midwifing patients," Della Rose said.

"She's pregnant?" Tess asked in a loud voice.

"Shh." Della Rose glanced back at her boys. "Jerome isn't sure that the baby is his."

"Just sure that it could be." Moira shook her head, her silky black hair whisking over the surface of her shoulders. "This is why I'm happily and preferably single. I get plenty enough romance from these books we read."

The conversation continued. Once Della Rose was exhausted from talking about her situation, it moved to Lucy.

"The brother of one of my patients asked me out this week," Lucy said.

"Did you say yes?" Tess wanted to know.

Lucy shrugged. "I said maybe. But I'm leaning more toward no."

"Cute?" Moira asked.

Lucy wobbled her head from side to side. "That's subjective, but I think he's average looking."

"Does he have a job?" Della asked. "Because that's important too."

Lucy nodded. "Yes, he's employed."

"How does he treat his mother?" Tess asked. "Also important."

Lucy laughed at this question. "I don't know. But he treats his sister well."

"That's a good sign." Tess reached for her glass of lemonade and picked it up. Then she looked around at the group of women, her gaze holding Trisha's for a moment, seemingly feeling Trisha out on if she wanted to say anything. When

Trisha stayed quiet, Tess said, "Okay, it's time for the book club toast."

Everyone raised their glasses as if this was a normal thing.

Trisha was the last to pick up her glass. She leaned in to hold it up with the others.

"What are we toasting to tonight?" Moira asked.

"Della Rose was the only one of us who wasn't single. And now she's joined the club," Lucy said. "We can officially name this gathering the Single Women's Book Club."

Everyone laughed.

"I still believe in happy ever afters," Tess objected.

"But for some, being single is considered living happily," Moira pointed out.

"True. How about we toast to being independent women?" Lucy suggested.

"Smart, independent women," Della Rose added.

"Beautiful, kind, smart, independent women who don't mess with another woman's husband," Moira amended.

"Amen to that!" Della Rose said.

"Anything you want to add before we tap glasses?" Tess asked Trisha.

Trisha felt put on the spot. She thought for a moment. "Strong," she said, which elicited a couple more cheers.

"Yes, indeed." Tess nodded approvingly. "We are strong, independent, smart, beautiful, book-loving women."

They all tapped glasses and drank the bittersweet lemonade. Afterward, they leaned back in their respective chairs and couch.

"As you can see, this is half support group, half book club," Tess finally explained to Trisha. "That's one of the reasons I invited you. You seem like you could use a good support group."

All eyes were on Trisha, the women waiting expectantly for

her to spill her guts the way the others had. What if she did tell these women her story? She certainly risked their judgment or the judgment of others when one of them inevitably told someone else. She also risked the gossip and the potential bullying of Petey.

But if she continued to hide, she risked never truly being home here in her new town. And that's what she wanted more than anything.

Trisha took a breath, her heart beating forcefully. She wasn't ready to talk about the past, but the future seemed less threatening. "Well, the cottages are really coming along. Della Rose came over this week and gave me some great advice on what I can do to make them more marketable for renters. I'm planning to take some pictures of the places now that they're all spruced up. I just need to figure out how to build a website for the property to showcase the cottages."

Moira raised her hand. "Oh, I can help you with that. That's easy."

"Really?" Trisha asked, shocked that every time she voiced a need, someone in this town volunteered to help her with it. "That would be amazing. Thank you."

"Of course. Just email the pictures to me. I have a lot of free time at my job so I'll just build the website in the long stretches of boredom." She laughed and held up a hand. "Don't get me wrong. I'm glad I'm bored because that means there are no crises happening that require nine-one-one services."

Trisha reached inside her purse and pulled out a pad of paper and a pencil. "What's your email address? I'll get those to you tomorrow."

Moira told her and assured her that building a free website was no big deal. "I've done it several times for other people in the community."

"Then once you get that website up," Della Rose said, "send

me the link. There are a lot of young medical folks in Magnolia Falls. They like to rent instead of buy because they're not sure where life is taking them just yet. I think those Somerset Cottages would be perfect for them." Della looked at Trisha. "Maybe take a few photos of the fun stuff you can do on that lake. That way we can lure those young people in."

Trisha wrote that down in her notepad as well. "Fun stuff," she said as she jotted down notes. Then she looked up. "Like what?" she asked.

"Oh, you know. Snap a picture of Jake's dog running on the beach. People love dogs. Or snap a few photos of someone paddleboarding. Boating. Fishing."

"Take a picture of Jake with his shirt off," Lucy said, waggling her eyebrows and making the women giggle. "That'll attract the women for sure."

Trisha laughed, too, her face growing hot.

"Of course, Jake is already taken by Trisha," Lucy added. "No hope for those hopeful women."

Trisha looked up from her notepad. She opened her mouth to speak but no words came out.

"You rendered her speechless," Tess said on a laugh. "Let's stop teasing poor Trisha. We might scare her away." She held up the book club selection for the night instead. "Now, let's get to business. Be honest, ladies. Who read this week's chapters?"

Trisha was the only one to raise her hand. Well, it looked like she had more to share with the group tonight than she'd thought.

* * *

Jake checked the time on his cell phone and tossed the ball for Bailey again. He was sitting below the deck of Peony

Cottage to provide Bailey lots of running space. It would also allow him to get up and go see Trisha faster when she arrived home.

She'd been gone for hours. What in the world took hours to talk about at a book club gathering? He wasn't sure because he'd never been part of such a group. The books he read weren't popular selections.

Bailey skidded and jumped, catching the ball in her mouth. Then she ran back, just as energetic on the twelfth time as she was on the first.

Jake tossed it. She brought it back. Tossed and fetched. Tossed and fetched.

Finally, headlights streamed along the gravel road behind the cottages. Jake felt his heart skip in his chest. He stood and turned to face the oncoming car. It wasn't Trisha's. Instead, he held his hand over his eyes, trying to get a better glimpse of the large SUV. Uncle Tim.

Please keep going. Keep going.

The SUV pulled in next to his truck behind the cottage. Jake didn't think they had anything to talk about tonight, but apparently, Uncle Tim thought differently.

"Jake," his uncle drawled as he headed in Jake's direction. Bailey met him halfway and propped her paws on Tim's thighs. He dutifully patted her head and looked at Jake. "After our conversation on Monday, I did a little research into the help around here."

Jake put his hands on his waist. His uncle was one of the best lawyers in his area. If Tim wanted to dig up dirt on someone, he'd have no problem doing so. "Oh? And what did you find?" he asked, a tinge of worry tightening his chest. Everyone had pasts. Everyone kept secrets.

"Your little girlfriend is divorced from a man who has made himself an enemy of our family."

Jake looked down at his feet. He kicked around a few pebbles, debating how he was going to handle this turn of events. "You can't say anything," Jake finally said, looking up at his uncle.

Tim's mouth dropped. For the first time ever, Jake thought his uncle, who was always one step ahead of everyone else, looked shocked. "You knew about this? Does Vi know?"

Jake shook his head. "No, and she doesn't need to. Trisha didn't do anything wrong."

Tim straightened the cowboy hat on his head. "Are you sure about that, Jake? Or is your lust for this woman making it hard for you to see clearly?"

"Her ex-husband is the one who stole from his clients."

"Stole from your grandmother," Tim corrected. "And that property manager benefited from what that man stole. You can't tell me she didn't know it was dirty money. She was probably living the high life while Vi was going bankrupt and her health was suffering."

Jake felt his blood pressure rise as his uncle threw out groundless accusations. "Trisha isn't like that. She's a good person."

Another set of headlights streamed down the path now. This time, Jake wished it wasn't Trisha. Not yet. But it just wasn't his lucky night. Trisha's car slowed and pulled in behind Juniper Cottage.

Jake looked at his uncle. "Please don't cause trouble for her. She's been through enough."

Tim followed his gaze to Trisha's car. "Then you need to do the right thing and stick to the original plan. I don't want to issue threats, but my family comes first." Tim narrowed his eyes as if to say that Jake didn't keep the same values. "If I have to, I'll tell Vi and the rest of the family who that woman is. And I promise you, it won't be pretty."

Tim turned to watch Trisha step out of her vehicle. Then

he headed over, stopping about six feet away. Trisha looked between them. "Hi," she said with a touch of uncertainty.

Petey got out of the back seat and ran over to Jake. "Hi, Jake!" he said eagerly. "This is your uncle?"

"That's right, Copilot," Jake said. He had to force a smile because Tim had threatened the people he cared about.

Petey didn't seem to notice. "Cool!"

Tim held out a hand for Petey to shake. "Whoa! That's a firm grip you got there, son," he said when Petey slid his hand in Tim's.

Petey laughed. "I like your big hat," he said. Then he headed over to pet Bailey.

Trisha looked between Jake and his uncle again. "Well, I don't want to interrupt whatever you two were talking about. Petey and I are going inside. We're worn out from book club." She laughed quietly.

"Was it fun?" Jake asked.

"It was. I'll tell you about it tomorrow," she said, looking between the two men. "Are you getting Mr. S up in the morning?" she asked Jake. "Or should I?"

"I will. I told you. It's my job while I'm here."

"If she's the property manager, sounds like it's part of her job," Tim said.

Trisha's smile slid away just a touch. "I can certainly do it."

"But you're not going to. I'm going to have a talk with Mr. S about staying fully clothed outside his own home." Jake turned to his uncle. "Trisha's job description for the cottages is handling maintenance issues and renting them out."

"There's seven open, right?" Tim asked.

"Six, because I'm staying in one," Jake said.

"Rent-free, I presume. And Trisha is also staying rent-free." Tim kept on smiling. "So that's eight cottages that are not making the family property money. In fact, last time I checked the statements for these rental properties, they were losing money."

Jake offered Trisha an apologetic look. "I'll wake Mr. S and meet up with you later," he told her. "We're almost done with renovations. Then they'll be ready to rent out," he said more for his uncle's sake than Trisha's.

"Yes. I have some news on that front. The ladies at the book club have offered to help me with a website," Trisha said, excitement flashing in her eyes. "I just can't believe how wonderfully things are coming together. It's almost too good to be true."

Guilt curled in Jake's stomach. He didn't want to disappoint her, but now that his uncle knew the truth about Trisha, Jake would have to get back on board with convincing Vi to sell the rentals. Or he risked having Tim reveal Trisha's past. Either way, Trisha got hurt. Either way, Jake lost her.

CHAPTER EIGHTEEN

Jake woke early the next day. He pulled on a pair of jeans and a T-shirt and then headed out the door to go wake Mr. S just like he'd told Trisha he would. The glow of the sun was lighting up the sky, even though it hadn't yet crested the mountainscape.

"Jake," his uncle drawled.

Jake took a few more steps before turning, his feet going faster than his mind this early in the morning. He hadn't yet drunk his coffee. He looked at Uncle Tim, who appeared as if he'd been up for a good while already. He was smiling and perky, dressed and sitting comfortably in one of the Adirondack chairs below Peony Cottage's deck. "Good morning, Uncle Tim."

Uncle Tim waved. "I need to talk to you."

Jake continued to walk as he called behind him. "All right. We can talk in a little bit. I have something I need to tend to first."

His uncle ignored the attempt to delay what he needed to say. "I was up all night, thinking about our conversation last night. I don't want to come off as the bad guy here, Jake. I really don't. You don't know all the facts, and I think it's time you did."

Jake stopped walking and turned to face him fully. "Oh? What facts am I missing?" Bailey nudged Jake's hand as it dangled by his side. Jake absently petted her.

"Well, for starters, that financial guru Vi hired did irreparable damage to this place. The storm tore up several of these cottages, and they've been sitting vacant for the past year. The only money coming in is from the four cottages that are inhabited, and the rent Vi is charging is far less than what she should be. She doesn't have the money to hire a property manager for this place. I love my mother and I want her to be happy, but she's still making bad business decisions."

Jake shifted on his feet. He already knew most of those things. "We'll raise the rent then. And Trisha and I have almost completed the repairs on the cottages. They'll be rented within a month's time."

Tim sighed. "You're not hearing me. The cottages are a dead weight. We're in the hole, boy, no thanks to that girlfriend of yours's ex-husband. Eventually Vi will lose these places anyway."

Jake wasn't buying that.

Tim offered an apologetic look. "I'm sorry, Jake, but the property manager needs to be let go. Vi is undercharging for rent and overpaying for that job. And she's giving the woman a free place to live on top of that. Vi didn't run that decision by the family. She just did it."

"She doesn't need to run it by the family. She's the trustee on the property." Jake felt all his defenses rising. He rubbed his hand across the back of his neck. He didn't like this. He wanted to keep arguing. Time and money. That's what this all came down to. But apparently, if he listened to his uncle, they'd run out of both. "Are you going to tell the family about Trisha?" Jake asked.

Tim frowned. "Whatever I do, I want you to know this isn't personal against her or you."

Jake put his hands on his hips and took in a breath. He turned to watch the lake for a long moment. "It is personal to me."

"Only because you let yourself have feelings for that woman."

Jake didn't deny his feelings for Trisha. They were growing and expanding with every breath. He didn't want to see Trisha get hurt. He didn't want to see Vi or his family struggle either though. And every turn he made, someone was putting more responsibility on his shoulders. It felt like everyone's happiness was riding on him—and he couldn't make everyone happy. "It doesn't matter if I get back on board and try to convince Vi. She won't agree."

Tim gave him a steady look. "We're a family of lawyers, Jake. We get paid to be convincing."

Bailey nudged Jake again, no doubt wanting to go down the beach so she could sniff the air.

And wake up Mr. S.

"Ah, geez," Jake muttered under his breath. "I have to do something." The sun was already up. If he didn't hurry, Jake wouldn't get to Mr. S before someone else saw him. And he didn't want that. Just like he didn't want the rest of the inevitable to happen.

* * *

Trisha was enjoying the sunshine on her face when her cell phone interrupted her quiet, peaceful moment. She reached for it, expecting it to be one of two people: Vi or Jake. Instead, the screen displayed an unknown number.

"Hello?" she answered.

"Hello, Trisha?"

"This is she."

"This is Deputy Bruno. Miles."

"Hi, Miles." Trisha assumed for a moment that this was a social call. "Thank you and the kids so much for helping out at the cottages this past week. They did an amazing job. I intend to bring over some goodies to the youth center to thank them."

"They would love that," Miles said. He cleared his throat. "I'm calling because there's an issue with one of your tenants."

Trisha stood and started pacing the front deck. "Oh?"

"I'm sorry to get your Friday morning started off like this, but I got a call to the lake about a man lying on the shore in the nude."

Trisha closed her eyes. *Nooo.* Jake was supposed to wake Mr. S up. "Mr. S. Yes, I'm so sorry, Miles. I will attend to that matter immediately."

"I've already gotten him up and back to his home. I just wanted to inform you about the situation."

Trisha stepped inside the cottage to get Petey. "Thank you. Can you tell me who called?" She was suddenly worried about what unfortunate person she needed to apologize profusely to.

"I'm afraid that's considered confidential information. We don't disclose who calls us, but the person was upset and rightfully so. Mr. S was awfully upset, too, when I escorted him back to Bear Cottage. Mainly because it was a bit of a scene. Law enforcement attracts attention, and he got his share. Anyway, this is a courtesy call to you. Mr. Santorini asked that I contact you instead of Vi. Says he's afraid of Vi." Miles chuckled. "I'd guess that word will probably get back to Vi anyway. There were a handful of people gathered. The talk will travel."

Ugh. Vi was going to be so disappointed in her. "I'll talk to Mr. Santorini."

"Thanks. If it happens again, I'll have to take him to jail. Just doing my job."

"I understand." And it probably would happen again. Mr. S was bound and determined to lie naked on the beach. Worst case, Vi might have to evict the Santorini family, which Trisha knew Vi wouldn't want to do. And ultimately, that was part of Trisha's duties. She would be the one to hand out the eviction notice.

"Thank you, Miles," Trisha said.

"You're welcome. Have a good day," the deputy said politely.

Trisha disconnected the call and turned toward Jake, who was coming up the steps.

He held up his hands. "I am so sorry." He glanced down at the phone in her hand. "The sheriff's department?" he asked.

"Deputy Bruno. Miles," Trisha confirmed. "He said next time he'll have to arrest Mr. S."

Jake rubbed the back of his neck. "Does Vi know?"

"Not yet."

Jake stepped closer to her. She looked around to see if Petey was watching. He was still in bed. She looked back up at Jake. "It was my responsibility, not yours."

"I promised to handle it for you. My uncle Tim met me at the bottom of the steps early this morning as I was heading that way. He had something he wanted to discuss."

Trisha felt something uncomfortable shift in her chest. She didn't think anything Jake's uncle wanted to discuss was probably a good thing.

Petey opened the back door and looked between them. "Hi, Jake! Are you here for breakfast?"

Breakfast. Right. Feeding her son came before putting out fires at the Somerset Rental Cottages.

"I don't know," Jake said slowly. He looked at Trisha. "I deserve to have you tell me to get off your deck and not show my face for at least another twenty-four hours."

She had never been the type to anger easily. She was forgiving and overlooking, maybe to a fault. "Well, then I'd have to finish up that last cottage on my own, which doesn't sound like any fun. And I'd have to go downtown to Sunset Over Somerset tonight by myself. I'm still an outsider here so I'd rather have you by my side."

Jake's blue eyes seemed to twinkle as he looked lazily at her. "I see. You're overlooking your anger for completely selfish reasons?"

There was a flirty swing to his tone, but Petey was too young to recognize it—hopefully. "Completely and utterly selfish," she confirmed.

Undoubtedly bored with their adult talk, Petey went back inside the house.

Trisha looked at Jake again. "That is unless your grandmother fires me for dropping the ball with Mr. S this morning, and I need to start packing my bags tonight."

"Not happening." Jake reached for her arm. "I'll pass on breakfast and go talk to her right now. Then I'll meet you over at the last cottage on our list."

"Sounds great." Trisha nibbled at her lower lip. "How upset do you think Vi will be?"

"She won't be mad at you," Jake promised. For a moment, it looked like he was about to lean down and kiss her. He stopped himself though, probably remembering that Petey was inside and possibly watching them.

Her heart melted a little. She wanted to kiss him. She wanted to step into his arms and allow herself to be held. "See you in a bit?"

"Yep."

As Jake walked away, Trisha wondered again who had called the law this morning. Her gaze caught on a man in a cowboy hat who was walking along the lakeshore. Uncle Tim.

Trisha's gut clenched, and a thought popped into her head. Or more of a question. Was Uncle Tim so eager to get Vi to sell the property and move that he'd call the sheriff's department? He'd heard Jake offer to wake Mr. S this morning. And he'd been the one to distract Jake from doing just that.

The thought felt paranoid. But as she watched him walk along the lake, it also rang true.

* * *

Jake had worked hard all day. He'd finished the floors and had installed all the appliances that he and Trisha purchased from the thrift store earlier in the week. He was bone tired, but his mind whirred with too many thoughts to allow him to rest. So instead, he got himself cleaned up and drove to Lakeside Books on Hannigan Street. He'd read all the manuals and how-to books in his collection. He needed something new to stimulate his mind.

He pushed through the front door and glanced around for Tess.

"I was wondering when you'd make your way here." Tess appeared from one of the tall aisles of books.

He headed in her direction. "I've run out of things to read. I've read the cereal box in my pantry at least ten times."

"Oh no." She laughed, the sound stirring memories from high school. Tess, Moira, Lucy, and Rachel had been close. Tess had always loved to laugh, and whenever she and Rachel had gotten together, that's all they'd seemed to do. Jake used to suspect half the time they were laughing about him. Or at him.

"Well, I have books that are more interesting than cereal boxes," Tess said. "If I remember correctly, you like those non-fiction instructional books."

"Guilty. Although at this point, I might have read them all."

"Doubtful." She shook her head on a laugh. "Do you know

how many books are published each week in each genre? It's so hard to decide what to order for a little bookstore like mine." She led him toward a wall of books with a sign overhead that read HOW TO. "So what do you want to learn? How to make a woman fall madly in love with you?" She lifted a brow.

Jake cleared his throat. He wasn't expecting the bluntness, but he should have been. Tess loved books, but she wasn't the stereotypical, face-in-a-book, shy type. She was outgoing and also incredibly perceptive.

"Or how about a book on how to come home again? Because they say you can never go home again, but that's just silly." Tess clucked her tongue.

"I'm only here for a few weeks," Jake said. At this point, the line felt tired and rehearsed. He didn't even believe it himself.

Tess folded her arms, her dark eyes narrowing. "The right woman might change your mind."

Jake looked at the spines of the books in front of him. "You never left. I was the one who was supposed to stay and marry my high school sweetheart. You were going to leave us all behind, if I remember correctly." He looked at Tess.

"And Rachel was supposed to live forever and become a teacher." Tess gave him a knowing look. She'd been one of Rachel's best friends. She'd also grieved after the accident. "Yes, I remember. Lucy was going to be a trophy wife. Instead, she's single and delivering babies, which is about the grossest thing I can imagine. I mean, she nearly passed out when we dissected a frog in biology. How did she ever become a midwife?"

Jake grimaced at the sudden mental images. "I don't know. It's just how life works, I guess. Nothing happens the way you think it will."

"Well, I'm a believer that things happen for a reason, even if they make no good sense to us mere humans." She angled her body toward him. "That's why I have a hunch that this summer excursion for you is more than a short trip down Memory Lane." When he didn't respond immediately, she gestured at the wall of books. "Anyway, these are the instructional books I have. I can order something different if you have a certain subject you want to learn about. Orders usually take about a week to come in."

Jake ran his gaze over the wall of guides. "I'm sure I can find something interesting here."

"I hope so. I'll be at the counter," Tess said. "Take your time, but I'm closing in ten minutes." She winked at him. "Sunset Over Somerset is calling. Are you coming out tonight?"

"I thought I would."

"You bringing Trisha?" she asked with a mischievous grin.

"And Petey," he confirmed.

"See? You were always meant to be a family man."

Trisha and Petey weren't Jake's family though. Vi was his family, and the rest of the Fletcher family was in Florida. Vi would have to move too. It was happening, whether she or Jake liked it or not. And when it did, Trisha would lose her job and her home. Everything she'd built over the last couple months would come crashing down.

Jake turned to the books, needing something to occupy his mind. He was hardwired to fix things, but he couldn't seem to figure out a way to stop what felt like an oncoming, out-of-control train.

He grabbed a guide on camping because he'd told Petey they could pitch a tent sometime this summer, and he wasn't one to do anything without knowing all the ins and outs and possible complications.

Next, he found himself reaching for a manual on photography. Not for himself, but for Trisha. She'd mentioned that she'd lost the instructional guide that came with her camera. She'd like this, and for a moment, he could make her happy.

Even if he was afraid he was about to turn into just another man who brought her to tears.

Jake carried the books to the counter and laid them down.

Tess looked between the books and back up to him. "I've always thought that men should bring a woman a book instead of flowers. Good choice."

Jake pulled out his wallet from his back pocket. "What makes you think one of those is for Trisha?"

"Because she was looking at that same book in here during our book club last night. She also told us she's interested in photography. That's about the only thing she disclosed. She seems like a private person."

"And you seem like one to ignore a person's privacy," he said, teasing her.

"It's the Southern way, Jake." She winked again and rang up the book. Then she picked up the camping book. "I'm guessing this one has to do with Petey." She lifted her gaze questioningly.

Jake nodded, but didn't say more. He liked his privacy as well. He paid and took his bag. "See you downtown. I think Mayor Gilbert is probably anxiously looking forward to punching your dance card."

"Stop!" she pleaded. "Gil has his eye on Moira anyway. Not me."

Jake chuckled. "See you later, Tess."

"Enjoy those books, Jake," she called as he turned to walk away.

Jake opened the door and stepped back onto Hannigan Street, thinking about Tess's words. She was right about him being a family man at heart. He just wasn't sure which family he would choose this summer.

Chapter Nineteen

Mom, you look pretty!" Petey stepped into Trisha's room and sat on her bed, watching as she fixed the tie on her sundress.

"Thank you, sweetie. It's just an old outfit that I purchased at your aunt's boutique a long time ago."

Petey's little mouth pinched as he gave her a thoughtful look. "You haven't worn those clothes in a long time," he observed.

Trisha turned and walked over to sit on the bed beside him. She waited for him to ask a question, as always. Instead, his gaze lingered on her clothes.

"Jake is going to think you look beautiful too," he said quietly.

Trisha felt her face warm. It would be naïve to think that Petey wouldn't notice something between her and Jake after all the time they'd been spending together lately. Yes, she and Jake had tried to keep their hands to themselves when Petey was around, but there'd been long glances, lots of laughing, and just a general vibe that even a seven-year-old would notice.

"He's not Dad. Or Uncle Chase."

Trisha swallowed as she shook her head. "No, he's not."

"But I like him." Petey picked at something on the leg of his shorts, most likely dried food from lunch, focusing there for a long moment. "Jake is different from them in a good way." He looked up at her. "I like his dog, and I like his plane. I like that he can answer most of my questions too. He's like a walking YouTube video."

This made Trisha laugh unexpectedly. "He does seem to know a lot of stuff, doesn't he?"

"He reads a lot of books," Petey added. "That's pretty cool. But most of all, I like that he makes you happy, Mom. You laugh a lot when he's with us."

Trisha's eyes burned. If she blinked, a tear might slip down her cheek, and she was tired of crying. They would be happy tears this time though.

She blew up a breath to dry her eyes. A second motivation for keeping her tears at bay was that she was wearing mascara tonight, and she didn't want to look like a raccoon. She wanted Jake to think she looked beautiful just like Petey had said.

Petey wasn't just inquisitive, he was also perceptive, and even though she'd intended to leave him out of whatever was going on with her and Jake, he'd seen through the facade. Which meant that if Trisha got her heart broken, he would too. When Jake left Somerset Lake as planned, she wouldn't be the only one crying.

"Jake and I enjoy each other's company," she said. "I guess you've picked up on that."

"If you're worried that I'll be sad because of Dad, I won't be." Petey looked down for a moment. "I mean, I miss Dad, and I wish he wasn't in prison. I wish he was here with us." His little mouth twisted to one side thoughtfully. "But then we wouldn't be here. We'd still be in Sweetwater Springs, which I guess would be okay, but I like it here."

"You do?" Trisha asked.

"Of course. I like that you don't work so much and have more time for me. Oh, and I like the twins. They're really cool. They told me all about the other kids who'll be in my class this fall. It's going to be pretty great." Petey was bubbling over with enthusiasm.

"That's great, sweetheart."

Petey looked shy for a moment. "Mom?"

"Yeah?"

"I need to tell you something." His voice tremored softly.

Uh-oh. Trisha felt a sense of dread rising through her chest and throat. "Okay. You can tell me anything. I hope you know that."

He rolled his lips together. "I told Justin and Jett about Dad."

Trisha blinked, trying to decipher how she felt about that. She'd told Jake, but she trusted him. Petey had told two little boys who, even with good intentions, would never be able to keep a secret.

"Are you mad?" Petey asked. His first real question of the night.

She sucked in a breath and let it out. "We talked about not telling people about your dad. You got picked on because of that. Why would you tell your new friends? They could pick on you too."

Petey's eyes were shimmering with tears that he was visibly trying to hold back. "Then they're not real friends. I only want true friends."

Trisha sucked in a shallow breath, finding it hard to pull enough air into her lungs.

"Mom, are you okay? Are you crying because you're upset with me?" Petey asked, the worry thick in his voice.

Trisha hadn't realized she was actually crying. She wrapped

her arm around his little shoulders. "No, I'm not mad. I'm very proud of you. You are growing up so fast, and you're so wise."

"It's all those books you make me read."

Trisha laughed. "No, it's you. You are a good boy and one day you're going to be a good man." She didn't have to worry about him landing himself behind bars like his father. Petey was okay. They were fine, and they were going to continue to be fine. "What did Justin and Jett say when you told them your dad was in prison?"

Petey squirmed under her arm. "They asked a bunch of questions. They wanted to know why he was there and if he was ever coming back. Then they asked about your divorce. Their mom and dad are getting one, too, but not because he's going to prison."

Trisha twisted her bracelet around her wrist as she listened. Della Rose said that she hadn't told the twins just yet, but it appeared the boys were as perceptive as Petey. "Right. So back to the subject of Jake. We like each other, but he's still leaving town. I want to make sure you understand that."

"I know. But his grandma lives next door," Petey argued. "And I left my grandma in Sweetwater Springs, and I'm going to visit her all the time. So when Jake leaves, it's not forever. He'll be back, Mom."

* * *

Jake had never enjoyed Sunset Over Somerset this much growing up.

He reached out for Trisha's hand. They were under the stars and being serenaded by music onstage. Petey had run off to Della Rose's blanket to be with his friends a half hour ago.

It was just Jake and Trisha. Yeah, 70 percent of the town was here tonight, but it felt like, here on this blanket, they were in their own little bubble. A bubble for two.

"Hey, you two." Lucy stepped over with Moira. "Are we interrupting?" She looked between them.

Jake wanted to say yes, but Trisha answered first.

"No, of course not. Not at all," Trisha said cheerily. She radiated happiness. When he'd first met her, she'd offered a reluctant smile. There'd been a guard that had fallen as quickly as he had for her.

"Good." Lucy and Moira sat down on the blanket.

"Okay, I have good news!" Moira said. "Your website is finished."

"Already? You just offered last night. I just sent you a couple pictures earlier today."

Moira shrugged. "It was easy. And the photos you sent me were amazing. I had no idea you were so talented."

Trisha shook her head and deflected the compliment. "I'm not really. I'm just playing around with my camera."

"Well, you have a great eye. They were terrific. The website is seriously very simple, but sometimes less is more. You want prospective customers to focus on what you're offering anyway. I emailed you the link to the website. Check it out later and tell me what you think."

"I will. Thank you so much," Trisha said.

"And send me the link too," Lucy told Moira. "I want to forward it to my friend Ainsley."

"You got it."

Lucy practically squealed. "I will be so happy to have my friend move closer to me. It would also be awesome to help you out. How many cottages are left to rent?" Lucy asked.

"Seven after Jake leaves," Trisha said quietly.

"Right." Lucy looked at him. "I guess some part of me

blocked out the fact that you were leaving soon. It's good to have you home. Anyway, we'll leave you two alone." Lucy gave Trisha a meaningful look that didn't escape Jake's notice. It was the kind of look that women gave each other when there was a new love interest.

Jake looked down at his hands. How did a couple short weeks turn into a love interest?

"Bye, guys," Lucy said, standing. "Going to save Tess. Gilbert is talking to her. He's probably looking for Moira." Lucy winked.

"Stop it!" Moira complained as she stood as well. Then she followed behind Lucy toward a nearby blanket.

Trisha laughed and looked at Jake. "I haven't met this Gilbert guy yet."

"He likes to be called Gil," Jake pointed out.

"Is that what his friends call him?" she asked.

"No, no." Jake shook his head on a laugh. "His friends definitely call him Gilbert just to mess with him."

Trisha laughed even more. "So I guess we might be about to rent out one of the six...seven cottages."

"I guess so."

"That's reason to celebrate."

"Well, I just so happen to have a present for the occasion. I didn't know this was going to happen, but it seems fitting." Jake reached into the picnic basket that Vi had packed for them again tonight.

"You got me a present?" Trisha asked. "It's not my birthday."

He slid his gaze to meet hers. "When is that, by the way? I don't want to miss it."

"October," she said, a hint of sadness in her voice.

He wouldn't be here in October. "I'll have to remember that." He pulled out the purchase from Tess's bookstore. "Sorry I didn't wrap it."

Trisha gasped as she looked at the book. "How did you know I wanted this?"

"I didn't. I was in there buying a book for myself."

Trisha tilted her head. "Let me guess, a how-to book on something interesting?"

"Camping. I promised Petey so..."

Trisha's lips parted. She fanned her eyes for a moment.

"You okay?"

"Yeah, I'm just emotional tonight it seems. I've already cried once with Petey." She placed the photography book in her lap. "He told the twins about his dad being in prison."

"Oh." Jake stiffened. "And?"

"And I'm proud of him, actually. His head and his heart are in the right space. I'm the one who needs to get with the program."

Jake reached for her hand again. "I think you're amazing, if that counts for anything."

She looked up. "It counts for a lot. Maybe too much. And I have a gift for you too," she said, reaching into her purse. "It's not a lot," she warned him.

"I don't need anything." *But you*, he wanted to say. All he needed was more time with her.

Trisha pulled out some pictures. "I printed off the pictures I've been taking. There were a few that I thought you might want." She chewed her lower lip as she handed them over.

Jake felt his throat tighten as he looked down at the photographs in his hand. "Wow." The first picture was one of him flying his plane last week. There was a huge smile on his face, and he knew it was because of Trisha. "This is great. I've never had a picture of myself piloting a plane."

"Well, you should. And now you do."

Jake looked at her. "Moira was right. Maybe you're just getting started, but you're talented."

"Look at the rest," Trisha said. "There's two more."

Jake moved the front picture to the back to see the next in the thin stack. It was a picture of him, Bailey, and Petey standing in front of the lake. Trisha took it a few days ago after they'd worked most of the day in the cottages. "I love it." He moved that picture to the bottom of the stack to see the last picture and his breath caught. It was a selfie of him and Trisha in one of the cottages. They were paint splattered and smiling like two people in love.

His heart kicked softly. He didn't know about her, but he was definitely falling in love.

"Thank you. Really. This is a great gift."

Trisha looked pleased that he thought so.

"I've been thinking about things," he found himself saying. "I know my family wants to sell the Somerset Cottages. They don't want Vi to be alone here and responsible for over a dozen properties. I was thinking that maybe she doesn't have to be alone though. What if I stay a while and help with things? How could they argue with that?"

Trisha was looking at him, her lips still parted, her eyes still shiny. He looked down at his hand on hers and then back up into her brown eyes. He didn't want to blink or breathe or move so that this moment between them didn't disappear.

"Vi needs me. And I know you don't need me, but..." He trailed off. He hadn't planned to say any of this tonight. It was just something he was thinking about. Not something he'd actually decided on. But it felt right. "I was hoping that maybe, even if you don't need me to stay, that you want me to."

"Jake," she said quietly.

"Yeah?"

Trisha nibbled on her lower lip, distracting him. She shook her head and then a tear slipped down her cheek. She swiped it away quickly. "See? I told you I was emotional this evening. I just don't want you to give up things for me."

"Why not?" Jake asked. "You don't think you deserve to have a guy make sacrifices for you?"

"Not for him to sacrifice everything for me. You'd be moving to a place you never wanted to return to. Giving up a good job with your family. All for what? For a woman you barely know?"

Jake ran his thumb along the back of her hand. "For a woman who, in a couple of weeks, has managed to heal a piece of my heart that's been broken for over a decade. How can I possibly walk away from a woman like that?"

Another tear slipped off her cheek. This time he lifted his hand and wiped it away, his gaze locking on hers.

"I never wanted to return to Somerset Lake because it hurt to be here. It almost felt like this place was haunted because all I could think of were the people I've lost here." He continued to touch her cheek, looking at her, loving her more with each passing moment. "But this time around, I still think of Rachel, my grandfather, too, but it doesn't hurt like it used to. In fact, it feels good to think of them. I feel like all the broken pieces of my heart that have been scattered around in my chest have come together. They found where they belong again." He probably sounded crazy right now, but Trisha's smile made him keep talking. "I feel like *I* found where I belong again." He lowered his hand from her cheek, bringing it to rest over her hand.

"Petey told me that he was okay with us getting close."

"Yeah? I have his permission to date you? No more hiding?"

"No more hiding," she agreed. She glanced down at the photography book. "Thank you for my gift. I love it."

"You're welcome. I love seeing you smile." He wanted to see more of it. More of her. He wanted to tell her that he loved more than just her smile.

It wasn't just an idea in his head any longer. He was staying. For Vi. For Trisha and Petey. For himself. And as long as Vi was capable of making her own decisions, which she was, there was nothing his uncle or his parents could do.

* * *

On Thursday evening of the following week, Trisha walked through the door of Lakeside Books and smelled the delicious aroma of whatever treats the women had brought.

Trisha suddenly felt empty-handed. All she'd brought with her was Petey, the current book selection, and a willingness to share pieces of her life, including her past, that she'd wanted so desperately to hide since she'd arrived.

Trisha's talk with Petey last Friday night had opened her eyes to a few things. Somerset Lake could never truly be their home if they were hiding. And yes, maybe some people would judge them, but others, hopefully, would accept them—skeletons in the closet and all. Like Petey had said, Trisha wanted true friends too—nothing less.

"Trisha!" Della Rose got up from her chair and gave Trisha a huge hug. Petey went to the back area to play LEGOs with the twins. "I'm glad you could make it."

"Me too." Trisha turned and said hello to Moira, who was seated on a small burgundy sofa. Tess was behind the counter, closing out the cash register for the day. She briefly looked up and waved. "Where's Lucy?" Trisha asked the women.

"Oh, I think one of her patients went into labor this afternoon," Della Rose said. She sat back down and glanced over her shoulder at the boys, who were making a ruckus in the kids' corner.

"Okay, I'm ready." Tess walked over and gave Trisha a hug

too. "Sit, sit. Looks like Moira has been to Choco-Lovers. What is that deliciousness?"

"Chocolate éclairs. Nobody makes them like Jana," Moira said.

"You know, if we could get Jana to finally agree to come to our little book club, she'd probably feed our sweet tooth for free," Della Rose conspired.

Trisha took a seat in a comfy lounge chair and listened to the women go back and forth in their easy conversation. She'd had friends in Sweetwater Springs, but since adulthood, she'd been so busy that she hadn't been afforded much time to join a group of women and just talk.

It felt good to be here.

Someone knocked on the front door. The women turned to see Lucy standing there and waving.

Tess hurried to open the door for her and gave Lucy a hug as she stepped inside. Then Tess locked the door behind her.

"False alarm," Lucy told the women. "My patient has had four false alarms in the last week," she said with exasperation. "New mom and all." Lucy stepped over to the group and took a seat beside Trisha. "Hey, you. Glad we didn't scare you away last week."

"Just the opposite," Trisha said. "I've been looking forward to being here all week."

"In between kissing Jake Fletcher," Tess pointed out, reaching for a chocolate éclair. She brought it to her mouth and prepared to take a bite. "How's that going? You two looked awfully cozy at Sunset Over Somerset last weekend."

The women didn't waste any time diving into Trisha's personal life. Last week, they'd been more reserved with Trisha's private life. Now they were no-holds-barred, and Trisha was ready.

"Well," Trisha said with a growing grin, "it's going well

enough that Jake has decided to stay in Somerset Lake a while longer."

"What?" the women all gasped at the same time.

"That's huge!" Moira said. "Jake left and made it clear that he was never moving back."

"You must be pretty special to him," Lucy said. She also held an éclair in her hand now. She bit into it, catching the crumbs with her opposite hand.

Trisha took in a breath and blew it out. She'd come ready to spill her guts. *Here goes nothing. Or everything.* "I never thought I'd fall for someone again after my divorce to Petey's dad. Certainly not for some guy who was basically trying to kick me out of my job and my home when he got here a couple weeks ago."

Trisha looked around the group. Apparently, that wasn't news to them. They all knew that Jake's family wanted Vi to sell. Uncle Tim had told everyone who would listen since he'd been here.

"I guess my ex-husband really did a number on my ability to trust," Trisha admitted. "The truth is, um…" This was harder than Trisha had expected. Somehow when she'd told Jake about Peter, it had felt easy. Like a confessional. She had trust issues, but she'd trusted that he wouldn't tell anyone. "My ex, Petey's father, was a financial planner. A prominent one in western North Carolina. He…" Trisha felt shaky suddenly. "He stole from his clients. A little bit here and some there. I had no idea what he was doing. I just thought he was earning more income every year because he was good at what he did. I trusted him just like his clients did. Then one day…" Trisha's eyes burned as she came to the part of the story she liked the least. She took a steadying breath and continued. "One morning, we were all still in our beds when the FBI came crashing through our front door. In a tiny town like Sweetwater Springs, that's a pretty big deal."

"In any town, that's a big deal," Lucy said.

"That must have been so terrifying for you," Moira said. There was no judgment in her eyes. None in any of the women's eyes. There was no surprise either. Why didn't these ladies look at least surprised by what Trisha was telling them?

Trisha looked around at each face. They all looked calm, as if she were telling them what she ate for breakfast this morning. They continued to eat their éclairs. Yes, they looked sympathetic, but in no way shocked. "Why do I get the feeling that none of this is news to you?"

Tess grimaced. She shared a look with Lucy that stopped Trisha's heart. She knew what that look meant.

"You guys already knew?" she asked breathlessly. "Jake told you?" The pain of that realization felt like a sharp knife to her chest. She resisted pressing her hand to her heart.

"No." Lucy shook her head. "Jake didn't tell us anything."

But Jake was the only one that Trisha had told. He must have told someone for Lucy, Moira, Tess, and Della Rose to know. Or maybe Della Rose's twin boys were the ones who told. Perhaps they'd told their mother, and she'd told the other ladies.

Trisha looked at Della Rose for answers.

"It was in Reva Dawson's blog today," Della Rose said gently. "It released a couple hours ago. We thought you saw it."

"I don't read the blog. I don't know Reva." Trisha felt panic rising within her. "But the whole town does. The whole town knows I was married to a thief? They all know that Petey's dad is a convicted felon?" Trisha asked, talking quickly as her thoughts jumbled. It felt like she was going to hyperventilate.

Tess placed a hand on her back. "Just breathe. It's going to be okay."

"It doesn't feel like it will be." Trisha had another thought. "Vi is going to see it. She might be upset."

"You didn't tell Vi when she hired you?" Lucy asked, shock playing in her voice for the first time.

"No. I mean, is that so wrong? I wanted a fresh start. My ex-husband's crimes shouldn't follow me everywhere I go for the rest of my life."

Tess's eyes went wide. She looked at Lucy, who looked at Moira, who looked at Della Rose.

"Why are you all looking at each other?" This was the reaction she'd thought she'd get when she'd told them about her past. Why was she getting it now? "What are you not telling me?" Trisha asked.

Tess stood, walked over to her counter, and grabbed her laptop. She brought it over, pulled up Reva's blog, and placed it on Trisha's lap.

Trisha blinked. Maybe she didn't want to read whatever was said about her. But it affected Petey so she needed to know what everyone in town now knew. Trisha blinked the screen into focus and started to read.

It was all very matter-of-fact, even friendly and shining a positive light on Trisha. She'd been through so much, and yet she was determined not to let it drag her down. She was a single mother, caring for her son. They were starting a new life here in Somerset Lake.

Trisha's brain stumbled over the last paragraph. She read it a second time. And a third time for it to process.

> We all knew our very own Vi Fletcher was an amazing woman. Hiring the ex-wife of the financial planner who robbed her and nearly sent her into bankruptcy is an act of sainthood.

Trisha finally looked up. "I don't understand." She could feel tears burning in her eyes. "Vi never said anything about a financial planner. She said there was a hurricane and her stroke."

"But first Vi hired a financial planner, who steered her wrong with her money after her husband died," Tess explained. "The guy almost put the Somerset Cottages in bankruptcy too. Vi couldn't afford to fix the damage because her financial planner had wiped out a huge chunk of the funds in the family's trust. Then she had her stroke, which some say was a direct result of the stress of the whole situation."

"It was a series of bad events," Lucy said quietly.

Trisha shook her head as she listened. "Why didn't Vi tell me?" And more importantly, why hadn't Jake told her these things? Surely, once Trisha had told him about her ex-husband, he would have wondered if Vi's finance guy was the same man that Trisha was once married to. "I mean, maybe it's not the same person," Trisha told the women. "I don't know Reva or where she got this information. It could be wrong."

Lucy shrugged. "Reva's information is usually pretty accurate. She was a journalist when she was young. I've never known her to get the facts wrong."

"I don't remember the name of the planner that was helping Vi," Tess said apologetically. "I just know that he wasn't from town."

"I'm sure your ex wasn't the same guy," Della Rose said. "I mean, what are the odds of that?" She laughed nervously.

The odds were pretty good in Trisha's mind. Peter's list of clients had been extensive and stretched beyond Sweetwater Springs. He'd always been on the phone. He was always working at his computer. He'd worked so hard, and she was so proud of him while the wool was still covering her eyes.

"Right," Trisha said. The only thing that gave her hope was that Jake wouldn't have kept this a secret if in fact Peter was the man who'd stolen from Vi. He'd have told Trisha the truth. Wouldn't he?

"I mean, no one likes to discuss a messy financial situation,"

Moira said, as if reading Trisha's mind. "That's private. I'm sure that's why Vi didn't tell you. And you didn't tell her about your past, so she wouldn't have known you two shared anything in common. We know that you didn't do anything wrong," Moira said.

The other women nodded in agreement.

"And the rest of the town is going to think the same thing," Tess assured her.

"Here." Della reached inside the box of goodies on the coffee table. "Have a chocolate éclair. Chocolate makes everything better, right, ladies?"

They all agreed.

All except Trisha. The only thing that would make things better right now was finding Jake. She needed to look him in the eye and ask him to tell her the truth. Was Peter Lewis Vi's financial planner? Did Jake know about this?

Trisha didn't really believe in coincidences, but she still desperately wanted to believe in Jake.

CHAPTER TWENTY

Jake pulled out his cell phone and checked for missed calls. It wasn't unusual for his parents not to answer or return his calls. They were retired and the type of people who decided to go somewhere on a whim, and quite often that somewhere didn't have cell phone service. They RV'd and camped all over the East Coast. They rented houseboats and lived on the ocean. Frankly, they inspired Jake.

And he wasn't much different from them. When his family had moved south, Jake headed north. He was the only one of his family to take up his grandfather's interest in flying planes, and he had often taken his plane on small expeditions and pitched a tent in remote areas off the grid.

Jake tapped his mom's contact in his phone again and held it to his ear, listening to the ring that finally went to his mom's voice mail.

Mad or out of touch? He was hoping for the latter.

Headlights streamed onto the gravel path. Jake's heart lifted in his chest. That would be Trisha returning home from the book club. He watched her pull in behind Juniper Cottage, noticing as she stepped out that Petey wasn't with her. He guessed that Petey had gone home with Della Rose and the twins.

Trisha looked up and spotted him on his deck. There was something off-kilter about her as she waved. He knew the women at the bookstore. They wouldn't have done anything to offend her. They were good folks with big hearts. He hadn't realized how much he'd missed the people here in Somerset Lake until being back this go-round.

Trisha walked around to the back of his cottage and headed up his steps. "Hey," she said when she'd reached the middle stair.

"Hey. Where's Petey?"

"Della Rose's for the night." Trisha continued climbing until she was standing on his deck. She walked over to the chair beside his, where she'd sat several times lately. It was her chair in the same way that the second chair on the deck of Juniper Cottage was his.

"Did you have a good time tonight?" he asked.

"For the most part." She hesitated. There was definitely something on her mind. Her hands fidgeted at her midsection while she chewed her lower lip. Jake waited patiently for her to decide to tell him what was going on. "Actually, no," she finally said. "Have you read Reva Dawson's blog today?"

Jake gave her a strange look. "I don't read Reva's blog on a daily basis. Or even a weekly basis. Why?"

Trisha inhaled. "Who did you tell about my ex-husband?"

Jake shook his head. "No one. I told you I wouldn't tell, and I didn't."

"You must have," Trisha said, "because Reva knew. She put it in her blog, and now everyone knows the truth about who I was married to and who Petey's father is." Trisha's eyes filled with tears.

Jake stood and went to her, putting his hands on the sides of her shoulders. "Hey, I didn't tell anyone. I promise. It wasn't me."

Trisha looked skeptical. "The blog mentioned something about Vi and a financial planner who stole from her?"

Jake hesitated as every muscle in his body tensed. "That's true," he finally said.

"The ladies at the book club didn't know his name," Trisha continued. "But I'm sure you do. I told you my ex's name and his story. So if it was the same person, you would have told me right away."

It wasn't a question, but it may as well have been.

She stared at him, her eyes narrowed, her expression pinched with worry. "Jake? Are you going to say anything?"

He'd intended to tell her the truth this week. He was just waiting for the right time and for his uncle Tim to leave.

Uncle Tim. He knew about Trisha's ex. His uncle pretty much threatened to expose Trisha, and it looked like he'd made good on those threats by going to the town's gossip blogger. "Trisha..." Jake said.

She sucked in an audible breath. "So it's true? Peter was the one who took Vi's money? He's the reason these cottages have been deteriorating since the storm? He's the reason Vi was so stressed before her stroke?"

Jake shook his head. "Slow down, okay? You are not responsible for what your ex-husband did. None of it."

Trisha's lips parted. "How could you know about all of this and hide it from me?" She pulled away from his arms and took a step backward.

"I didn't hide it necessarily."

"Well, you didn't tell me. That's hiding it," she countered, her voice climbing an octave.

"Only because I didn't want you to blame yourself. And I

didn't want you to leave. Not until I had a chance to convince you that you belong here. With me." Jake's heart was pounding against his ribs. This conversation had taken a turn down a path that led nowhere good.

"This is your home, Trisha. When you told me your story, I understood that you were just as much a victim as Vi was. And the last thing I wanted to do was inflict more pain on you and Petey." Jake reached out to comfort her, but she stiffened under his touch. "I was planning to tell you."

Trisha walked to the deck railing, looking out on the lake, her body shaking as she took audible breaths.

Jake walked over to stand beside her. "I'm sorry. Maybe I should have told you sooner. But if I had, would you have stayed?"

She looked at him, her expression full of pain. "That's not the point, Jake. I shared something with you because I felt like I could trust you."

"You can," Jake said. "I would never tell anyone."

"Not even me," she said softly.

Jake reached out for her, relieved when she didn't pull away immediately. "Trisha, I know you're upset. And I'm sorry. I'm *really* sorry. But I'm not your ex. I'm not your parents. I'm never going to do anything that I know will hurt you. I'm not going anywhere. I'm here to stay."

She blinked back tears. One slipped past her control and slid down her cheek. "Yeah, well, maybe I'm not," she said quietly.

The words kicked Jake in the center of his chest. "What?"

"I don't know." She stepped back. "I need to be alone. I need to think."

Jake was at a loss for words for a moment. He wanted to argue. He wanted to plead. "Okay," he finally said, unable to do either. Sometimes time and space was enough to allow someone a different perspective. He knew that firsthand. "Let's have breakfast in the morning."

She hesitated for just a moment. "All right. I'll wake Mr. S and come over here."

"I told you I'd take care of Mr. S."

Trisha shook her head and took another small step away, creating more distance between them. "It's my job. At least for the moment."

* * *

Trisha woke with a splitting headache. The tension that she'd hoped would ease while she slept hadn't gone anywhere. It was resting right at the center of her forehead. She squinted and lifted her hand to shield her eyes from the small splice of light coming through her blinds.

Time to get up and face the day. To face all the problems she'd briefly left behind in the hours before.

She sat up in her bed and turned her body to drape her legs off the side. She suddenly felt twenty years older. Worry and fear would do that to a person. On a yawn, she stood and shuffled down the hall to use the bathroom. She quickly dressed and slipped out the back door, across the deck, down the steps, and along the beach to wake Mr. S.

Because Jake had failed to do that last week. Because this wasn't his job. It was hers. Because Jake had kept something so important from her that her chest ached right along with her head this morning.

Tears burned her eyes. Was she overreacting? She wasn't sure, but this felt like a huge betrayal. It hurt because of the way she felt about Jake. Every bone, every breath, everything hurt.

Mr. S was lying on the shore about ten feet away. Trisha clutched her towel and walked faster, noticing that something was different about him this morning. It took a second for her mind to register what it was.

She reached him and looked down. No need to shield her eyes this morning because for the first time since she'd started working for Vi, he was wearing clothes. Just a pair of long shorts, but still. Clothes!

He cracked an eye and looked up at her. "Don't ask me to leave this morning, T. I'm dressed so I can stay as long as I want to."

Trisha smiled, which felt odd considering she was currently nursing a small heartache that felt like a crater in her chest. "You are free to stay as long as you want today, Mr. S."

"Good. I'll be in this spot every morning wearing these shorts. So if you don't mind, stop waking me up and sending me home to my cottage."

A laugh bubbled up, passing over Trisha's lips. "You got it. Have a great morning." She turned and headed back to her cottage. She felt like laughing and crying at the same time. It was going to be a long day with her emotions giving her whiplash.

When she reached Juniper Cottage, she kept walking until she was standing in front of Vi's steps. One thing Trisha had decided before going to bed last night was that she needed to talk to Vi as soon as possible. She couldn't keep her past a secret any longer, especially now that she knew the truth about Peter's connection to the Fletcher family. If Trisha had known that Vi was one of Peter's clients, she never would have applied for the job. And now that she did know, she wasn't sure she could stay.

Vi was an early riser so she'd be awake right now. And since Petey was at Della Rose's house, this was the perfect time to have a heart-to-heart with Vi.

Trisha climbed the steps, taking them slowly as her thoughts and emotions warred internally. The main thing she wanted to tell Vi was that she was sorry for what Peter did to her. Because there was still some part of Trisha that felt responsible for not realizing what her ex-husband was doing. She'd just turned a blind eye to everything that was going on right in front of her.

Trisha reached the deck's landing and walked to Vi's lake-side door. There was a light on inside. Vi usually enjoyed her coffee out on the deck, but maybe she'd decided to have it at her kitchen table instead. Trisha knocked and waited. She knocked again, louder this time. Something tightened inside her chest.

Why isn't Vi answering the door? Is she still asleep? Is something wrong?

Trisha tried the door's handle, and it opened easily. Vi only locked it at night. That meant she'd already come out this morning or that she hadn't gotten a chance to lock the door before bed.

"Vi?" Trisha's breaths felt shallow as she stepped inside and walked through the living area to the kitchen. "Vi?" The coffee maker wasn't on. That was the first thing Vi did when she woke up. Trisha's steps quickened as she walked through the house, calling her boss's name. Her friend's name. Then she paused and cried out as she found Vi lying on the floor beside her bed. She rushed to Vi's side. "Vi!"

The older woman didn't stir or respond to Trisha's voice or touch. Trisha shook Vi's shoulders. There was no sign of blood or injury. It just looked like Vi had fallen asleep on the floor next to her bed.

Trisha lifted Vi's wrist and checked her pulse, holding her own breath as she waited to feel a small thump under her fingertips.

She's alive!

But something was definitely wrong.

Trisha pulled her cell phone out of her pocket. Her first instinct was to call 911, but Jake had told her that paramedics were slow getting to this stretch of the lake. Vi would get to the hospital faster if Jake drove.

Trisha pulled up Jake's contact with shaking hands and connected the call. He answered after two rings.

"I was hoping you'd call—" he began.

She cut him off. "Something's wrong with Vi! She needs to go to the hospital, now!"

* * *

Jake shot out of bed. He hadn't been sleeping, but he didn't want to crawl out from under the covers just yet either. Now he was moving as fast as he could, yanking on his jeans and a T-shirt from the dresser.

He shoved his wallet and his cell phone into his pockets and grabbed his keys as he hurried out the door. Bailey followed him onto the deck. "Sorry, girl. You can't come. You're free to run the lake today," he called behind him as he nearly stumbled down the steps.

Once his feet hit the ground, he ran as fast as he could to Vi's house and took the steps two at a time. The door was already open. He barged in and looked around. "Trisha!"

"Back here!" she called from the far end of the house.

Jake raced in that direction. When he entered Vi's bedroom, he stopped for a moment to assess the scene. "What happened?"

"I don't know," Trisha said, tears shimmering along her cheeks. "She was just lying like this when I got here. Her eyes have fluttered a few times, and she's moaned but she's not waking up, Jake. She needs to go to the hospital, and we need to hurry."

Jake crouched down beside Vi and slid his arms underneath her body. Then he gently lifted her and headed out of the room, carrying his grandmother as fast as he could.

Trisha followed behind him. As much as he wanted to resolve things between them, Vi's life was hanging in the balance. Trisha hurried ahead of him and opened his passenger truck door. He loaded Vi in the seat, her body slumping. He secured her with a seat belt and shut the door.

Trisha wasn't standing there anymore. She was halfway back to her cottage with Bailey at her side.

"I'll put Bailey in my place!" she called to him. "I'll meet you there. Just hurry!"

Jake didn't waste a second. He dipped into the driver's side of his truck, slammed the door, and cranked the engine. Then he drove, faster than ever, down the private gravel path, his tires spitting rocks as they spun out.

He looked over at Vi. "Hang in there, Grandma. I can't lose you too." His words reminded him that there was always someone for him to lose in Somerset Lake. First Rachel, then his grandfather. *Please not Vi.*

Vi groaned weakly. Her eyes fluttered to meet his as he glanced over. "I'm not...going anywhere," she slurred.

Was she having another stroke? He knew there was a higher risk now that she'd had the first.

Jake couldn't bear the thought. He pressed the gas pedal harder. There was an urgent care in Somerset Lake, but the closest hospital was in Magnolia Falls. That was one of the problems living in a small town. Emergency crews had a longer trip getting to you.

"I'm sorry," Vi said.

"What? There's no reason to apologize."

"I wanted to keep...the cottages...for you." Her words stopped and started.

Jake reached over and grabbed her hand. "Just worry about yourself right now, Grandma. That's all I'm concerned about."

He understood what she was saying though. She wanted to stay in Somerset Lake and keep the cottages. But another stroke meant that probably wouldn't happen now. She was going to lose more of her independence. The next generation of Fletchers was going to take over. And they were going to do what they'd been pressing for all along—sell out.

CHAPTER TWENTY-ONE

*J*ake was drinking his fourth cup of stale coffee in the hospital's waiting room. The doctors were running tests on Vi so here he was worrying and waiting for the rest of his family to arrive.

Waiting for Trisha to arrive too.

She was supposed to be following behind him, but she'd never shown up.

He pulled out his cell phone and tapped out another text to her.

> You okay? Where are you?

He didn't want to be here alone. He didn't want to be here at all.

His phone lit up with an incoming text.

> I turned around and went home. Family should be with Vi right now. How is she?

Jake blew out a breath and texted back. Vi would want you here. He added, I'm not sure how she is. They're running tests. I'm in the waiting room. Just me.

Was Trisha still upset with him? Is that why she wasn't here? Did she blame herself for what was happening? He couldn't begin to guess at what was going on in her mind. He texted a message.

You should come to the hospital.

Jake stared at his screen, willing a speedy response. Instead, his phone remained inactive for a long moment.

Petey will be home from Della Rose's place soon. Please keep me updated on Vi's condition, she finally texted back. Which was basically a no. She wasn't coming. She didn't feel like she belonged here. And maybe she was second-guessing whether she belonged in Somerset Lake altogether.

Jake threaded his fingers through his hair. He felt like he was suddenly on the verge of losing everything that mattered right now.

"Jake?" A woman's voice filled the waiting room.

Jake looked up and stood to greet his mom. "Mom. How'd you know to come?"

"We got your message. We were already en route to Somerset Lake so we didn't have far to travel."

"I didn't know you were coming."

"Didn't Vi tell you?" his mom asked.

Jake shook his head. "No."

"Well, she probably wanted to surprise you. You know how your grandmother is."

His dad stepped up behind his mom. Jake headed over and hugged him too.

"How is Vi?" his mom asked once they'd pulled away from each other.

"They're running tests. It looks like she may have suffered another stroke, but there's no definitive answers," Jake told his parents. "They want us to wait here for the doctor to come out."

Jake gestured at the seats. He moved back to the one he'd been seated in, his parents following and sitting on his left side. "You haven't been returning my calls."

His dad crossed one leg over his knee. "Well, we figured we'd talk to you when we got here. It's not really a conversation to have over the phone. Or in a hospital waiting room."

Jake looked between his parents. "Vi doesn't want to sell. She doesn't want to move."

His mom offered a small grimace. "We know. And we had decided to be supportive of that. But now..." She trailed off. "Well, I guess we'll need to wait and see what the doctor says. Her health is what's important."

Jake agreed. He just wished it didn't mean that Vi's wishes and Trisha's plans had to fall apart.

"Have you called Tim?" his dad asked. "He's still in the area, right?"

Jake nodded. "I left a voice mail for him right after I called you. I haven't heard from him though." Jake guessed that maybe Tim was avoiding his calls, expecting that Jake would be angry with him about leaking Trisha's story to Reva. "I'm happy that you guys are here," Jake told his parents.

His mom reached for his hand. "Of course, dear. I'm glad you're not here waiting for news by yourself." She gave him a pointed look.

The night of Rachel's accident, Jake had been here, waiting alone. Rachel's family was out of town that weekend. Jake's parents had been asleep in their bed. That night had been long, and Jake had been the only one waiting when the doctor came out, looking for next of kin.

Jake wasn't family though. He was just the boyfriend who'd planned to marry Rachel one day. Jake's eyes had connected with the doctor's as he stood before him. In that moment, he didn't need to be told. He could see the news that the doctor was waiting to tell Rachel's parents. It was written in the unmistakable sympathy carved into the doctor's eyes.

"Can I see her?" Jake had asked anyway, ignoring his gut. Rachel was young. Young people didn't die. They lived.

The doctor shook his head. "I'm afraid not, son. I'll come back to talk to the family when they arrive." Then the doctor turned and walked away, leaving Jake to wait and hope the doctor's grim look was just in his imagination.

A doctor walked into the waiting room now and looked at Jake and his parents. Jake swallowed thickly, wondering if this doctor held the same bad news.

* * *

There were a million things on Trisha's to-do list today, but all she could manage right now was sitting in the Adirondack chair on her deck and watching the water. Petey had returned from his sleepover an hour ago, and he was inside reading Jake's camping guide. Jake had finished it and passed it on to him the other day.

Trisha was grateful that Petey was occupied. She needed time. She needed an update on Vi. She needed...something.

Just when this lake was starting to feel like home, it felt like the sky was falling, piece by painful piece.

Her cell phone lit up with another text from Jake. She'd lost count of how many he'd sent. She'd returned maybe one for every five. And all she could say or ask about was Vi's condition. She couldn't talk to Jake about anything else. She still wasn't sure how to feel about yesterday's revelations.

Jake knew that Peter had been Vi's financial planner. He knew there was a ticking time bomb waiting to explode on her and Petey's new life. That was the part that hurt the most. She didn't want to uproot Petey. She didn't want him to be hurt again. Her heart couldn't take watching him cry himself to sleep for weeks on end again.

"Mom?"

She turned to Petey, who was now standing in the doorway. "Yeah?"

Petey closed the door behind him and walked out on the deck. He sat in the chair beside hers. "Is Vi going to die?" he asked in a small voice.

"No." Trisha shook her head, and then she thought better of her answer. "I mean, I don't think so. Jake took her to the hospital, and I'm sure the doctors are taking good care of her."

"Can we go see her?" Petey asked.

Trisha reached for his hand and squeezed it. "She has her family there with her right now. And even the family isn't allowed inside her room for a while. The best thing we can do for Vi is to continue working on the cottages and pray for her."

Petey leaned back in his chair and sighed. "Okay."

"So I guess we should get up and back to work." It was a lot easier to do that when she realized that Petey was moping too.

"The cottages are done, aren't they?" Petey asked. "Jake fixed the holes in the roofs. The kids from the youth center helped clean. Deputy Bruno too," he added. "You and Jake painted, and Mrs. Moira made that website for you, which is really cool. What else is there?"

Trisha brought up her mental list. Petey was right. For the most part, everything was checked off. "I want to hang the pictures I took on the living room walls. Decorating is the fun part. You can help me."

Petey didn't look enthused.

"And when we're done, we'll go to Choco-Lovers for a treat. I've been wanting to try that place out."

Now his eyes lit up. "Can we stop at Tess's bookstore too?"

"I guess so." Trisha needed a distraction as much as Petey.

"We can get Vi a get-well present and bring it to the hospital," Petey added. "Wouldn't she like that?"

Trisha patted Petey's hand. "I'm sure she would." She wasn't sure she was ready to face Vi yet. It had crossed her mind that Vi might have read Reva's blog yesterday too. And that maybe that contributed to her being in the hospital again. Trisha knew Vi had underlying health conditions that were in no way her fault, but she couldn't help blaming herself anyway.

Petey hopped off his chair with renewed spirit at the mention of chocolate and a new book. "I'll get your camera for you in case you want to take more pictures. Be right back." He disappeared inside.

Trisha stood, wishing her mood could swing back to high so easily. Instead, her insides seemed to throb. She felt emotionally sucker-punched, and her body was having sympathy pains.

Petey returned a minute later, handed her the camera, and headed down the steps with Bailey trailing behind him. "Come on, Mom!"

"I'm right behind you." Her spirit and body were heavy as she went down the steps. What if Vi died? What then?

"Good morning."

Trisha looked up, surprised to see Tim walking toward them. "Morning," she said. It certainly wasn't a good one. She was actually surprised to see Tim smiling so brightly, considering that his mother was in the hospital. "Why are you here?"

Tim gave a quick head shake, looking completely baffled by Trisha's question.

"Why aren't you at the hospital?" she clarified.

Tim narrowed his eyes. "What are you talking about?"

"You don't know? Jake rushed Vi to the emergency room a couple hours ago."

Tim reached into his pocket, coming out empty-handed. "I must have left my phone in my truck." He looked a shade paler. "Is she okay?"

"Jake said they're running tests," Trisha said. "There's nothing definitive yet, but it might have been another stroke. That's all I know."

Tim massaged a hand over his face, a few choice words rolling off his tongue.

Trisha glanced at Petey to make sure he couldn't hear. He was occupied with Bailey though.

Tim rubbed a hand across the back of his neck. "This is all that financial planner's fault. That caused her first stroke," Tim said, looking up at Trisha. "At least in part. After that guy, I vowed I'd research anyone my mom hired again. I would know everything about them, to make sure they had Mom's best interests at heart."

The way he was looking at her told Trisha that Tim had done just that in her case. He was a lawyer just like the rest of the Fletchers. He knew how to dig into a person's background. He'd dug into hers, and it was probable that he'd been the one to leak her past to Reva for the town's blog.

Trisha looked at Petey again. She didn't want him to witness what might be a messy conversation. Then she looked back up at Tim. "I would never hurt Vi. I'm grateful to her for all that she's done for me."

Tim looked at Trisha for a long second. "You know, I believe that might be true. But the best thing for Mom is to put that guy and everything associated with him in the past." Tim gestured back to the cottage where his truck was parked. "I'm gonna grab my phone and call Jake to check on my mom."

"Of course. You should be there." And she wanted to be as far away from him as possible.

Tim started to walk away and then turned back. "If you truly mean it when you say you'd never hurt Vi, and if you want what's best for her, then you'd walk away."

Trisha swallowed. She didn't speak. What could she say? Tim was a man who was looking out for his family. She couldn't fault him for that. She would do anything for her family as well. She'd do whatever it took to spare Petey pain. That's why they'd moved here. And it was why they might need to move again.

"Mom?" Petey asked as Tim walked away. "What did he mean that you should walk away?"

Trisha usually encouraged Petey's inquisitive nature, but right now she didn't have any answers. She lifted the camera off her chest and handed it to Petey. "Why don't you take the pictures today?" she said, distracting him instead.

Petey's face lit up. "Really?"

"Mm-hmm. I'll teach you how." Anything to change his viewpoint for the day, which hadn't been that good so far. Trisha's camera didn't have a rose-colored lens, but she could really use one right now.

* * *

Jake's senses were accosted as he stepped into his grand-mother's hospital room. The harsh smells and sounds were abrasive enough on his already fragile senses. Seeing Vi lying there was too much.

"Stop it," she said with a drooped smile, a result of her CVA—cerebrovascular accident. The doctor said that this one was bigger than the last. "I'm not dead," she said with a thick slur. "I thought I was a goner for a moment there."

"I'm glad you're still here." Jake took a seat in the chair beside her bed. "You worried me." He was still worried.

Vi reached for his hand. "Jake, it's over. I've turned the Somerset Cottages over to my kids. They're going to sell."

Jake wasn't surprised. He'd heard Tim in the waiting room talking to his parents half an hour ago. "We don't need to discuss this right now."

"We do. I want you to hear it from me. I'm sorry, Jake."

"You're moving to Florida?" he asked. "Even though that's not what you want."

"Life is full of things you don't want. You know that as well as I do. We just have to take our lemons and sweeten them up as best we can."

"No." Jake shook his head. "You don't have to do that, Grandma. I'll stay and run the property for you. I'll move into your house so you won't be alone. I'll—"

Vi rested a hand over his. "The property in the trust is a financial mess. Your parents and uncles were right about it being time to sell. It's theirs now. I'm tired, Jake. This is what's best for everyone involved."

Jake wanted to argue, but all the arguments fizzled out inside him. Along with hope. Vi couldn't manage the properties. She couldn't even manage her own health right now.

"You don't need to be caring for an old woman anyway. You need to be finding the right person to care for you. And you for her. You need to start your own family." Her words were slow, and they stumbled over each other. He understood everything she said though.

"Trisha," Vi finally said. "She's the one for you, Jake. I could tell the first time I saw you together."

"We're, uh...Trisha isn't talking to me right now."

Vi's expression was serious, but her eyes were warm. She held his gaze, silently urging him to continue.

"She found out that I kept something from her. Something kind of important."

Vi's eyes narrowed now. "That her ex-husband stole money from me and from the family's trust?" she asked in a quiet voice.

Jake blinked as his lips parted. "You know?"

"Of course I do. I learned my lesson after Peter Lewis." She spoke slowly, sucking in deep breaths between every few slurred words.

"You knew, and you hired her anyway?" Jake asked, and then nodded. "Of course you did."

"We needed each other."

Trisha needed a home. And Vi needed someone to help her save hers.

Jake sighed. "I'm not sure if she's mad at me for not telling her the truth or if she's just blaming herself now that she knows. A little of both, I guess. Anyway, I should probably cut my losses and bury that heartache in Lost Love Cemetery." Jake massaged a hand over his face. "Before it gets sold right along with everything else." He blew out a breath. "I can't believe this is happening. Just when I was ready to come home again."

Vi's hand squeezed his. Tears glimmered in her eyes as she looked up at him. "Home isn't as much a place as a feeling. You can have that anywhere."

A doctor walked in the room, knocking only as an afterthought. Vi turned to look at him, giving him her full attention. The conversation was over. For now.

"I'll be back later, Grandma." Jake had been here since he'd brought her in early this morning. He needed a little fresh air to clear his head and to think about everything Vi had told him.

They were selling the cottages.

She was moving to Florida.

Trisha was the one.

He loved Trisha. He was *in* love with her, but he didn't know how to mend things between them other than to give her time and space. There was no time or space to give right now though. He needed to find her. The least he could do was make sure she heard the latest news from him. If the cottages were being sold, Trisha would be out of a job. She'd be out of a place to live too. Her life would be upheaved, and there was nothing he could do about it.

He walked out of the hospital and toward his truck. Once he was inside, he slammed the door behind him. He was on his way to see Trisha, rehearsing every word he'd say. If he could just convince Trisha that his heart had been in the right place. Then what? It was still over, right? There was no reason for either of them to stay in Somerset Lake after Vi left and the cottages were sold. He could ask Trisha to come to Florida with him. He could follow her to wherever she went—if she'd let him.

A half hour later, he pulled behind Peony Cottage and sat in his truck for a long moment. Trisha's car was still here. That was a good sign. He'd just go up those steps, knock on her door, and they'd sit down and talk.

Jake blew out a breath, got out of his truck, and did just that. Except no one answered the door. Trisha and Petey weren't inside, even though their car was parked below the cottage.

Jake turned and looked down the lakeshore to see if he could spot them. Since he couldn't, he decided to head down the lake. He needed to clear his thoughts. He needed to find Trisha. He needed this day to never have happened.

CHAPTER TWENTY-TWO

The sun was going down. It had been one of the longest days that Trisha could remember. At least since the day the FBI had stormed her home and taken Peter away in handcuffs. That day might have been longer than this one by a few perceived hours.

Trisha had gone on today, completing the duties that her job required. Thankfully, Petey was with Della Rose and her boys again. Della Rose seemed to be filling a void for her boys with Petey, and right now Trisha was grateful that Petey had his friends to keep him occupied as well.

Trisha was finishing up one last item on the afternoon's checklist before she would return home for the evening. Mrs. McLauren was a widow who stayed in Orange Blossom Cottage. She'd called earlier because her home was being invaded by tiny ants.

"Oh, thank you so much, sweetheart," Mrs. McLauren said as Trisha prepared to leave. "You're so kind to handle this for me."

"Just doing my job," Trisha told her. Maybe she'd only been in this job for a brief time, but she loved doing it.

"You go above and beyond your duties as property manager, in my opinion. Can I get you a glass of lemonade?" Mrs. McLauren asked.

"No, thank you. Maybe next time. Let me know if the ants return, okay?" But Trisha might not be here if the older woman had problems again. "I'll see myself out."

Trisha opened the back door and stepped onto the deck. She took the steps but instead of turning toward Juniper Cottage, she headed in the other direction, stepping into the woods and following the path toward the Lost Love Cemetery.

She still had her camera around her neck, and she thought maybe she would take a few pictures since this might be the last time she saw this place. Depending on who purchased the property, this might become collateral damage.

The thought of that broke Trisha's heart as she stepped past the sign that read: FOR ROMANTICS ONLY. CYNICS TURN BACK.

Trisha was leaning toward the latter these days, but she continued forward anyway until she reached the clearing in the woods. She stood for a moment and looked at the place. Then she lifted her camera to her eyes and snapped a few pictures. There was something special about this makeshift memorial for the brokenhearted.

She started moving again and opened the gate. As she walked inside, she stayed between the narrow rows, stopping periodically to take a few pictures.

A plastic rose—*click*.

A WORLD'S BEST HUSBAND coffee mug—*click*. She wondered what the story behind that mug was. Maybe it belonged to Della Rose's soon-to-be ex.

Trisha found an empty space in the Lost Love Cemetery and stared down at it for a heartbeat. This place was for lost love. She was in love with Jake, and she'd lost him.

Squatting over the empty spot, she wondered what she could

leave here to symbolize their relationship. She reached into her pockets, finding them empty. She lifted the flap of the bag she wore draped across her body and went through the contents. There was only one item that would do. The photography book he'd given her at Sunset Over Somerset on Friday night.

She didn't want to part with it, but she guessed that was the point. It was hard to let go of something, someone, you cared about so deeply. But it was necessary in order to move on.

Trisha pulled the book out and laid it down on the empty spot. She was more of a learn-by-experience than a learn-by-studying kind of girl anyway. And now that she and Jake were parting ways—it was inevitable—she wouldn't be able to read this manual anyway. It would only remind her of him.

She blew out a breath and released the book to the ground. It wasn't weatherproof. Rain and time, especially being near the lake air, would wear on this book. Trisha looked around at the other items, some of which were rusting and breaking down. If whoever purchased this property wasn't from Somerset Lake, they might just see this place as a small junkyard.

Trisha stood and turned to leave, stopping short at the sound of something approaching through the woods. She heard sticks break beneath something heavy. *A bear?* Her heart stopped for just a moment as Jake came into view. She'd rather confront a bear right now.

She swiped at a lock of hair as butterflies fluttered in her belly. Didn't they know the romance was over? "Hi."

"Hey." He continued walking toward her, stopping just shy of the gate. His gaze fell on the book at her feet for a moment. Then he looked back up and met her gaze. Her heart sped up. Leaving the book on the ground here in the Lost Love Cemetery said more than she'd intended to in this moment.

It said that she loved him. And it said that she was saying goodbye.

Jake's gaze was serious. "You were supposed to read that."

She folded her arms, applying pressure to her achy heart. "I'm going to be busy moving and finding a new job. I'm guessing that's what you're going to tell me."

He gave her a steady look. "You wouldn't know because you haven't answered your phone to talk to me."

Even so, Jake had still texted Trisha reports on Vi throughout the day. She knew the rest. Selling the cottages was inevitable. Firing her and kicking her and Petey out of their home was too.

Jake opened the gate and stepped inside, walking inside the rows of lost things and lost loves. When he made his way to her, he bent and picked up the book. He held it out to her. "This doesn't belong here."

She swallowed painfully, trying not to cry. "It does. This thing between you and me..." She shook her head as a tear slid down her cheek. "You and I can't do this anymore."

"This?"

She narrowed her eyes at him. "We can't date. Can't kiss. Can't..."

He glanced down at the book and back up to her. "Be in love?"

Everything froze inside her. She couldn't profess love for him when they were breaking up. And that's what they were doing.

She took the book from his hands. "You're right. I can't leave this here. This place is only for lost love. We were never..."

Jake flinched subtly.

Trisha tucked the book back into her bag and took a breath. She didn't meet his gaze again. It hurt too much to look into those sky-blue eyes. "Anyway, I'll start packing my stuff. We can't afford to live in Juniper Cottage if I'm not working as the property manager."

Jake cleared his throat. "I'd like to tell you that you're wrong,

268 *Annie Rains*

but it's true. My parents and uncles are selling the cottages. And Vi is going to Florida once she's healthy enough for travel. But you never know. Maybe whoever buys the property will keep them as rentals and keep you employed here."

Trisha shook her head. "I've been thinking. If I had known the truth about Peter and his connection to Vi, I never would have moved me and Petey here. Some part of me always knew that this deal was too good to be true." She dared to meet his gaze again. "All of it."

"Don't say that," he said quietly.

She swallowed past a fresh surge of pain. "So I think Petey and I are going to return to Sweetwater Springs. At this point, I can't stand the thought of starting over again somewhere new. And there's no guarantee that my ex-husband doesn't have a connection to any new place we go anyway." Tears burned in her eyes. The sudden hopelessness she felt was like a black hole in the center of her chest. This wasn't what she wanted, but she didn't feel like there was another choice.

"What about us?" Jake asked.

Trisha stiffened, willing her emotions at bay. "Like I said, none of this should have ever happened. It was always too good to be true."

"That's not the way I see it." Jake reached out for her.

Trisha stepped back, letting his arm drop into empty air. "If you understood what a leap of faith it was for me to trust you, you wouldn't have kept me in the dark." Jake started to talk, but she held up a hand to stop him. "I know you were just doing what you thought was best for me and Petey. But that's what my ex said too. His crimes were all because he wanted to provide a good life for us. He said it was all for us."

"Trisha, listen to yourself. I didn't commit any crime." Jake shook his head.

"No, but you did break my trust. And my heart." Her voice

cracked. *Don't cry, don't cry, don't cry.* "And I don't know how to come back from that. I don't know how to forgive you or myself." Tears thickened in her eyes until all she saw was a blurry image of the man she'd accidentally kissed... and fallen in love with.

She sniffled and fought to maintain her composure. If she melted down, Jake would wrap his arms around her. And if he did, she didn't think she had the willpower to push him away. In fact, she was pretty sure she didn't. "Jake, I'm going home. To Sweetwater Springs."

He shook his head. "Trisha, you've made a home here. You can stay. We can figure this out."

"Haven't you been listening? There is no *we*," she said, her voice cracking. "There never was." Then she stepped past him and kept walking. She didn't look back.

* * *

Jake didn't move or breathe as he watched Trisha walk away. His chest hurt as he stood in this symbolic place.

He looked down at his feet where Trisha was going to leave the photography book he'd given her. She'd taken it back and told him it was never love. But it was for him. He had been falling in love with Trisha since the moment he met her. He was in love with her at this very moment, and it wasn't going to go away.

He sat down before his knees gave out. Then he pulled the photograph that Trisha had given him from his pocket. It was the selfie of them together. He'd been carrying it around for some silly reason like, oh, say, he was in love with her. Madly, deeply, unregrettably in love.

He'd trade this photograph in his hand to have that moment back. But time couldn't be reversed. He'd learned that lesson with Rachel. Time only marched forward, leaving loss and regret in its wake.

Jake laid the picture down on the open row in Lost Love Cemetery. Then he stood and headed back to Peony Cottage. He climbed the steps, forcing himself not to look over at Juniper Cottage, where he might see Trisha.

The dream of saving Somerset Cottages was over. The dream of staying and having something real—love—was over too. Now it was time to move on.

* * *

Jake's body felt like he had been in a battle when he woke up the next morning. His chest hurt. Everything hurt. He reached for his cell phone to see if he'd gotten any calls or texts during the night.

He blinked a text message from his mom into focus.

> Vi is doing well. She's seeing speech therapy this morn-
> ing. The doctor thinks she'll be okay for discharge in
> two days.

Two days. In two days, his parents would drive to Florida with Vi. His uncle Tim would go as well. And a FOR SALE sign would likely be at the entrance to the Somerset Rental Cottages.

Jake double-checked to see if there were any more missed messages. Maybe one from Trisha? Nothing.

He stood and shuffled down the hall to make coffee. When it was prepared, he carried it out onto the deck and drank it while he watched the early morning lake activity. His gaze fell on his plane bobbing beyond the pier, calling for him the way it often did.

He finished his coffee and dressed, and then he and Bailey headed in that direction. Flying had always been the solution to every problem since he was fifteen. He cranked the engine, let the propeller spin for several minutes, and then took off, skimming along the water until he propelled the plane into the sky.

This was his grandfather's favorite pastime. His grandfather had been a lawyer, too, but he'd quit practicing in his forties. When Jake asked Gramps later why he'd quit, his grandfather had taken his time in answering. "Because I realized just how short life can be. Why waste your time doing something you don't love?"

So his grandfather had spent the rest of his life running the Somerset Rentals with Vi and flying his plane. They didn't have a lot, but it was enough, and they were happy.

Jake looked down at the lake below, passing over the cottages, the woods beyond, and circling around to the other side of the lake. He passed over Hannigan Street and The Village, thinking about life, love, and loss.

"I don't want to leave this place," he whispered under his breath. The first time he said it, it still felt like he was saying goodbye. He said it again, mumbling the words like a prayer. "I don't want to leave this place." This time it felt like he was second-guessing any plans to go to Florida.

He continued to fly, the engine's steady hum soothing him.

"I don't want to leave this place." The third time he said it, it felt like a realization. A decision. A resolution. Why go somewhere he didn't want to be? Why do something he didn't want to do?

Jake glanced over at Bailey. "We're not leaving," he said without a shred of doubt about what he planned to do. As he flew his plane back to the pier, his thoughts felt clearer than ever before. And he knew exactly what he needed to do to fix things. He just hoped it wasn't already too late.

* * *

The next afternoon, Trisha turned to watch a vehicle pull in behind Juniper Cottage. She didn't recognize the large SUV. It wasn't Tim's. Maybe it was more of Jake's family arriving to see Vi. That thought made Trisha feel nauseous. Vi was still in the hospital. Some part of Trisha felt guilty for not going to visit her yet.

Trisha watched the SUV park, and four women stepped out.

Lucy, Moira, Tess, and Della Rose were standing outside her house, looking up at her on the deck.

Della Rose waved first. Then the four friends headed up the steps.

"What are you doing here?" Trisha asked, sniffling and barely able to hold back her tears. This wasn't a good time for a book club visit. She needed to be packing and planning how to get over the next speed bump in her life.

There was only one chair on the deck beside Trisha. Della Rose took it. The three other women leaned against the deck railing, sunglasses shading their eyes. Trisha wished she had a pair of glasses to cover hers right now, too, because her mascara—the one makeup item she never skipped—was about to become a runny mess.

"We heard about Vi," Lucy said. "Reva Dawson put it in her blog for the town."

Trisha shook her head. "Of course she did. So if you know about Vi, why are you here with me instead of at the hospital with Vi?" Trisha asked. "Or with Jake. I think that's where he is." She'd seen him leave in his truck early this morning.

"Because Jake told us you were here," Lucy said. "And as your friends, we felt like we needed to come make sure you were all right."

Trisha's instinct was to tell them she was fine. Her instinct was to smile and push them away. "Why wouldn't I be okay? I'm not the one who's in the hospital."

"We know your ex turned out to be Vi's financial planner," Della Rose said gently. "Jake told us, but only because he's concerned about you."

"Jake confirmed that fact for me the other night when I got back from book club. He already knew." Tears spilled off Trisha's cheeks now. She couldn't seem to stop crying lately. "I don't know why I feel so betrayed by that but I do. I just...I thought Petey and I had a second chance at happiness here. If I had just..." Trisha tried to pull in a deep breath, but she couldn't seem to get one. "If I had known the truth before..." She trailed off, unsure of what she was about to say. She was unsure of everything. Her thoughts and emotions were a jumbled mess.

"Before what?" Lucy asked.

Trisha blinked up at her friend. "Before I got attached to this town. Before I got attached to you guys."

"And to him too," Lucy said.

Trisha took a steadying breath. What was the point of hiding the truth? It always came out anyway. "Yeah. I didn't mean for that to happen. I was ready to find a new home for me and Petey. But I was never looking for anything romantic again. That was the furthest thing from my mind."

"That's usually when it happens," Tess said. "When you least expect it."

Trisha laughed sadly. "It's absurd to think I'm in love after just a few weeks, right? I mean, we just met, and I barely know him. We've gone on a few dates and kissed a few times, but nothing more than that." And why was she telling these women all this information?

She looked between them, her breaths shallow, her heart breaking. It didn't matter that they'd only just gotten to know each other. It didn't matter that she didn't know everything there was to know about the women in front of her. These ladies were friends. And they were here for her right now when she needed them.

"Love is a heart-thing. Calculations and logistics are a mind-thing." Tess shrugged.

"All I know," Lucy added, "is that Jake left town when he was eighteen, and we've barely seen him since. Then he came back this summer, and he's different. Because of you. That's what love does. It changes people. I see it all the time with my patients. Yeah, it's usually the love between a parent and a child, but sometimes it's between the parents too. When you see it, it's an unmistakable thing."

Trisha glanced behind her to check on Petey inside. He was sitting at the kitchen island still reading the book that Jake had given him. "Well, it doesn't matter. I will undoubtedly lose my job and my home. Petey and I will probably be leaving town soon."

"What?" Moira asked. "You just got here."

"No job and no home equals no choice." Trisha sniffled.

Tess shook her head. "That would just be your excuse to run. Because you're scared and you came here to hide," she said pointedly.

Trisha's lips parted as her gaze darted from Tess to a nodding Lucy, Moira, and Della Rose. She thought these women were here to support her, but Tess's words felt like an attack.

"It's true. You left Sweetwater Springs so that you could come here and be free from your past," Lucy agreed. "But pasts follow you wherever you go. Talking from experience."

"So you might as well stay," Moira said.

"You can live with me," Della Rose offered. "I just kicked my husband out, so there's plenty of room for you. The twins and Petey can be like brothers."

"Or you can stay with me," Lucy said. "I'm in my parents' huge house in The Village all by myself. Why do I need a house that big for just one person?"

"See? You'd be helping Lucy out," Moira agreed. "She's already started talking to herself."

Lucy elbowed her friend in the side.

"And," Tess said, "you can work at the bookstore with me. I need some part-time help. It doesn't pay much, but if you don't have a mortgage or rent, then it would be enough to live on."

Trisha was on the verge of dissolving into the best kind of ugly cry. "Why would you all go out of your way to help me?" She really shouldn't be surprised. Everyone had done the same when they'd realized she'd needed a hand renovating the rental cottages.

Della Rose leaned in and gave her a tight hug. "Oh, sweetie, I think I'm talking for everyone when I say we see ourselves in you. All of us have been where you are. Some of us are still there. We women need to stick together."

Tess stepped toward them and wrapped her arms around Trisha from the other side. Then Moira and Lucy joined the group hug, too, smothering Trisha until she couldn't breathe, but she didn't care.

"So it's final," Lucy said after they'd all pulled away. They all had tears on their cheeks, leaving mascara streaks on their faces. "No matter what happens with these cottages and Jake, you're staying. Somerset Lake is your home now, and we're your friends, which is thicker than family in some cases."

Trisha's nose was running right along with her eyes. All she ever wanted was a home and family and good friends. A place to belong. She had that here. "Okay. I'll stay."

CHAPTER TWENTY-THREE

Jake had spent the last three and a half hours making life-changing decisions.

First, he had called his parents and asked what the fair market value for the cottages was and what the family planned to sell them for. Then he'd asked them to sell the family's rental properties directly to him. He had a nice-sized nest egg that he'd planned to use to buy a home and settle down in Florida. He planned to use that money as a down payment and get a real estate loan for the rest.

"Why on earth would you want to take over those cottages when you can be in Florida with us?" his mom asked. "Once upon a time, you couldn't wait to leave this lake."

"Yeah, but now I can't wait to stay." Jake meant every word. He would spend his last dime trying to make this new dream of his come true. It was that important to him.

"Jake, Vi has already agreed to move to Florida. She'll live with Aunt Dawn and Uncle Tim. It'll be good for her."

"Okay," Jake said. He wasn't sure that was true, but it

didn't change his mind. His mind was made up, and he wasn't changing it.

"Are you sure you're doing this for the right reasons?" his mom finally asked.

"I am. Somerset Lake is my home. My heart is here. There's no better reason that I can see. If you say no to my request, I can wait for you to put the property on the market. I'll make an offer on day one."

His mom hesitated on the other end of the line. "All right. Let me talk to the rest of the family. I'll call you back."

"Thanks, Mom. I love you."

She hesitated again, and he wondered if she was going to make another argument. "When you were a boy, Somerset Lake was a part of you. Calling you in from the lake was a feat every night. Then you started flying with your grandfather, and, I don't know, you were such a free spirit. What happened to Rachel...I know that took some of that spirit away. Then you lost your grandfather here. But it feels like maybe you've gotten that spirit back this summer. Being on the lake has been good for you."

Jake pressed his head into the back of his driver's seat. "Yeah." He could only manage one word. His emotions were raw and frayed. The last couple days had wrecked him, but sometimes that's what it took to change directions and mind-sets.

"As soon as I discuss your plans with the others, I'll call you. I'm proud of you, son."

"Thank you, Mom. That means a lot."

After they'd disconnected the call, Jake contacted a few of his guy friends. In exchange for hamburgers, hot dogs, and unlimited soda, he'd gotten Gil and another high school friend named Luis to agree to come over this weekend and help him paint the exteriors of the cottages. The insides were done. The cottage exteriors were all that was left to do. And since he was going to be the new owner, he wanted them to look good.

Finally, there was only one thing left on his agenda. He pulled onto Lakeshore Drive, following the gravel path up to Juniper and Peony Cottages.

Bailey greeted him at his truck door. Jake didn't go to his place. Instead, he climbed the steps to Juniper Cottage, feeling energized and hopeful. Every sense was heightened as he knocked on Trisha's door. He had no idea what he'd say when he saw her. *I'm sorry? Forgive me? I love you? Spend your life with me?*

He waited. There was no sign of life inside. Now he realized that Trisha's blue sedan wasn't parked behind the house. What if she'd already left? What if she'd already packed up her belongings and moved away?

* * *

Darkness was falling, but the moon was coming up and showering light over the lake. Trisha followed the gravel path toward the tiny blue cottage where she'd lived for the last two months. She would miss this place, but change seemed to be the only constant in life.

"Why are you dragging your feet like that?" Trisha asked as she followed Petey up the steps.

"Because I'm tired. You dragged me all over town today, Mom."

For Petey to say he was tired meant she really had worn him out today. "Sorry." She reached forward and ruffled his hair. "But we had important things to do."

He glanced back over his shoulder. "I like living here."

"We've already talked about that. Discussion over." They reached the deck landing, and Petey turned back to Trisha with his lower lip turned slightly down. "Why don't you take a bath?" she suggested. "I'll make dinner, and we'll relax in front of the TV for the rest of the night."

Excitement flickered in Petey's expression. "Can Jake come over too?"

Trisha hadn't yet gotten around to telling him that she and Jake weren't hanging out anymore. When he'd asked questions, she'd redirected and ignored. Eventually she'd tell him, but first she wanted to find them a new place to stay in Somerset Lake and a new job to keep them afloat. "Probably not. He's very busy making sure Vi is okay."

Petey nodded. "We need to visit Vi soon."

"We can do that tomorrow," Trisha promised. She wanted to give Vi time with her family, and she was worried that she'd just be a painful reminder of Peter Lewis and all that Vi had lost partnering with him. And then partnering with Trisha too. "Get yourself ready for bed," Trisha said.

"Okay, Mom." Petey walked inside, leaving her on the deck. She turned toward the water. She liked living here too. She loved the calming view of the lake. Loved the quaint little cottage. Loved the work she'd done here on this property. But she would love whatever came next too. Hopefully.

A dog barked, and Trisha redirected her gaze to Bailey on the ground below. And Jake. She'd tried her best to ignore him since they'd broken up in Lost Love Cemetery. Hopefully, he would just wave and keep walking.

Keep walking, keep walking, keep walking.

Instead, he climbed the steps with Bailey at his heels. "Hey," he said when he reached the top.

"Hi. How's Vi?" she asked. She wanted to know, yes, but it was also the only safe subject between them.

"Going home tomorrow."

Vi wasn't going home though. Not really. Home was in the house next door. Vi was going to Florida with the rest of the Fletchers. "That's great."

"It is. I was worried that you'd skipped town," he said. "I've been looking for you this afternoon."

"Oh?" She fidgeted with her hands. "I was actually looking for a place to stay. Here in Somerset Lake."

"You're staying?" Jake's face lit up.

"Yeah. Petey has friends here, and so do I." She smoothed her hair out of her eyes as the wind played around her, coming off the lake. "I found a few promising places. I applied for a couple jobs too."

"I see." Jake shifted back and forth on his feet. "Well, if you haven't committed to anything just yet, I think I know the perfect place for you to live. The perfect job too."

She narrowed her eyes. "Oh? Where?"

"Here."

Trisha shook her head. "Jake, we've already discussed this. The new owner might not even want to have a property manager right away. At least not until these cottages are out of the red."

"I have it on good authority that he does."

Trisha's lips parted. "The cottages have already sold?" Something ached deep inside her chest. She'd known this would happen, but it was so soon.

"There's a buyer. And he wants a property manager. He wants you to stay," Jake said.

Trisha didn't want to get her hopes up. "How do you know that?"

He shoved his fingers in his pockets the way he always did. "Because it's me."

Trisha pulled her head back slightly. "What are you talking about?"

"I spoke to my family today. I'm taking out a loan and paying fair market price for the Somerset Rental Cottages."

"You can't..." She shook her head. "How can you afford that, Jake?" It would cost a small fortune to buy the entire property. And he didn't have that kind of money, as far as she knew.

"I made a few sacrifices. I used pretty much every cent in my nest egg for settling down in Florida." He shook his head, a lazy smile crossing his lips. "But I guess it's not a sacrifice if you do it for love. This place is my home. I don't want to lose it." His gaze was heavy on her. "I don't want to lose you."

"Jake..."

He held up a hand. "Just hear me out. I'm glad you're sticking around so I can make my best effort to show you that I'm a man you can trust. I'm a man who will always be there for you. Who will always love you, whether you want to love me back or not.

"I've loved and lost before," he continued. "I thought loving someone again would hurt too much, but the truth is, it's not loving that hurts. It's losing the one you love." He ran a hand through his hair. "I'm not sure if any of that made a lick of sense."

Her heart was beating so hard she could barely breathe. "It made perfect sense actually."

Jake smiled back at her. Then he reached into his pocket and pulled out the selfie of her and him, handing it over. "I was gonna leave this in the Lost Love Cemetery. I did actually. But I took it back because I'm not ready to lose you. I don't want to say goodbye."

She blinked away tears, trying to look at him more clearly. The tears kept springing up though. "What if I hadn't told you I was staying, Jake? What if I had decided to leave town?"

"Then I would have begged you to change your mind. I would have traveled to wherever you were every chance I got to convince you to come home."

The h-word made tears spill onto her cheeks. "I guess that's the nice thing about being a pilot. You can go wherever you want whenever you want." She laughed quietly, pressing a hand to her chest, trying to steady her heartbeat so she could think clearly.

"This isn't just my home, Trisha. It's yours and Petey's too."

Trisha's ex would have taken someone's last dime or their last bite to eat. But Jake had given up something special. He was selfless and true.

He lifted a hand and used the pad of his thumb to wipe away one of her tears. "So I have a question for you."

"The answer is yes," she said, her words coming out rushed and eager.

"You haven't even heard what I'm asking yet." Jake grinned.

"You want me to stay and be your property manager again?" she asked. "Now that you're the sole owner."

Jake shook his head. "No."

"Oh." Trisha's chest deflated with that one word. She felt foolish, too, but he'd already said that the new owner—him—wanted her to stay and manage the cottages.

Jake reached for her hands and held them in his. "I want you to stay and be my partner in this business."

Trisha's lips parted. "What?"

"I want you to be my partner in life too," he said.

She sucked in a shocked breath.

Jake looked out at the lake for a moment and then back at her. He looked resolute, peaceful. "I know it's soon. This isn't a proposal. Not yet." He gave her a meaningful look. "But life can be short, and even if we live to be one hundred years old, that wouldn't be enough time together. Why waste another moment searching when I've already found what I'm looking for? It's you. It's Petey. It's a family and this home."

Trisha looked at the man in front of her. She loved him more than she'd even known she could. There'd always been a small feeling of emptiness in her chest, as if something was missing. He'd filled that emptiness, past overflowing. When she was with him, she felt complete and loved. She felt like there was no other place she was meant to be than beside him.

Jake squeezed her hand. "What do you say?"

"You didn't actually ask me a question yet."

"I see. Well, it's more of a request really. I want you to stay. Here. With me."

"Yes," she said, blinking past the blur of tears in her eyes. She laughed. "I say yes to all of those things. I want it all. With you."

Jake wrapped his arms around her, kissing her until her knees felt like they might buckle. Inside she was soaring though, high above the clouds where he'd taken her before. And she never wanted to come down.

Jake pulled away, just enough to look at her again. "I already have it all, as long as I have you."

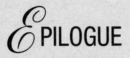PILOGUE

*I*t was a perfect fall day. The air was cool and thick with all the things that made this time of year Trisha's favorite.

"Mom?"

Trisha glanced over at Petey, who was walking alongside her up the lakeshore on their way back home to Juniper Cottage. All but one of the cottages were rented now, which kept Trisha busy, but she didn't mind. She looked over at her son. "Yes?"

"Can I go ahead of you? You're walking so slow," he complained, his tone halfway teasing.

She laughed and made a shooing gesture. "Go." It was Friday afternoon, and Petey had big plans for the night. School had started last month, and he'd been making good grades and lots of new friends. Jake had spent most of his week at his new law office in Magnolia Falls. And Trisha had managed things here at the rental cottages. It'd been an uneventful week, but perfect nonetheless.

Trisha watched him race Bailey, leaving footprints in their wake. She continued at her slow, steady pace until she was standing in front of Vi's cottage. Then she climbed the steps until she was on the deck. "Mind if I join you?"

Vi looked up from her outdoor rocking chair. "Of course not."

Trisha walked over and sat in the neighboring rocker, soaking in the view for a long moment. "I thought I heard you talking to someone when I was coming up?"

"Oh yes. Just my late husband." Vi chuckled to herself. Her gaze slid to give Trisha a look. "And, no, I'm not crazy."

Trisha held up her hands. "I don't think you are. No need to explain."

Trisha visited Vi a couple times a day. For the moment, Vi was independent. Home health workers came into her home to provide speech, physical, and occupational therapy. Jake had put in a few safety features and an emergency call button that Vi could quickly access too.

And when the time came, *if* the time came, they would move into Vi's house with her. It was far bigger than any of the cottages on the property. "And what did your late husband have to say?" Trisha asked.

One corner of Vi's mouth drooped as she smiled. "I do all the talking. He just listens. That's the way it always was when he was alive too."

Trisha reached over and rested her hand over Vi's as it draped across the rocker's arm. "You okay? You need anything?"

"I'm fine, dear. All I need is this chair and this view. I'm glad to have you, Petey, and Jake next door. My heart is full."

"Mine too," Trisha said, meaning it.

They both looked out onto the water again for a long time. Then a buzzing sound hummed softly in the distance, growing steadily louder before the plane came into view. Trisha's pulse jumped.

"Jake needs the open sky almost as much as he needs you."

Vi winked. Then she patted her other hand over Trisha's. "Go on. I'm fine."

"Okay. I'll be back in the morning though. Or sooner if you need me. I can stay over."

"No need to do that. Join me for coffee tomorrow?" she asked.

"You got it." And that first cup would happen a lot later now that Mr. S slept on the shore with his clothes on. Trisha wondered if he would've done that anyway come winter, but she was grateful she didn't have to wait to find out.

She stood and headed down the steps, her pace quickening as the plane skimmed over the lake and came to a stop at the end of the pier. Jake stepped out with the sun at his back. Her heart filled with so much love at the sight of him. "How'd it go up there?" Trisha asked as she drew closer, talking about the plane.

"Amazing." He took long strides up the pier until his arms were wrapped around her.

"We have an audience. Your grandmother is watching," Trisha warned.

"I'm not concerned about that. Vi isn't your boss anymore, remember?" Jake dipped and kissed Trisha's lips. "Where's Petey?" he asked once they'd pulled away.

"Packing. He's so excited about this camping trip you guys have planned for tonight."

"Me too." Jake gazed into her eyes. "I just wish you were coming."

Trisha shook her head. She was staying to be near Vi just in case. "It's a boys' trip. I wouldn't belong."

Jake kissed her again. "With me is exactly where you *always* belong. No matter what."

She tilted her head. "We can have our private trip for two next weekend. Just you and me." Petey was staying with his aunt Sophie and uncle Chase next weekend. They were taking him to see his dad in prison. And the book club ladies had offered to take turns checking on Vi while Jake and Trisha went off together.

"I'm looking forward to having you all to myself for a couple of days," Jake said.

"You still haven't told me where we're going."

His blue eyes twinkled in the morning light. "We have to fly to get there."

"I suspected as much." Trisha swatted a playful hand to his chest.

"Do you trust me?" he asked.

Trisha's head tipped back, her eyes searching his as she grinned. "Yes, but I still want to know. How else can I pack? A woman needs to be dressed in the right clothing," she added.

Jake held her close. "All right. I'll tell you. It's off-season in the Outer Banks. I was thinking we'd fly down and spend some time collecting shells and making memories."

"The ocean." Trisha expelled a contented sigh. "That sounds wonderful."

"My thoughts exactly. And it'll be the perfect place to ask you a very important question." His gaze held hers, the blue of his eyes bluer than the sky or lake backdrop.

Trisha's lips parted. She'd been suspecting that he was planning to propose for a while now. He'd been dropping hints and testing the proverbial waters. "My answer is yes."

"You don't even know what the question is yet." A corner of his mouth quirked. "You'll have to wait until next weekend. At the coast."

Trisha loved the western side of North Carolina where the mountains bordered the state. She'd rarely been on the eastern side where the land was flatter and the Atlantic Ocean roared. That excited her, but the reason she suspected that Jake was taking her there was even more appealing.

Trisha lifted on her toes and kissed his lips softly. "Yes," she said again, her gaze fluttering up to meet his. "It doesn't matter what the question is. I trust you, Jake Fletcher, with all my heart and soul. My answer is always yes."

Jake grinned. "Good to know. First, I need to ask permission from the other man in your life." They shared a look. Trisha didn't have a father for Jake to ask. But she did have a son.

"Jake! Jake!" Petey came running down the pier, an overnight bag flopping off his back and Bailey at his side. "Is it time yet? I'm so excited!"

Jake chuckled as he stepped away from Trisha. "Me too, buddy. We are going to have the best time ever."

Trisha's heart melted as she watched her son and the man she loved together. How had her life gone from being so messed up to becoming a beautiful, overflowing, happy mess in such short order? How had she gotten so lucky?

"Hug your mom and hop in the plane, Copilot," Jake told him.

Petey rushed Trisha's waist, his arms squeezing her until a laugh bubbled out of her. Then he hurried to the plane with Bailey hopping up onto the seat ahead of him.

Jake turned back to Trisha. He kissed her cheek and stared at her a long moment. "We'll be home tomorrow."

"I'll be home waiting for you."

A warmth radiated from her chest as she watched Jake turn and climb into the plane with her son. She continued to stand there as the plane skimmed the water and finally took off. They were going camping.

Jake was going to ask Petey for permission to marry her. They were all going to live happily ever after. The three of them here on Somerset Lake, where they belonged.

If you've enjoyed
The Summer Cottage,
please turn the page for a
sneak peek at the next book in
Annie Rains's series,
The Christmas Village.

FOREVER

CHAPTER ONE

A noise woke Lucy Hannigan. She peered into the darkness of her bedroom, heart thumping beneath her heavy quilt, and waited to hear it again.

Or hopefully *not* hear it again.

Another loud bang had her body shooting upright in bed. It sounded like something had been knocked over outside. Was someone at her back door?

Lucy grabbed her iPhone on the bedside table and looked at the time. Five a.m. wasn't the hour for friendly visitors. But if this were just a friendly guest, then whoever was making the ruckus would ring the doorbell. From the back side of the house, someone would need to open Lucy's fence, which was secured by a lock.

Lucy eyed her French bulldog Bella, who was snoring soundly in the corner of the room. "Some guard dog you are," she whispered, standing on shaky legs, her ears tuned to anything that went bump in the night—*er*, early morning.

Lucy had been out late, helping to deliver a baby at Maria

Fernandez's house. Being a midwife, she was used to keeping late hours, but she'd hoped to sleep in this morning. Now she was wide awake with adrenaline pumping through her veins.

Something scraped against Lucy's back porch. She stood frozen for a moment. This time, Bella opened her eyes and lifted her head.

"Bella, bark," Lucy whisper-shouted. Perhaps the sound of a ferocious canine would frighten the intruder away. "Bark!"

Lucy had inherited her mom's old French bulldog along with this excessively large home in The Village, the oldest neighborhood in Somerset Lake, North Carolina. The house had belonged in her family for generations along with half the businesses in town. Along the way, families had grown smaller, businesses had been sold off, and all that was left in the Hannigan family now was Lucy and this pink house.

"Bella, bark!" she ordered again.

Instead, Bella lowered her head, closed her eyes, and huffed softly. Once upon a time, Bella had been trained to be a watch dog. Now she could barely hear or see. She could still catch a scent though. That wasn't helpful at this moment.

Lucy stepped out of her bedroom. It was the only one downstairs. She did everything on the first floor because Bella couldn't climb the stairs anymore. For the most part, Lucy just pretended that the second level of the house didn't exist. This house was big enough for two large families to live comfortably. It felt a bit wasteful to have so much unused space.

She shuffled quietly down the hall in socked feet, her heart pumping as she clutched her cell phone in her hand.

What did she really think she was going to do if she ran into a burglar? Invite him in for coffee?

The noise happened again. Lucy gasped. Then she simultaneously pressed the POWER button and the volume button on her iPhone four times in quick succession—the shortcut to dial nine-one-one. The phone immediately began to sound an alarm that punctured the darkness. This time, Bella scurried out of the bedroom with a few loud barks.

Lucy held the phone to her ear, her hand shaking so hard she could barely keep from dropping it.

"Nine-one-one, what's your emergency?" a familiar woman's voice asked.

"Moira?" Lucy whispered. Moira was one of Lucy's best friends, and she worked as an emergency services dispatcher in town.

"Lucy?" Moira asked. "Why are you calling me here? This line is for emergencies only."

Lucy leaned against the wall in the hallway, one hand pressed to her chest. Her heartbeat forcefully thumped the pads of her fingers. "This *is* an emergency. I think someone is breaking into my home. There are noises on the back porch. Can you send a deputy? Or the whole Sheriff's department?"

Moira asked a few more questions and kept Lucy on the line. She was so professional that Lucy almost forgot that the woman helping was her sarcastic best friend. Minutes felt like hours and then someone rang her front doorbell.

Bella ran ahead of Lucy, stopping behind the front door and barking in a deep, misleading baritone.

Lucy followed and went up on her tiptoes to look out the peephole. A Somerset Lake Sheriff's deputy was standing on her porch. She wobbled on her toes until she could also see the man's face. Black hair, dark eyes.

"Is that a deputy?" Moira asked, her tone continuing to exude calm professionalism.

"Yes." Lucy returned to flat feet. Her heart was racing for a whole other reason now.

"So you're safe to disconnect this call?" Moira asked.

"Yes. Thank you. We'll have coffee later?" Lucy asked.

Moira audibly sighed. "These calls are recorded, Luce. Just text my cell."

"Right." Lucy tapped END on her phone's screen, reached for the door knob, but hesitated. Of all the deputies at the Somerset Lake Sheriff's Department, why was Miles Bruno the one who responded to the call?

The doorbell chimed again.

This time, Lucy sucked in a breath and turned the knob. She opened the door and peered back at Miles, almost forgetting that she was terrified of whatever was making the noises on her back porch. This man still had a hold over her, even twelve years after he'd broken off their brief engagement.

"What's going on?" he asked, his tone just as professional as Moira's had been.

Lucy pointed in the opposite direction. "The back porch. There's a noise." She hugged her arms around her chest, realizing that she was wearing a too-thin cotton pajama top and pants. It was late November, and the chilly air zipped right past Miles, through her door, and penetrated her clothing.

Another noise had Lucy whirling in the direction of her kitchen which led to the back door. "Did you hear that?" she asked breathlessly.

Without answering, he stepped over the threshold and walked past her.

What kind of egotistical burglar continued to break in once a sheriff's car had pulled into the driveway?

Lucy locked the front door behind Miles, just in case the burglar decided to run around to the other side of the house. She heard Miles open the back door and braced herself for a fight. Good guy versus the bad one. What if the bad guy won? What if he had a weapon?

I should hide.

Lucy looked around the living room, which still housed her

parents' furniture. Everything she owned had belonged to her mom. Her father had passed away when she was in college. One morning, he'd had a heart attack in his sleep and never woke up. Lucy had been devastated at the time, but losing her mom last year hurt even more.

Lucy hurried over to the couch and squatted down, sandwiching herself between it and the end table. She'd always been horrible at Hide and Seek as a child. Anyone with two good eyes would find her, especially since her breathing was so shallow that her lungs were making a scraping sound. She momentarily tried to stop breathing, but that only resulted in an audible gasp a minute later and more shallow breaths.

She listened for what felt like an eternity. Then she heard heavy footsteps approaching.

Please be Miles. Please be Miles.

She squeezed her eyes shut and then jumped as Miles called her name.

"Lucy? I've dealt with your burglar. It's safe to come out now."

The breath whooshed out of her lungs. The good guy had won. Miles had always been one of the good guys, even when her broken heart had told her he was one of the bad.

* * *

As soon as Miles heard the address, he'd known whose house he was in route to. Lucy Hannigan had lived in the pink house on Christmas Lane since she was a kid. And since they were teenagers all tangled up in the thrill of first love.

Lucy peered up at him from her hiding place behind the couch.

"There was never a burglar," he said. "But if there was, that would be an awful hiding spot."

Lucy frowned up at him. "Well, I didn't have a lot of time to find a better one."

He chuckled and offered his hand to help her stand.

She hesitated, and he knew she was just stubborn enough not to take it. Lucy was independent—that's something he'd always admired about her. All the women in his life had that in common. His mom, his sister Ava. His Aunt Ruth. Not that Lucy was a woman in Miles's life anymore. She was more of a friend who kept him at an arm's length. He couldn't say he blamed her.

Lucy surprised him by extending her arm and slipping her hand in his, palm to palm. He tugged gently, and she came up fast and close, her green eyes narrowing in. Her soft pink lips puckered and made a small "o" of surprise. "Thank you," she said a little breathlessly—probably because she was still calming down from the scare.

"You're welcome." He didn't release her hand immediately. She didn't let go either. Instead they looked at each other for a long moment. Once upon a time, Miles could swear he saw forever in those eyes of hers, reaching across time to old age. He'd been able to imagine Lucy's red-toned hair turning a soft white and her sitting on a front porch swing still holding his hand somewhere.

Lucy pulled her hand away and dropped it down by her side. Her gaze flitted past him, a look of uncertainty crossing her expression. "If it wasn't a burglar," she said, "what was making all that noise?"

"An opossum. The little guy had his head stuck in a mason jar on your back porch. Want to see?"

Lucy looked horrified. She shook her head quickly. "No, that's okay. The mason jar is to harvest rain water," she explained. "My mom used it to—"

"Wash her face and hair." He nodded. "I know."

It was a Hannigan family beauty secret. That beauty secret had been common knowledge since Reva Dawson had put it up on her town blog a couple years ago, boasting something about pH levels and minerals and referencing the Hannigan beauty. Miles had seen a lot of rainwater jars out on folks' back porches since then. Then the Hannigan name had always been able to sell anything in this town. Even an old wives' tale.

"The creature is still in my jar?" Lucy folded her arms in front of her. Either because she was cold—the house was a little drafty—or because she was protecting herself and not from a burglar this time.

"Yes. You had a plastic bin on your porch. I contained it inside to make sure it didn't run off while I talked to you." Miles grimaced. "I'll try not to break the jar, but I wanted to make sure you won't be upset if I do."

Her arms loosened and dropped by her side. Lucy looked from him to the back door and the critter beyond. "Those jars cost less than a dollar. The thing needs to breathe."

"He's getting enough to stay alive right now."

"No. You should free him." She shook her head. "It's just a jar. I can get another at the store—really."

But Miles suspected the jar held sentimental value. It was her mother's, just like the house and her dog. He'd been worried about Lucy since her mother passed. He saw something sad when he looked into her eyes. He'd wanted to reach out to her many times over the last twelve months, but he'd always hesitated. She had close friends, and he doubted she wanted to hear from him.

"Go. I don't want that thing to die on my watch." Lucy gave his shoulder a little shove, the unexpected touch shooting unexpected warmth through him.

Miles started walking toward the back door, sending up a little prayer that he could save the opossum, the jar, and Lucy's heart. He stepped outside with Bella at his heels. She hurried over and sniffed the thing with its head in the jar.

When it swung wildly toward her, she took off, running back inside.

Miles chuckled to himself. "Don't worry, little guy. I got you. You're creating quite the commotion this morning, you know," he told the opossum. It was gray with a white face and bright pink nose. Kind of cute, maybe, but this wasn't the first opossum Miles had come in contact with. He knew they had teeth like razor blades, and he didn't really want those teeth to come anywhere near him. The last thing he needed this holiday season was rabies.

"Okay, you grab the jar. I'll grab the opossum," he told Lucy, whose eyes grew wide. "Unless you'd rather touch the critter," he said, knowing full well she wouldn't.

She shook her head quickly, making him chuckle.

He grabbed the opossum's backside first. Then Lucy bent and secured the jar. They both straightened and looked at one another. Of all the ways Miles imagined he might get close to Lucy Hannigan again, having an opossum in a rainwater jar between them wasn't one of them. "On my count," he said.

She nodded, her green eyes still locked on his. She stepped away from the jar now, holding it far away from her body as if the creature might escape and launch itself at her.

They both lowered back to the ground and prepared to pull in opposite directions.

Miles's fingers tightened just enough around the creature to keep it still. As soon as its head was free, he was going to let go and let it scurry off this porch. "One. Two. Three." He pulled the critter. Lucy pulled the jar. The opossum was free with a quick pop of its head. Miles's fingers flung open, almost tossing the creature in the direction of the steps so that Lucy didn't freak out. From his peripheral vision, he could see that she was dancing on her feet, freaking out anyway as she watched the scene unfold.

Miles smiled to himself. It took all of five seconds for the opossum to disappear into the night.

Miles looked over at Lucy. "You okay?"

She looked a bit shell-shocked. "Yes. That was certainly an adventure for one night."

"Well, it's kind of already morning." He tipped his head at the scattering of light rising behind the mountain skyline. The mountains of North Carolina were softer than those on the west coast. These rolled like a lazy river along the clouds. Any which way you turned in Somerset Lake, the view was the same—all sky and Blue Ridge peaks.

"I guess it is," Lucy said. She hugged the mason jar to her body. "And I will be wide awake for the rest of the morning. I was hoping to sleep in."

"Late night?" he asked.

"Nine hours of labor and delivery," Lucy confirmed. "But at the end of it, there was a healthy baby and two very exhausted and happy parents."

"A tired midwife too," Miles added.

"Yes." Lucy broke into a yawn. "But after all this excitement, there's no hope of going back to bed now."

Miles couldn't take eyes off her as she fidgeted with the strings of her pajama pants and patted down her long auburn hair. "The bright side is you can enjoy your coffee while watching the sunrise."

Lucy noticeably stiffened. No, he hadn't been referring to the time they'd done that when they were eighteen—hers had been decaf because of the baby. Judging by her face, however, that's exactly what she was thinking about.

Time to leave.

Miles walked past Lucy, back inside, and toward the front of the house. "I'm still on duty," he said as if to explain his rush. Not that she'd invited him to stay and catch up or enjoy a cup of coffee with her. "Do you think I can wash my hands at your sink?"

"Of course. After rescuing me from my burglar, that's the least I can do," she said, following him inside the kitchen.

"You didn't need rescuing," he called behind him. "Although, I guess you would still be crouched between the wall and the couch right now if not for me," he teased. He turned on the faucet and pumped some soap from the dispenser into his palm.

After getting cleaned up, he headed toward the front of the house. He opened the door and stepped out onto the porch. "See you later, Lucy," he called over his shoulder.

"Goodbye. And Miles?"

He stopped walking and turned back. "Yeah?"

"Thank you."

"Just doing my job. And I'm glad I was the one who got the call. It's good to see you, Luce. Have a good day." He headed down the steps and made quick strides to his cruiser.

Once he was inside, he blew out a breath and flicked his gaze to Lucy who was still standing in her open doorway. After a second, she turned back and closed the door behind her. Miles reversed out of her driveway to finish his shift. After that, he'd be going straight to the youth center, where he volunteered regularly.

With Thanksgiving coming next Thursday, the kids at the center were finishing up charity meal baskets. Once upon a time, Miles's family had been the one in need. These days, the Bruno family was doing all right, even if they'd never lived in a fancy mansion-sized house like Lucy's in The Village. Miles had a good job with a stable income. Next on his list was to purchase a house of his own. Maybe after that, he'd finally be ready to settle down.

The problem was that he'd ruined any chances with the only

person he'd ever been interested in spending his life with. It was kind of hard to take back telling your ex-fiancé that the reason you'd proposed was because you'd felt obligated.

Ouch.

But telling Lucy the truth would sting a whole lot more—which was why he never would.

CHAPTER TWO

Lucy stepped into Sweetie's Bake Shop later that morning, dragging her feet and in desperate need of a double expresso. She'd just left a client's home and really wanted something stiffer than her usual French roast brew.

The mother-to-be that Lucy had just visited didn't respect Lucy's time. The TV in her living room had been blaring, and the future mom was doing laundry in between Lucy's mid-wifery services, making what should have been a thirty-minute house call last well over an hour. This was one of those times, rare as they were, that Lucy missed being an obstetric nurse in a hospital setting.

"Hey, sweetie." The café's owner, Darla, waved from behind the counter. Never one to mince words, she said, "You look rough. Are you meeting my daughter here this morning?"

"Yes. Moira said she'd stop by after her shift." The shift where Moira had answered Lucy's nine-one-one call. *How embarrassing.* Lucy was never going to live this down with her best friend. "Can I get a double expresso please?"

"Of course, you can. And I'll go ahead and make Moira's coffee too."

Lucy had no doubt that Darla knew exactly how her daughter drank her brew. Moira had always been an old soul, drinking black coffee since she was seven and reading the newspaper before she'd ever reached double-digits.

"And what'll you have to eat?" Darla wanted to know. "How about a Sweetie Pastry?" Instead of naming the bakery after herself, Darla had titled it in honor of the Sweetheart Tree on the edge of Somerset Lake where lovers sometimes carved their initials.

Lucy looked at the food in the display longingly. Everything looked as good as it tasted. Lucy knew this firsthand because she'd sampled every cookie, pastry, and muffin on the menu. "A pastry sounds delicious, but I think today I'll have a French baguette."

"You got it." Darla took Lucy's debit card, ran it through the scanner, and handed it back. Then she prepared Lucy's expresso and slid it across the counter along with the baguette wrapped in a square of parchment paper. "I'll bring Moira's breakfast over in just a sec."

Lucy thanked her and then found a seat along the wall of the bakery, which was decorated in soft pastel colors. Lucy settled at her table and took a sip of her expresso, looking up when someone called her name.

"Morning, Lucy," Mayor Gil Ryan said as he walked toward the counter.

"Hey, Gil." Lucy didn't harass the poor guy by calling him Gilbert the way that the guys in town did, knowing how much he hated that. Lucy thought it was a nice name though. It brought back memories of her teenage years reading *Anne of Green Gables* and falling hopelessly and helplessly for the character Gilbert Blythe.

Lucy pulled a piece off her baguette and popped it into her mouth, almost sighing at the cottony texture of the bread that practically dissolved when it hit her tongue. She hoped Gil would get his breakfast and move on quickly before Moira arrived. Moira always got a little frustrated with Gil's attention. He wasn't flirty or inappropriate in any way. He was just nice. And he was *extra* nice to Moira.

Darla, knowing her daughter and probably thinking the same thing, was quick in giving the good mayor his coffee and Danish. As Gil headed out with his breakfast in hand, he waved to Lucy. "See you later."

"Bye, Mayor Gil," she called back.

A moment later, Moira strolled in with their friend Tess at her side. Tess owned Lakeside Books and led the book club they attended every Thursday night.

"Thank goodness Gil is gone," Moira huffed as she laid her purse on the chair across from Lucy's. She sat down, and Tess took the seat right next to Lucy.

"I saw Somerset's friendly mayor come in and waited around the corner to avoid him," Moira explained.

Tess rolled her eyes and shook her head. "And I caught her in the act on my way here."

Lucy giggled, nearly choking on another bite of her baguette. "Gil is nice. Handsome." She ticked off the mayor's positive qualities on her right hand. "He's smart. Rich. A genuinely good person. What am I missing?"

"You're missing the fact that I'm not romantically interested in him."

Darla stepped over with Moira's coffee, bagel, and a kiss on the cheek for her only daughter, leaving a bright pink lipstick print in her wake. She also placed a coffee and bagel in front of Tess. "Morning, Tess. I'm assuming you want your usual?"

Tess reached for the drink. "Thank you, Darla."

"Of course." Darla looked at Moira. "How was the nightshift?"

She blew out a breath as her bottom lip poked out. "Awful. I can't wait for Celia to get back from her honeymoon so I can return to working days."

"She's a newlywed. They should be up all night for entirely different reasons," Darla said with a snicker.

Moira reached for her coffee. "Thank you for this, Mom. I need it so much." She sipped it gratefully.

"Of course. Let me know if you three ladies need anything else." Darla turned and headed back to the counter.

"So..." Moira said. Judging by the grin on her face, she knew what had happened with Lucy's burglar. "An opossum, huh? Did he steal anything valuable?"

"Only my pride." Lucy rolled her eyes and sipped her expresso. "I'm guessing Moira told you what happened this morning?" she asked Tess.

Tess nodded. "I never knew you were so jumpy."

"The opossum was loud, okay? Very loud. And I live alone in a huge house with a ton of things that someone might want to take. How was I supposed to know it was an animal?"

Moira cackled and bit into her bagel with a loud crunch. "And Miles was the one who responded," she said after chewing and swallowing. "How did that go?" She waggled her eyebrows.

Lucy was beginning to regret asking Moira to meet her here. "He saved the creature and left."

Tess looked disappointed. "That's it? I thought there might be something juicier to that story." Although a widow, Tess was the romantic of the group. All the books she chose for book club always had a happy ending. She wouldn't hear of it otherwise. Lucy guessed it was because Tess's own love story hadn't ended happily.

"Like what?" Lucy asked.

"I don't know." Tess shrugged. "Like a brush of the hand or better yet a kiss."

Lucy's mouth dropped even though she wasn't a bit surprised. "I hate to break it to you two, but Miles and I are friends."

"Boring." Moira took another bite of her bagel, hazel eyes rolling upward.

"If you want exciting, find a book in Tess's store," Lucy muttered.

After a quiet minute of eating, the conversation moved to other things.

"So, any leads on renting out your garage apartment?" Tess asked.

Lucy shook her head. "I've had that sign for renting my garage apartment out in the yard forever. Not one person has inquired. I was hoping the extra money would help me pay the last of my mother's bills."

"Bummer," Moira said. "I've heard of inheriting valuables after a loved one passes, but never their debt too."

In Lucy's case, the bills were all related to the house. It was so unlike her mom to be irresponsible with finances. Her entire life, Lucy's mom had been frugal. In her last few years though, she'd hired several contractors before she'd gotten sick and had failed to pay half of them. Funny, they'd all come collecting when Lucy was still grieving this time last year.

There was a roofer. A plumber. A painter who'd painted the entire house in a fresh shade of pink. There were so many unpaid bills for Lucy to take care of along with that of her mother's funeral.

Lucy had promised herself that she'd wipe them all out by the New Year, which by her calculation was only six weeks away. And for the most part, she had. There was only one outstanding bill left on Lucy's radar. "I really should sell the house. That would give me plenty of money to pay off the last debt my mom owes. But..." She trailed off for a moment. "Giving up the house feels like I'd be saying goodbye to my mom completely. And there's Bella. That's her house."

"Bella is a dog," Moira pointed out, eyes rolling again. "She'd adjust to a change of scenery just fine."

There was also the fact that Lucy loved living in the pink house. Even as a little girl, being there felt like having her own, life-sized doll house. It had felt magical to her, and in some ways, it still did. Every corner of the house was special in some way, from the abalone shell backsplash of the downstairs sink to the antique oak stair baluster that to the expansive upper level. Even the attic felt special with its stained glass windows that let streamed in jewel-colored light on stored away things.

"It's too bad no one's biting on the garage apartment," Tess said. "The passive income would be great."

Lucy leaned back in her chair and folded her arms in front of her. "And a couple months' rent would take care of the hot tub bill that my mom left me." She'd never even seen her mom use a hot tub. When Lucy had come home to be a nurse to her ailing mother, she'd just assumed it was paid for. Like everything else. Her mother's health had gone from bad to worse so quickly that there'd been no time to talk about frivolous things like bills and finances. Lucy's mom had barely been able to talk at all as the throat cancer metastasized through her body. One month her mom had been bustling with the energy of a dozen five-year-olds. The next, she'd struggled to open her eyes.

"Just be careful who you do decide to rent to." Moira popped the last of her breakfast in her mouth and chewed. "Getting a terrible tenant could make your life miserable. They might blare music at all hours, have parties, or have a dog that poops all over your property."

Lucy felt her eyebrows raise.

Moira dabbed her mouth with a crisp white napkin. "Trust me, I've heard it all on the dispatch."

"I'm sure you have," Lucy said, sharing a look with Tess.

"You could ask Reva to spread the word about the rental," Tess suggested. Reva Dawson ran a blog online about the town. She spread all the news she could get her hands on, which was why everyone in Somerset Lake read it as faithfully as they would any newspaper.

"That's not a bad idea," Lucy said. *Geesh. I must really be desperate to consider spreading the word on Reva's blog.* "Now that it's the holidays, it might be hard to find someone. People don't usually make big life changes this time of year."

Moira looked at her seriously. "It's a hard time of year for some people. The call center gets more calls than usual."

Lucy narrowed her eyes. "I know where this is coming from, and you don't need to worry about me. I'm fine."

"Great." As if to prove a point, Moira asked, "So what are you doing for Thanksgiving next week then?"

Lucy hugged her arms around herself even tighter. "Bella and I are, um, planning to stay home for a quiet day of reading. I have a huge stack of books that I've been meaning to get to."

"As much as I promote reading, doing so while home alone on Thanksgiving isn't the best idea," Tess said.

"Not home alone. I have Bella." Lucy understood that her argument was weak.

Moira gave her a serious look. "Just know that my offer for you to come to my family's home still stands. My mom owns a bakery. There'll be lots of breaded things."

"You can also feel free to join me at my parents' home," Tess offered. "I'm the only single person there so bringing an ally would be a good thing."

These weren't Lucy's first invitations. She knew her friends meant well. But it was somehow sadder to sit around everyone else's dinner table and pretend to be having a good time—when all you really wanted to do is be alone to count your losses, which for Lucy, felt immeasurable in the last year.

* * *

Miles had worked all day, starting early at Lucy's house. Now his shift was over, but instead of going home, he was in the next best place. In his mind, at least.

He stood at the head of one of three long tables with kids of various ages. The kids were bused from the school to the youth center every afternoon, where they completed home-work, played games, and worked on projects that taught them team-building skills while also benefiting the community.

Right now, they were working hard on making Thanksgiving cards to accompany the food baskets that they'd put together for the holiday delivery that always happened the weekend before the big day.

Miles walked between two of the tables, commenting on the colorful drawings as he passed through. The children on this side of the room were mostly younger, except for Charlie Bates. Charlie was thirteen, but he liked to help out with the younger kids.

"Hey, Charlie. How're you doing?" Miles stepped over to where the boy was seated.

Charlie looked up, lifting his lanky shoulders to the ears he hadn't quite grown into yet. "Just hanging out, Deputy Bruno."

"Is your sister here?" Miles asked. Charlie's sister Brittney was fifteen and had the attitude of three teenaged girls.

"Nah. Mom doesn't make her ride the bus here anymore. She gets to hang out with her boyfriend," Charlie said.

"Boyfriend? Already?" Miles shook his head. "Well, thanks

for helping out, bud. It's appreciated. How's your mom and dad?"

Charlie's eyes dulled. His father had been laid off last month, and from what Miles had heard, they were struggling. Even so, he hadn't seen the Bates family on the list of homes that would be receiving holiday food baskets this weekend.

"They're good," Charlie said in a less than convincing tone of voice.

"Glad to hear that. Let me know if I can help, okay? Don't hesitate to ask for anything you need."

"Sure." Charlie wasn't looking at him anymore. Instead, he was back to drawing bubble letters on a piece of paper for the little girl beside him.

Miles patted a hand on his shoulder and kept walking. "Keep working on the cards. We need them to be finished by this weekend," he said as he walked back down the aisle to join the other adult volunteers, one of whom was Jake Fletcher.

Miles had gone to school with Jake. They hadn't exactly been friends, but since Jake had moved back to town this past summer, they had gotten closer. Jake worked as a lawyer in Magnolia Falls, and he also helped his fiancé Trisha Langly run the Somerset Cottages down on the south side of the lake.

"How's Charlie?" Jake asked.

Miles's gaze moved to the boy sitting at the table with the younger kids. "He seems to be doing okay, considering."

"His dad is having a hard time finding work. I spoke to him the other day," Jake said.

Miles couldn't help thinking about his own childhood and father. "I wish the Sheriff's Department was hiring."

"Lack of jobs can be a drawback of such a small town. Hopefully something will turn up soon."

Hopefully before the family got into dire straits. When Miles was growing up and his own father had lost his job, it had a domino effect that ended with his father walking out on Miles, his sister, and their mother. After that, hard times had gotten even tougher.

Miles glanced over at Jake. "So, have you and Trisha set a date for the wedding yet?"

Jake grinned from one ear to the other. "New Year's."

"This coming one?" Miles raised his eyes. "That's fast."

"When you know, you know," Jake said. "And Trisha and I don't need anything big or fancy."

Miles listened to Jake go into a few details. He and Lucy had decided the same thing when they were briefly engaged. They didn't need a big church filled to the brim with people. They'd wanted to do things simply. Lucy had said she wanted to get married at dusk in the backyard of the pink house "with fairy lights everywhere" And she'd wanted to wear a white dress trimmed in lavender ribbon because, at eighteen, that had been her favorite color.

Miles smiled to himself, wondering for a moment if it still was.

"I was thinking…"—Jake said, pulling Miles from his memories—"maybe you would agree to be one of my grooms-men."

Miles felt his jaw drop. "You hated me in high school."

"True. But I like you now."

Miles chuckled. "I'd love to stand up there with you, buddy."

Jake offered his hand for Miles to shake. "Thanks. I would appreciate it."

"Well, I'm honored." Miles smiled back at his friend, even if something inside his chest felt a little achy.

Miles had seen a lot of his friends settle down in the last couple years. He didn't buy into the whole biological clock; all he knew was that he liked the idea of spending his life with someone. But not until he was one hundred percent certain he could support them. He didn't want to take any chances that he'd let a family down the way his own father had. That's why he'd hesitated about dating seriously until this point in his life.

Miles had the stable job and income now. The last thing on his list of criteria was a house that he owned instead of rented. His dad was always delinquent on rent. Miles's family had been kicked out of three homes before his dad left their family. It was always his mom's dream to own a house. A place that no one could take from them. Miles had adopted that goal for himself. He'd been saving money for a down payment, and he was gearing up to make it happen. Not today, but maybe next year.

For the next couple hours, Miles encouraged, played, and joked with the youngest members of his community. At six p.m., when the youth center closed, Miles headed out to his truck. His cell phone rang as he slid behind the steering wheel. He pulled it out of his pocket and read the caller's name.

Tony Blake.

It was so infrequent that Miles's landlord ever called that he picked it up and answered right away, worried that maybe the older man was sick or needed help. "Hello, Mr. Blake. How are you?"

"Good. And yourself?" Mr. Blake asked.

"I can't complain. I have all my needs met, including a roof over my head." Miles laughed because it was supposed to be a joke.

Mr. Blake remained quiet. "About that," his landlord finally said, clearing his throat, "your lease is up at the end of month." That wasn't news to Miles. For the last several years, he'd re-upped his lease every November after Thanksgiving. "The thing is, I'm downsizing my life, and I've decided that I won't be leasing out that house anymore. I'm going to move into it myself."

Miles took a moment to process what Mr. Blake was telling him. "I'm being kicked out?"

"I'm sorry, Miles. You've been a great tenant. But I'm afraid to say, I need you to move out. As soon as possible."

* * *

The next day, Lucy woke to her alarm clock instead of a frisky opossum with its head in her rainwater jar. She had her coffee first and then showered and dressed for the day. After that, she went to the counter of Sweetie's Bake Shop for another cup of brew and a bite to eat before sitting alone at a table along the wall and pulling out her laptop.

She took a huge bite of her bagel as she pulled up Reva Dawson's blog for the town. Reva liked to use bullet points to list the town's goings-on. That way you could read it more easily, digesting the gossip in small increments so that you were sure to remember it all and pass it on.

It wasn't all gossip, of course. Listed today, for example, was that Lakeside Books was having a sale on children's titles, Choco-Lovers was having a chocolate tasting on Thanksgiving weekend, and the youth center was helping with the Thanksgiving meal baskets that were handed out every year. And...

Lucy nearly choked on her bite of bagel. It lodged at the back of her throat before she could swallow effectively. She slapped a hand on her breastbone, helping it along, and reached for her coffee to wash it completely down. The coffee was too hot though, and it burned the roof of her mouth. She supposed that was better than choking.

When she could breathe again, she read the bullet point with her name again.

- *Lucy Hannigan had a break-in on Thursday morning. Deputy Miles Bruno was called to the scene and he handled the little rascal who turned out to be a raccoon.*

"It was an opossum!" Lucy practically yelled at her computer screen.

Darla set a glass of water in front of Lucy. "Here you go, sweetie. Don't want you to keel over in my bakery. That's bad for business."

"And then it would make a bullet point in Reva's blog," Lucy said sarcastically. "Thank you." She reached for the glass of water and drank half before setting it down. Darla was still standing there.

"Can I get you something else?" she asked.

Lucy checked the time on her phone. "I have a client appointment in fifteen minutes." Lucy looked at Darla. "Can I get another one of these? For my client."

"Sure you can." Darla headed behind the counter, talking behind her. "Pregnant women love baked items. Who is this for?"

"Mandy Elks."

Darla glanced back, her mouth forming an exaggerated "o." "She's ready to pop any day, isn't she?"

"Not soon enough," Lucy muttered under her breath. Mandy was sweet, but pregnancy had made her a bit demanding. She was high maintenance, which meant that Lucy was making daily house visits to check on her now. And to bring her breakfast.

Lucy paid Darla for the extra bagel, grabbed the bag, and headed out. Ten minutes later, she pulled into the driveway of Mandy Elks' house. After doting on Mandy just enough to maintain a pleasant relationship, she headed back to her car. Then she headed home for a small break. She noticed that the FOR RENT sign in the front yard had fallen—again. She walked over, picked it up, and drove it back into the ground, using the force of all her weight.

As she was struggling to get the stake deeper into the dirt, she was vaguely aware of a vehicle approaching, slowing, and stopping.

Lucy turned toward the deputy cruiser now parked on her curb. She straightened at the sight of Miles getting out, her heart betraying her with an extra beat or two. She supposed Miles would always have that effect on her. "Everything okay?" she asked.

"That's my line." He stepped toward her, all tall, dark, and handsome.

"I came by to check on you after yesterday's scare."

Lucy straightened. "I'm fine. Just a little embarrassed, that's all."

"I also came to ask about that sign in your yard. I saw it when I was here."

"Yeah. I'm trying to rent out the garage apartment," she said. "I've had this sign up for a while, but no one is biting."

"Mind if I ask how much the rent is?" Miles asked.

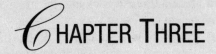

CHAPTER THREE

*L*ucy straightened as the implications of that question circulated in her mind. "Why do you want to know how much I'm charging?"

Miles shrugged. "Well, it appears that I'm about to be homeless. At least temporarily. Mr. Blake is downsizing and wants to move back into the house that I've been living in for the last seven years."

"When?" Lucy asked, trying not to notice how Miles's uniform hugged his shoulders and biceps just right.

"He wants to move in on Thanksgiving weekend."

Lucy gasped. "That's not even a two-week notice. Can he do that?"

"I guess I could fight it, but it sounds like Mr. Blake needs the place more than me. He's had two knee operations this year, and he can't climb stairs anymore." Miles shoved his hands in his pockets. "I can get my stuff out and store it temporarily at my mom's place. I guess she'd let me stay on her couch for a while." His gaze dropped to the sign.

Lucy really wished he didn't know about her garage apartment. She didn't want him living so close by. That would be awkward, right? An ex-fiancé living on the same property? "I haven't decided how much to charge yet," she said. "I think there might be vacancies at the Somerset Cottages. Trisha fixed them up over the summer. That would be a nice place to live."

"They're all full," Miles said. "I called as soon as I got off the phone with Mr. Blake." He looked at her for a long moment. Then he pulled his hands from his pockets and presented open palms. "I just need a temporary place while I look for something else. I'm thinking it might be time for me to buy a small house of my own. I've been saving money with that in mind."

"Wow. Buying a house is a big decision."

"It is. I was going to start my search in the new year, but I guess my timeline has sped up...I'm a great tenant. Mr. Blake can vouch for me."

This is so awkward.

"It would be handy to have a deputy sheriff living on your property. In case of break-ins," he said it in a teasing tone.

"That's true. It's just..." Lucy trailed off.

Miles narrowed his dark brown eyes as his expression turned serious. "Because we used to date? Because we were engaged?"

"That was a long time ago," Lucy said, maybe a little too quickly.

"Right," Miles agreed. "And we're friends now. So it shouldn't be weird at all."

"Right." She didn't have this tightly coiled tension in her chest with anyone else though.

Miles held up his hands. "But we'll still be friends if you tell me no. I promise."

"Can I think about it?" Lucy asked. "I mean, I haven't

even decided how much I want to charge or if I'm really even doing this."

They both knew that was a lie. The sign had been out for a month.

"Sure. Think about it. And in the meantime, I'll keep looking for a place to avoid sleeping on my mom's couch. I love my mother, but she loves to get into my business a little too much, always asking who I'm dating, why I'm not dating so and so, and when I'm going to settle down with a nice woman."

Just that little bit of information was enough to make Lucy feel awkward. Seeing Miles all the time would definitely be weird.

Miles's radio buzzed to life at his hip.

Shoplifting at Hannigan's Market.

He took a few retreating steps toward his vehicle at the end of her driveway. "I need to go. I'll talk to you later?"

"Yeah." Later. And hopefully by then she'd have a different renter in place and a reason to tell Miles he couldn't live here.

He paused before getting into his car. "Hey, Luce?

"Hmm?"

"You know my mother makes enough food at Thanksgiving to feed the entire lake. She insists that I invite friends. I've already invited the other volunteers at the youth center. Jake Fletcher is bringing Trisha. Reese Whitaker said maybe. What do you say? Want to join us on Thursday at two o'clock?"

Lucy hesitated. "Um."

"Do you already have plans? Because Thanksgiving Day is not the time to stay home alone."

Lucy wondered if he'd been talking to Moira or Tess. Or maybe Reva had broadcast in her blog that Lucy was orphaned this year.

- *Someone please adopt lonely Lucy Hannigan for the holidays.*

Miles opened his car door and stood behind it. "Mom has this challenge," he continued before she could argue with him. "Whoever invites the most people to Thanksgiving dinner gets an entire pumpkin pie to bring home."

Lucy laughed softly. "I remember that challenge."

"And agreeing to dinner doesn't mean agreeing to renting the apartment to me. It's two separate things."

"Thanks for the invitation, Miles. The truth is, I actually already have plans."

His eyebrows drew up on his forehead. "Oh. Okay."

That was two small fibs she'd told Miles this visit. She was definitely not landing herself on Santa's good list this year. Once Miles was gone though, she'd go inside her house and make plans. Then what she'd just told Miles would be true.

His radio buzzed again.

"You better go," she said.

Miles glanced at his radio. "Yeah, shoplifting in Somerset Lake is a rarity."

"Thank goodness for that. I'll let you know about the apartment," she promised—already knowing her answer would be no.

* * *

Miles flipped on the sirens of his car, which he rarely ever did, and sped to the scene. Shoplifting wasn't necessarily an emergency and he suspected it was more of a misunderstanding than anything. He couldn't remember the last time he'd truly caught someone stealing.

Within minutes, he pulled up to the curb in front of Hannigan's Market and cut the engine. He quickly got out and strode inside to meet the manager, Sandy Dunkin. She was sitting at a little counter along the store wall, separate from the cash registers.

Miles's heart sank when he saw who was sitting alongside her.

"Hey Sandy." He stepped up to the counter and glanced over at Charlie Bates, the thirteen-year old boy who helped the younger kids at the youth center. What had Charlie done? Now Miles was even more sure that this whole incident was a misunderstanding.

"Thank you for coming, Deputy Bruno." Sandy's expression was regretful as she glanced over at the teenager. "Charlie here had some store items in his pockets as he tried to head out. I caught him last week and had a talk with him already. I told him, if I caught him again, I'd have to call the law. He promised he wouldn't lift again, but..." She trailed off. "So, this time I called you. I had to keep my word."

Miles folded his arms in front of him. "Keeping your word is important. Hey, Charlie," he said, addressing the boy whose chin was tipped down, nearly touching his chest.

Charlie mumbled something that Miles thought might be a hello.

"I'll give him a ride to the station, and then I'll have him call his parents," Miles told Sandy.

Now Charlie's face whipped up to meet Miles's eyes. "No! You can't do that!"

Miles faced the boy. "Why not?"

Charlie looked at Sandy and back at him. Miles took the hint. They needed to talk privately.

"I'll take him from here, Sandy. Thanks for calling," Miles said.

"Thanks for getting here so quickly. I'm sorry, Charlie," Sandy said regretfully. "You left me no choice."

"Let's keep this just between us, can we?" Miles asked Sandy as an afterthought. Sandy wasn't one to gossip, but sometimes word got out to the folks who were. Gossip wouldn't help Charlie or his family.

Sandy nodded solemnly. "I won't say a word."

"Thanks." Miles walked alongside Charlie out of the store and to his cruiser. The chilly late November air made him fold into his coat deeper as they walked. They didn't talk until they were both seated inside the warmth of his vehicle. "All right, Charlie. What's going on?"

Charlie's chin was resting on his chest again. "Please don't call my parents," Charlie pleaded.

Miles thought that maybe he heard tears in the boy's voice. "Give me one good reason."

"Because... Because my mom lost her job a couple days ago too. My dad was supposed to be looking for work, but the truth is he took off last week. My mom said he'll be back and we'll be okay, if we can just get through this rough patch."

"Rough patch," Miles repeated. That was an understatement.

"If I cause trouble for my family, I'll just make things worse."

"Then why were you shoplifting?" Miles asked. He still hadn't started his car yet.

"Because we don't have snacks. My sister and I just get peanut butter sandwiches and Ramen Noodles right now. I wanted to get something else, just so Brittney would stop frowning so hard. I was going to pay for it later, I promise."

The story felt so similar to Miles's own. His family had struggled, and his dad had finally broken under the pressure and left. Miles had been older than Charlie at the time though. He'd been able to get a job, at least. "Stealing is a crime."

Charlie was pale. "Yes, sir."

Miles suspected the poor kid was envisioning himself going to jail from now until next January. "I'll make you a deal. I'll buy your family a little bit of food right now. But you have to do something for me."

Charlie's eyes widened as he looked over. "What?"

"I haven't figured that out just yet," Miles said. "No

more stealing though. If that happens again, I will call your mom."

Charlie's gaze slid over to meet Miles's. "Yes, sir."

"Okay." Miles pushed the car door back open. "Let's go inside the market and get some snacks and maybe a box of mac and cheese for you and your family tonight. Then I'll drive you home."

"What'll you tell my mom? She'll wonder why you're buying us food."

"I'll tell her that you and I have struck a deal. I'm delivering food baskets this weekend. Think your mom will be okay with you helping? I can pick you up."

"Yeah. She won't mind."

"Good."

They went back inside the store, Miles waved at Sandy, and they perused the aisles, putting several items in a cart before checking out and leaving the store with a couple of bags of groceries. Then Miles drove Charlie home and walked him to the door.

"What's all this?" Mrs. Bates asked with a surprised smile.

"Well, I asked Charlie to help me with a few things. I hope that's okay. In exchange, he wanted to buy food. This is a good kid you got here."

The mother turned to her son. "That's very thoughtful, Charlie."

"It is," Miles agreed, rubbing his chin thoughtfully. "I was wondering if you could spare Charlie on Saturday to help me deliver food baskets in the community."

Mrs. Bates looked between Miles and her son. "Well, he's babysitting a friend's six-year-old at one-thirty. But he can help you in the morning, I suppose. This is a lot of groceries just for a few hours of work though." She gestured for Miles to follow her inside.

Miles walked through the living room and into the kitchen, where he laid the bags on the table. "I've been needing help here and there. I'm sure I'll find something else for Charlie to help me with."

Mrs. Bates nodded again. "Of course I can spare Charlie if you need him."

Miles turned to leave.

Charlie followed him to the door. "Thanks, Deputy Bruno," the boy said a bit shyly.

"You're welcome. You might regret this arrangement though, kid. I'm gonna make you work for it."

"I don't mind," Charlie said, a small smile touching the corners of his mouth. "I just want to help my family until my dad gets back."

"All right. I'll see you at the Youth Center at 9:00 Saturday morning, Charlie." Miles turned and headed back to his cruiser. When he got inside, he checked his cell phone before pulling back onto the road. He still hadn't heard from Lucy about that garage apartment. If she didn't call back, it looked like he might be sleeping on his mom's couch for Thanksgiving and maybe Christmas too. How was that for motivation to go ahead and make his dream of being a homeowner come true?

* * *

Ashley Herring should have been a movie star. She was a high maintenance diva misplaced in a small-town void of all the extravagancies she seemed to think she was due. Lucy kind of felt bad for Ashley's husband, Allen, who was doting on his pregnant wife the best he could, and yet he seemed to keep falling short of Ashley's expectations.

"You want me to take a birthing class?" Ashley asked Lucy as if the idea was a foreign concept.

"Like Lamaze?" Allen asked.

"Kind of," Lucy said. "I teach the expectant mother's class over at The Village's Community Building on Tuesday nights. It's more than just breathing lessons. It's how to eat healthy for the baby and what to expect during the various stages of pregnancy. It's so important that an expectant mother take good care of herself. The father too."

"Can't you just teach me that stuff during our appointments?"

Lucy maintained her smile, despite her fraying patience. "This is more in-depth. The information I provide at the community building is on top of what I'm already teaching you during our home visits. You don't have to come, of course. I'm just letting you know that it's an option."

Allen put his hand on Ashley's shoulders. "It'll be fun. Kind of like a date night."

Ashley's face scrunched up. "Date night is a nice dinner over candlelight. It's not commiserating with other swollen-ankled moms-to-be over acid reflux and Braxton Hicks pains."

Lucy's smile wobbled just a touch. "That's not what this is. Allen, you are free to come on your own if you'd like. It's good for husbands to be involved in everything going on during this special time."

"Well, he's not going without me," Ashley whined, her hands flattened over the mound of her belly, roughly the size of a basketball. Was Ashley like this before she'd gotten pregnant? Lucy wasn't sure because they'd only been acquaintances before Ashley had become her client.

"Great, then you two can come together. Tuesday nights at seven."

"What if I go into labor on a Tuesday night?" Ashley asked. "You'll be teaching a class. Who will help me?"

Lucy took a breath, drawing it deep into her lungs before answering. "If you go into labor on a Tuesday night," she explained, "then I will, of course, cancel or reschedule the class and meet you at the birthing center. The participants are all pregnant. They understand that labor is unpredictable."

"Thank you, Dr. Hannigan," Allen said.

Lucy had already told Allen several times over, but it was worth repeating. "I'm not a doctor. I'm a nurse practitioner. If a real doctor hears you call me that, they might get offended. I didn't go to school as long as they did."

"Got it," Allen said, a small grimace lining his lips. "Sorry. We'll see you on Tuesday night."

Ashley didn't look happy about this new plan which she was treating like an inconvenience. Lucy suspected that Ashley would be happy to have the knowledge as she progressed into her pregnancy though.

After leaving the Herring house, Lucy went by Hannigan's Market for groceries before going home. Hannigan's used to be owned by her family, but like everything else in Somerset Lake, it now belonged to someone else. Except for the pink house on Christmas Lane and Bella.

Note to self: Bella needs more treats.

Lucy pushed her buggy down the market aisles, heading toward the pet section. Groceries for one was quick and easy. That was the upside to being a single woman. The downside was that she shopped alone and ate alone. Everything she did, for the most apart, was in solitude. She was the very image of an independent woman, which she was proud of, but sometimes she took it to such an extreme that she felt a bit lonely.

This close to the holidays, the aisles were extra crowded, and folks were chattier than usual. Lucy managed to make it out with just a few waves and hellos. Then she loaded the bags in her backseat and got into the driver's seat. She cranked the car and made a mental to-do list for the remainder of the day.

One of the items gave her a pang of guilt. She still hadn't called Miles back about the apartment above her garage because she didn't have a good excuse to say no.

But she did have two good reasons *not* to say no. First, saying no implied that she wasn't comfortable with Miles. That there was still sexual attraction between them. That maybe she still harbored feelings for the man who had once broken her heart. He didn't just break one tiny little piece. He'd shattered it with all the gentleness of a sledgehammer.

Secondly, if she didn't say yes, she'd be carrying her mom's debt into the New Year, which she'd promised herself, no matter what, she wouldn't do. She needed to move on from the heavy weight of it. Somehow, staying in her mother's debt kept her stuck in her grief as well. She couldn't fully move on until the last bill was paid.

Lucy reached for her phone, took a breath, and started to call Miles. She hesitated. Just the thought of holding a conversation with him made her anxious.

This is silly. They'd dated a million years ago. They were friends now. Just friends. Even so, instead of calling, she tapped out a text.

Lucy: I've decided to charge $850 for rent through the end of the year.

Lucy: Not sure if you're interested.

The rent Lucy was asking was fair, in her opinion. The garage apartment was complete with an open kitchen, living area, bedroom, and a bathroom. Lucy had lived there after high school and when she'd come back and forth during college.

The dots on her screen started bouncing.

She held her breath, part of her hoping that Miles wasn't interested. The other part needed him to say yes.

Miles: That sounds good. I'll take it.

Lucy swallowed. Her mouth was suddenly parched. She was also shaking a little bit. Her ex- fiancé was moving in next door. This was probably an epically bad idea.

Lucy: Okay then. When do you think you'll start moving in?
Miles: I'm delivering holiday food baskets on Saturday for the Youth Center. I'll be there Sunday, if that's okay.

Sunday. As in two days from now. Two days from now, Miles Bruno would be living next door.
Lucy texted back.

Lucy: Perfect. Sunday sounds good.

Have you missed Annie Rains's
Sweetwater Springs series?

Please turn the page to read
the bonus story
"Kiss Me in
Sweetwater Springs."

FOREVER

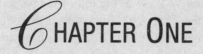

CHAPTER ONE

$\mathscr{L}$acy Shaw looked around the Sweetwater Springs Library for the culprit of the noise, a "shhh" waiting on the tip of her tongue. There were several people reading quietly at the tables along the wall. A few patrons were wandering the aisles of books.

The high-pitched giggle broke through the silence again.

Lacy stood and walked out from behind her counter, going in the direction of the sound. She wasn't a stickler for quiet, but the giggling had been going on for at least ten minutes now, and a few of the college students studying in the far corner kept getting distracted and looking up. They'd come here to focus, and Lacy wanted them to keep coming.

She stopped when she was standing at the end of one of the nonfiction aisles where two little girls were seated on the floor with a large book about animals in their lap. The *shhh* finally tumbled off her lips. The sound made her feel even more like the stuffy librarian she tried not to be.

The girls looked up, their little smiles wilting.

Lacy stepped closer to see what was so funny about animals and saw a large picture of a donkey with the heading "Asses" at the top of the page. A small giggle tumbled off Lacy's lips as well. She quickly regained control of herself and offered a stern expression. "Girls, we need to be quiet in the library. People come here to read and study."

"That's why we're here," Abigail Fields, the girl with long, white-blond curls, said. They came in often with their nanny, Mrs. Townsend, who usually fell asleep in the back corner of the room. The woman was somewhere in her eighties and probably wasn't the best choice to be taking care of two energetic little girls.

"I have to write a paper on my favorite animal," Abigail said.

Lacy made a show of looking at the page. "And it's a donkey?"

"That's not what that says," Willow, Abigail's younger sister, said. "It says…"

"Whoa!" Lacy held up a hand. "I can read, but let's not say that word out loud, okay? Why don't you two take that book to a table and look at it quietly," she suggested.

The little girls got up, the older one lugging the large book with both hands.

Lacy watched them for a moment and then turned and headed back to her counter. She walked more slowly as she stared at the back of a man waiting for her. He wore dark jeans and a fitted black T-shirt that hugged muscles she didn't even have a name for. There was probably an anatomy book here that did. She wouldn't mind locating it and taking her time labeling each muscle, one by one.

She'd seen the man before at the local café, she realized, but never in here. And every time he'd walked into the café, she'd noticed him. He, of course, had never noticed her. He was too gorgeous and cool. There was also the fact that Lacy usually sat in the back corner reading a book or people-watching from behind her coffee cup.

What is he doing here?

The man shifted as he leaned against her counter, his messenger bag swinging softly at his lower hip. Then he glanced over his shoulder and met her gaze. He had blue crystalline eyes, inky black hair, and a heart-stopping smile that made her look away shyly—a nervous remnant of her high school years when the cool kids like him had picked on her because of the heavy back brace she wore.

The brace was gone. No one was going to laugh at her anymore, and even if they did, she was confident enough not to find the closest closet to cry in these days.

"Hey," he said. "Are you Lacy Shaw, the librarian here?"

She forced her feet to keep walking forward. "I am. And you are?"

He turned and held out a hand. "Paris." He suspended his hand in midair, waiting for her to take it. When she hesitated, his gaze flicked from her face to her hand and then back again.

She blinked, collected herself, and took his hand. "Nice to meet you. I'm Lacy Shaw."

Paris's dark brows dipped farther.

"Right," she giggled nervously. "You didn't need me to introduce myself. You just asked if that's who I was. Do you, um, need help with something? Finding a book maybe?"

"I'm actually here for the class," he said.

"The computer skills class?" She walked around the counter to stand behind her computer. "The course instructor hasn't arrived yet." She looked at the Apple Watch on her wrist. "It's still a little early though. You're not late until you're less than five minutes early. That's what my mom always says."

Lacy had been wanting to offer a computer skills class here for months. There was a roomful of laptops in the back just begging for people to use them. She'd gotten the computer skills teacher's name from one of her regular patrons here, and she'd practically begged Mr. Montgomery over the phone to take the job.

"The class runs from today to next Thursday. It's aimed toward people sixty-five and over," she told the man standing across from her, briefly meeting his eyes and then looking away. "But you're welcome to attend, of course." Although she doubted he'd fit in. He appeared to be in his early thirties, wore dark clothes, and looked like his idea of fun might be adding a tattoo to the impressive collection on his arms.

Paris cleared his throat. "Unless I'm mistaken, I *am* the instructor," he said. "Paris Montgomery at your service."

"Oh." She gave him another assessing look. She'd been expecting someone...different. Alice Hampton had been the one to recommend Paris. She was a sweet old lady who had sung the praises of the man who'd rented the room above her garage last year. Lacy never would've envisioned the likes of this man staying with Mrs. Hampton. "Oh, I'm sorry. Thank you for agreeing to offer some of your time to our senior citizens. A lot of them have expressed excitement over the class."

Paris gave a cursory glance around the room. "It's no problem. I'm self-employed, and as I told you on the phone, I had time between projects."

"You're a graphic designer, right?" she asked, remembering what Alice had told her. "You created the designs for the Sweetwater Bed and Breakfast."

"Guilty. And for a few other businesses in Sweetwater Springs."

Lacy remembered how much she'd loved the designs when she'd seen them. "I've been thinking about getting something done for the library," she found herself saying.

"Yeah? I'd be happy to talk it over with you when you're ready. I'm sure we can come up with something simple yet classy. Modern. Inviting."

"Inviting. Yes!" she agreed in a spurt of enthusiasm before quickly feeling embarrassed. But that was her whole goal for the library this year. She wanted the community to love coming in as much as she did. As a child growing up, the library had been her haven, especially during those years of being bullied. The smell of books had come to mean freedom to her. The sound of pages turning was music to her ears.

"Well, I guess I better go set up for class." Paris

angled his body toward the computer room. "Five minutes early is bordering on late, right?" he asked, repeating her words and making her smile.

He was cool, gorgeous, *and* charming—a dangerous combination.

* * *

Paris still wasn't sure why he'd agreed to this proposition. It paid very little, and he doubted it would help with his graphic design business. The librarian had been so insistent on the phone that it'd been hard to say no to her. Was that the same woman who'd blushed and had a hard time making eye contact with him just now? She looked familiar, but he wasn't sure where or when they'd ever crossed paths.

He walked into the computer room in the back of the library and looked around at the laptops set up. How hard could it be to teach a group of older adults to turn on a computer, utilize the search engine, or set up an email account? It was only two weeks. He could handle that.

"You're the teacher?" a man's voice asked behind him.

Paris whirled to face him. The older man wore a ball cap and a plaid button-down shirt. In a way, he looked familiar. "Yes, sir. Are you here for the class?"

The man frowned. "Why else would I ask if you were the teacher?"

Paris ignored the attitude and gestured to the empty room. "You have your pick of seats right now, sir,"

Paris told him. Then he directed his attention to a few more seniors who strolled in behind the older man. Paris recognized a couple of them. Greta Merchant used a cane, but he knew she walked just fine. The cane was for show, and Paris had seen her beat it against someone's foot a couple of times. She waved and took a seat next to the frowning man.

"Paris!" Alice Hampton said, walking into the room.

He greeted her with a hug. After coming to town last winter and staying at the Sweetwater B&B for a week, he'd rented a room from Alice for a while. Now he had his own place, a little cabin that sat across the river.

All in all, he was happy these days, which is more than he could say when he lived in Florida. After his divorce, the Sunshine State had felt gloomy. He hadn't been able to shake the feeling, and then he'd remembered being a foster kid here in Sweetwater Springs, North Carolina. A charity event for bikers had given him an excuse to come back for a visit, and he'd never left. Not yet, at least.

"I told all my friends about this class," Alice said. "You're going to have a full and captive audience with us."

Nerves buzzed to life in his stomach. He didn't mind public speaking, but he hoped most were happy to be here, unlike the frowner in the corner.

More students piled in and took their seats, and then the timid librarian came to the door. She nibbled on her lower lip, her gaze skittering everywhere but to meet his directly. "Do you need anything?"

Paris shook his head. "No, we have plenty of

computers. We'll just get acquainted with them and go from there."

She looked up at him now, a blush rising over her high cheekbones. She had light brown hair spilling out of a messy bun and curling softly around her jawline. She had a pretty face, made more beautiful by her rich brown eyes and rose-colored mouth. "Well, you know where I am if you do need something." She looked at the group. "Enjoy!"

"You hired a looker!" Greta Merchant hollered at Lacy. "And for that, there'll be cookies in your future, Ms. Lacy! I'll bring a plate next class!"

The blush on Lacy's cheeks deepened as her gaze jumped to meet his momentarily. "Well, I won't turn down your cookies, Ms. Greta," she said.

Paris watched her for a moment as she waved and headed back to her post.

"The ink in those tattoos going to your brain?" the frowner called to him. "It's time to get started. I don't have all day, you know."

Paris pulled his gaze from the librarian and faced the man. "Neither do I. Let's learn something new, shall we?"

An hour later, Paris had taught the class of eleven to turn on and turn off the laptops. It'd taken an excruciating amount of time to teach everyone to open a browser and use a search engine. Overall, it'd gone well, and the hour had flown by.

"Great job," Alice said to him approvingly. She patted a motherly hand on his back that made him feel warm and appreciated. That feeling quickly dissipated as the frowner headed out the door.

"I already knew most of what you taught," he said.

Who was this person, and why was he so grouchy?

"Well, then you probably didn't need this class," Paris pointed out politely. "Actually, you probably could've taught it yourself."

The frowner harrumphed. "Next time *teach* something."

Paris nodded. "Yes, sir. I'll do my best."

"Your best is the only acceptable thing," the man said before walking out.

Paris froze for a moment, reaching for the memory that the frowner had just stirred. *Your best is the only acceptable thing.* His foster dad here in Sweetwater Springs used to say that to him. That man had been nothing but encouraging. He'd taught Paris more about life in six months than anyone ever had before or since.

Paris hadn't even caught his student's name, and there was no roster for this computer skills class. People had walked in and attended without any kind of formal record.

Paris watched the frowner walk with slow, shuffled steps. He was old, and his back was rounded. A hat sat on his head, casting a shadow on his leathered face. All Paris had really seen of him was his deep, disapproving frown. It'd been nearly two decades since Paris had laid eyes on Mr. Jenson, but he remembered his former foster dad being taller. Then again, Paris had been just a child.

When Paris had returned to Sweetwater Springs last year, he'd decided to call. Mrs. Jenson had been the one to answer. She'd told him she didn't remember a boy named PJ, which is the name Paris had gone by back then. "Please, please, leave us alone! Don't call here again!" she'd pleaded on the line, much to Paris's horror. "Just leave us alone."

The memory made Paris's chest ache as he watched the older man turn the corner of the library and disappear. He resisted the urge to follow him and see if it really was Mr. Jenson. But the Jensons had given Paris so much growing up that he was willing to do whatever he could to repay their kindness—even if it meant staying away.

* * *

Lacy was checking out books for the Fields girls and their nanny when Paris walked by. She watched him leave. If you flipped to the word *suave* in the dictionary, his picture was probably there.

"I plan to bring the girls to your summer reader group in a couple weeks," Mrs. Townsend said.

Of course she did. That would be a convenient nap time for her.

"I always love to see the girls." Lacy smiled down at the children. Their father, Granger Fields, and his family owned Merry Mountain Farms in town where Lacy always got her blue spruce for the holidays.

Lacy waved as the little girls collected their bags of books and skipped out with Mrs. Townsend following behind them.

For the rest of the afternoon, Lacy worked on ongoing programs and plans for the summer and fall. At six p.m., she turned off the lights to the building and headed into the parking lot.

She was involved with the Ladies' Day Out group, a gaggle of women who regularly got together to hang out and have fun. Tonight, they were meeting at Lacy's house to discuss a book that she'd chosen for everyone to read. They were in no way a book club, but since it was her turn to decide what they did, Lacy had turned it into one this time.

Excitement brimmed as she drove home. When she pulled up to her small one-bedroom house on Pine Cone Lane, she noticed two of her sisters' cars already parked in the driveway. Birdie and Rose had texted her during the day to see what they could do to help. Seeing the lights on inside Lacy's home, they'd evidently ignored Lacy's claims that she didn't need anything and had used her hideaway key under the flowerpot.

"Honey, I'm home!" Lacy called as she headed through the front door.

Birdie, her older sister by one year, turned to face her. "Hey, sis. Rose and I were just cleaning up for you."

"Great." Lacy set her purse down. "Now I don't have to."

"What is this?" Rose asked, stepping up beside Birdie. Rose was one year younger than Lacy. Their mom had been very busy those first three years of marriage.

Lacy looked at the small postcard that Rose held up.

"You were supposed to RSVP if you were going to your ten-year class reunion," Rose said. "You needed to send this postcard back."

"Only if I'm going," Lacy corrected.

"Of course you're going," Birdie said. "I went to my ten-year reunion last year, and it was amazing. I wish we had one every year. I wouldn't miss it."

Unlike Lacy, her sisters had been popular in school. They hadn't had to wear a bulky back brace that made them look like a box turtle in its shell. It had drawn nothing but negative attention during those long, tormenting years.

"It's not really a time in my life that I want to remember," Lacy pointed out as she passed them and headed into the kitchen for a glass of lemonade. Or perhaps she should go ahead and pour herself something stronger. She could tell she might need it tonight.

A knock on her front door made her turn. "Who is that?" Lacy asked. "I scheduled the book discussion for seven. It's only six." Lacy set down the glass she'd pulled from the cabinet and went to follow her sisters to the door.

"About that," Birdie said a bit sheepishly. "We changed the plan at the last minute."

Lacy didn't like the sound of that. "What do you mean?"

"No one actually read the book you chose," Birdie said as Rose let the first arrivals in. "Instead, we're playing matchmaker tonight. What goes together better than summer and love?"

Lacy frowned. "If you wanted summer love, I could've chosen a romance novel to read instead."

Birdie gave her a disapproving look. Lacy doubted anyone was more disappointed about tonight's shift in festivities than her though.

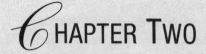

CHAPTER TWO

*P*aris hadn't been able to fully concentrate for the last hour and a half as he sat in front of his computer working on a job for Peak Designs Architectural Firm. His mind was in other places. Primarily the library.

The Frowner, as he'd come to think of the old man in his class, was forefront in his mind. Was it possible that the Frowner was Mr. Jenson?

It couldn't be. Mr. Jenson had been a loving, caring guy, from what Paris remembered. Granted, loving and caring were subjective, and Paris hadn't had much to go on back then.

Mrs. Jenson had been the mother that Paris had always wished he had. She'd doted on him, offering affection and unconditional love. Even though Paris had been a boy who'd landed himself in the principal's office most afternoons, Mrs. Jenson had never raised her voice. And Mr. Jenson had always come home from his job and sat down with Paris, giving him a lecture that had proved to be more like a life lesson.

Paris had never forgotten those lessons. Or that man.

He blinked the memories away and returned his attention to the design he was working on. It was good, but he only did excellent jobs. *Your best is the only acceptable thing.*

He stared at the design for another moment and then decided to come back to it tomorrow when he wasn't so tired. Instead, he went to his Facebook page and searched Albert Jenson's name. He'd done so before, but no profiles under that name had popped up. This time, one did. The user had a profile picture of a rose instead of himself. Paris's old foster dad had loved his rose gardens. This must be him!

Paris scrolled down, reading the most recent posts. One read that Mr. Jenson had gone to the nursing home to visit his wife, Nancy.

Paris frowned at the news. The transition must have been recent because Mrs. Jenson had been home when he'd called late last year. She'd been the one to pretty much tell him to get lost.

He continued to scroll through more pictures of roses and paused at another post. This one read that Mr. Jenson had just signed up for a computer skills class at the Sweetwater Library.

So it was true. Mr. Jenson, the foster dad who'd taught him so much, was also the Frowner.

* * *

Lacy had decided to stick to just lemonade tonight since she was hosting the Ladies' Day Out group. But plans were meant to be changed, as evidenced by the fact that the book discussion she'd organized had turned into the women sitting around her living room, eyes on a laptop screen while perusing an online dating site.

"Oh, he's cute!" Alice Hampton said, sitting on the couch and leaning over Josie Kellum's shoulder as she tapped her fingers along the keys of Lacy's laptop. Not that anyone had asked to use her computer. The women had just helped themselves.

Lacy reached for the bottle of wine, poured herself a deep glass, and then headed over to see who they were looking at. "I know him," she said, standing between her sisters behind the couch. "He comes into the library all the time."

"Any interest?" Josie asked.

Lacy felt her face scrunch at the idea of anything romantic with her library patron. "Definitely not. I know what his reading interests are and frankly, they scare me. That's all I'll say on that."

She stepped away from her sisters and walked across the room to look out the window. The moon was full tonight. Her driveway was also full, with cars parked along the curb. She wasn't a social butterfly by any means, but she looked like one this evening and that made her feel strangely satisfied.

"So what are your hobbies, Lacy?" Josie asked. "Other than reading, of course."

"Well, I like to go for long walks," Lacy said, still watching out the window.

Josie tapped a few more keys. "Mmm-hmm. What's your favorite food?"

Lacy turned and looked back at the group. "Hot dogs," she said, earning her a look from the other women.

"Do you know what hot dogs are made out of?" Greta wanted to know.

"Yes, of course I do. Why do I feel like I'm being interviewed for one of your articles right now?"

"Not an article," Birdie said. "A dating profile."

"What?" Lacy nearly spilled her glass of wine as she moved to look over Josie's shoulder. "What are you doing? I don't want to be up on Fish In The Sea dot com. Stop that."

Birdie gave her a stern look. "You have a class reunion coming up, and you can't go alone."

"I'm not going period," Lacy reiterated.

"Not going to your class reunion?" Dawanda from the fudge shop asked. She was middle-aged with spiky, bright red hair. She tsked from across the room, where she sat in an old, worn recliner that Lacy had gotten from a garage sale during college.

Lacy finished off her wine and set the empty glass on the coffee table nearby. "I already told you, high school was a miserable time that I don't want to revisit."

"All the more reason you *should* go," Birdie insisted. Even though she was only a year older, Birdie acted like Lacy's mother sometimes.

"Why, so I can be traumatized all over again?" Lacy shook her head. "It took me years to get over all the pranks and ridicule. Returning to the scene of the crime could reverse all my progress."

"What progress?" Rose asked. "You never go out, and you never date."

Lacy furrowed her brow. "I go to the café all the time."

"Alone and you sit in the back," Birdie pointed out. "Your back brace is gone, but you're still hiding in the corner."

Lacy's jaw dropped. She wanted to argue but couldn't. Her sister was right.

"So we're making Lacy a dating profile," Josie continued, looking back down at the laptop's screen. "Twenty-eight years old, loves to read, and takes long walks in the park."

"I never said anything about the park," Lacy objected.

"It sounds more romantic that way." Josie didn't bother to look up. "Loves exotic fruit…"

"I said hot dogs."

This time Josie turned her head and looked at Lacy over her shoulder. "Hot dogs don't go on dating profiles…but cute, wagging dogs do." Her fingers started flying across the keyboard.

"I like cats." Lacy watched for another moment and then went to pour herself another glass of wine as the women created her profile at FishInTheSea.com.

After a few drinks, she relaxed a little and started feeding Josie more details about herself. She wasn't actually going to do this, of course. Online dating seemed so unromantic. She wanted to find Mr. Right the old-fashioned way, where fate introduced him into her life and sparks flew like a massive explosion of fireworks. Or at least like a sparkler.

* * *

An hour later, Lacy said goodbye to the group and sat on the couch. She gave the book she'd wanted to discuss a sidelong glance, and then she reached for her laptop. The dating profile stared back at her, taking her by surprise. They'd used a profile picture from when she'd been a bridesmaid at a wedding last year. Her hair was swept up and she had a dipping neckline on her dress that showed off more skin than normal. Lacy read what Josie and her sisters had written. The truth was disregarded in favor of more interesting things.

Lacy was proud of who she was, but the women were right. She wasn't acting that way by shying away from her reunion. She was acting like the girl in the back brace, quietly sitting in the far corner of the room out of fear that others might do something nasty like stick a sign on her back that read KICK ME! I WON'T FEEL IT!

"Maybe I should go to the reunion," she said out loud. "Or maybe I should delete this profile and forget all about it."

The decision hummed through her body along with the effect of one too many glasses of wine. After a moment, she shut the laptop and went to bed. She could decide her profile's fate tomorrow.

* * *

The next morning, Paris woke with the birds outside his window. After a shower and a quick bite, he grabbed his laptop to work on the deck, which served as his office these days. Before getting started on the Peak Designs logo, he scrolled through email and social media. He clicked on

Mr. Jenson's profile again, only to read a post that Paris probably didn't need first thing in the morning.

> The computer skills class was a complete waste of time. Learned nothing. Either I'm a genius or the instructor is an idiot.

The muscles along the back of his neck tightened. At least he didn't need to wonder if Mr. Jenson would be back.

He read another post.

> Went to see Nancy today. I think she misses her roses more than she misses me. She wants to come home, and this old house certainly isn't home without her.

Paris felt like he'd taken a fall from his bike, landing chest-first and having the breath knocked out of him. Why wasn't Mrs. Jenson home? What was wrong with her? And why was Mr. Jenson so different from the man he remembered?

Paris pushed those questions from his mind and began work on some graphic designs. Several hours later, he'd achieved much more than he'd expected. He shoved his laptop into its bag, grabbed his keys, and rode his motorcycle to the library. As he walked inside, his gaze immediately went to the librarian. Her hair was pulled back with some kind of stick poking through it today. He studied her as she checked books into the system on her desktop.

She glanced up and offered a shy wave, which he returned as he headed toward the computer room. He would have expected Mr. Jenson not to return to class today based on his Facebook comments, but Mr. Jenson was already waiting for him when he walked in. All the other students from the previous day filed in within the next few minutes.

"Today I'm teaching you all to use Microsoft Word," he told the group.

"Why would I use Microsoft Word?" Alice Hampton asked. Her questions were presented in a curious manner rather than the questions that Mr. Jenson posed, which felt more like an attack.

"Well, let's say you want to write a report for some reason. Then you could do one here. Or if you wanted to get creative and write a novel, then this is the program you'd use."

"I've always wanted to write a book," Greta told Alice. "It's on my bucket list, and I'm running out of time."

"Are you sick?" Alice asked with concern, their conversation hijacking the class.

"No, I'm healthy as a buzzard. Just old, and I can't live forever," Greta told her.

"Love keeps you young," Edna Baker said from a few chairs down. She was the grandmother of the local police chief, Alex Baker. "Maybe you should join one of those online dating sites."

The group got excited suddenly and turned to Paris, who had leaned back against one of the counters, arms folded over his chest as he listened.

He lifted a brow. "What?"

"A dating site," Edna reiterated. "We helped Lacy Shaw join one last night in our Ladies' Day Out group."

"The librarian?" Paris asked, his interest piquing.

"Had to do it with her dragging and screaming, but we did it. I wouldn't mind making a profile of my own," Edna continued.

"Me too." Greta nodded along with a few other women.

"I'm married," Mr. Jenson said in his usual grumpy demeanor. "I have no reason to be on a dating site."

"Then leave, Albert," Greta called out.

Mr. Jenson didn't budge.

"We're here to learn about what interests us, right?" Edna asked Paris.

He shrugged. There was no official syllabus. He was just supposed to teach computer literacy for the seniors in town. "I guess so."

"Well, majority rules. We want to get on one of those dating sites. I think the one we were on last night was called Fish In The Sea dot com."

Paris unfolded his arms, debating if he was actually going to agree to this. He somehow doubted the Sweetwater Springs librarian would approve, even if she'd apparently been on the site herself.

"Fine, I'll get you started," Paris finally relented, "but tomorrow, we're learning about Microsoft Word."

"I don't want to write a report or a novel," Mr. Jenson said, his frown so deep it joined with the fold of his double chin.

"Again, don't come if you don't want to," Greta nearly shouted. "No one is forcing you."

Paris suspected that Mr. Jenson would be back regardless of his opinions. Maybe he was lonely. Or maybe, despite his demeanor, this was his idea of a good time.

After teaching the group how to use the search bar function and get to the Fish In the Sea website, Paris walked around to make sure everyone knew how to open an account. Some started making their own profiles while others watched their neighbors' screens.

"This is Lacy's profile," Alice said when he made his way to her.

Paris leaned in to take a closer look. "That's not the librarian here."

"Oh, it is. This photo was taken when she was a bridesmaid last year. Isn't she beautiful?"

For a moment, Paris couldn't pull his gaze away from the screen. If he were on the dating site, he'd be interested in her. "Likes to hike. Loves dogs. Favorite food is a hot dog. Looking for adventure," he read. "That isn't at all what I would have pegged Lacy as enjoying."

Alice gave him a look. "Maybe there's more to her than meets the eye. Would you like to sit down and create your own profile? Then you could give her a wink or a nibble or whatever the online dating lingo is."

He blinked, pulled his gaze from the screen, and narrowed his eyes at his former landlord. "You know I'm not interested in that kind of thing." He'd told Alice all about his past when he'd rented a room from her last year. After his messy marriage, the last thing he wanted was to jump into another relationship.

"Well, what I know is, you're young, and your heart can take a few more beatings if it comes to it. Mine, on the other hand, can't, which is why I'm not creating one of these profiles."

Paris chuckled. "Hate to disappoint, but I won't be either." Even if seeing Lacy's profile tempted him to do otherwise.

* * *

At the end of the hour, Paris was the last to leave his class, following behind Mr. Jenson, who had yet to hold a personal conversation with him or say a civilized thing in his direction.

He didn't recognize Paris, and why would he? Paris had been a boy back then. His hair had been long and had often hung in his eyes. His body had been scrawny from neglect and he hadn't gotten his growth spurt until well into his teen years. He hadn't even had the same last name back then. He'd gone by PJ Drake before his parents' divorce. Then there was a custody battle, which was the opposite of what one might think. Instead of fighting *for* him, his parents had fought over who *had* to take him.

"Mr. Jenson?" Paris called.

The older man turned to look at Paris with disdain.

"How was the class?"

"An utter waste of time."

Paris liked to think he had thick skin, but his former

foster dad's words had sharp edges that penetrated deep. "Okay, well what computer skills would you like to learn?"

The skin between Mr. Jenson's eyes made a deep divot as he seemed to think. "I can't see my wife every day like I want to because I don't drive. It's hard for an old man like me to go so far. The nurses say they can set up Skype to talk to her, but I don't understand it. They didn't have that sort of thing when I was old enough to learn new tricks."

"Never too late," Paris said. "A great man once taught me that."

That great man was standing in front of him now, whether he knew it or not. And he needed his own pep talk of sorts. "Come back tomorrow, and we'll get you set up for that."

Mr. Jenson frowned back at him. "We'll see."

* * *

Lacy was trying not to panic.

A blue circle had started spinning on her laptop screen five minutes ago. Now there were pop-up boxes that she couldn't seem to get rid of. She'd restarted her computer, but the pop-up boxes were relentless. She sucked in a breath and blew it out audibly. Then another, bordering on hyperventilation.

"You okay?" a man's voice asked.

Her gaze lifted to meet Paris's. "Oh. Yeah." She shook her head.

"You're saying yes, but you're shaking your head no."

His smile was the kind that made women swoon, and for a moment, she forgot that she was in panic mode.

"My computer seems to be possessed," she told him.

This made Paris chuckle—a sound that seemed to lessen the tension inside her. "Mind if I take a look?"

She needed to say no. He was gorgeous, charming, and cool. And those three qualities made her nervous. But without her computer, she wouldn't be able to pay her bills after work. Or delete that dating profile that the Ladies' Day Out group had made for her last night. *Why didn't I delete it right away?*

"Yes, please," she finally said.

Paris headed around the counter. "Did you restart it?" he asked when he was standing right next to her. So close that she could smell the woodsy scent coming off his body. She could also feel a wave of heat radiating off him, burning the superficial layer of her skin. He was gorgeous, charming, cool, *and* he smelled divine. What woman could resist?

"I've restarted it twice already," she told him.

"Hmm." He put his bag down on the floor at his feet and stood in front of her computer. She couldn't help a closer inspection of the tattoos that covered his biceps muscles. They were colorful and artistically drawn, but she could only see parts of them. She had to resist pulling back the fabric of his shirt to admire the artwork there. What was wrong with her?

Paris turned his head to look at her. "Is it okay if I close out all the programs you currently have running?"

"Of course."

He tapped his fingers along her keys, working for

several long minutes while she drifted off in her own thoughts of his muscles and tattoos and the spicy scent of his aftershave. Then he straightened and turned back to her. "There you go, good as new."

"Wow. Really? That was fast."

He shrugged a nonchalant shoulder. "I just needed to reboot and run your virus software."

"You make it sound so easy."

"To me it is. I know computers. We have a kinship."

Lacy felt the same way about books. She reached for her cup of coffee that she'd purchased this morning, even though a jolt of caffeine was probably the last thing her nerves needed right now.

Paris pointed a finger at the cup. "That's where I know you from. You're the woman at the café. You always sit in the back with a book."

Her lips parted as she set her cup down. "You've noticed me?"

"Of course. Why wouldn't I?"

She shrugged and shook her head. "We've just never spoken." And she'd assumed she was invisible in the back corner, especially to someone like him. "Well, thank you for fixing my computer."

"Just a friend helping a friend." He met her gaze and held it for a long moment. Then he bent to pick up the strap of his bag, hung it over his shoulder, and headed around to the other side of the counter. "Be careful on those dating sites," he said, stopping as he passed in front of her. "Always meet at a safe location and don't give anyone your personal information until you know you can trust them."

"Hmm?" Lacy narrowed her eyes, and then her heart soared into her throat and her gaze dropped to her fixed computer. Up on the screen, first and foremost, was FishInTheSea.com. She giggled nervously as her body filled with mortification. "I didn't...I'm not..." Why wouldn't her mouth work? "This isn't what it looks like."

Paris grinned. "The women in my class told me about last night. Sounds like you were forced into it."

"Completely," she said with relief.

He shrugged. "I doubt you need a website to find a date. They created a really attractive profile for you though. It should get you a lot of nibbles from the fish in the sea."

She laughed because he'd made a joke, but there was no hope of making intelligible words right now. Instead she waved and watched him leave.

"See you tomorrow, Lace," he called over his shoulder.

* * *

That evening, Paris kicked his feet up on the railing of his back deck as he sat in an outdoor chair, laptop on his thighs, watching the fireflies that seemed to be sending him secret messages with their flashing lights. The message he needed right now was "get back to work."

Paris returned to looking at his laptop's screen. He'd worked on the graphic for Peak Designs Architectural Firm all evening, and he was finally happy with it. He sent it off to the owner and then began work on a

new agenda for tomorrow's class. He'd be teaching his
students how to Skype, and he'd make sure Mr. Jenson
knew how to do it on his own before leaving.

Paris liked the thought of reuniting Mr. and Mrs.
Jenson through technology. It was the least he could
do for them. Technology shouldn't replace person-to-
person contact, but it was a nice substitute when two
people couldn't be together. Paris suspected one of the
main reasons Mr. Jenson even came to the library was
because it was one of the few places within walking
distance from his house.

Creating an agenda for live communication technology took all of ten minutes. Then Paris gave in to his
impulse to search FishInTheSea.com. He found himself
looking at Lacy's profile again, staring at the beautiful
picture on the screen. Her brown hair was down and
spilling over one shoulder in soft curls. She had on
makeup that accentuated her eyes, cheekbones, and lips.
And even though she looked so different from the person
he'd met, she also looked very much the same.

"Why am I on a dating site?" he muttered, his voice
blending with the night sounds. And for that matter,
why was he staring at Lacy's profile? Maybe he was
just as lonely as Mr. Jenson.

CHAPTER THREE

"I love the design," Pearson Matthews told Paris on Friday afternoon as Paris zipped down the gently winding mountain road on his bike. The pavement was still wet from the rain earlier this morning. Puddles splashed the legs of his jeans as he hit them.

He had earbuds in place under his helmet so he could ride hands-free and hold a conversation without the roar of the engine interfering. "I'm glad you like it, sir."

"Love. I said love," Pearson said. "And I plan to recommend you to everyone I know. I'm part of the Chamber of Commerce, so I have business connections. I'm going to make sure you have enough work to keep you in Sweetwater Springs for years to come."

Paris felt a curious kick in his heart. He loved this town and didn't like to think about leaving...but he had never been one to stick anywhere for long either. He credited the foster system for that. "Thank you."

"No need for thanks. You did a great job, and I want others to know about it. You're an asset here."

Paris resisted saying thank you a second time. "Well,

please make sure anyone you send my way tells me that you referred them. I give referral perks."

Pearson was one of the richest men in the community, so he likely didn't need any perks. "Sounds good. I'll talk to you soon."

They hung up, and Paris continued down the road, slowing at the entrance to the local library. His heart gave another curious kick at the thought of Lacy for a reason he didn't want to investigate. He parked, got off his bike, and then walked inside with his laptop bag on his shoulder.

Lacy wasn't behind the counter when he walked in. His gaze roamed the room, finding her with two little girls that he'd seen here before. She was helping them locate a book. One little girl was squirming as she stood in place, and Paris thought maybe she needed to locate a restroom first.

"Here you go. I think you girls will like this one," he heard Lacy tell them. "Abby, do you need to use the bathroom?"

The girl bobbed her head emphatically.

"You know where it is. Go ahead." Lacy pointed to the bathroom near the front entrance's double doors, and both girls took off in a sprint. Lacy watched them for a moment and then turned back to her computer. She gasped softly when she saw Paris. "You're here early. Do you need something?" she asked.

Need something? Yeah, he needed an excuse for why he'd been standing here stupidly waiting to talk to her.

"A book maybe?" Lacy stepped closer and lowered her voice.

"Yeah," he said. "I'm looking for a book."

"Okay. What exactly are you looking for?" she asked.

He scanned the surrounding shelves before his gaze landed back on her. "Actually, do you have anything on roses?"

Lacy's perfectly pink lips parted.

Paris had been trying to think of something he could do for his former foster parents, and roses had come to mind. Albert Jenson loved roses, but his wife, Nancy, adored the thorny beauties. "I was thinking about making a flower garden at the nursing home, but my thumbs are more black than green."

Lacy giggled softly. "Follow me." She led him to a wall of books in the nonfiction area and bent to inspect the titles.

Paris tried and failed not to admire her curves as she leaned forward in front of him. *Get it together, man.*

"Here you go. *The Dummie's Guide to Roses.*" She straightened and held a book out to him.

"Dummie's Guide?"

Her cheeks flushed. "Don't take offense. I didn't title it."

Paris made a point of looking at the other titles that had sandwiched the book on the shelf. "No, but you didn't choose to give me the one titled *Everything There Is to Know About Roses* or *The Rose Lover's Handbook.*" He returned to looking at her, fascinated by how easily he could make her blush. "Any luck on Fish In The Sea dot com?"

She looked away, pulling her hands to her midsection to fidget. "I've been meaning to cancel that. The ladies had good intentions when they signed me up, albeit misguided."

"Why did they choose you as their victim?"

Lacy shrugged. "I have this high school reunion coming up. They thought I'd be more likely to go if I had a date."

"You're not going to your own reunion?" Paris asked.

"I haven't decided yet," she said as she inched away and increased the distance between them.

Unable to help himself, Paris inched forward. He told himself it was because they had to whisper and he couldn't hear her otherwise.

"Have you gone to one of yours?" she asked.

"No." He shook his head. "I never stayed in one place long enough while I was growing up to be considered an official part of a class. If I had, I would." He looked at her. "You should go. I'm sure you could find a date, even without the dating site." Part of him was tempted to offer to take her himself. By nature, he was a helpful guy. He resisted offering though because there was another part of him that wanted to be her date for an entirely different reason.

He lifted *The Dummie's Guide to Roses*. "I'll just check this out and get set up for my class."

Lacy headed back behind the counter and held out her hand to him. "Library card, please."

"Library card?" he repeated.

"I need it to check you out."

He laid the book on the counter. "I, uh, I..."

"You don't have one?" she asked, grinning back at him.

"I do most of my reading on the computer. I guess it's been a while since I've checked a book out."

"No problem." She opened a drawer and pulled out a blank card. "I can make you one right now. Do you have a driver's license?".

He pulled out his wallet and laid his license on the counter. He watched as she grabbed it and got to work. Then she handed the card back to him, her fingers brushing his slightly in the handoff. Every nerve in his body responded to that one touch. If he wasn't mistaken, she seemed affected as well.

There was the real reason he hadn't offered to be her date for her class reunion. He was attracted to Lacy Shaw, and he *really* didn't want to be.

* * *

Lacy lifted her gaze to the computer room in the back of the library where Paris was teaching a class of unruly elders. From afar, he actually seemed to be enjoying himself. She'd called several people before Paris, trying to persuade them to teach a class here, and everyone had been too busy with their own lives. That made her wonder why a guy like Paris was able to accept her offer. Did he have any family? Close friends? A girlfriend?

She roped in her gaze and continued checking in books from the pile beside her. Paris Montgomery's personal life was none of her business.

"Ms. Shaw! Ms. Shaw!" Abigail and Willow Fields came running toward the checkout counter.

"What's wrong, girls?" Lacy sat up straighter, noting the panic in the sisters' voices.

"Mrs. Townsend won't wake up! We thought she was sleeping, but she won't wake up!"

Lacy took off running to the other side of the room where she'd known Mrs. Townsend was sleeping. Immediately, she recognized that the older woman was hunched over the table in an unnatural way. Her skin was a pale gray color that sent chills up Lacy's spine.

Panic gripped Lacy as she looked around at the small crowd of people who'd gathered. "Does anyone know CPR?" she called. There were at least a dozen books here on the subject, but she'd never learned.

Everyone gave her a blank stare. Lacy's gaze snagged on the young sisters huddled against the wall with tears spilling over their pale cheeks. If Mrs. Townsend died in front of them, they'd be devastated.

"Let's get her on the floor," a man's voice said, coming up behind Lacy.

She glanced back, surprised to find Paris in action.

He gently grabbed hold of Mrs. Townsend and laid her on the floor, taking control of the situation. She was never more thankful for help in her life.

"Call 911!" Lacy shouted to the crowd, relieved to see a young woman run toward the library counter where there was a phone. A moment later, the woman headed back. "They're on their way."

Lacy nodded as she returned to watching Paris perform chest compressions. He seemed to know exactly what to do. Several long minutes later, sirens filled the parking lot, and paramedics placed Mrs. Townsend onto a gurney. They revived her just enough for Mrs. Townsend to moan and look at the girls, her face seeming to contort with concern.

"It's okay. I'll take care of them, Mrs. Townsend," Lacy told her. "Just worry about taking care of yourself right now."

Lacy hoped Mrs. Townsend heard and understood. A second later, the paramedics loaded the older woman in the back of the ambulance and sped away, sirens screaming as they tore down the street.

Lacy stood on wobbly legs and tried to catch her breath. She pressed a hand against her chest, feeling like she might collapse or dissolve into tears.

"You all right?" Paris asked, pinning his ocean-blue gaze on hers.

She looked at him and shook her head. "Yes."

"You're contradicting yourself again," he said with a slight lift at one corner of his mouth. Then his hand went to her shoulder and squeezed softly. "Why don't you go sit down?"

"The girls," Lacy said, suddenly remembering her promise. She turned to where the sisters were still huddled and hurried over to where they were. "Mrs. Townsend is going to get help at the hospital. They'll take good care of her there, I promise."

Abby looked up. "What's wrong with her?"

Lacy shook her head. "I'm not sure, honey. I'm sure everything will be okay. Right now, I'm going to call your dad to come get you."

"He's at work," Willow said. "That's why we were with Mrs. Townsend."

"I know, honey. But he won't mind leaving the farm for a little bit. Follow me to the counter. I have some cookies up there."

The girls' eyes lit up, even as tears dripped from their eyelashes.

"I can call Granger while you take care of the girls," Paris offered.

How did Paris know that these sweet little children belonged to Granger Fields? As if hearing her thoughts, he explained, "I did some graphic design work on the Merry Mountain Farms website recently."

"Of course. That would be great," Lacy said, her voice sounding shaky. And she'd do her best to calm down in the meantime too.

* * *

Thirty minutes later, Granger Fields left the library with his little girls in tow, and Lacy plopped down on her stool behind the counter. The other patrons had emptied out of the library as well, and it was two minutes until closing time.

"Eventful afternoon," Paris said.

Lacy startled as he walked into view. She hadn't realized he was still here. "You were great with the CPR. You might have a second career as a paramedic."

He shook his head. "I took a class in college, but I'll stick to computers, thanks."

"And I'll stick to books. My entire body is still trembling."

Paris's dark brows stitched together. "I can take you home if you're not up for driving."

"On your bike?" she asked. "I'm afraid that wouldn't help my nerves at all."

Paris chuckled. "Not a fan of motorcycles, huh?"

"I've never been on one, and I don't plan to start this evening. It's time to close, and my plans include calling the hospital to check on Mrs. Townsend and then going home, changing into my PJs, and soothing my nerves with ice cream."

Paris leaned against her counter. "While you were with the girls, I called a friend I know who works at Sweetwater Memorial. She checked on things for me and just texted me an update." He held up his cell phone. "Mrs. Townsend is stable but being admitted so they can watch her over the next forty-eight hours."

Lacy blew out a breath. "That's really good news. For a moment there, she looked like she might die. If we hadn't gone over to her when we did, she might have just passed away in her sleep." Lacy wasn't sure she would've felt as safe in her little library ever again if that had happened.

"Life is fragile," Paris said. "Something like this definitely puts things into perspective, doesn't it?"

"It really does." Her worries and fears suddenly seemed so silly and so small.

Paris straightened from the counter and tugged his bag higher on his shoulder. "See you tomorrow," he said as he headed out of the library.

She watched him go and then set about to turning off all the lights. She grabbed her things and locked up behind her as she left, noticing Paris and his motorcycle beside her car in the parking lot.

"If I didn't know you were a nice guy, I might be a little scared by the fact that you're waiting beside my car in an empty parking lot."

"I'm harmless." He hugged his helmet against him. "You looked a little rattled in there. I wanted to make sure you got home safely. I'll follow you."

Lacy folded her arms over her chest. "Maybe I don't want you to know where I live."

"The end of Pine Cone Lane. This is a small town, and I get around with business."

"I see. Well, you don't need to follow me home. Really, I'm fine."

"I'd feel better if I did."

Lacy held out her arms. "Suit yourself. Good night, Paris." She stepped inside her vehicle, closed the door behind her, and cranked her engine. It rolled and flopped. She turned the key again. This time it didn't even roll. "Crap." This day just kept getting better.

After a few more attempts, Paris tapped on her driver's side window.

She opened the door. "The battery is dead. I think I left my lights on this morning." It'd been raining, and she'd had them on to navigate through the storm. She'd forgotten her umbrella, so she'd turned off her engine, gotten out of her car, and had darted toward the library. In her rush, she must've forgotten to turn off her lights.

"I'll call Jere's Shop. He can jump your battery or tow it back to your house," Paris said.

Lacy considered the plan. "I can just wait here for him and drive it back myself."

"Jere is dependable but slow. You don't need to be out here waiting for him all evening. Leave your keys in the ignition, and I'll take you home."

Lacy looked at the helmet that Paris now extended toward her, her brain searching for another option. She didn't want to be here all night. She could call one of her sisters, but they would then follow her inside, and she didn't want to deal with them after the day she'd had either.

She got out of the car and took the helmet. "Okay," she said, shaking her head no.

This made Paris laugh as he led her to his bike. "You are one big contradiction, Lacy Shaw."

* * *

Paris straddled his bike and waited for Lacy to take the seat behind him. He glanced over his shoulder as she wrung her hands nervously. She seemed to be giving herself a pep talk, and then she lunged, as if forcing herself, and straddled the seat behind him.

Paris grinned and waited for another long second. "You know, you're going to have to wrap your arms around my waist for the ride."

"Right," he heard her say in a muffled voice. Her arms embraced him, clinging more tightly as he put the motorcycle in motion. Before he was even down the road, Lacy's grasp on him was so tight that her head rested on his back. He kind of liked the feel of her body hugging his, even if it was because she was scared for her life.

He knew the way to her house, but at the last second, he decided to take a different route. Lacy didn't speak up, so he guessed her eyes were shut tightly, blocking out the streets that zipped past.

Instead of taking her home, he drove her to the park, where the hot spring was. There were hiking trails and a hot dog vendor too. On her profile, Lacy had said those were among her favorite things, and after this afternoon, she deserved a few guilty pleasures.

He pulled into the parking lot and cut the engine. Slowly, Lacy peeled her body away from him. He felt her shift as she looked around.

She removed her helmet. "Why are we at the park?"

Paris glanced back. "Surprise. I thought I'd take your mind off things before I took you home."

She stared at him, a dumbfounded expression creasing her brow. "Why the park?"

"Because you love to take long hikes. And hot dogs, so I thought we'd grab a couple afterward. I didn't wear my hiking boots, but these will work for a quick half mile down the trail. Your profile mentioned that you love the hot spring here."

Lacy blinked. "You read my dating profile?"

"Great late-night reading." He winked.

She drew her hand to her forehead and shook her head. Something told him this time the head shake wasn't a yes. "Most of the information on my profile was exaggerated by the ladies' group. Apparently, they didn't think the real Lacy Shaw was interesting enough."

"You don't like hiking?"

"I like leisurely walks."

"Dogs?" he asked.

"Cats are my preference."

Paris let his gaze roam around them briefly before looking back at her. "What *do* you like?"

"In general?" she asked.

"Let's start with food. I'm starving."

She gave him a hesitant look. "Well, the hot dog part was true, but only because I added that part after they left."

Paris grinned, finding her adorable and sexy at the same time. "I happen to love a good chili dog. And there's a stand at the far side of the park." He waited for her to get off the bike and then he climbed off as well. "Let's go eat, shall we?"

"Saving someone's life works up an appetite, I guess."

"I didn't save Mrs. Townsend's life," he said as they walked. "I just kept her alive so someone else could do that."

From the corner of his eye, he saw Lacy fidgeting.

He reached for her hand to stop the motion. "I brought you here to take your mind off that situation. Let's talk about something light."

"Like?"

"You? Why did you let the Ladies' Day Out group make you a dating profile if you don't want to be on the site?"

Lacy laughed softly as they stepped into a short line for hot dogs. "Have you met the Ladies' Day Out group? They are determined and persistent. When they want something, they don't take no for an answer."

"You're part of the LDO," he pointed out.

"Well, I don't share that same quality."

"You were persistent in getting me to agree to teach a class at the library."

"True. I guess when there's something I want, I go after it." They reached the front of the line and ordered two sodas and two hot dogs. One with chili for him and one without for her.

Lacy opened the flap of her purse, and Paris stopped her. "I brought you here. This is my treat."

"No, I couldn't—"

She started to argue, but he laid a ten-dollar bill in front of the vendor. "It's just sodas and hot dogs." He glanced over. "You can treat me next time."

Her lips parted. He was only teasing, but he saw the question in her eyes, and now it was in his mind too. Would there really be a next time? Would that be so bad?

After collecting the change, they carried their drinks and hot dogs to a nearby bench and sat down.

"I didn't think I'd like teaching, but it's actually kind of fun," Paris confessed.

"Even Mr. Jenson?" she asked before taking a huge bite of her hot dog.

"Even him. But he didn't show up today. Maybe he dropped out." Paris shrugged. "I changed the syllabus just for him. I was planning to teach the class to Skype this afternoon."

"You didn't?"

He shook his head. "I went back to the lesson on Microsoft Word just in case Mr. Jenson showed up next time."

"Maybe he didn't feel well. He's been to every other class this week, right?"

Paris shook his head. "But he's made no secret that he doesn't like my teaching. He's even blasted his opinions all over Facebook."

Lacy grimaced. "Oh my. He treats everyone that way. I wouldn't take it personally. It's just how he is."

"He wasn't always that way. He used to be really nice, if memory serves me correctly."

Lacy narrowed her eyes. "You knew him before the class?"

Paris looked down at his half-eaten hot dog. "He and Mrs. Jenson fostered me for a while, but he doesn't seem to remember me."

"You were in foster care?"

"Yep. The Jensons were my favorite family."

Her jaw dropped. "That's so interesting."

Paris angled his body toward her. "Do you know what's wrong with Mrs. Jenson?"

Lacy shrugged. "I'm not sure. All I know is she's forgetful. She gets confused a lot. I've seen her get pretty agitated with Mr. Jenson too. They used to come into the library together."

"Maybe that's why he's so bitter now," Paris said, thinking out loud. He lifted his hot dog to his mouth and took another bite.

"Perhaps Mr. Jenson just needs someone to help him."

Paris chewed and swallowed. "I'm not even sure how I could help Mr. Jenson. I've been reading up on how to make a rose garden, but that won't make his wife well again."

Lacy hummed thoughtfully. "I think Mr. Jenson just needs someone to treat him nicely, no matter how horrible he is. No matter what he says to me, I always offer him a big smile. I actually think he likes me, although he would never admit it." She giggled to herself.

Paris looked at her. "You seem to really understand people."

"I do a lot of people-watching. And I had years of being an outcast in school." She swiped at a drop of ketchup at the corner of her mouth. "When you're hiding in the back of the classroom, there's not much else to do but watch everyone else. You can learn a lot about a person when they think no one is paying attention."

"Why would you hide?" he asked, growing increasingly interested in Lacy Shaw.

She met his gaze, and he glimpsed something dark in her eyes for a moment. "Childhood scoliosis. I had to wear a back brace to straighten out my spine."

His gaze dropped to her back. It was long and smooth now.

"I don't wear it anymore," she told him. "My back is fixed. High school is when you want to be sporting the latest fashion though, not a heavy brace."

"I'm sure you were just as beautiful."

She looked away shyly, tucking a strand of brown hair behind her ear with one hand. "Anyway, I guess that's why I know human nature. Even the so-called nice kids were afraid to be associated with me. There were a handful of people who didn't care. I'm still close with them."

"Sounds like your childhood was less than desirable.

Kind of like mine," he said. "That's something we have in common."

She looked up. "Who'd have thought? The librarian and the bad boy biker."

"Bad boy?" he repeated, finding this description humorous.

Her cheeks blossomed red just like the roses he'd studied in the library book. She didn't look away, and he couldn't, even if he wanted to. Despite himself, he felt the pull between them, the sexual tension winding around its gear, cranking tighter and tighter. "Perhaps we have a lot more in common."

"Like what?" she asked softly.

"Well, we both like hot dogs."

She smiled softly.

"And I want to kiss you right now. Not sure if you want to kiss me too but…" What was he doing? It was as if something else had taken control of his mind and mouth. He was saying exactly the opposite of what he intended.

Lacy's lips parted, her pupils dilated, and unless he was reading her wrong, she wanted to kiss him too.

Leaning forward, he dropped his mouth and brushed his lips to hers. A little sigh tumbled out of her, and after a moment, she kissed him back.

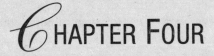

CHAPTER FOUR

*S*parks, tingles, the whole nine yards.

That was what this kiss with Paris was. He was an amazing kisser. He had a firm hand on her thigh and the other gently curled around the back of her neck. This was the Cadillac of kisses, not that Lacy had much experience recently. It'd been a while since she'd kissed anyone. The last guy she'd briefly dated had run the library in the town of River Oaks. They'd shared a love of books, but not much else.

Paris pulled back slightly. "I'm sorry," he said. "I didn't mean to do that."

She blinked him into focus, a dreamlike feeling hanging over her.

"All I wanted to do tonight was take your mind off the afternoon."

"The afternoon?" she repeated.

"Mrs. Townsend?"

"Oh." She straightened a touch. Was that why he'd kissed her? Was he only taking her mind off the trauma of what happened at the library? "I definitely forgot about that for a moment."

"Good." Paris looked around the park. Then he stood and offered her his hand. "Want to take a walk to the hot spring before we leave?"

She allowed him to pull her to standing. "Okay."

She followed him because he'd driven her here. Because he'd kissed her. Because she wasn't sure what to think, but one thing she knew for sure was that she liked being around Paris. He was easy to talk to, and he made her feel good about herself.

"Penny for your thoughts?" he asked a couple of minutes later, walking alongside her.

She could hear the subtle sound of water as they drew closer to the hot spring. "Oh, I was just thinking what a nice night it is."

Paris looked around. "I don't think there's a single season in this town that I don't like. The air is easier to breathe here for some reason." She watched him suck in a deep breath and shivered with her body's response.

"I've always wanted to get in a hot spring," Lacy admitted, turning her attention to the water that was now in view.

"You've never been in?" Paris asked.

Lacy shook her head. "No. That was another fabrication for the profile. I've read that a spring is supposed to help with so many things. Joint and muscle pain. Energy levels. Detoxification."

"Do you need those benefits?" he asked.

Lacy looked up at him. "Not really." All she really needed was to lean into him and press her lips to his once more.

Paris sighed as they walked. "So what should I do?"

A dozen thoughts rushed Lacy's mind. "Hmm?"

"I want to help Mr. Jenson somehow, like you suggested."

"Oh." She looked away as she swallowed. "Well, he didn't show up at today's class. Maybe you could stop by and see him. Tomorrow is Saturday, so there's no class anyway. You could check on him and make sure he's okay."

Paris stared at her. "I have to admit, that old man kind of scares me."

Lacy giggled softly. "Me too." She gasped as an idea rushed into her mind. She didn't give herself time to think before sharing it with Paris. "But I'll go with you. It's my day off."

He cocked his head. "You'd spend your day off helping me?"

"Yes, but there's a condition."

He raised a questioning brow. "What's that?"

"I'll go with you if you'll be my date to my class reunion." Seeing Mrs. Townsend at death's door this afternoon had shaken her up more than she'd realized. "I don't want to hide anymore. I want to go, have a blast, and show everyone who tried to break me that they didn't succeed." And for some reason, Paris made her feel more confident.

Paris grinned at her. "Are you asking me out, Lacy Shaw?"

She swallowed. "Yes. Kind of. I'm offering you a deal."

He shoved his hands in his pockets. "I guess Mr. Jenson might be less likely to slam the door on my face tomorrow if I have a beautiful woman by my side. You said he likes you, so..."

Her insides fluttered to life. "My old bullies might be less likely to pick on me if I have a hot graphic designer as my escort."

This made him laugh. Then Paris stuck out his hand. "Want to shake on it?"

She would prefer to kiss on it, but that first kiss had come with an apology from him. This deal wasn't romantic in nature. It was simply two people helping one another out.

* * *

Even though Paris worked for himself, he still loved a Saturday, especially this one. He and Lacy were spending the day together, and he hadn't looked forward to something like this in a while. He got out of bed with the energy of a man who'd already had his coffee and headed down the hall to brew a pot. Then he dressed in a pair of light-colored jeans and a favorite T-shirt for a local band he loved.

As he sipped his coffee, he thought about last evening and the kiss that probably had a lot to do with his mood this morning. He hadn't planned on kissing Lacy, but the feeling had engulfed him. And her signals were all a go, so he'd leaned in and gone for it.

Magic.

There'd be no kissing today though. He didn't like starting things he couldn't finish, and he wasn't in the market for a relationship. He'd traveled that path, and his marriage had been anything but the happy ending he'd envisioned. He couldn't do anything right for his ex, no matter how hard he'd tried. As soon as he'd realized she was having an affair, he'd left. He didn't stick around where he wasn't wanted.

Paris stood and grabbed his keys. Then he headed out the door to go get Lacy. He'd take his truck today so that he didn't need to torture himself with the feel of her arms around his waist.

A short drive later, he pulled into her driveway on Pine Cone Lane, walked up the steps, and knocked. She opened the door, and for a moment, he forgot to breathe. She wore her hair down, allowing it to spill softly over her shoulders just like in her profile picture. "You look, uh...well, you look nice," he finally said.

She lifted a hand and smoothed her hair on one side. "Thanks. At the library, it's easier to keep my hair pulled back," she explained. "But since I'm off today, I thought I'd let loose."

It was more than her hair. A touch of makeup accented her brown eyes, and she was wearing a soft pink top that brought out the colors in her skin. If he was a painter, he'd be running for his easel. If he was a writer, he'd grab a pen and paper, ignited by inspiration.

But he was just a guy who dabbled on computers. A guy who'd already decided he wasn't going to act on his attraction to the woman standing in front of him.

"I'm ready if you are," she said, stepping onto the porch and closing the front door behind her. She looked out into the driveway. "Oh, you drove something with four wheels today. I was ready for the bike, but I admit I'm kind of relieved."

"The bike grew on you a little bit?"

She shrugged one shoulder. "I could get used to it. My mother would probably kill you if she knew you put me on a motorcycle last night."

"I was rescuing you from being stranded in a dark parking lot," he pointed out.

"The lesser of two evils."

Paris jumped ahead to open her door, winning a curious look from her as well as a new blush on her cheeks—this one not due to makeup.

"Thanks."

He closed the door behind her and then jogged around to the driver's side. Once he was seated behind the steering wheel, he looked over. "Looks like Jere got your car back okay." He gestured toward her Honda Accord parked in front of a single-car garage.

"He left it and texted me afterward. No charge. He said he owed you." Lacy's brows subtly lifted.

"See, it pays to hang around me." Paris started the engine. "I was thinking we could stop in and check on Mrs. Townsend first."

Lacy pointed a finger at him. "I love that idea, even though I'm on to you, Paris Montgomery. You're really just procrastinating because you're scared of Mr. Jenson."

He grimaced as he drove toward the Sweetwater hospital. "That's probably true."

They chatted easily as he drove, discussing all of Lacy's plans for the library this summer. She talked excitedly about her work, which he found all kinds of attractive. Then he pulled into the hospital parking lot, and they both got out.

"We shouldn't go see Mrs. Townsend empty-handed," Lacy said as they walked toward the main entrance.

"We can swing by the gift shop before we go up," he suggested.

"Good idea. She likes magazines, so I'll get her a couple. I hope Abby and Willow are okay. It had to be confusing for them, watching their nanny being taken away in an ambulance."

"The girls only have one parent?" he asked.

"Their mother isn't around," Lacy told him.

Paris slid his gaze over. He wasn't sure he wanted to know, but he asked anyway. "What happened to their mom?" He'd heard a lot of stories from his foster siblings growing up. There were so many reasons for a parent to slip out of the picture. His story was rather boring in comparison to some. His parents didn't like abiding by the law, which left him needing supplementary care at times. Then they'd decided that another thing they didn't like was taking care of him.

"Their mother left right after Willow was born. There was speculation that maybe she had postpartum depression."

Paris swallowed as they veered into the gift shop. "It's good that they have Granger. He seems like a good dad."

"I think so too. And what kid wouldn't want to grow up on a Christmas tree farm? I mean, that's so cool." Lacy beelined toward the magazine rack in the back of the shop, picking out three. They also grabbed some chocolates at the register.

Bag of presents in hand, they left the shop and took the

elevator up to the third floor to Mrs. Townsend's room. Lacy knocked, and they waited for Mrs. Townsend's voice to answer back, telling them to "come in."

"Oh, Lacy! You didn't have to spend your Saturday coming to see me," Mrs. Townsend said as they entered her room. "And you brought a friend."

"Mrs. Townsend, this is Paris Montgomery. He did CPR on you in the library yesterday."

Mrs. Townsend's eyes widened. "I didn't even know I needed CPR. How embarrassing. But thank you," she told Paris. "I guess you were instrumental in saving my life."

"It was no big deal," he said.

"To the woman who's still alive today it is." Mrs. Townsend looked at Lacy again, her gaze dropping to the bag in her hand. "What do you have?"

"Oh, yes." Lacy pulled the magazines out and offered them to Mrs. Townsend, along with the chocolates.

Mrs. Townsend looked delighted by the gifts. "Oh my goodness. Thank you so much."

"Are you doing okay?" Lacy asked.

Mrs. Townsend waved a hand. "The doctors here have been taking good care of me. They tell me I can go home tomorrow."

Lacy smiled. "That's good news."

"Yes, it is. And I'll be caring for the girls again on Monday. A little flutter in the heart won't keep me from doing what I love."

Lacy's gaze slid to meet Paris's as worry creased her brow. He resisted reaching for her hand in a calming gesture. His intentions would be innocent, but they could also confuse things. He and Lacy were only out today as friends. Nothing more.

They stayed and chatted a while longer and then left, riding down the elevator in silence. Paris and Lacy walked side by side back to his truck. He opened the passenger side door for her again and then got into the driver's seat.

"I'm glad Mrs. Townsend is okay," Lacy said as they pulled back onto the main road and drove toward Blueberry Creek Road, where Albert Jenson lived.

"Me too," Paris told her.

"But what happens next time?"

"Hopefully there won't be a next time."

"And if there is, hopefully you'll be around," Lacy said. Something about her tone made him wonder if she wanted to keep him around for herself too.

A few minutes later, he turned onto Mr. Jenson's street and traveled alongside Blueberry Creek. His heart quickened as he pulled into Mr. Jenson's driveway.

"I can't believe he walks from here to the library," Lacy said as he cut the engine. "That has to be at least a mile."

"He's always loved to walk." Paris let his gaze roam over the house. It was smaller than he remembered and in need of new paint. The rosebushes that the Jensons loved so much were unruly and unkempt. He was in his seventies now though. The man Paris knew as a child had been middle-aged and full of energy. Things changed. He looked over. "All right. Let's get this over with. If he yells at us, we'll know he's okay. The buddy system, right?"

"Right."

Except with each passing second spent with Lacy, the harder it was for him to think of her as just a buddy.

* * *

Lacy had never been to Mr. Jenson's home before. She'd known that the Jensons kept foster children once upon a time, but it surprised her that one of them was Paris.

"Strange, but this place feels like home to me," Paris said as he stood at the front door.

"How long did you live here with the Jensons?"

"About six months, which was longer than I lived with most."

"Makes sense why you'd think of this place fondly then." She wanted to ask more about his parents, but it wasn't the time. "Are you going to ring the doorbell?" she asked instead.

"Oh. I guess that would help." Paris pushed the button for the doorbell with his index finger and let his hands clasp back together in front of him.

"If I didn't know better, I'd think Mr. Cool was nervous," she commented.

"Mr. Cool?" He glanced over. "Any relation to Mr. Clean?"

This made her giggle until the front door opened and Mr. Jenson frowned back at them.

Lacy straightened. From the corner of her eye, she saw Paris stand more upright as well.

"Mr. Jenson," Paris said. "Good morning, sir."

"What are you doing here?" the old man barked through the screen door.

"Just checking on you. You missed a class that I put together just for you."

"I hear you were trying to kill people at the library yesterday," Mr. Jenson said, his frown steadfast. "Good thing I stayed home."

"Mrs. Townsend is fine," Paris informed him. "We just checked on her at Sweetwater Memorial."

"And now you're checking on me?" Mr. Jenson shook his head, casting a suspicious glare. "Why?"

Paris held up his hands. "Like I said, I missed you in yesterday's class."

Mr. Jenson looked surprised for a moment, and maybe even a little happy with this information. Then his grumpy demeanor returned. "I decided it wasn't worth my time."

Lacy noticed Paris tense beside her. "Actually, the class is free and taught by a professional," she said, jumping in to help. "We're lucky to have Mr. Montgomery teaching at Sweetwater Library."

Mr. Jenson gave her a long, hard look. She was prepared for him to take a jab at her too, but instead he shrugged his frail shoulders. "It's a long walk, and my legs hurt yesterday, okay? You happy? I'm not a spring chicken anymore, but I'm fine, and I'll be back on Monday. If for no other reason than to keep you two off my front porch." Mr. Jenson looked between them, and then he harrumphed and promptly slammed the door in their faces.

Lacy turned to look at Paris. "Are you sure you're remembering him correctly? I can't imagine that man was ever very nice."

"Did you see him smile at me before he slammed that door though? I think he's softening up."

Lacy laughed, reaching her arm out and grabbing Paris momentarily to brace her body as it shook with amusement. Once she'd realized what she'd done, she removed her hand and cleared her throat. "Okay, our well-check visits are complete. Mrs. Townsend and Mr. Jenson are both alive and kicking."

"I guess it's time for me to keep my end of the deal now," Paris said, leading her back to his truck.

Lacy narrowed her eyes. "But my reunion isn't until next Saturday."

"Yes, but I'm guessing you need to go shopping for something new to wear, right? And I can't wear jeans and an old T-shirt." He opened the passenger door for her.

"You can wear whatever you want," she told him as she stepped inside. Then she turned to look at him as he stood in her doorway.

"I want to look my best when I'm standing beside you. And I hear that Sophie's Boutique is the place to go if you want to dress to impress." He closed the door behind her and walked around to get in the driver's seat.

"Are you seriously offering to go dress shopping with me right now?" she asked once he was seated. "Because guys usually hate that kind of thing."

Paris grinned as he cranked the truck. "Sitting back and watching you come in and out of a dressing room, modeling beautiful clothes, sounds like a fun way to spend an afternoon to me." He winked before backing out of the driveway.

For a moment, Lacy was at a complete loss for words. "I mean, I'm sure you have other things to do with your Saturday afternoon."

He glanced over. "None as fun as hanging out with you."

She melted into the passenger seat. No one in her life had made her feel quite as interesting as Paris had managed to do last night and today. Just the opposite, the Ladies' Day Out group, while well-meaning, had made her feel boring by elaborating on the truth.

Paris made her feel other things as well. Things that were too soon to even contemplate.

CHAPTER FIVE

*E*very time Lacy walked out of the dressing room, Paris felt his heart kick a little harder. The dresses in Sophie's Boutique were gorgeous, but they paled in comparison to Lacy.

"You're staring at me," she said after twirling in a lavender knee-length dress with small navy blue polka dots. "Do you like this one or not?" She looked down. "I kind of love it. It's fun, and that's what I want for my reunion." She was grinning when she looked back up at him. "I want to dance and eat all the foods that will make this dress just a little too tight the next morning." A laugh tumbled off her lips.

Paris swallowed, looking for words, but they all got stuck in his throat. His feelings for Lacy were snowballing with every passing second—and it scared him more than Mr. Jenson did.

"Well?" she said again.

"That's the one for sure." He tore his gaze from her, pushing away all the thoughts of things he wanted to do to her in that dress. He wanted to spin her around on the dance floor, hold her close, and kiss her without apology next time.

Next time?

"Oh, wow! You look so beautiful!" Sophie Daniels, the boutique's owner, walked over and admired Lacy in the dress. "Is that the one?"

Lacy was practically glowing. "I think so, yeah."

Sophie turned to look at Paris. He'd met Sophie before, and she'd flirted mildly with him. He hadn't returned the flirting though because, beautiful as she was, he wasn't interested.

But he couldn't deny his interest in Lacy.

"Now it's your turn," Lacy said.

Sophie gestured to the other side of the store. "I have a rack of men's clothing in the back. Let's get you something that will complement what Lacy is wearing but not steal her show."

"As if I could steal the attention away from her," he said while standing.

Sophie's mouth dropped open. With a knowing look in her eyes, she tipped her head, signaling for him to follow her while Lacy returned to the dressing room to change.

"You seem like a nice guy, Paris, and Lacy deserves someone who will treat her well," Sophie said to him over her shoulder as she led the way.

"It's not like that between us." He swiped a hand through his hair. "I mean, Lacy is terrific, but the two of us don't make sense."

Sophie started sifting through the men's clothes on the rack. "Why not? You're both single and attractive.

She avoids the spotlight, and you kind of grab people's attention wherever you go."

"I do?" he asked.

Sophie stopped looking through the clothes to give him another knowing look. "Opposites attract is a real thing, and it makes perfect sense." She pulled out a dark purple button-down shirt that would match Lacy's dress. "Do you have black pants?"

"I have black jeans," he told her.

She seemed to think about this. "Yes, black jeans will work. You just need to dress up a little bit. You're a jeans and T-shirt kind of guy, so let's keep the jeans." She nodded as if making the decision. "You, but different."

"Me, but different," he agreed, taking the shirt from her. That's how he felt with Lacy. He was still him but more grounded. And Lacy was still reserved but also coming out of her shell, and he loved watching it happen. "Do you have any bathing suits?" he asked on a whim. "One for me and one for Lacy?"

Sophie's eyes lit up, a smile lifting at the corners of her mouth. "Of course I do."

"I'll take one for each of us then. And this shirt for the reunion," Paris said.

Sophie gave him a conspiratorial wink. "I'll take care of it."

* * *

Lacy felt like Julia Roberts in *Pretty Woman*. She loved the dress she'd picked out, and she'd enjoyed the way

Paris had stared at her as she'd modeled each one before it.

They left the boutique and walked back to Paris's truck. He opened her door, and she got in, tucking her bag in the floorboard at her feet. "That was so much fun. Thank you."

He stood in the open doorway of his truck, watching her. His gaze was so intense, and for a moment, her heart sped up. Was he going to kiss her again?

"I want to take you somewhere else," he said.

She furrowed her brow. They'd already spent nearly the entire day together, not that she minded. "Where?"

He placed a second bag in her lap and winked before shutting the door behind her and walking around the truck.

Lacy peeked inside the bag and gasped as he opened his own door and got behind the wheel. "This is a bathing suit."

"You said you always wanted to go to the hot spring. You and I are on one big adventure today, so I thought it'd be fitting to end our expedition by doing something on your bucket list."

"I don't actually have a bucket list," she noted, looking down at the bathing suit again, "but if I did, this would be on it. I can't believe you got me a bathing suit." Underneath her bright pink suit in the bag was a pair of men's board shorts. "Are we really going to do this?"

Paris looked over. "Only if you agree. Will you go on a date with me to the hot spring?"

A date? Had he meant that the way it'd sounded?

Because a date implied that they were more than friends, and that's the way she felt about him right now.

* * *

The night was alive with sounds of nature. In the past hour, the sun had gone down behind the mountains, and stars had begun to shimmer above as darkness fell.

Lacy came out of the changing room with her bathing suit on and a towel wrapped around her waist. Paris was waiting on a bench for her, bare chested and in a pair of swim shorts.

Her mouth went dry. This wasn't her. She didn't visit hot springs with gorgeous men. Her idea of fun on a Saturday night was curling up on her front porch swing with a good book. This was a nice change of pace though, and with Paris beside her, she didn't mind trying something new.

"Ready?" he asked, standing and walking toward her. He reached for her hand and took it. The touch zinged from her heart to her toes, bouncing back up through her body like a ball in a pinball machine.

The sound of water grew louder as they approached the hot spring. They were the only ones here so far this evening, which she found odd and exciting.

Paris stood at the steps and looked at Lacy. "You're going to have to drop that towel," he said, his gaze trailing from her face and down her body toward her hips.

"Right." She swallowed and let go of his hand. She was about to remove her towel, but he reached out for her and did the honors. There was something so intimate about the gesture that her knees weakened. The towel fell in his hand, leaving her standing there in just her suit. She felt exposed and so alive.

He met her gaze for a long moment and then folded the towel and left it on a bench. Turning back to her, he reached for her hand again. "Careful," he said quietly, leading her down the steps and into the water.

She moaned softly as the hot water lapped against her skin. "This is heavenly," she finally said once she'd taken a seat inside. He was still holding her hand, and that was heavenly as well. They leaned back against the spring's wall, and both of them looked up at the stars.

"Anywhere I've been in my life," Paris whispered after a moment, "I've always been under these same stars. I've always wished I was somewhere different when I looked up, but tonight, there's nowhere else I'd rather be." He looked over, his face dangerously close to hers.

She swallowed. "Are you going to kiss me again?"

His blue eyes narrowed. "Do you want me to kiss you again?"

"Ever since that first kiss."

His eyes dropped to her mouth. Her lips parted for him. Then he leaned just a fraction, and his lips brushed against hers. He stayed there, offering small kisses that evolved into something deeper and bigger. One of his hands slid up her thigh, anchoring midway. The touch completely undid her, and if they weren't in a public setting, she might have wiggled until his hand slid higher.

"Are you going to apologize again?" she asked once he'd pulled away.

He shook his head. "I'm not sorry."

"Me neither," she whispered. Then she leaned in and kissed him this time. Who was she these days? This wasn't like her at all.

They didn't stop kissing until voices approached the hot spring. Lacy pulled back from Paris. Another couple appeared and headed toward the spring. They stepped in and sat across from Lacy and Paris.

"We have to behave now," Paris whispered in Lacy's ear.

"Easier said than done." She grinned at him.

"And I'm not leaving until this little problem I have has gone down."

"What problem?" she asked, looking down through the clear bubbles. Then she realized what he was referring to, and her body grew impossibly hotter.

They returned to looking at the stars and talking in whispers, sharing even more details about themselves. Lacy could've stayed and talked all night, but the hot spring closed at ten p.m. When she finally stepped out of the water, the cool air was a harsh contrast.

After toweling off and changing in the dressing room, Lacy met Paris outside and got into his truck. He drove slowly as he took her home, their conversation touching various subjects. And the more she learned about Paris, the more she wanted to know.

Finally, he pulled into her driveway and looked at her.

"I'm not sure you should walk me to my door," Lacy said. "I'd probably end up asking you if you wanted to come inside." She nibbled softly on her lower lip. "And, well, that's probably not the best idea."

"I understand." He reached for her hand. "Thank you for the best day that I can remember."

She leaned toward him. "And the best night."

She gave him a brief kiss because there was still the risk that she might invite him inside. She was doing things that were surprising even herself. "The library is closed tomorrow. I can make lunch if you want to come over."

He hesitated.

"I mean, you don't have to, if you have something else to do."

He grinned. "I have work to do tomorrow, but a man has to eat, right? Lunch sounds nice. I'll be here."

"Perfect." She pushed the truck door open before her hormones took over and she climbed over to his side of the truck instead. "Good night, Paris."

"Good night, Lace."

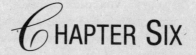HAPTER SIX

*L*acy wasn't thinking straight last night. Otherwise, she would've remembered that a few members of the Ladies' Day Out group were coming over for lunch after church. No doubt they wanted to nag her about one thing or another. Today's topics were most likely the dating site and her reunion.

Then again, that was all the more reason for Paris to join them for lunch. His presence would kill two birds with one stone. She didn't need a dating site. And she and Paris were going to have an amazing time at her reunion next weekend.

She heard his motorcycle rumble into her driveway first. She waited for him to ring the doorbell, and then she went to answer. Butterflies fluttered low in her belly at the sight of him.

"Come in." She led him inside the two-bedroom house that she'd purchased a couple of years ago. "It's not much, but it's home."

"Well, sounds cliché, but I've learned that home really is where the heart is," he said.

She turned to look at him, standing close enough that she could reach out and touch him again. Maybe pull him toward her, go up on her tiptoes, and press her lips to his. "By cliché, you mean cheesy?"

Paris pretended to push a stake through his heart. "When you get comfortable with someone, your feisty side is unleashed. I like it." He leaned in just a fraction, and Lacy decided to take a step forward, giving him the not-so-subtle green light for another kiss. He was right. She was feisty when she was with him, and she liked this side of her too.

The sound of another motor pulling into her driveway got her attention. She turned toward her door.

"Are you expecting someone else?" Paris asked, following her gaze.

"Yes, sorry. I didn't remember when I invited you last night, but I have company coming over today."

"Who?" Paris asked.

"My mom."

He nodded. "Okay."

"And my two sisters, Birdie and Rose," Lacy added. "*And* my aunt Pam."

Paris started to look panicked. "Anyone else?"

"Yeah. Um, Dawanda from the fudge shop. They're all part of the Ladies' Day Out group. I got a text earlier in the week telling me they were bringing lunch."

"Well, I'll get out of your guys' hair," he said, backpedaling toward the door.

She grabbed his hand, holding it until he met her gaze. "Wait. You don't need to leave. I want you here."

Paris grimaced. "Family mealtime has never really been my strong point."

Lacy continued to hold his hand. She wanted to show the women outside that she could find a guy on her own. She didn't need FishInTheSea.com. She also wanted to show them this new side of herself that seemed to take hold when she was with Paris. "They're harmless, I promise. Please stay."

Paris shifted on his feet, and she was pretty sure he was going to turn down the invitation. "You didn't take no for an answer when you wanted me to teach the computer class at the library," he finally said. "I'm guessing the same would be true now, huh?"

She grinned. "That's right."

"You're a hard woman to resist."

"Then stop trying," she said, going to answer the door.

* * *

The spread on Lacy's table was fit for a Thanksgiving dinner by Paris's standards. Not that he had much experience with holidays and family gatherings. He'd had many a holiday meal with a fast-food bag containing a burger, fries, and a small toy.

"I would've brought Denny if I'd known that men were allowed at lunch today," Mrs. Shaw said, speaking of her husband. She seemed friendly enough, but Paris also didn't miss the scrutinizing looks she was giving him when she thought he wasn't looking. He was dressed in dark colors and had tattoos on both arms. He also had a motorcycle parked in the driveway. He probably wasn't the kind of guy Mrs. Shaw would have imagined her sweet librarian daughter with.

"Good thing you didn't bring Dad," Lacy's sister Birdie said. "He would've grilled Paris mercilessly."

"Paris and I aren't dating," Lacy reiterated for the tenth time since she'd welcomed the women into her home. She slid her gaze to look at Paris, and he saw the question in her eyes. *Are we?* When the ladies had come through the front door, they'd all immediately began calling him Lacy's secret boyfriend.

"Sounds like I'd be in trouble if you and I did get together," Paris said. "Your dad sounds strict."

Lacy laughed softly. "Notice that my sisters and I are all still single. There's a reason for that."

Lacy's other sister, Rose, snorted. "Dad crashed my high school prom when I didn't come home by curfew. Who has a curfew on prom night?" Rose slid her fork into a pile of macaroni and cheese. "I thought I'd never forgive Dad for that. I liked that guy too."

"What was his name again?" Mrs. Shaw asked.

Rose looked up, her eyes squinting as she seemed to think. "I can't remember. Brent maybe. Bryce? Could've been Bryan."

"You couldn't have liked him too much if you can't remember his name," Mrs. Shaw pointed out.

Everyone at the table laughed.

"Don't you worry, Rose," Dawanda said, seated beside Mrs. Shaw. "I've read your cappuccino, and you have someone very special coming your way. I saw it in the foam."

"Well, I'll be sure to keep him away from my dad until the wedding," Rose said sarcastically, making everyone chuckle again.

Whereas some read tea leaves, Dawanda read images formed in the foam of a cappuccino. She'd done a reading for Paris last Christmas. Oddly enough, Dawanda had told him he was the only one whose fortune she couldn't read. Dawanda had assured him it wasn't that he was going to fall off a cliff or anything. His future was just up in the air. He had shut his heart off to dreaming of a life anywhere or with anyone.

He didn't exactly believe in fortune-telling, but she was spot-on with that. Some people just weren't cut out for forever homes and families. He guessed he was one of them.

"Dad's first question any time he meets any of our dates is 'What are your intentions with my girl?'" Rose said, impersonating a man's deep voice.

"He actually said that while sharpening his pocket-knife for a date I brought home in college," Birdie said. "I didn't mind because I didn't like the guy too much, but what if I had?"

"Then you would've been out of luck," Lacy said on a laugh.

The conversation continued, and then Mrs. Shaw looked across the table at Paris. "So, Paris," she said, her eyes narrowing, "tell us about yourself. Did you grow up around here?"

Paris looked up from his lunch. "I spent a little time in Sweetwater Springs growing up. Some in Wild Blossom Bluffs. My parents moved around a lot."

"Oh? For their jobs? Military maybe?" she asked.

Paris shifted. Ex-felons weren't allowed to join the

military. "Not exactly. I was in foster care here for a while."

"Foster care?" Mrs. Shaw's lips rounded in a little O. "That must've been hard for a young child."

Paris focused his attention back on his food. "I guess I didn't really know any different. Most of the places I landed were nice enough." And there'd been somewhere he'd wished he could stay. Six months with the Jenson family was the longest amount of time he'd ever gotten to stay. It was just enough time to bond with his foster parents and to feel the loss of them to his core when he was placed back with his real parents.

He picked up his fork and stabbed at a piece of chicken.

"And what brought you back to Sweetwater Springs? If I recall, you moved here last year, right?" Dawanda asked. "You came into my shop while you were staying at the Sweetwater Bed and Breakfast."

Paris swallowed past the sudden tightness in his throat. He didn't really want to answer that question either. He looked around the table, his gaze finally landing on Lacy. "Well, I guess I decided to come back here after my divorce."

Lacy's lips parted.

Had he forgotten to mention that little detail to her? When he was with Lacy, he forgot all about those lonely years in Florida. All he could think about was the moment he was in, and the ones that would follow.

"That sounds rough as well," Mrs. Shaw said.

Paris shrugged, feeling weighed down by the truth. "Well, those things are in the rearview mirror now." He tried to offer a lighter tone of voice, but all the women looked crestfallen. Mrs. Shaw had already seemed wary of him, but now she appeared even more so.

"And since my husband isn't here to ask"—Mrs. Shaw folded her hands in front of her on the table—"what are your intentions with my daughter?"

"Mom!" Lacy set her fork down. "Paris and I aren't even dating." She looked over at him. "I mean, we went on a date last night. Two if you count that night at the park."

"Last night?" Birdie asked.

All the women's eyes widened.

"It wasn't like that." Lacy looked flustered. "We didn't spend the night together."

Mrs. Shaw's jaw dropped open, and Lacy's face turned a deep crimson.

Guilt curled in Paris's stomach. Lacy was trying her best to prove herself to everyone around her. Now her family and Dawanda were gawking at her like she'd lost her mind. It was crazy to think that she and Paris would be dating. Sophie Daniels had told him at the boutique that opposites attract, but he and Lacy had led very different lives.

"Sounds like you're dating to me. Are you going to go out again?" Rose asked.

"Well, Paris offered to go with me to my reunion," Lacy said.

Mrs. Shaw's smile returned. "Oh, I'm so glad you decided to go! That's wonderful, dear. I want all those bullies to see that you are strong and beautiful, smart and funny, interesting—"

"Mom," Lacy said, cutting her off, "you might be a little partial."

"But she's right," Paris said, unable to help himself.

Lacy turned to look at him, and something pinched in his chest. He'd tried to keep things strictly friendly with her, but he'd failed miserably. What was he going to do now? He didn't want a relationship, but if they continued to spend time together, she would.

"So, Paris, how did you get our Lacy to agree to go to this reunion of hers?" Mrs. Shaw asked. "She was so dead set on not attending."

"Actually, Lace made that decision on her own," he said.

"Lace?" Both Birdie and Rose asked in unison.

The nickname had just rolled off his tongue, but it fit. Lace was delicate and beautiful, accentuated by holes that one might think made it more fragile. It was strong, just like the woman sitting next to him. She was stronger than she even knew.

"Well, I'm glad she's changed her mind. High school was such a rough time for our Lacy," Mrs. Shaw said. "I want her to go and have a good time and show those bullies who treated her so badly that they didn't break her."

Paris glanced over at Lacy. He wanted her old classmates to see the same thing.

Mrs. Shaw pointed a finger at Paris, gaining his attention. "But if you take her, it won't be on the back of that motorcycle in the driveway. Lacy doesn't ride those things."

"Actually, Mom, I rode on the back of it with Paris two days ago."

Mrs. Shaw looked horrified.

"Maybe he'll let me drive it next time," Lacy added, making all the women at the table look surprised.

"Lacy rode on the back of your bike?" Birdie asked Paris. "This is not our sister. What have you done with the real Lacy Shaw?"

He looked over at the woman in question. The real Lacy was sitting right beside him. He saw her, even if no one else did. And the last thing he wanted to do was walk away from her, which was why he needed to do just that.

* * *

An hour later, Lacy closed her front door as her guests left and leaned against it, exhaling softly.

"Your mom and sisters are great," Paris said, standing a couple of feet away from her. "Your aunt too."

She lifted her gaze to his. "You almost sound serious about that."

"Well, I'm not going to lie. They were a little overwhelming."

"A little?" Lacy grinned. "And they were subdued today. They're usually worse."

Paris shoved his hands in his pockets. "They love you. Can't fault them for that."

The way he was looking at her made her breath catch. Was he going to kiss her again?

"I guess not."

"They want what's best for you," he continued. Then he looked away. "And, uh, I'm not sure that's me, Lace."

She straightened at the sudden shift in his tone of voice. "What?"

He ran a hand over his hair. "When we were eating just now, I realized that being your date might not be doing you any favors. Or me."

"Wait, you're not going to the reunion with me anymore?" she asked.

He shook his head. "I just think it'd be better if you went with someone else."

"I don't have anyone else," she protested, her heart beating fast. "The reunion is in less than a week. I have my dress, and you have a matching shirt. And you're the one I want to go with. I don't even care about the reunion. I just want to be with you."

He looked down for a moment. "You heard me talking to your family. I've lived a different life than you. I'm an ex-foster kid. My parents are felons." He shrugged. "I couldn't even make a marriage work."

"Those things are in the past, Paris. I don't care about any of that."

He met her gaze again. "But I do. Call me selfish, but I don't want to want you. I don't want to want things that I know I'll never have. It's not in the cappuccino for me, Lacy." His expression was pained. "I really want you to believe me when I say it's not you, it's me."

Her eyes and throat burned, and she wondered if she felt worse for herself or for him. He obviously had issues, but who didn't? One thing she'd learned since high school was that no one's life was perfect. Her flaws were just obvious back then because of the back brace.

She'd also learned that you couldn't make someone feel differently than they did. The only feelings you could control were your own. The old Lacy never stood up for herself. She let people trample on her and her feelings. But she'd changed. She was the new Lacy now.

She lifted her eyes to meet Paris's and swallowed past the growing lump in her throat. "If that's the way you feel, then I think you should go."

CHAPTER SEVEN

On Monday afternoon, Paris looked out over the roomful of students. Everyone had their eyes on their screens and were learning to Skype. But his attention was on the librarian on the other side of the building.

When he'd driven to the library, he'd lectured himself on why he needed to back away from Lacy Shaw. Sunday's lunch had made that crystal clear in his mind. She was smart and beautiful, the kind of woman who valued family. Paris had no idea what it even meant to have a family. He couldn't be the kind of guy she needed.

Luckily, Lacy hadn't even been at the counter when he'd walked in and continued toward the computer room. She was probably hell-bent on avoiding him. For the best.

"Does everyone think they can go home and Skype now?" Paris asked the class.

"I can, but no one I know will know how to Skype with me," Greta said.

Janice Murphy nodded beside her.

"Well, you could all exchange information and Skype with each other," Paris suggested.

"Can we Skype with you?" Alice asked.

Warmness spread through his chest. "Anytime, Alice."

"Can I Skype you if my wife doesn't want to talk to me?" Mr. Jenson asked. "To practice so I'm ready when she does?"

Paris felt a little sad for the older man. When Paris had been a boy in their home, they'd been the happiest of couples. "Of course. If I'm home and free, I'll always make time to Skype with any one of you," he told the group, meaning it. They'd had only a few classes, but he loved the eclectic bunch in this room.

When class was over, he walked over to Mr. Jenson. "I can give you a ride home if you want."

Mr. Jenson gave him an assessing stare. "If you think I'm climbing on the back of that bike of yours, you're crazy."

Paris chuckled. "I drove my truck today. It'll save you a walk. I have the afternoon free too. I can take you by the nursing home facility to see Mrs. Jenson if you want. I'm sure she'd be happy to see you."

Mr. Jenson continued to stare at him. "Why would you do that? I know I'm not that fun to be around."

Paris clapped a gentle hand on Mr. Jenson's back. "That's not true. I kind of like being around you." He always had. "And I could use some company today. Agreeing would actually be doing me a favor."

"I don't do favors," the older man said. "But my legs are kind of hurting, thanks to the chairs in there. So walking home would be a pain."

Paris felt relieved as Mr. Jenson relented. "What about visiting Mrs. Jenson? I'll stay in the truck while you go in, and take as long as you like." Paris patted his laptop bag. "I have my computer, so I can work while I wait."

Mr. Jenson begrudgingly agreed and even smiled a little bit. "Thank you."

Paris led Mr. Jenson into his truck and started the short drive toward Sweetwater Nursing Facility.

"She sometimes tells me to leave as soon as I get there," Mr. Jenson said as they drove.

"Why is that?"

Mr. Jenson shrugged. "She says she doesn't want me to see her that way."

Paris still wasn't quite sure what was wrong with Mrs. Jenson. "What way?"

"Oh, you know. Her emotions are as unstable as her walking these days. That's why she's not home with me. She's not the same Nancy I fell in love with, but she's still the woman I love. I'll always love her, no matter how things change."

"That's what love is, isn't it?" Paris asked.

Mr. Jenson turned to look out the passenger side window as they rode. "We never had any kids of our own. We fostered a few, and that was as close as we ever got to having a family."

Paris swallowed painfully.

"There was one boy who was different. We would've kept him. We bonded and loved him as our own."

Paris glanced over. Was Mr. Jenson talking about him? Probably not, but Paris couldn't help hoping that he was. "What happened?"

"We wanted to raise him as part of our family, but it didn't work out that way. He went back to his real parents, which I suppose is always best. I lost him, and now, most days, I've lost my wife too. That's what love is. Painful."

Paris parked and looked over. "Well, maybe today will be different. Whatever happens, I'll be in the truck waiting for you."

Mr. Jenson looked over and chuckled, but Paris could tell by the gleam in his eyes that he appreciated the sentiment. He stepped out of the truck and dipped his head to look at Paris in the driver's seat. "Some consolation prize."

* * *

Two nights later, Lacy sat in her living room with a handful of the Ladies' Day Out members. They'd been waiting for her in the driveway when she'd gotten home from the library and were here for an intervention of sorts.

"Sandwiches?" Greta asked, her face twisting with displeasure.

"Well, when you don't tell someone that you're coming, you get PB&J." Lacy plopped onto the couch beside Birdie, who had no doubt called everyone here.

"You took your online profile down," Birdie said, reaching for her own sandwich.

"Of course I did. I'm not interested in dating right now."

"You sure looked interested in Paris Montgomery,"

Dawanda said, sitting across from them. "And you two looked so good together. What happened?"

All the women turned to face Lacy.

She shrugged. "My family happened. No offense. You all behaved—mostly," she told her mom and sisters. "We just decided it'd be best to part ways sooner rather than later."

Birdie placed her sandwich down. "I thought you were the smart one in the family."

Rose raised her hand. "No, that was always me." A wide grin spread on her face. "Just kidding. It's you, Lacy."

Birdie frowned. "I was there last weekend. I saw how you two were together. There's relationship potential there," she said.

Lacy sighed. "Maybe, but he doesn't want another relationship. He's been hurt and..." She shrugged. "I guess he just doesn't think it's worth trying again." That was her old insecurities though so she stopped them all in their tracks. "Actually, something good came out of me going out with him a few times."

"Oh?" Birdie asked. "What's that?"

"I'm not afraid to go to my reunion, even if I have to go on my own."

"Maybe you'll meet someone there. Maybe you'll find 'the one,'" Rose said.

"Maybe." But Lacy was pretty sure she wouldn't find the *one* she wanted. He'd already been found and lost.

"I'll go with you if you need me to," Josie offered. She wasn't sitting on the couch with Lacy's laptop this time. Instead, she held a glass of wine tonight, looking relaxed in the recliner across the room.

"I wonder what people would think about that," Birdie said.

Lacy shrugged. "You know what, I've decided that I don't care what the people who don't know me think. I care about what I think. And what you all think, of course."

"And Paris?" Dawanda asked.

Lacy shook her head, but she meant yes. Paris was right. Her gestures often contradicted what she really meant. "Paris thinks that we should just be friends, and I have to respect that."

Even if she didn't like it.

CHAPTER EIGHT

*P*aris was spending his Saturday night in Mr. Jenson's rosebushes—not at Lacy's class reunion as he'd planned. He'd clipped the bushes back, pruning the dead ends so that they'd come back stronger.

Over the last couple of days, he'd kept himself super busy with work and taking Mr. Jenson to and from the nursing facility. He'd read up on how to care for rosebushes, but that hadn't been necessary because Mr. Jenson stayed on the porch barking out instructions like a drill sergeant. Paris didn't mind. He loved the old man.

"Don't clip too much off!" Mr. Jenson warned. "Just what's needed."

"Got it." Paris squeezed the clippers again and again, until the muscles of his hand were cramping.

Despite his best efforts, he hadn't kept himself busy enough to keep from thinking about Lacy. She'd waved and said hi to him when he'd gone in and out of the library, but that was all. It wasn't enough.

He missed her. A lot. Hopefully she was still going

to her reunion tonight. He hoped she danced. And maybe there'd be a nice guy there who would dance with her.

Guilt and jealousy curled around Paris's ribs like the roses on the lattice. He still wanted to be that guy who held her close tonight and watched her shine.

"Done yet?" Mr. Jenson asked gruffly.

Paris wiped his brow and straightened. "All done."

Mr. Jenson nodded approvingly. "It looks good, son."

Mr. Jenson didn't mean anything by calling him son, but it still tugged on Paris's heartstrings. "Thanks. I'll come by next week and take you to see Mrs. Jenson."

"Just don't expect me to get on that bike of yours," the older man said for the hundredth time.

"Wouldn't dream of it." As Paris started to walk away, Mr. Jenson called out to him.

"PJ?"

Paris froze. He hadn't heard that name in a long time, but it still stopped him in his tracks. He turned back to face Mr. Jenson. "You know?"

Mr. Jenson chuckled. "I'm old, not blind. I've known since that first computer class."

"But you didn't say anything." Paris took a few steps, walking back toward Mr. Jenson on the porch. "Why?"

"I could ask you the same. You didn't say anything either."

Paris held his hands out to his sides. "I called last year. Mrs. Jenson answered and told me to never call again."

Mr. Jenson shook his head as he listened. "I didn't

know that, but it sounds about right. She tells me the same thing when I call her. Don't take it personally."

Paris pulled in a deep breath and everything he'd thought about the situation shifted and became something very different. They hadn't turned him away. Mr. Jenson hadn't even known he'd tried to reconnect.

Mr. Jenson shoved his hands in the pockets of his pants. "I loved PJ. It was hard to lose him...You." Mr. Jenson cleared his throat and looked off into the distance. "It's been hard to lose Nancy, memory by memory, too. I guess some part of me didn't say anything when I realized who you were because I was just plain tired of losing. Sometimes it's easier not to feel anything. Then it doesn't hurt so much when it's gone." He looked back at Paris. "But I can't seem to lose you even if I wanted to, so maybe I'll just stop trying."

Paris's eyes burned. He blinked and looked down at his feet for a moment and then back up at the old man. He was pretty sure Mr. Jenson didn't want to be hugged, but Paris was going to anyway. He climbed the steps and wrapped his arms around his foster dad for a brief time. Then he pulled away. "Like I said, I'll be back next week, and I'll take you to go see Mrs. Jenson."

"See. Can't push you away. Might as well take you inside with me when I go see Nancy next time. She'll probably tell you to go away and never come back."

"I won't listen," Paris promised.

"Good." Mr. Jenson looked relieved somehow. His body posture was more relaxed. "Well, you best get on with your night. I'm sure you have things to do. Maybe go see that pretty librarian."

Paris's heart rate picked up. He was supposed to be at Lacy's side tonight, but while she was bravely facing her fears, he'd let his keep him away. His parents were supposed to love him and stand by him, but they hadn't. His ex-wife had abandoned him too. He guessed he'd gotten tired of losing just like Mr. Jenson. It was easier to push people away before they pushed him.

But the Jensons had never turned their back on him. They'd wanted him and he wished things had gone differently. Regardless of what happened in the past, it wasn't too late to reconnect and have what could've been now.

As he headed back to his bike, Paris pulled his cell phone out of his pocket and checked the time. Hopefully, it wasn't too late for him and Lacy either.

* * *

Lacy looked at her reflection in the long mirror in her bedroom. She loved the dress she'd found at Sophie's Boutique. She had a matching pair of shoes that complemented it perfectly. Her hair was also done up, and she'd put on just a little bit of makeup.

She flashed a confident smile. "I can do this."

She took another deep breath and then hurried to get her purse and keys. The reunion would be starting soon, and she needed to leave before she changed her mind. The nerves were temporary, but the memories from tonight would last. And despite her worries, she was sure they'd be good memories.

She grabbed her things and drove to Sweetwater

Springs High School where the class reunion was taking place. When she was parked, she sat for a moment, watching her former classmates head inside. They all had someone on their arm. No one was going in alone. Except her.

She imagined walking inside and everyone stopping to stare at her. The mean girls from her past pointing and laughing and whispering among each other. That was the worst-case scenario and probably wasn't going to happen. But if it did, she'd get through it. She wasn't a shy kid anymore. She was strong and confident, and yeah, she'd rather have Paris holding her hand, but she didn't need him to. "I can do this," she said again.

She pushed her car door open, locked it up, and headed inside. She opened the door to the gymnasium, accosted by the music and sounds of laughter. It wasn't directed at her. No one was even looking at her. She exhaled softly, scanning the room for familiar faces. When she saw Claire Donovan, the coordinator of the event, standing with Halona Locklear and Brenna McConnell, she headed in that direction. They were always nice to her.

"Lacy!" Brenna exclaimed when she saw her walking over. "It's so good to see you." She gave her a big hug, and Lacy relaxed a little more. "Even though we all see each other on a regular basis," she said once they'd pulled apart.

Lacy hugged the other women as well.

"So you came alone too?" Lacy asked Halona.

"Afraid so. My mom is watching Theo for a few hours. I told her I really didn't need to come, but she insisted."

Brenna nodded as she listened to the conversation. "Sounds familiar. Everyone told me that you can't skip your high school reunion."

"This is a small town. It's not like we don't know where everyone ended up," Halona said. "Most everyone anyway."

"Don't look now," Summer Rodriquez said, also joining the conversation, "but Carmen Daly is veering this way."

Lacy's heart sank. Carmen was the leader of her little pack of mean girls. How many times had Lacy cried in the girls' bathroom over something Carmen had said or done to make her life miserable?

Lacy subtly stood a little straighter. Her brace was gone, and whatever Carmen dished out, she intended to return.

"Hi, ladies," Carmen said, looking between them. She was just as beautiful as ever. Lacy knew Carmen didn't live in Sweetwater Springs anymore. From what Lacy had heard, Carmen had married a doctor and lived a few hours east from here. Her vibrant smile grew sheepish as she looked at Lacy. "Hi, Lacy."

Every muscle in Lacy's body tensed. "Hi, Carmen."

Then Carmen surprised her by stepping forward to give her a hug. For a moment, Lacy wondered if she was sticking a sign on her back like she'd done so long ago. KICK ME. I WON'T FEEL IT.

Carmen pulled back and looked Lacy in the eye while her friends watched. "Lacy, I've thought about you so many times over the years. I'm so glad you're here tonight."

Lacy swallowed. "Oh?"

"I want to tell you that I'm sorry. For everything. I'm ashamed of the person I was and how I acted toward you. So many times I've thought about messaging you on Facebook or emailing you, but this is something that really needs to be done in person." Carmen's eyes grew shiny. "Lacy, I'm so sorry. I mean it."

Lacy's mouth dropped open. Of all the things she'd imagined about tonight, this wasn't one of them. She turned to look at Summer, Brenna, and Halona, whose lips were also parted in shock, and then she looked back at Carmen.

"I've tried to be a better person, but the way I behaved in high school has haunted me for the last ten years."

Lacy reached for Carmen's hand and gave it a squeeze. "Thank you. Looks like we've both changed."

"We grew up." Carmen shrugged. "Can you ever forgive me?"

"Definitely."

Carmen seemed to relax. "Maybe we can be friends on Facebook," she said. "And in real life. Maybe a coffee date next time I come home."

"I'd like that." Lacy's eyes burned as she hugged Carmen again and watched her walk over to her husband. Then Lacy turned her back to her friends. "Is there a sign on my back?"

"Nope," Brenna said. "I think that was sincere."

Lacy faced them again. "Me too. It was worth coming here tonight just for that." Someone tapped her shoulder and she spun again, this time coming face-to-face with Paris.

"Sorry to interrupt," he said, looking just as sheepish as Carmen had a few minutes earlier.

She noticed that he was dressed in the shirt he purchased from Sophie's Boutique. "Paris, what are you doing here?"

"Hoping to get a dance with you?" He looked at the dance floor, where a few couples were swaying.

"I...I don't know," she said.

Summer put a hand on her back and gave her a gentle push. "No more sitting on the sidelines, Lacy. When a boy asks you to dance, you say yes."

Lacy took a few hesitant steps, following Paris. Then they stopped and turned to face each other, the music wrapping around them. "Paris"—she shook her head—"you didn't have to come. As you can see, I didn't chicken out. I'm here and actually having a great time. I don't need you to hold my hand."

He reached for her hand anyway, pulling her body toward his. The touch made her grow warm all over. "You never needed me. But I'm hoping you still want me."

Lacy swallowed. *Yeah*, she definitely still wanted him. She looked at his arms looped around her waist. They fit together so nicely. Then she looked back up at him. "I lied when I said that we could still be friends, Paris. I can't. I want things when I'm with you. Things I shouldn't want, but I can't help it."

"Such as?" he asked.

Lacy took a breath. She might as well be honest and scare him off for good. "I want a relationship. I want to fall in love. I want it all. And I just think it would be too hard—"

Paris dropped his mouth to hers and stopped her words with a soft kiss.

"What are you doing?" she asked when he pulled back away.

"I want things when I'm with you too," he said, leaning in closer so she could hear him over the music. "I want to kiss you. Hold your hand. Be the guy you want a relationship with. To be in love with."

Lacy's lips parted. Since they were being honest... "You already are that guy. I mean, not the love part. We haven't known each other very long, so it's too soon for that. That would be crazy."

"Maybe, but I understand exactly what you mean," he said.

She narrowed her eyes. "Then why are you smiling? You said you didn't want those things."

"Correction. I said I didn't *want* to want those things." He tightened his hold on her as they danced. "But it appears it's already too late, and you're worth the risk."

"So you're my date to this reunion tonight," Lacy said. "Then what?"

"Then tomorrow or the next day, I was thinking I'd go to your family's house for dinner and win over your dad."

Lacy grimaced. "That won't be easy. He'll want to know what your intentions are with his daughter."

Paris grinned. "My intention is to put you on the back of my bike and ride off into the sunset. What do you think he'll say to that?"

She grinned. "I think he'll hate that response. But if you're asking what I think..."

"Tell me," Paris whispered, continuing to sway with her, face-to-face, body-to-body.

"I love it." Then Lacy lifted up on her toes and kissed him for the entire world to see, even though in the moment, no one else existed except him and her.

DON'T MISS A SINGLE ROMANTIC MOMENT OF THE SWEETWATER SPRINGS SERIES!

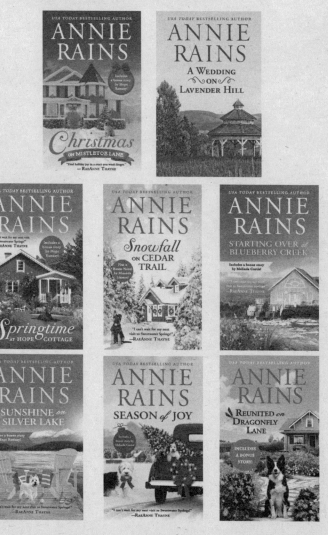

About the Author

Annie Rains is a *USA Today* bestselling contemporary romance author who writes small-town love stories set in fictional places in her home state of North Carolina. When Annie isn't writing, she's living out her own happily ever after with her husband and three children.

Learn more at:

AnnieRains.com
Twitter @AnnieRainsBooks
Facebook.com/AnnieRainsBooks
Instagram @AnnieRainsBooks

Want more charming small towns?
Fall in love with these
Forever contemporary romances!

THE SUMMER COTTAGE
by Annie Rains

Somerset Lake is the perfect place for Trisha Langly and her son to start over. As the new manager for the Somerset Cottages, she's instantly charmed by her firecracker of a boss, Vi—but less enchanted by Vi's protective grandson, attorney Jake Fletcher. If Jake discovers her past, she'll lose this perfect second chance. However, as they spend summer days renovating the property and nights enjoying the town's charm, Trisha may realize she must trust Jake with her secrets …and her heart. Includes a bonus story!

FALLING IN LOVE
ON WILLOW CREEK
by Debbie Mason

FBI agent Chase Roberts has come to Highland Falls to work undercover as a park ranger to track down an on-the-run informant. But when he befriends the suspect's sister to get nearer to his target, Chase finds that he's growing closer to the warm-hearted, beautiful Sadie Gray and her little girl. When he arrests her brother Elijah, Chase risks losing Sadie forever. Can he convince her that the feelings between them are real once Sadie discovers the truth?

A WEDDING ON LILAC LANE
by Hope Ramsay

After returning home from her country music career, Ella McMillan is shocked to find her mother is engaged. Worse, she asks Ella to plan the event with her fiancé's straitlaced son, Dr. Dylan Killough. While Ella wants to create the perfect day, Dylan is determined the two shouldn't get married at all. Somehow amid all their arguing, sparks start flying. And soon everyone in Magnolia Harbor is wondering if Dylan and Ella will be joining their parents in a trip down the aisle.

FRIENDS LIKE US
by Sarah Mackenzie

When a cancer scare compels Bree Robinson to form an *anti*-bucket list, she decides to start with a steamy fling. Only her one-night stand is Chance Elliston, the architect she's just hired to renovate her house. Bree agrees to a friends-with-benefits relationship with Chance before he returns to the city at the end of the summer. But as their feelings for each other grow, can she convince him to risk it all on a new life together?

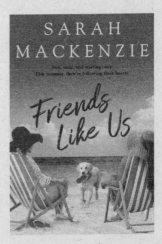

Discover bonus content and more on
read-forever.com

SANDCASTLE BEACH
by Jenny Holiday

What Maya Mehta really needs to save her beloved community theater is Matchmaker Bay's new business grant. She's got some serious competition, though: Benjamin Lawson, local bar owner, Jerk Extraordinaire, and Maya's annoyingly hot arch nemesis. Turns out there's a thin line between hate and irresistible desire, and Maya and Law are really good at crossing it. But when things heat up, will they allow their long-standing feud to get in the way of their growing feelings? Includes the bonus story *Once Upon a Bride*, for the first time in print!

DREAM SPINNER
by Kristen Ashley

There's no doubt that former soldier Axl Pantera is the man of Hattie Yates's dreams. Yet years of abuse from her demanding father have left her terrified of disappointment. Axl is slowly wooing Hattie into letting down her walls—until a dangerous stalker sets their sights on her. Now he's facing more than her wary and bruised heart. Axl will do anything to prove that they're meant to be—but first, he'll need to keep Hattie safe.